This
is
Life

This is Life

DAN RHODES

CANONGATE
Edinburgh · London

Thanks to Blondelle Woods, Jenita Colganova and
M.E.M. Rhodes for early readings; F. Bickmore and all other
humans of Canongate; Christine Glover; the American Academy
of Arts and Letters; The Society of Authors; a cormorant in Cork;
another cormorant in Paris; The Laugharne Weekend; Aberdeen
Art Gallery (which is where Eugène Carrière's *Enfant avec casserole*
really lives); parents, and family in general.

Special thanks are due to the true author of this work,
the petite, beautiful and forever young Danuta de Rhodes – cruelly
felled in her prime.

And thanks most of all to Arthur.

This book was written in Buxton, Derbyshire, through the long,
cold winter of 2010 & 2011.

First published in Great Britain in 2012 by Canongate Books Ltd,
14 High Street, Edinburgh EH1 1TE

1

www.canongate.tv

British Library Cataloguing-in-Publication Data
A catalogue record for this book is available on
request from the British Library

ISBN 978 0 85786 245 7

Typeset in Sabon by Palimpsest Book Production Ltd,
Falkirk, Stirlingshire

Printed and bound in Great Britain by
CPI Group (UK) Ltd, Croydon, CR0 4YY

For Wife-features and Arthur

MERCREDI

I

Aurélie Renard was standing on the west side of the small square. She struck a match against the wall, lit her fourth cigarette of the morning and tucked the dead stick back into the box. It was the tail end of the rush hour, and a stream of people rose from the exit of the Métro station and walked past her on their way to jobs in the streets beyond. On the other side of the square, intermittently visible through the passing bodies, sat a thick-bearded old man, wrapped in a heavy and ancient brown coat as he played a hurdy-gurdy. She enjoyed the rattle and drone they made together, and remembered it well. He wore a Russian hat, and it was because of this that Aurélie had always thought of him as *The Russian*. She really had no idea where he was from, or what his instrument was called. To her it was just *that Russian instrument*, and she didn't want to risk spoiling its magic by finding out too much about it.

The previous evening she had taken off her blindfold, walked over to the map of Paris that she had pinned to her wall and been pleased to see that the dart had landed somewhere familiar. The summer before last, when she was nineteen and had just arrived in the city, she had found a job in a kitchen shop a few streets away, selling expensive pots and pans to people who seemed to have no idea that they lived in splendour. This had been the nearest Métro station to her work, and for a while she had walked across the square almost every day. She liked the idea that she had once been a part of this same flow of people. She pictured herself as she would have been back then; bleary-eyed and walking fast, almost running, as she tried to get to the shop on time after a muddled start to the day. Now, though, she stood still, cigarette in hand, as she waited for the right moment to begin.

The Russian had been there every morning, and he had always worn his coat and hat, even at the height of the summer, when any clothes at all felt like a hindrance. Just looking at him on such days had made Aurélie feel a dull throb of heat exhaustion. Today, there was a real chill in the air, and this was the first day this autumn when his clothes would have seemed appropriate. Aurélie could even see her breath, and some of the people walking by were wearing thick jackets, even winter coats and gloves. Others, the ones the weather had caught by surprise, were trying not to look uncomfortable as they hurried along faster than usual on their way to work.

Nobody seemed to be paying any attention to the hurdy-gurdy man. Most of them would have walked past him several days a week, just as she had done, and they had long since stopped noticing him. She had never known anyone to stop and listen, or throw him a coin, and she had even wondered whether he was really busking; maybe he had a landlady whose nerves couldn't stand the noise, and who sent him out of the house to practise. Though his case was open, it was on the bench beside him rather than in the traditional buskers' spot, on the ground by his feet. These ambiguities had stopped her from ever giving him a euro or two, and even now she felt half bad about it. It seemed a strange way to try and make money though, playing for the same horde of hurrying, inscrutable commuters every day.

She considered her own clothes for a moment. She had given a lot of thought to what she was going to wear. First impressions were going to be crucial, and she had wanted to look like an artist in a way that was plausible without being overbearing. She was confident that she had done a good job. Almost everybody walking by was wearing ordinary clothes for a working day, just as she had whenever she had walked through the square, but today she stood out, wearing black work boots that were spotted with various colours from her recent failed experiment with oil paint, black jeans and a brand new red quilted jacket, a last minute addition thanks to the temperature. Her hair, after years of changes, had finally returned to its natural colour, a colour which in her early teenage years she had condemned as *mousy* before attacking it with bleach and dye, but which she had lately come to think of as a pleasing dirty blonde. She had yet to decide whether to grow it out properly, but for now it was just long enough to tie back, which was what she had done. She knew she looked right. The first impression was going to be a good one.

She smoked her cigarette as far as it would go, then ground it out on the wall and put the stub in the matchbox. The time had come. A new batch of passers-by was spilling from the Métro, and they were augmented by the passengers of a bus that had just pulled up. She switched on her video camera, and rested it on her shoulder. It was quite heavy, an old-style one that used VHS tape, and she hoped its antiquity would help towards the *mixed-media* aspect of her assessment. She took the stone from her pocket.

She had chosen it carefully. It was a smooth pebble about the size of a small grape, and so dark grey that it might as well have been black. She had decided that a dark one would be ideal for the task, because it wouldn't be lost against the backdrop of light stone apartment buildings. She had taken it from the collection of interesting stones she had built up as a young girl, most of them found on beaches on family trips to the seaside. She couldn't remember which beach this one had come from, but it must have been the combination of its smoothness and darkness that had marked it out from its neighbours and inspired her to pick it up and take it home.

She had spent the preceding Sunday afternoon practising in the Bois de Boulogne. When she was growing up, her father had often told her he wasn't prepared to raise a daughter who couldn't throw, and over the years she had developed a good right arm. The problem was going to be capturing the stone on film. She had begun with horse chestnuts, throwing them as high as she could and trying to locate them in the viewfinder at the same time, following their trajectory as they rose and fell. Once she had practised enough with horse chestnuts she had moved on to stones. She had been so lost in her task that by the time she gave up, her arm aching so much she could no longer throw, the park was growing dark, and unusually beautiful silhouettes had begun to appear along the roadside.

It was a clear morning. Yesterday's rain and clouds had gone, leaving only a few puddles. The sky was blue, and the light was good. She held the stone as she pressed the *record* button, closed her eyes, counted slowly to fifteen, pulled back her right arm and threw.

She knew before it had left her hand that the throw was a good one, high and true. She opened her eyes and immediately caught the small black dot in the viewfinder, just as she had practised. It rose to its apex, and seemed for a split second to hover, completely still, before beginning its descent. It was at this moment that her doubts set in: she went from a state of absolute confidence in her plan to a feeling of wretched stupidity. *This is art*, she had thought, exhilarated as the stone had left her hand. But she no longer felt that way, and she had no idea what it was, apart from a ridiculous and ill-thought-out thing to do.

She had intended to stay silent, but she couldn't. Even so, she had no idea that she had spoken. It was only much later, when she played the tape back, that she heard, above the music of the hurdy-gurdy, the words she had uttered as she saw where the black dot was heading.

Oh God. Oh shit . . .

She realised with horror that the stone – smooth and black and the size of a small grape – was about to land, hard, on a baby's face.

II

It had been a long day for Professor Papavoine, the one he dreaded more than any other in the academic calendar. The students had been given free rein to come up with a personal project, and it was his job to listen to their ideas and either sanction them or not. As always on this day of the year he was running late, but at last he had almost made it through. He had only a handful of ten-minute tutorials left in a day that had been full of ten-minute tutorials. The door opened, and his latest student walked in. His heart thumped as if she had pulled a gun on him, and he stopped breathing.

He coughed as air rushed back into his lungs, and tried his best to pull himself together. 'Sit down,' he invited, his tone welcoming, just as it had been for all the other students. He looked at his schedule. 'Aurélie Renard?'

'Yes.'

'Aurélie Renard. Aurélie . . .' He left a deliberate gap, smiled and rolled the *r* for as long as his tongue would allow. '. . . Renard.' This double repetition had become traditional, and he did it without thinking. It was a friendly touch that was designed, successfully, to put the student at ease and give the misleading impression that he was going to be fully engaged in the conversation that was to follow, listening very carefully to every word of their proposal. This time, though, he added a third repetition which, it struck him halfway through, was for his own benefit, to imprint her name in his memory. 'Aurélie Renard,' he mumbled, his eyes glazed. It was a repetition too far, and his intonation left its meaning unclear.

She looked confused. 'Er . . . yes?'

He shuddered as if waking from a trance, which, he supposed, was just what was happening. He knew he had to turn this situation around. 'Hello, Aurélie Renard!' he cried. He realised too late that this was over-friendly. He had even raised his hand in a cheery wave, as if she had been a small child and he a dental surgeon about to perform an appalling procedure upon her. He cleared his throat, and for a moment he allowed himself to just look at her. She was quite short, three or four centimetres below average height he guessed, and slim, with breasts that were palpable, yet unobtrusive. She was very pretty, in a no-make-up kind of way. She was what his colleague Professor Boucher would have called a *compact blonde*.

Professor Boucher took pride in putting all the female students into chauvinistic categories, and whenever a *compact blonde* was in the vicinity he took the opportunity to pull faces, wink and bug his eyes out, implying that she would be Professor Papavoine's *type*. Sometimes his grey chain smoker's tongue would even dart out of his mouth and moisten the lips that lurked below his unruly beard. Professor Papavoine was always exasperated by these displays, and what exasperated him more than anything was that Professor Boucher was right; he supposed the compact blonde *was* his type, insofar as he had one.

'So,' he said, taking care now to sound at least a little bit professorial, 'you have an idea for your project?'

'Yes.' Aurélie swallowed hard, and began. Until a few minutes earlier she had been determined to stick to her original plan of spending the coming weeks producing a series of line drawings. Drawing had been her first love; it was what had led to her being singled out by her art teacher as an exceptional student, and it had won her prizes at school. It was her love of drawing that had driven her to apply to art college, to leave the industrial town she had grown up in and come to Paris to learn about materials and technique, and to become as accomplished as she possibly could at the only thing she had ever been really good at, apart from making mashed potato.

Her idea for the project had been to wander around her neighbourhood and draw people, animals and objects: anything she saw that she thought would make a good subject. She'd had a feeling, though, that telling the professor she wanted to draw a series of pictures would not be enough, that he was going to be looking for an *angle*. She had one ready. It was bold, perhaps even audacious: she was going to look him in the eye and tell him that she planned to make these line drawings really, really good. She would leave it at that.

As she had waited for her name to be called, she had

joined her fellow students outside the professor's office, and her confidence began to drain away. Sitting in a circle of much criticised plastic chairs, she had listened quietly as they talked at length about their own proposals. They seemed to come from a different planet from hers. Their talk was of *recontextualising found objects*, of *blurring the boundary between art and the everyday*, and of *provoking extreme reactions*. One of the students, Sébastien, was saying something about *subverting the zeitgeist*.

She watched him as he took his turn to hold court. On the last day of college before the summer break everyone had gone out for drinks, and she had ended up inviting him back to her apartment, and they had spent the night together. He had left first thing in the morning, and hadn't called her once over the summer. He was tall, and had good bones, and she had liked him from the moment she had set eyes on him. She had spent more time than she should have done wondering whether he had lost her number, or whether she had written it down incorrectly as he hurried to gather his things and go.

When she saw him again at the start of the current term, as scores of students milled around waiting to be allowed into a lecture hall, she had sought him out, gone up to him and said hello. He had given her only a cursory greeting before returning to the intense conversation he had been having with a fellow student about something she didn't understand, and had no particular interest in understanding. He was acting as if nothing had ever happened between them, as if she was just another slight acquaintance from his course, as if she had never slept in his arms, and as if he had not lightly pinched her chin as he told her that her eyes were just the right shade of blue. He hadn't even asked her how her summer had been.

She had stood there for a minute or two, and when she realised he wasn't going to acknowledge her further she had gone away and leaned against a wall by herself. He hadn't been her first, but he had been her third, and she had hoped it would be a case of third time lucky. He was with another girl now, a sculptor with waist-length black hair, who never smiled. She had seen them around together.

On visits home, Aurélie had endured several identical conversations with various aunts, uncles and neighbours about the apparent horrors of a monstrous thing called *modern art*.

—*So you're at art college?*

'Yes.'

—*What kind of work do you do? It's not modern art, is it?*

'I mainly do line drawings, but I'm starting to work with oil paint too.'

—*So, it's not modern?*

'Er . . . not particularly.'

—*Thank God for that.*

Every time this happened she felt like grabbing the aunt, uncle or neighbour and shaking them. She didn't like the idea that what she did was automatically considered to be better than everything that they lumped together under the banner of *modern art*. She was also frustrated by the implication that because she chose to work in a conventional way, then what she produced must be old-fashioned and unoriginal. By their standards, being old-fashioned and unoriginal were virtues, and they didn't even feel the need to see any of her work before declaring her superiority, purely because of her perceived refusal to embrace anything that might be considered to be in some way progressive.

She was very impressed with a lot of the work her fellow students were producing, and some of this work would doubtless be considered *modern art* by these aunts, uncles and neighbours. She knew how much care and thought went into it, and though some of it ended up plain, ugly or nowhere near as original as the artist thought it was, a lot of it worked incredibly well, and it dismayed her to see it all dismissed by people who would never be open-minded enough to give it a chance. She was always looking for different ways to approach her work, and she had ideas for new perspectives and techniques, and had plans to seek out unusual subjects, all of which would amount to something that would be seen as undeniably *modern* to her supporters.

She also had plenty of aunts, uncles and neighbours who were more open-minded about art, but listening to Sébastien, who was still going on, she knew he would stretch even their patience. He was saying something about *mapping territory beyond the beyond*. He wasn't doing himself, or anyone else, any favours at all.

She had never been able to work out what this kind of talk had to do with anything. It seemed designed only for the artists to elevate themselves into positions of intellectual unassailability before they had even taken the time to put brush to canvas, or smash the bricks, or saw the hooves off the freeze-dried donkey. She couldn't see what it could ever do but alienate people, and turn them away from all art, good and bad, and it was this that had driven her to keep her proposal as straightforward as possible, as uncluttered with explanations and justifications.

She supposed the simplicity of her proposal had, at least partly, been a kind of protest against the sort of thing she had been listening to, as well as the excruciating artists' statements she often read on exhibition programmes, words that turned her against the work before she had even seen it. But whatever her intentions, her plan to announce that she was going to simply draw some pictures no longer seemed bold and combative; it just seemed very small, as if she hadn't given it any thought at all. She worried that she would be laughed out of the professor's office, or castigated for having a lack of ambition or for being unable to articulate her ideas. Her courage evaporating, she did what she always did at times like this: she asked herself what her friend Sylvie would do.

Sylvie was always breezing into difficult situations, and she had a knack for escaping them. Aurélie began to consider feigning a fainting fit to get out of the appointment, but she decided that Sylvie would have come up with something more creative and far less transparently fraudulent than this. Then, as if from nowhere, a plan came into her mind. She knew at once that she had found a way to present the professor with the kind of proposal he would be looking for. She had no idea whether or not it was any good, but at least it was something other than saying she was going to draw some pictures.

Sébastien's soliloquy was still going on. By now he was furiously bemoaning the blindness of the public, how unable they are to even *see* brilliance, let alone comprehend it. By this, she knew he meant that they were unable to see or comprehend *his* brilliance. She had seen his latest piece, and it had looked like something torn from a children's colouring book; if it had any worth she was blind to it as well. She was annoyed with herself for having let him make her so unhappy, and even more annoyed that she still found him so attractive, that she still wished he had called, and that it had been her, and not the unsmiling sculptor, by his side. She made a mental note to have a word with herself about him, to write a list of everything that was wrong with him and stick it to her fridge door with a magnet.

She left him to his monologue and continued to pull her plan into shape. She even started to feel quite pleased with it. It had still been forming in her mind when the professor's secretary called her through to his office.

Every year Professor Papavoine began this day with the intention of listening hard to what his students were saying, but it had never happened. In the opening seconds of his first appointment it would strike him that there was really no point, and unable to get away from this truth his concentration lost focus and only odds and ends of the students' ideas ever registered with him. These sessions barely counted as tutorials; being only symbolic, they were a way of acknowledging that the students had made it through to the second year of study and were now ready to have their projects approved by an authentic professor. The faculty's primary aim in this was for news of these encounters to reach the parents, who would, they hoped, be satisfied that their offspring were receiving an acceptable standard of education. Whatever the students' proposals for their personal projects, Professor Papavoine waved them through, wished them all the best and sent them on their way. He didn't see what else he could do.

The only time he had ever come close to vetoing a suggestion was when a student had proposed a project in which he would publicly collect, categorise and display everything that came out of his body over a twelve-week period. A big glass vat would contain his urine, another would house his excrement, and smaller demijohns and specimen jars would hold snot, earwax, semen and sweat. He had planned on presenting this as an exhibition called, simply, *Life,* during which he would be on display himself twenty-four hours a day, naked and publicly topping up the exhibits as the weeks went by, while microphones picked up the sound of his bodily functions and a series of speakers amplified them around the room in near-deafening surround sound.

Professor Papavoine had pulled a slightly quizzical face and said he wasn't quite sure about this idea, at which the student had turned white with rage and stormed out, vowing to leave the college, turn his back on Paris and make his name in London, which he had promptly done with this very concept. In interviews he had derided the conservatism of his forsaken home city, and announced that he had embraced the English way of art, which he confirmed by selling the completed work to an oligarch for three quarters of a million pounds and gaining member-ship of a number of private drinking clubs.

He had gone on to present *Life* in San Francisco, Tokyo and São Paolo, and with each new staging its popularity had increased. It had become acknowledged as a sensation of the international art world, and it was due to open in Paris any day now: the return of the Prodigal Son. Everybody was talking about it. Since his meeting with

Professor Papavoine he had shaved off all his hair, even his eyebrows, and changed his name to *Le Machine*. There were posters all over the city of the artist naked among the empty receptacles, his genitalia only just obscured by a carefully positioned specimen jar. Bold letters across the top said, simply: *Le Machine: Life*. Were it not for the booking information at the foot of these posters, they could almost be mistaken for advertisements for a gentlemen's fragrance. Professor Papavoine spoke to nobody about his encounter with the star of the event.

In every case other than Le Machine's, though, Professor Papavoine had expressed neither doubt nor discomfort, and he made a point of offering no praise. He would think no more of the ideas he heard until weeks later, when the time came time for him to sit on the assessment panel.

Aurélie carried on. Professor Papavoine really wanted to hear what she had to say, and he worked hard at concentrating. She told him her plans to blindly throw a dart into a map, and how the nearest suitable public space to where it landed would become the starting point of the project. Then she started saying something about small stones, and strangers, and random selection, but he lost the thread. As he looked at her, he was only just able to stop himself from sighing. She was so pretty. Her shortish hair was tied back, and he noticed that one of her ears stuck out a bit more than the other, and her teeth were a little uneven. He guessed she would have been offered braces when she was a teenager, but refused to have them fitted. *Oh, petulant child*, thought Professor Papavoine.

She wasn't quite beautiful, but she was really, really

close. To him, her extreme prettiness combined with her rough edges to make her even more incredible to look at than if had she been the conventionally beautiful, airbrushed type.

He realised he was no longer listening, and tuned back in. He heard the phrase *mixed media*, and immediately tuned back out. He was mesmerised. He wanted to . . . he wanted to do all sorts of things with her.

Professor Boucher would have made fun of the feelings he was experiencing for Aurélie Renard. 'When are we going to get a decent midlife crisis out of you?' he had asked Professor Papavoine with depressing frequency. 'You're in danger of leaving it too late – what are you? Fifty-what?' He was fifty-seven. Professor Boucher habitually mocked him for never having taken a mistress. There had never even been a fleeting clandestine romance, or a tortuous, humiliating episode of unrequited obsession. 'And you are *definitely* French?'

'There are rumours in my family that I had an English great-grandfather.'

'Maybe that explains it. But even so, could you not just fuck a student every once in a while? For the faculty's sake? This is an art college, after all – we have our reputation to consider.'

Professor Papavoine liked to think he had a high threshold when it came to vulgarity, but he often found his colleague to be almost unbearable, and sometimes he wondered how they had ever become such close friends. His working days would have passed so much more serenely if Professor Boucher had been a personal and professional adversary.

He was pleased to see that Aurélie Renard seemed

to be looking a little unsure about the words she was saying, avoiding eye contact as she spoke about *making a statement*, and *the importance of social documentary*, and how she aimed to *capture the essence of somebody's time, because, er, I suppose, er, everybody lives in their own time*. As with all the ideas he had half-listened to that day, it didn't seem to make much sense, and, as with all of them, it could go either way. It would be good, bad or, as was almost always the case, somewhere in between. He had heard plans to *appropriate the now*, to *create tension between the artist and the work*, and one desperate case had even risen to his feet as he announced his plan to *subvert the zeitgeist*.

More often than not, he felt sorry for the students as they made their proposals. It was as if they really believed that their work wouldn't count as art unless it had a paragraph of awful words behind it. He longed for one of them to tell him that they were going to paint a picture, and work really hard to make it a good picture, and leave it at that. This never seemed to happen.

At least Aurélie Renard's proposal seemed, if he had understood any of the fragments to which he had paid attention, to be about something. So many of the concepts he heard were so abstract as to be unintelligible. It struck him that she had stopped talking. It was his turn.

He said what he had said to the others: 'That sounds fine. I wish you all the best with it. I look forward to seeing the result.'

'Me too,' she said. 'I hope it'll be interesting.' Relieved at having made it through, her guard came down, and she smiled. 'I suppose I just want to make something beautiful.' As soon as the words came out she felt she had made a mistake. That would have been the last thing the professor wanted to hear.

She rose to leave, but Professor Papavoine gestured for her to sit back down. He opened a desk drawer, and pulled out a card. It carried the university's crest. He shook his head, put the card back and pulled out another one. 'I would like to hear how things are going. Any time you would like to talk about it, just call me.' Knowing he was crossing a line, and trying not to tremble, he handed it to her.

She took it, and looked at it. It was a personal card, with the professor's home address and phone number on it, along with a personal email address. She had a pretty good idea that this was unusual, and wondered whether or not she should start to become suspicious of his motives. She put it in her pocket. 'Thank you, professor,' she said.

He paused, looked straight into her eyes, and said, 'Any time.' He looked down at his hands, which were clutching the edge of the desk. 'Day or night.'

'Yes,' she said, quietly. She looked sadly at the dull gold band on his ring finger. 'Of course.'

He watched her go, and when the door had shut behind her he picked up the framed photograph that faced him throughout his every working day. It was a picture of his wife. He smiled. She would have been about the same age as this Aurélie Renard when it was taken. She too was a little below average height, and slim, and very pretty, in a no-make-up kind of way. She was what Professor Boucher would have called a *compact blonde*.

At last, he allowed himself a sigh.

III

Weeks later, when she watched the footage, Aurélie Renard calculated that when the stone smashed into the baby's face it would have been travelling at somewhere between sixty-five and seventy kilometres per hour. The impact made little sound, just a dull smack that had been buried by the sound of the traffic and the hurdy-gurdy before it could reach the built-in microphone. She found it strange that something so terrible had made so little noise.

People were still making their way through the square. Some of them glanced her way, having caught an unexpected flash of movement and noticed her video camera. Uninterested, and just wanting to get out of the cold, they walked on. To her, they might as well have not been there. She saw only the baby, reclining in his buggy. There was a terrible stillness. Perhaps she had killed him.

She put her hand to her heart with relief when his little hands rose and clenched into fists. She hoped that this meant he was fine. She hadn't spent a great deal of time with babies, and had no idea that this moment of calm was usual when they are hurt, that it takes a while for the shock to subside and the pain to register. Three seconds after the event, the child's face crumpled in confusion and despair, and tears spilled from his eyes. His mouth opened wide, but there was still no sound. Then, on the seventh second, it came, a bottomless howl.

Aurélie lowered the video camera from her shoulder. She put a hand to her mouth as she shook with worry. The possibility of such an outcome had not crossed her mind, and she realised just how stupid she had been. She had no idea what to do next, and it was only then that it occurred to her that the baby had not been making his own way across the square. He came as part of a package with a mother, and she was leaning over him, dabbing his face with a cloth. Only when this was done did the mother turn away from the inconsolable child and give Aurélie a look of disgust that she would never forget.

She knew she deserved it. She wanted to turn and run, to get out of there as quickly as she could, and try to convince herself that this had never happened. She couldn't, though. She had to say sorry, to the howling child and to his mother. Burning with shame, she made her way over to the scene she had created.

She stood silently, cringing as the mother made a point of ignoring her, choosing instead to lean over the buggy and apply a folded baby wipe as a compress to the child's face. It wasn't until minutes later, when the baby had at last stopped crying, that she turned to Aurélie, gave her an

ice-cold smile and said, softly, 'You did a good job. Look
. . .' She lifted the makeshift compress, and pointed to a
red blotch on his face. 'That'll bruise nicely. Very nicely,
indeed. Another centimetre in this direction,' she pointed,
'and you'd have put his eye out. Just imagine that! And
I don't mean that as a figure of speech – I want you to
really imagine it.'

Aurélie pictured a shattered eyeball, and it was awful.
She couldn't think of anything to say. She and the baby's
mother were around the same age. She liked the way
she was dressed; perhaps under different circumstances
they would have become friends. She had been on the
lookout for a new scarf, and she could have asked
her where she had bought hers. She liked it a lot, and
thought the turquoise complemented her colouring. She
could have gone to the same shop and bought herself
one, but in a different colour so it wouldn't be copying.
An image flashed before her of the two of them in their
scarves, drinking coffee and laughing as the baby looked
on from his buggy. But instead she stood there feeling
like a child as she accepted her scolding. She wondered
whether this was the right moment to explain herself
and apologise.

The woman hadn't finished. 'Better luck next time.' Her
eyes narrowed. Her sarcasm exhausted, she exploded in
anger. 'You make me sick.'

Aurélie nodded. She made herself sick too.

'What did you think when you got out of bed this
morning? *I know – I've got a brilliant idea: I'll go out into
the street and throw a stone at a baby.* You're a genius.
Round of applause!' She clapped and clapped, and Aurélie
stood still, looking at the ground as she accepted this

bitter ovation. 'Bravo!' cried the baby's mother. 'Bravo!' Just when it seemed this would never end, she pulled her phone from her pocket. 'And when the police come, what will you tell them? I can't wait to hear . . . One moment.' The stone had fallen nearby, and she took out her handkerchief and gently picked it up between gloved fingers. 'Fingerprints. In case you make a run for it.'

Aurélie nodded. She wasn't going to make a run for it.

The baby's mother seemed to be examining her. Then, in a single motion, she reached out and yanked a stray hair from Aurélie's head. She held it up, and said, 'DNA.' She placed the hair next to the stone on the handkerchief, which she folded and put in her coat pocket.

'So what will you tell them? Why did you do it?'

Aurélie rubbed the spot on her head where the hair had been plucked. She knew she owed her a full and honest explanation. She looked at the ground. 'It's an art project,' she said. 'I'm at art college.'

'Art!? Painting a picture, that's art. Carving a statue, that's art too. There's a guy coming to town who thinks that shitting into a bottle is art. Maybe it is, I don't know. But this is the first time I've ever heard that attacking a baby can be a work of art. You know what? I think it might even catch on. You'll get full marks for your project. You'll be rich. You'll be just like Monet, only instead of painting lily ponds you'll be hurting children. Here comes one now – quick, go and kick her in the face.'

The square was no longer busy with commuters, and a toddler was nearby, holding her father's hand. She looked as if she had only just learned to walk – her legs were stiff and wide apart, her steps faltering. She was a picture of delight as she put her new-found skills to work. The last thing Aurélie wanted to do was kick her in the face.

'I didn't know I was going to hit a baby,' she said. 'I could have hit anyone.'

'Oh, that makes it better. That makes it fine.'

'I thought it would just land in front of someone, and they would stop and look at it. Or maybe it would bounce off their shoulder or their back without hurting them. People are wearing quite thick clothes at the moment.'

'And you gave no thought to it hitting someone's head?'

She had done. She had worked out that it would be very unlikely, and had supposed that if it did hit someone on the head it would only give them a surprise and maybe sting a bit, but nothing more. It was a small stone, after all, and she hadn't thought for a moment that any of the people going past would be looking to the sky, like the baby.

'And what was next? Once you had blinded a random passer-by, or given them brain damage? What was next for your art project?'

'I was going to rush over to them and explain my idea.'

'I'm sure they would have been dying to hear about it. In fact, why am I standing in the way of your assignment? Here he is. Here's your random passer-by. Introduce yourself, and tell him all about it.' She pointed at the baby, who had calmed down and was sitting in his buggy looking melancholy. 'Go on.'

Aurélie hesitated for a moment, then crouched to his level. She felt she owed him at least this much. 'Hello,' she said. 'I'm Aurélie. Aurélie Renard. I'm the one who threw the stone at you. I'm really sorry about that.' She reached out and tentatively touched the baby's shoulder.

'Don't touch him.'

Aurélie withdrew her hand and lowered her eyes. 'No,' she said. 'Of course not.' She addressed the baby again. 'As I said, I'm sorry. With hindsight I can see it was a mistake – I should have used a different random selection process. What I was supposed to do was make you my subject for one week. I was hoping you would grant me permission to follow you around and take photos of you, and make short films and draw pictures of you. That sort of thing. It was going to be a depiction of everyday life. *Your* everyday life. The randomness of throwing a stone into a crowd was going to stop it from being a premeditated selection, and retain the purity of the . . .' She couldn't go on. She sounded so stupid. There was nothing good about this idea. She looked at the mark on the baby's face, and fought tears as she thought of how sad her dad would be if he ever found out what she had done.

The child's mother looked sidelong at Aurélie. Then she looked at the baby. She seemed to be thinking hard. 'One week, you say?' Her manner had softened.

'Yes.'

'Wait here.' She walked over to a secluded part of the square, and pulled out her phone. She made a call. Aurélie couldn't hear what she was saying, but the conversation seemed to be making her happy. She hung up, and walked back to where they were.

'Let me look at you.' She gestured for Aurélie to stand up. She obeyed, and they stood nose to nose. The child's mother turned a finger and thumb into a clamp, and gripped Aurélie by the chin. Aurélie noticed how soft her gloves were. She liked them too. The mother moved her face left and right, then up and down and round and round, examining her from a number of angles. 'You have a kind face,' she said. She flicked one of her ears. 'This ear sticks out a bit more than the other one, but I can't see that being too much of a problem. And you do seem to be genuinely sorry.'

'I am. I'm really, really sorry.'

'I think you might even mean it . . .' She moved Aurélie's head around a little more. 'Yes. Yes, you do mean it. You are sorry. It was a stupid thing to have done, really stupid, but anybody can make a mistake. It wouldn't be right for me to judge you too harshly.'

Aurélie had never been more relieved. She had been convinced that she would be kicked out of college and sent to jail. 'Thank you,' she said. 'Thank you so much.'

'You're not from Paris, are you? I can tell from your accent.'

'No. I've been here about a year and a half.'

'So would it be safe to say that you're a simple country girl with honest country ways?'

'I, er . . .' Aurélie had no idea what to say to this. She had never lived in the countryside, but the child's mother was making her sound as if she had just stepped out of a Raymond Depardon documentary; she felt she ought to be holding a shepherd's crook, her cheeks ruddy after a lifetime in the wind. Her home town was certainly small compared to Paris, though, and she told herself she was only lying a little bit when she said, 'I hope so.'

The mother gave her a sideways stare, as she continued to size her up.

'If there's anything I can do to make it up to you and the baby,' said Aurélie, 'just tell me.'

'Anything? Really?'

Aurélie nodded, in so far as she was able with somebody else's hand clamped to her chin. She truly wanted to make amends.

The woman stared at her for while. She seemed to be weighing up a big decision. At last, she let go of Aurélie's face. 'Do you know how one of these things works?' she asked, pointing.

'The buggy? No, not really. I think I could push it along, but I wouldn't know how to fold it, or get it down steps, or anything like that.'

'I'm not talking about the buggy. I mean what's in it. The thing you just threw the stone at: the baby.'

Aurélie shook her head. She had no idea how babies worked. She had occasionally had a small child lowered on to her lap for a photograph, then lifted off as soon as it had been taken, but beyond that she had never held one. 'No,' she said. 'Not really.'

'Never mind,' said the mother. 'They're quite straightforward. Now, I want to show you something.' She gestured for Aurélie to join her at the back of the buggy. There was a big bag hanging off the back, in coordinated red fabric. 'In here is everything he needs to get through the day. It goes everywhere with him whenever he leaves the house. You need to be prepared for all eventualities.'

Aurélie nodded, wondering where this was going.

The mother continued. 'It'll be easy. I changed him about twenty minutes ago. All you have to do is keep him alive. Sterilise his bottle, don't let him roll off the bed, all that kind of thing. Just use your common sense and rustic intuition. Just imagine he's one of your sheep.'

Aurélie had never so much as touched a sheep.

The mother went on. 'He's a good child. He won't give you any trouble.' She thought for a while. 'Well, he has his moments, but I doubt he'll give you *much* trouble. No more throwing stones at him, and I'll see you back here exactly one week from now.' She looked at her watch. 'At nine twenty-two next Wednesday.'

The woman crouched, and said a brief goodbye to the boy, telling him that the nice lady who had given him the bruise was going to be his mummy for a week. She didn't kiss him, or even touch him. She stood up, and turned to leave.

'But . . .' Aurélie was dazed. She felt herself lose her balance, and she held on to the buggy for support.

The mother turned back, her eyes cold and narrow. 'But what? Suddenly you don't want to do your project? What happened to the you of a moment ago, the you who was such a dedicated artist? Don't tell me you've given up? Would you rather I called the police? Is that how you want your project to end, before a judge, being handed a conviction for assaulting an infant? Would that be art? Would it?' She took her phone from her pocket.

Aurélie had no idea whether or not it would be art, but she pictured herself in jail and was desperate not to end up behind bars. 'No, I mean . . . But . . . what's he called?'

'His name is Herbert.'

'Herbert?' Aurélie pronounced it the French way, with no H at the beginning and no t at the end: *Air-bear.*

'No,' snapped the mother. 'Not *Air-bear.* Herbert. Repeat after me – *Herbert.*'

'*Air-bear.*'

The mother closed her eyes, pinched the top of her nose and shook her head. She reached into her shoulder bag and pulled out a compact mirror. She held it in front of Aurélie's mouth and made the *H* sound.

Aurélie did as she was instructed, and made the sound.

'See, there's mist on the mirror. Now say his name.'

'H-H-Hair-bear'

'Herber*t*. *T-t-t*.'

'T-t-t.'

'After me: Herber*t*.'

Aurélie closed her eyes in concentration as she tried to get her tongue around these unfamiliar sounds. 'Herber*t*,' she said.

'Close. Again, though.'

'Her-bert. Her-bert. Herbert.'

'Almost perfect. You're a fast learner, I'll give you that.'

'Is he English?'

'Does he look English to you?'

Aurélie scrutinised the child. She couldn't tell.

'Now don't do anything stupid. I've got your DNA, remember?' She patted the pocket where she had put the stone and the hair. 'I'll see you back here in one week. Right there.' She pointed at the bench where The Russian had been playing his hurdy-gurdy. Aurélie hadn't noticed until that point that he had packed up and gone. The mother walked away.

As she watched her go, Aurélie realised that all she knew about the baby was his name. She needed to know a little bit more about him. She called after her, 'How old is he?'

Without looking back, she replied, 'He's Aquarius.'

She called again. 'One last thing . . .'

Herbert's mother stopped, turned and glared at her. 'What?'

Aurélie's head swam with questions. After what seemed

like an age, one of them rose to the surface. The woman was some way away, and she had to shout. 'Where did you get your scarf?'

'La Foularderie. It's one of those shops in Le Marais. You'll find it.'

'I really like it.'

'Thank you. Me too.'

And with that she was gone.

The square was empty now, and quiet. Aurélie stood beside the buggy, and looked at the baby. His battered face was peeping out from under his hat. 'Hello *Air-bear*,' she said. She corrected herself. 'I'm sorry. I mean hello . . . *Her-ber*t. *Herber*t. Herbert.' She had to get his name right. She owed him at least this. She knelt over him. 'So . . . Herbert,' she said. At last she felt able to rest her hand on his shoulder. She gave it a squeeze. 'Do you think we can be friends?'

He looked at her, then did something she hadn't expected: he smiled. It was amazing. He seemed to smile with his whole face, and even his arms and legs joined in, flapping up and down and side to side. He made a sound as well, a kind of squelchy giggle. She took that for a *yes*. She knew this ought to be a cue for her to grab her digital camera and take a photo, but she didn't. She just looked at him and smiled back. There would be plenty of time for photos.

She tried to work out what to do next. She took stock of the situation. It was a nice buggy, a sleek, bright red three-wheeler with a black frame. It looked expensive. She was pleased to see that the buggy and the baby's bag matched her new coat. She needed to cling to something, and she told herself that this colour coordination was a clear sign that this unexpected turn of events was meant to be. As she crouched beside her new friend she lit her fifth cigarette of the morning, in the hope that it would help her think things over.

She put her used match back in the box, and made a point of blowing the smoke away from Herbert's face. She had responsibilities now.

IV

Monsieur Eric Rousset, proprietor of Le Charmant Cinéma Érotique, had fallen on hard times. His establishment, situated on a narrow backstreet just off the Boulevard de Clichy, had been opened in the late nineteen forties by his grandfather, another Monsieur Eric Rousset, who had handed it down to Monsieur Rousset's father, also Monsieur Eric Rousset, who in turn had the pleasure of steering it through its heyday of the sixties and seventies. The latest and last Monsieur Eric Rousset, though, had found to his dismay that there was little he could do but oversee its decline.

It seemed to him that the precise moment he had taken the reins of the family business, the home video phenomenon had arrived to lure away row after row of his audience. Then came DVDs, their picture so clear that it was possible to freeze each frame and make out beads of sweat, even individual hairs, and as if this wasn't bad enough, televisions had become larger and larger until they began to resemble cinema screens. Just as he had started to feel like a beleaguered ship's captain saluting the flag as water lapped around his ankles, the Internet had caught on, the driving force of this revolution in communications technology being its seemingly endless supply of free porn for all.

The changing world had siphoned his customers away until they were all but gone. He often sighed at the thought of how devalued the erotic movie had become, but knowing that there were few sights more pathetic than that of a short, fat, middle-aged bald man sighing, he took care to do so only in private, and at all other times he maintained as cheery a facade as he could.

Monsieur Rousset did not want to close his cinema. As well as it being the only livelihood he had ever known, he was unable to escape a nagging loyalty to the memory of his father and grandfather, and to his remaining clientele. He knew his regulars by sight, but not name; conversation was not expected in his business. Sometimes a familiar character would fail to show up for a few weeks in a row, and he knew he would not be seeing them again, that they had been claimed by a nursing home, taken in by concerned relatives or bundled into a box and fed into an incinerator. He was always saddened when this happened. Though many would have dismissed them as *dirty old men*, to him they were no better or worse than anybody else. Life had not been easy for them, and they were making the best of what it had to offer. He saw no shame in them answering their body's urges, but it always made him melancholy to see the loneliness in their eyes. As he turned a deaf ear to the rustling, the heavy breathing and the throaty gasps that came out of the dark, he was thankful that he had Madame Rousset waiting for him in their apartment a few streets away.

He was not immune to the charms of the films he showed, but he had never once slipped into the stalls to entertain himself alongside his customers, or misbehaved in his office or a projection room. He loved his wife, and always waited until he got home before giving in to his amorous urges. Just as short, plain, dumpy and middle-aged as her husband, Madame Rousset was well aware of the genesis of his romantic tendencies, but she was happy to accept things the way they were. She couldn't imagine there being a more regularly serviced wife in the whole of Paris, and theirs was a happy marriage that had produced one child, a daughter named Élise who had recently qualified as a doctor and who for innumerable reasons, none of them prudish, had never had any interest in taking over the family business.

Élise was proud of her parents, and to her father's delight she would often turn up at the cinema unannounced, with a group of colleagues on a night out. She would introduce them all, and he would shake their hands and usher them in for free, and they would take their pick of whatever happened to be showing. The last time they had dropped by he had been pleased when they had chosen a revival of the 1973 Inuit classic *Cut Not a Circle in the Ice Tonight*. It was one of his all-time favourites; the cinematography was faultless, the haunting score, played on a single chauyak, raised the hairs on the back of his neck, and the lesbian scene was up there with the best.

There was still a trickle of passing trade to bolster the

dwindling numbers of regulars, but year on year this too was diminishing, which made him very downhearted, not only for himself and the state of the business, but also because of the thought that there were so many people out there who had no idea what they were missing. He refused to show the kind of films that had come to be associated with the genre, with their weak punning titles and lack-lustre camera work. There had never been any question in his mind that his was the finest cinema of its kind in the city. He personally vetted each film for quality, and in this age, where it seemed as if everybody was making their own sex tapes, he refused to let his standards slip and took pride in showing only work of the highest order, sourced from the most committed film-makers from around the world. These were people who really cared about what they did, and he often told himself that if the films they made weren't art, then nothing was. His 35mm rule had kept him, aesthetically at least, streets ahead of rivals who had lazily resorted to video projectors, but he sometimes wondered whether his customers noticed this, or cared.

Inevitably, the cinema had slid into a state of disrepair. What had once had the feel of an exclusive gentlemen's club was becoming like any other sex flick fleapit: the deep red carpet was worn down, and paths of grey ran from the box office to the screens; the once plush velvet-textured wallpaper had been rubbed smooth to shoulder height; and the handyman had not been called in to replace fallen chandelier crystals.

In dark moments, Monsieur Rousset had thought about pulling down the shutters for the last time, putting the place out of its misery while it still had a shred of dignity left, but then he would see one of his regulars shuffling in, avoiding eye contact with him and with the rest of the world, and every time his sentimentality got the better of him. He knew that to close would be to tear the heart out of their lives. What else would they do? Where would they go? He knew he would struggle on, doing his best for them until the lights went out. He also knew, though, that this day would not be far away.

One afternoon in April, while he was dwelling a little more than was healthy on this sad state of affairs, he had taken a call in his office. 'Rousset,' he had said, rubbing his temple in anticipation of bad news as he did every time he answered the phone. From the other end came an unfamiliar voice, a woman who spoke perfect French with an unplaceable international accent. She told him she was the representative of an individual who had taken an interest in his premises.

Property developers, he thought. He supposed he might as well humour her. He would always have bills to pay, and if he was going to leave the business with anything at all to show for it he would have to sit down with her kind at some point.

'So,' he said, 'what can I do for you?'

Fifteen minutes later he put down the phone, having made the biggest decision of his working life: the cinema was to close. He had agreed to relinquish the building from early September until the end of January, during which time he would make enough money to restore the place to its former glory. And what's more he would be able to raise its profile and completely relaunch it – to let people know what Le Charmant Cinéma Érotique was: the only place to come for serious, hand-picked, properly projected grumble flicks from around the world. Out of nowhere had risen a new beginning.

He usually steered clear of the Internet. For a long time he had considered it an enemy whose sole intent was to bring Le Charmant Cinéma Érotique to its knees, but that day Monsieur Eric Rousset delightedly swept a pile of papers off his keyboard, opened a search engine and typed in his saviour's name: *Le Machine*.

Monsieur Rousset had the patrons of the major art museums to thank for the uplift in his fortunes. Le Machine's fame had made its way back to his forsaken home city, and when he announced his intention of bringing *Life* to Paris, a scramble had begun as the main players raced to be the one to host the work.

The scramble was followed by a swift retreat as, one by one, the city's art-minded philanthropists made discreet phone calls in which they made it quite clear that they could not be seen to support such an exhibition, and that they would have no choice but to reconsider their relationship with their favoured gallery were it to go ahead. Likewise, the controllers of government budgets were wary of a press backlash, and made it clear that they were not prepared to release funds in support of this installation. Within days of the announcement, it had become clear to everybody involved that *Life* had not found a home.

Le Machine's management had anticipated this outcome, and could not have been more delighted: their star's outsider status was confirmed beyond doubt, and though the organisational burden and initial investment would be greatly increased, they would be able to take full control of the marketing and the money. A few numbers jotted on the back of an envelope showed them that they would be on course to make around twice as much this way. All they needed was to find the right venue. And that, it turned out, was easy.

So, in early September, Le Charmant Cinéma Érotique had closed its doors, and Le Machine's management had moved in. They worked fast. A giant billboard heralding the exhibition now covered the front of the building, and the largest of the screens had been chosen as the main exhibition space. A four-hundred-seater, which Monsieur Rousset had used exclusively for lesbian porn (a speciality of the house, as well as being his personal favourite – he was a man of simple tastes), it had not contained more than thirty lost souls at any one time for well over a decade. The three hundred and twenty lower seats were stripped out and replaced with a sloping floor, which would accommodate four hundred and fifty standing spectators, with just enough room for them to mill around. A raised platform with a ramp was built to one side of the room, to allow access for people in wheelchairs. The eighty seats on the small balcony had been left just as they were. The screen had been removed, and the stage cleared to make way for the exhibits, and the walls had been painted black.

Just as he had on every other day, Monsieur Rousset had come in to see how things were going. Various items of apparatus were being moved into their final positions, and he watched as technicians rushed around sorting out the lighting, the surround sound and the positioning of eight discreet cameras. The projection room had been converted into an editing suite: every moment of this performance was to be filmed. All two thousand and sixteen hours were due to be released in a signed, limited edition, six hundred and seventy-two disc, cadmium-plated box set which would sell for thirty thousand euros apiece. Forty had already been reserved, and they were already close to breaking even on its production costs. Judging by the rate of enquiries coming in, Le Machine's management was confident that the remaining one hundred and sixty would be sold out before the end of the run.

The toilets had been gutted and refurbished; the ladies' had been used solely as a storage cupboard for decades, and it was emptied of clutter, mainly old flyers and posters. As well as the main auditorium there were two smaller screens: Screen Two had been used for man–woman porn, predominantly S&M, and this was stripped out to make way for the exhibition shop (selling, among all the Le Machine memorabilia, the seats that had been removed and the posters that had been excavated from the ladies' toilet, which an astonished Monsieur Rousset had been told were now collectable items, and after a seventy/thirty split they would provide him with further revenue for his relaunch). Screen Three – shemale, feet, German, miscellaneous deep fetish – was taken over by the organisation. The press office was based here, and today everybody was frantically busy because, with just two days left until the exhibition began, Le Machine himself was coming to look the place over, to get a sense of it for the first time, and to talk through any misgivings he might have.

It was crucial that he be comfortable with the arrangements. Everybody wanted things to be just right for him, nobody more so than Monsieur Rousset.

* * *

He had been expecting Le Machine to arrive at the venue like a boxing star, surrounded by an entourage, but he came unaccompanied, and apparently on foot. He was fully clothed, wearing a big coat, a black beanie hat and dark glasses. It looked as though he hadn't shaved in a couple of weeks. On being introduced to Monsieur Rousset, he shook his hand and quietly thanked him for allowing the use of his cinema. Monsieur Rousset was delighted by his soft-spoken graciousness, even more so when he was personally invited by Le Machine to accompany him and his management as they toured the venue.

They went from room to room before finishing on the stage. Le Machine was concerned about temperature control, and made a few technical enquiries about the refrigeration of certain phials, and the positioning of the heaters and air conditioners. Once he was satisfied that it was all going to be fine, he inspected the on-stage equipment, making sure its quality was up to scratch. He always commissioned brand new custom-made vessels for each show, and he had to make sure everything was just right. They had been fitted with valves to ensure that while his bodily excretions were fully visible, very little of the smell made it as far as the exhibition's visitors. He turned to Monsieur Rousset, and said, 'I wouldn't want to make your cinema smell like a sewer.'

'No. No, of course not.'

Le Machine and his team were always working on new approaches to *Life*, and an innovation for this run was a gas collection mechanism, which would be connected to a single-ring hob in the on-stage kitchen. Le Machine's plan was to do as much cooking as he could by using gas that had risen from his faeces.

He completed his inspection, and was reassured by his manager that the technicians had made sure everything was working perfectly, that they were ahead of schedule and had a full forty-eight hours to run double checks on all the equipment. He sat on the on-stage bidet to check it for comfort, then lay for a while on the single bed, after which he requested a firmer mattress. He stood close to his sound designer, whom Monsieur Rousset had come to learn was his closest collaborator, and made some hushed enquiries about something they referred to as *the new device,* then he stood in silent contemplation.

After a minute of this, he almost inaudibly addressed the people around him. 'Now, if I may . . .' At this, everybody scuttled down from the stage. Monsieur Rousset took his cue, and followed. He made his way to a seat in the balcony, where he sat and watched Le Machine as he paced up and down, apparently lost in concentration. He was overcome with admiration for the man.

V

Aurélie Renard was delighted by the ease with which she adjusted to motherhood. There were still some technical issues to overcome, but she took them in her stride. The first thing that struck her was that she had no idea how to deal with a buggy on the Métro or the bus, so to get around this she had simply chosen to walk the five kilometres back to her apartment.

Aurélie went everywhere with a big, full bag. She was always in awe of women who were able to live out of tiny bags; she couldn't work out how it was possible. She always had a sketchpad, a selection of pencils and charcoal and a camera with her, and she knew that not everyone needed those, but along with them she would carry around more everyday things like a snack, a paperback book, a packet of cigarettes, a bottle of water, a street atlas, a box of matches, a magazine, an emergency concealer pencil, tissues, a small mirror, chewing gum, lip balm and a spare packet of cigarettes just in case. To her this was as minimalist as it was possible to be; she couldn't imagine how anyone could get by with less. Her friend Sylvie was the same; she didn't have artistic leanings, so she was able to do without the sketchbook and things, but even so her bag was medium-sized, and was always overflowing. Many times they had sat outside cafés and watched in wonder as women with small bags passed by. The ones who amazed them the most were those who wore immaculate make-up and held cigarettes. How they compressed so much of their life into such a tiny space was a wonder of the world. There must have been a secret that they weren't being let in on.

Her bag was as full as ever, and with the ancient video camera adding to her burden she soon started to feel weighed down. Every few blocks she stopped for a rest, and to check in with Herbert. She would sit on a bench or a wall, and tap his nose, pinch his cheeks (avoiding the bruise, which was already starting to darken), sing half-remembered nursery rhymes and pull faces for his amusement. More often than not he would be indifferent to her efforts, but sometimes she would be rewarded with a smile or a gurgle. She began to take photographs.

Whenever they passed another woman pushing a buggy, Aurélie was confident that she didn't look any less natural a custodian of a small child than the genuine article. Her maternal instinct still needed some fine-tuning though, and it wasn't until she saw a passing baby with a bottle in its mouth that she realised Herbert might be thirsty. She found his milk in an outer pocket of the big bag, handed him the bottle and realised she had done the right thing when he drained it in one go. Shortly afterwards, he fell asleep. Sitting on a step, she pulled out a pencil and pad, and sketched him. She was fairly pleased with the result, but still hoped to do better the next time.

It was only as she got to her neighbourhood and neared her building that serious misgivings started to creep into her mind. She knew it would be best for her to keep him a secret, and she didn't want her neighbours asking awkward questions. She lived on the fourth floor and there was no lift, so getting him up without being seen would be difficult.

It took her a while to work out that the best way to get through the heavy street door was to push it open with her back, and pull the buggy after her. Once they were in the lobby she was faced with the stairs. She thought for a moment about taking her bag and the video camera up first, then coming back for the baby, but she supposed it wouldn't be ideal to leave him alone in the hall. She didn't want to leave her things unattended either, particularly not the video camera, which she had borrowed from the college. It wasn't worth anything, but if she lost it they would still make her pay to replace it. She found she didn't have a choice but to get everything up in one go.

She sized up the buggy, and took hold of the frame, top and bottom. She lifted it, and started walking up. It took all the strength she had, and by the time she reached her door she could feel sweat on her forehead, and could hardly breathe. She half-heartedly vowed to give up smoking as she found her key and pushed the buggy inside. Not one of her neighbours' doors had opened to reveal a quizzical face; even Old Widow Peypouquet was nowhere to be seen.

Herbert had slept through it all. She closed the door behind them, and at last they were safe at home.

Her apartment was tiny, and shabby, and a long walk from the Métro in an unfashionable neighbourhood. Because of all this, the rent wasn't too terrible, and with her wages from her summer work and her weekend shifts in a bar, along with help from her dad and a steadily mounting debt, she was just about able to afford to live alone. There was one main room, most of which was taken up by a double bed, a chest of drawers with a small television on top and an easel by the window. Off this was a shower room barely large enough to turn around in, and in the corner was a kitchen that had been built into what must once have been a closet.

She loved the place, and had never felt claustrophobic. When she first came to Paris she had shared an apartment with a group of other students, but now she was glad to have somewhere she could keep to herself, uninterrupted by the drama of the shared living space. She loved never having to justify her movements, or her lack of movements, to anyone else. She knew, though, that she was now going to have to relinquish her treasured privacy. It was going to be OK though. It would only be for a week.

The buggy took up most of the available floor space, and she wondered what she was going to do with her new companion, where she was going to put him. She flopped on to the bed, and thought.

In a box at the back of her kitchen cupboard was her sickness kit. Her dad sent her new items for it every term; he hated the thought of not being there to take care of her if she was ever unwell, of her languishing alone. He made sure she always had enough supplies to see her through a few days of being housebound: some dry crackers, powdered soup, spaghetti, rice, paracetamol, vitamin pills and an emergency toilet roll. She had dipped into this kit a few times, when she'd had a cold or an upset stomach, but more often for hangovers, and those times when she had nothing else in and hadn't wanted to go out shopping in the rain. It had always been a comfort to her though, just being there, and now it was going to be a life saver.

She had her usual supply of potatoes, too. She and Herbert were going to be OK; they could just hunker down for the week, indoors and out of trouble. This plan wouldn't provide her with much in the way of photo opportunities, but she would just have to make do. She wondered whether he liked spaghetti, soup and mashed potato. 'I know it sounds boastful,' she whispered to the sleeping child, 'but I make really good mash. There's no point in pretending otherwise – if it's mash you're after, you've come to the right place.'

She took the bag from the back of the buggy, and emptied it on to the bed. There was a spare set of clothes, three disposable nappies, a plastic spoon, moist wipes, two jars of pureed food, a bag of maize snacks, a pot of grapes, a kind of cloth, a first aid box, a plastic mat, a toothbrush, a small tube of toothpaste, some mysterious thin plastic bags and an unopened bottle of some special kind of milk. There were also some items that she couldn't identify, and she supposed their functions would be revealed as she went along. If this was all he needed, this was going to be easy.

She gazed at him for a while. She could smell something, and in seconds the room was filled with a thick, awful fug.

Oh shit, she thought. *I hadn't thought about that. Why didn't I think about that?* It made her wonder whether there was anything else she hadn't thought about.

He opened his eyes, took one look at her and his mouth became a chasm, from which came a blood-curdling howl. Maybe it wasn't going to be quite so easy after all.

'It's OK, Herbert,' she said softly, reaching out to squeeze his shoulder. 'It's OK. It's me. It's your brand new auntie Aurélie.'

Herbert's cries cut through to her marrow, and the smell thickened and thickened. She looked through the bag's contents, still strewn across the bed, for the things she would need to change him. She found a clean disposable nappy and a packet of wipes. She couldn't see what else she would need. She examined the nappy, and with an artist's eye she quickly saw how it would attach to the baby. Those long summer days spent indoors folding paper birds while the other children played in the shadow of the power station had not gone to waste after all. After a few attempts, she managed to unclip the safety belts that were keeping him in the buggy.

She tried to work out how to get him out of the buggy and on to the bed. She didn't want to go anywhere near his bottom, and the most practical way she could think of would be to clamp one hand under his chin and the other behind his head, and lift him out that way. She had never seen a baby carried like that though, and decided it would probably be best not to try it. She put her hands under his arms, and he struggled to get free. She retreated, steeled herself and tried again, and a moment later he was there before her, dangling and wailing as she held him at arm's length. She tried to breathe only through her mouth, but even so the stench was inescapable. She laid him on the bed, and took off his shoes, socks and trousers, and there it was: her first nappy. The cartoon characters on it seemed incongruous with the seriousness of the task at hand.

She undid the Velcro fastenings, and opened it. It was full to bursting with a stinking orange-brown slime. It was the most disgusting thing she had ever known, and she felt sick. She lifted his legs, and moved the nappy to one side. Only then did she realise she hadn't taken any of the wipes out of their packet, and with one hand grabbing the baby's squirming legs, she tried to extract one. Herbert broke free, and as he landed on the duvet he smeared it with a coating of sludge. She gave up trying to keep him still, and the duvet clean, and with two hands now available she was able to take out a wipe. She lifted a leg, and ran the moist cloth across his bottom. Straight away the wipe turned from white to orange-brown, and she knew she was going to need several more. She looked for somewhere to put the soiled one. There was nowhere obvious, so she piled it on top of the dirty nappy, which had started to leak on to the duvet. The last man to lie on her bed had been Sébastien, and it seemed consistent that his successor would leave it covered in shit. At least Herbert was straightforward about it.

She got hold of a handful of fresh wipes, and after much struggling from both of them she completed her task. At last, Herbert was clean and in a fresh nappy. She had done it. The duvet cover had been bundled into a plastic shopping bag, ready to go to the laundry along with his original trousers, which had somehow been caught up in the general slurry, and the dirty nappy and wipes had been put in one of the no-longer-mysterious small plastic sacks she had found in Herbert's bag. She opened the window, and as she breathed in the fresh air she was filled with a sense of accomplishment. At last she and the baby could relax and get to know each other.

She looked at him for a while as he lay on the bed. The time had come to work out how to hold him properly. She scooped him up, and jostled him around, trying various ways of lifting him until she found one that seemed natural, with her right hand under his bottom and her left cradling his back. She held him close as she walked up and down on the tiny patch of available floor. He was still wearing his hat. She took it off, and saw for the first time that on his head was a coating of fine, golden hair. She stroked it, and was amazed by its softness.

'You're blonde,' she said, 'just like me. Only you're a little bit fairer. But it's OK, I'm not jealous. Well, that's not entirely true – I am a bit jealous, but I think I'll get over it. Either way, with that hair and those blue eyes everyone will think I'm your real mother.' She gave him a squeeze, kissed the top of his head, and he looked up at her.

She noticed details she hadn't registered before. A few teeth were sticking out of his gums, and she couldn't believe how white they were. Maybe there was something to be said for leading a life free of coffee, cigarettes and red wine. She felt she was starting to get to know the *real* Herbert, and getting the hang of having him around. Then she heard a rumble and felt a squelch against her right hand. This was followed by a terrible, but by now familiar, smell. It had all begun again.

The second time, it was easier. She knew what was required of her, and she laid him on the plastic mat and got everything ready before the nappy came off. She was hoping that the new pair of trousers hadn't caught it, because there wasn't a spare pair after this. She was in luck.

It was looking as though she was going to have to abandon her plan of spending a week indoors. As well as the room being far too small for the two of them, particularly when one of them was making such violent smells, she was already running low on supplies. She had been wondering whether the baby's mother had been planning on handing him to a stranger for the week all along, but from the evidence it looked as if she probably hadn't. There really did seem to be only just enough things in the bag to see him through the day. They would have to go out and get some more.

Something else she knew was that there was no way she could cope with this on her own. With Herbert dressed again, and propped into a sitting position on the bed, she opened the window. With one hand she held a cigarette, directing as much of the smoke as she could into the outside air, and with the other she sent a text to Sylvie: *Want to go shopping?*

VI

For reasons that she told herself (and others if they asked, which they often did because she made no secret of it) were nobody's business but her own, Sylvie Dupont wanted to find a husband. It was what she had wanted more than anything for as long as she could remember. She had read somewhere that the most common way to meet your life partner is in the workplace, and this was one of the reasons she had taken on so many jobs: a different one each day, seven days a week. As well as providing her with a varied working life and just enough money for her to always be able to wear nice dresses and not have to worry too much about the rent and bills, this strategy broadened her field of prospective spouses quite considerably.

She made a point of taking on jobs that she thought would be interesting and unusual, partly so her shifts wouldn't seem too much like work, but also because this way she was much more likely to meet interesting and unusual people. She had no image in her mind of her ideal man, and she was ready to be surprised when he came along, but if he was to be interesting and unusual then she would have no problem with that. If anything, she thought it would be a bonus.

If a job ever got her down, if her colleagues were tiresome or customers rude, she would walk out and find one she liked better, and as a result she was usually happy at work, and often to be seen smiling. This rare trait, combined with her looks, which had never been a cause of concern for her (she knew she took after her mother, and she counted her mother as the most beautiful woman she had ever seen) drew her to the attention of an apparently endless stream of young men who thought they had finally, after years of longing, found their own personal Godard-era Chantal Goya, a sweet, smart and smiling dark-haired angel. As they found out fragments from the story of her life, any defences they might have had crumbled to nothing, and they were lost. When she told them, as casually as anything and usually on a first date, that her dream was to marry and have children, the thought of anyone but them being her husband or the father of those children made their blood run cold. If anybody could truly be said to have their pick, it was Sylvie Dupont. However, she had yet to take her pick.

Today she was in Montmartre, at the top of the hill, sitting in the driver's seat of a white 1963 Citroën 2CV and waiting to be assigned her next batch of tourists to take around the city. The morning had been pleasant but unexceptional, just a few short runs around the neighbourhood, and the afternoon had begun in the same way. She had a feeling that this wouldn't be the day she was going to meet her future husband, and the sight of her next passengers did nothing to change this. They were a retired Japanese couple and their interpreter, a young French man. There wasn't anything wrong with the interpreter, if anything he wasn't bad-looking in a gawky kind of way, but a gut feeling told her she wasn't going to be marrying him. She made a mental note to make him aware of this at the earliest opportunity, should he reveal the slightest hint of amorous intentions.

She took no pleasure in reducing men to husks, but when she knew there was no alternative she was able to do so with lightning efficiency. She had come to learn that this was the kindest way: several of the boys she had let down gently over the years still lived in hope, and she wasn't going to let herself be bothered with that kind of thing any more; it was just too time consuming.

The Japanese couple lowered themselves into the back seat and fastened their seatbelts, and the interpreter settled in beside Sylvie. She smiled, and greeted them, and asked them where they wanted to go.

The interpreter turned to them, and asked the same question in Japanese. The woman answered. 'They just want to go around the city,' he said. 'They want to see the sights.'

'That can be arranged.'

Sylvie pulled away, and off they went. She had been born in Paris twenty-two and a half years earlier, and had never lived anywhere else. She knew it inside out, but she had never taken it for granted. She had not always lived in the best of neighbourhoods, but the city had always been there for her to escape into and lose herself in, filling her life with incredible places to go and things to do. She had also found that it had provided her with endless opportunities for getting into trouble, but she had grown tired of sticky situations and had begun to learn how to avoid them, so they were coming along with less and less frequency. One of her motivations for working so much was that she had that much less free time in which to go off the rails. She had learned to accept that there was really no one there to watch over her. She had friends, but she had let very few of them get really close, and those few knew her well enough to understand that she didn't appreciate anybody interfering with her life. And besides, even the best of friends would never be the same as family, and she knew she had to be her own stabilising influence, that she had to watch over herself. She was quite pleased with how she had been doing lately. She was keeping her life together better than ever before.

As they crept through the narrow streets, then raced down the hill, she was looking forward to the next few hours. She always liked to know who she was driving. 'Aren't you going to introduce us?' she asked the interpreter. She looked in the rear-view mirror. 'What are you called?'

The slightly gawky interpreter passed this on, and she learned that the stern-looking man was Monsieur Akiyama, and his smiling wife was Madame Akiyama. Further questions revealed that they had come all the way from somewhere called Funabashi, that they were on their second full day of a week-long trip to Paris, and had spent the entire day beforehand in the Louvre, sheltering from the rain, and they had been faintly disappointed by the Mona Lisa but spellbound by plenty of the other exhibits. Now that the sun was shining they were looking to broaden their horizons. It had been Madame Akiyama's idea to head to Montmartre without any firm plans, just as it had been her very sudden idea to hire a classic car and go for a spin around the city. Monsieur Akiyama had yet to be convinced that such impulsive behaviour would not result in disaster.

Sylvie told them her own name, and wished them an enjoyable stay. 'And how about you?' she asked the interpreter. 'Who are you?'

'Lucien,' he said.

'And how come you're so good at speaking Japanese?'

'Would you like an honest answer, or would you rather I hid the truth from you?'

She thought for a moment. 'Hide the truth.'

'OK. It's because I find it a fascinating language.'

They drove on in silence for a while, until Sylvie could bear it no longer. 'I'm starting to wonder whether an honest answer might have been a bit more interesting.'

'Well, it is a fascinating language. But if you must know, the main reason is because I just really like Japanese girls. I always have done, and I realised early in life that if I was ever to meet one there would be a language barrier, so I started teaching myself at thirteen, that was twelve years ago, and now I've pretty much got it nailed, the conversational side at least. I've been taking on gigs like this to keep me on my toes.' He gestured towards the holidaymakers in the back seat. 'I've got these two for the whole week.'

Sylvie was delighted to find out that Lucien was obsessed with Japanese girls, and that he wouldn't be falling in love with her. It was always such a relief when she knew she was in the clear and could talk to a boy without the possibility of his impending misery hanging over her. She sympathised with his situation, too. She supposed that if she had been a man there would have been a strong possibility that she would be preoccupied with Japanese women. Why wouldn't she be? What was not to like about jet-black hair, porcelain skin, slim bodies and delicate features? 'Any luck yet?' she asked.

He pulled a face. 'I'm going to move there next year. I've got a job lined up at a university, as a French language and literature teaching assistant.' He sounded melancholy.

'What's the problem? I think you'll do fine. You'll be ploughing through them.'

Lucien went quiet.

'What? I thought that's what you wanted.'

'Well, no. I don't want to plough through them. That's the thing. There's something very wrong with me, you see. I tend not to talk about it, but since I already seem to have decided to use you as confessor I might as well tell you. My problem is that I only want to meet one girl, the right one for me. It's all I've ever wanted.'

'Hey, I'm a bit like that, only not for Japanese girls – I've got no interest at all in being with someone I can't see myself marrying. I've had a bunch of boyfriends, but the moment I realise I'm not going to marry them I drop them like a hot brick. It's got me into all sorts of trouble, some really deep shit, as a matter of fact – we're talking guns and knives, even ropes – but at least I'm honest with them. I'm getting pretty good at telling now. It used to take me ages, but these days I can usually see straight away if a man's not going to be the one. Take you, for example

– the moment I saw you I knew we wouldn't be getting married. But enough about me . . .' She was distracted, and noticed a red light just in time. She slammed on the brakes, and stopped millimetres from the car in front. She heard gasps coming from the back seat. She could see in her rear-view mirror that Monsieur and Madame Akiyama were looking alarmed. She turned to Lucien. 'Tell them it's the French way of driving.'

He did this, and Monsieur Akiyama spoke sternly for a while, after which Madame Akiyama spoke softly.

Lucien translated. 'Monsieur Akiyama wishes you to know that he worked for a large corporation for many years, rising through the ranks to a senior position. He says that if any of his company's chauffeurs had ever driven in the French way while transporting one of their employers, they would have been subject to the most stringent disciplinary procedures.'

'Oh, OK. It's always interesting to learn about different cultures. That's partly why I do this job.'

'And Madame Akiyama wishes you to know that her husband needs to relax and remember he's on holiday.'

Sylvie laughed. She was becoming a big fan of Madame Akiyama. The light turned green, and she drove on. She and Lucien continued their conversation.

'My theory is that most people only want one person,' she said, 'but people of our generation aren't prepared to admit it because they don't want everyone to think they're desperate. I'm not desperate, though. There's no way I would marry anyone unless I knew he was absolutely right for me. I would rather die than get stuck with the wrong man.'

'So you would rather die than marry me?'

'Yes.'

He shrugged. 'Fair enough.'

'But what's your problem anyway? Why are you so miserable? I can't see why you're all . . .' She let out a long moan, and mimicked his voice. '*Boo hoo, poor me, I'm going to Japan to be surrounded by Japanese student girls who will all have big crushes on me.*'

'I've hit a difficulty with my plan.'

'What's that?'

He lowered his voice, and looked sheepish. 'I think I've just fallen in love – even though I'm clearly not husband material.'

Sylvie was exasperated. She had really thought she was in the clear with this one, and she had certainly let him know where she stood. Her hair wasn't black, but it was dark brown and very straight. Her eyes were dark brown too, she was slim, and her complexion was clear. She had never thought of herself as looking Japanese, but maybe she looked just Japanese enough for Lucien. 'Listen, I've already told you – I'm not going to marry you, OK? How many more times will I have to tell you before it sinks in? Don't take offence, but I just know you're not the one. Stick with your Japanese girls. You'll be fine.'

'No, no. I'm not in love with *you*.'

Sylvie was relieved, but also a little put out. 'Oh, really?'

'Yes, really.'

'Good. I'm glad.'

'I'm glad you're glad. It would never have worked out with you, even if you had liked me. I've tried being with girls who aren't Japanese – I suppose I was hoping it would somehow *cure me of my affliction* – and I even really liked some of them, but it's never ended well. It's not right for me, and it's not fair on them. I've embraced the way I am, and there's no turning back. There were times when I saw it as a curse, but not any more – now I see it as a blessing.'

'That's good. So who is she then? Who is this *Mademoiselle Wonderful* who you just can't live without?'

'I think I'm in love with the Akiyamas' daughter.'

Sylvie was quiet for a while, as she pondered Lucien's predicament. 'You only *think* you're in love with her?'

'No, it's no use. I can't fight it – I *am* in love with her.'

'That's better. So where is she now?'

'In Japan. They showed me a picture of her yesterday. I could hardly sleep last night, and when I finally did I dreamt only of her.'

'I see.' Sylvie didn't subscribe to fashionable notions that in order to love somebody you need to know them. Love, she knew for sure, was stranger than that. One summer, when she was ten years old, she had been sent to stay with a distant aunt, who had shut her in her room for the entire school holidays with nothing but a copy of *Les Misérables* for company. She had read it over and over again, empathising with Cosette as she huddled under the Thénardiers' table, and glorying in her story as her happiness unfolded. When Marius had first set eyes on her he had felt no pressing need to take her out for coffee to find out her likes and dislikes, or to live with her on a trial basis just to be sure they were right for one another. And had Cosette reserved judgement until she had worked out whether or not Marius was going to fit in well with her existing social circle? Had she held back until she'd had a chance to interrogate him at extreme length about whether or not he still harboured residual feelings for any girls he had known before? No, they just saw each other and fell in love, and everything else melted away.

Sylvie saw no reason why Lucien's feelings shouldn't be as deep and poetic as theirs. She was by no means a starry-eyed romantic, though; while she believed absolutely in true love, she knew how hard it was to find, and how easy it was for tender-hearted boys to be fooled by their feelings. She had even allowed herself to be fooled enough times, but she had always been OK; only disappointed, not devastated. She could see that Lucien had a tender heart, and she didn't want to see him make a terrible mistake. He reminded her of several of her exes, and she didn't want to see him ending up like them. 'Just one picture?' she asked.

'Yes, just one.'

'You should probably see a few more, just to be double sure that it's true love and not just a crush.' After all, Marius and Cosette would at least have had the opportunity to observe one another from a number of angles at their first encounter. She was worried that this might have been the Akiyama girl's best photo by a long way, the only one her mother ever showed to people.

'One was enough. I can't get her out of my mind. Her name is Akiko.' He smiled. 'Akiko! Do you know what that means?'

'Er, no.'

'It means *sparkling child*. Sparkling child! And does Akiko sparkle? Yes, she sparkles. Akiko Akiyama sparkles, and so much more.' He sighed.

'It's a really nice name.' Sylvie put *Akiko* on her list of possibilities for her first daughter. She wanted three or four children, a mixture of girls and boys.

'The problem is, she lives three hundred miles away from where I'm going to be working. The course of true love isn't going to be easy for us. Oh, Akiko. Akiko! Akiko Akiyama!' He sighed again, and a stern voice came from the back seat. Lucien looked embarrassed, craned his neck around and a brief conversation ensued.

'What was that about?' asked Sylvie when at last they were quiet again.

'They wanted to know why I kept calling out their daughter's name, and smiling and sighing.'

'What did you tell them?'

'I couldn't stop myself. I revealed my feelings. I told them very sincerely that I was in love with her, and that my intentions towards her were entirely honourable. I don't think they're too happy about it, at least not Monsieur Akiyama. He says she has just graduated with honours from a prestigious university and has started in a junior position at a large corporation, and he expects her to find a husband from among the workforce.'

'Have you been able to work out if there's already a particular member of the workforce who has captured her heart?'

He sighed again. 'Not yet. They've not mentioned anybody.'

'Maybe they think it's none of your business. Or maybe they don't know. There's no reason why she should tell her parents who she's dating.'

'Thank you for that upbeat contribution to my love story.'

'Sorry.'

They drove on. Sylvie was having a good afternoon. She really liked Lucien, and was going to see what she could do to win the Akiyamas over to his cause. He and

Akiko belonged together, she just knew it, and she was going to make it her business to see that the obstacles that lay between them were overcome. But first she had to get back to the job in hand.

'Ask them if they'd like to go through the tunnel where Lady Di died.'

They did, of course.

Three and a half hours later, the 2CV was back in Montmartre and making its way up the steep and narrow west end of rue Norvins. Sylvie had had a great afternoon racing through the streets, pointing out her favourite places, and stopping here and there so they could all stroll around. At no point had it seemed like work. The Akiyamas had enjoyed themselves, and she and Lucien had been making one another laugh as they compared notes on their romantic lives and recounted some of the many pitfalls they had faced. They were both delighted to have met someone who didn't think that there was something wrong with them for wanting what they wanted.

At one point a passer-by had approached them and asked if she could take their photo. 'You are the happiest couple I have ever seen,' she had said. 'You look so right together.' Not wishing to disillusion her, they had posed with their arms around each other, and made up a story about how they had met while skiing three years earlier and been inseparable ever since. The wedding, booked for the coming spring, was to be a low-key event on a mutual friend's llama farm in Avignon.

They were both keen to keep in touch, and had exchanged numbers on the Île Saint-Louis while the Akiyamas were buying ice cream, and when she took her phone out of her bag she picked up a text from her friend Aurélie, asking her if she wanted to go shopping. She didn't want to go shopping, but she knew she wouldn't have to. This was just a euphemism. She knew that what Aurélie really wanted was to sit in a bar and have a drink and a talk, and that suited Sylvie just fine.

She had arranged to meet her after work, which was going to be any minute now. They were nearly back where they had started.

Without warning, the car slowed to a halt. Sylvie put her foot on the gas pedal and pumped the clutch, but there was no response. The engine was going, but the car wasn't. It just sat there, blocking the road. She worked the clutch again, but there was still no bite. 'Right,' she said. 'Everybody out.'

Lucien and the Akiyamas got out and went around to the back of the car. Monsieur Akiyama didn't seem particularly pleased by this, and delivered a brief monologue to Lucien, which was relayed to Sylvie through the open driver's window: 'Monsieur Akiyama wishes you to know that he worked for many years at a senior position in a large corporation, and has gone to great lengths to ensure that his wife, Madame Akiyama, has always had an adequate lifestyle, one free from the necessity of physical exertion. He requests, therefore, that in the interests of preserving his honour, she be exempt from this task.'

'No,' said Sylvie. 'She's in France now. We need her muscle.'

Madame Akiyama smiled when she heard this, and answered by putting both hands on the car and bracing herself. Monsieur Akiyama looked furious, but he too put his weight to the car.

'Now, get ready. I'm going to take my foot off the brake. After three: one . . . two . . . three . . .' Lucien translated as she went along. She lifted her foot, but for all their pushing the car didn't move forward. She braked again, before it had a chance to roll back. 'We'll try again. One . . . two . . . three . . .' Again, the car wouldn't move. A line of traffic was starting to build up behind them. They just had to get it to the brow of the hill, where the road widened, and the other cars would be able to pass. Her boss could arrange to have it towed from there. She looked in her wing mirror, and saw Aurélie trudging up towards them. 'Hey,' she called. 'Give us a push.'

Aurélie stuck her cigarette in the corner of her mouth, wedged Herbert's buggy against a lamppost so it wouldn't roll down the hill, and joined the gang at the back of the car. Together they pushed, and at last the car began to crawl upwards. A pair of passers-by joined in, and two minutes later it was tucked in at the side of the road at the top of the hill. Everyone was elated at having come through a crisis. Madame Akiyama announced that she hadn't had so much fun in decades, and even Monsieur Akiyama allowed himself a smile of satisfaction.

Sylvie hadn't seen Aurélie for two weeks. Never having been a great one for metropolitan reserve, she gave her an enthusiastic hug. She introduced her to the Akiyamas, and then Lucien. 'You don't have to worry about him hitting on you, because he's obsessed with Japanese girls.'

'Not *girls*, not any more. Just one girl,' he said.

'That's right,' clarified Sylvie. 'Just one girl he's never met.'

Aurélie thought it was a shame that he was an obsessive deviant. She could have done with someone to put his arms around her, and he was good-looking, in a gawky kind of way, and he seemed nice enough. Herbert could have benefited from a father figure for the next few days as well. But this was typical. She had grown quite used to not having much luck with men. Unlike Sylvie, she wasn't looking for a husband, not yet at least, but a boyfriend would have been nice.

When it was Madame Akiyama's turn to be introduced to Aurélie, she said something in Japanese, which Lucien translated.

'She says you have a very adorable child.'

Aurélie smiled, vicariously flattered by the compliment. 'Thank you,' she said. She looked down, hoping that Herbert had taken the praise graciously. She turned white. He wasn't there. She looked around, and there was no Herbert to be seen. She had completely forgotten that she had left him wedged against a lamppost somewhere down the hill. 'Oh shit – *Air-bear!* I mean, oh shit – Herbert!' She ran back down the hill. 'Herbert!' she cried. 'Herbert!'

Air-bear? thought Sylvie, remembering that Aurélie had indeed been pushing some kind of cart. She hadn't given much thought to it at the time, she had just wanted her to hurry up and start helping with the car. *I wonder what that's all about.*

The Akiyamas looked disconcerted by these events. Sylvie came to Aurélie's rescue, and told Lucien to inform them that forgetting you've left your baby halfway down a hill is normal for France.

He obliged, and they seemed to accept this. They all waited for her to return.

A small crowd had gathered around the buggy, and Herbert was charming them with a sequence of amusing faces as they tried to work out what they ought to do with the abandoned child. They were starting to debate various possibilities when Aurélie arrived, out of breath.

'Ah,' she said to the baby. 'There you are.' Everyone stared at her as she puffed and panted. 'He's always running off,' she explained. They kept staring at her. 'Come along, Herbert,' she said.

'*Air-bear*?' said one of the onlookers.

'No – Herbert. H-H-H. Herbert. Say after me: *Herbert.*'

They all had a go at pronouncing his name. Some did better than others, but none of them came close to getting it right. Even though they still had so much to learn, Aurélie decided to cut the lesson short. She wasn't about to go rooting through her bag for her mirror.

'Very good, everyone,' she lied. 'Now say goodbye to all your nice new friends, Herbert.'

Herbert crossed his eyes and blew a bubble, and the crowd of onlookers waved and wished him well.

As Aurélie fumbled with the buggy, they started talking among themselves, as if she wasn't there.

Air-bear? Isn't that an English name? He doesn't look English to me. He looks just like his mother, and she's definitely not English – maybe the poor girl married an Englishman. I had a cousin who did that . . .

She left them to it, and made her way back up the hill.

To Monsieur Akiyama's dismay, Madame Akiyama had insisted on buying everybody a drink, and after reporting the broken-down car to an embattled boss, they side-stepped the crowds of the Place du Tertre and made their way to a backstreet restaurant where they sat together under a gas heater in the courtyard, exchanging questions about each other's homelands and ways of life. Sylvie had a cup of coffee, and Aurélie had a glass of wine. She popped Herbert on her lap, and gave him some grapes and a bottle of milk. When he had had enough, she handed him over to a delighted Madame Akiyama, who bounced him on her knee as Aurélie sketched the pair of them. She gave one sketch to the Akiyamas and kept another for her project.

When she could contain her curiosity no longer, Sylvie asked Madame Akiyama if she could see a picture of her now legendary daughter. Monsieur Akiyama was not delighted about this, but his wife gladly pulled out her phone, selected a photo and handed it to her. Sylvie could see at once where Lucien was coming from. Akiko was lovely, and you really did only need one picture to tell. Her skin, her smile, her eyes: everything about her was just right.

'She's beautiful,' she said, and Lucien gladly passed this on. 'May we see some more?'

Madame Akiyama agreed, and Lucien leaned over Sylvie's shoulder as she looked through the album. There was Akiko petting a small dog, Akiko beside a lake, Akiko in a restaurant . . . With each new photograph Lucien let out a gasp, a sigh, a moan or a whimper. 'It's official,' whispered Sylvie. 'You love her. And I can completely see why.' She continued scrolling through the photographs until disaster struck. There she was, the lovely Akiko, standing in what looked like a forest. This would have been fine, had it not been for the fact that beside her stood a young man, his arm resting around her shoulder. And this was not just any young man; he was a young man so handsome it was unbearable. He looked like an old school movie star.

Lucien buried his face in his hands. He tried not to cry. As well as learning the language, he had studied Japanese manners, and he knew that breaking down in front of the father of the woman you hoped to marry was considered a sign of weakness in their culture. As he held back the tears it struck him that breaking down in front of the father of the woman you hoped to marry was probably considered a sign of weakness all over the world – except in England, where that kind of thing was positively encouraged.

It was Sylvie who spoke. 'And who is this?' she asked Madame Akiyama.

Lucien was only just able to utter a translation, but when Madame Akiyama replied, his face radiated joy. 'It's Akiko's brother, Toshiro.' He turned back to the woman he hoped would one day be his mother-in-law. 'Madame Akiyama, why didn't you tell me you had a son?'

'You only asked us if we had a daughter.'

'Oh.' He turned red. She was right, of course.

Sylvie was no longer listening. She was scrolling through Madame Akiyama's photo collection, looking for more pictures of Toshiro. There were plenty. She was able to study him from a number of angles. After a long silence, she looked up. 'You have wonderful children,' she said to Monsieur and Madame Akiyama.

They accepted this, Monsieur Akiyama with a nod, and Madame Akiyama with a smile.

VII

For the run-up to his latest presentation of *Life*, Le Machine had taken an unremarkable apartment on rue Eugène Carrière. He hadn't visited the place before moving in, but his manager had shown him a list of available properties, and the moment he saw the name of the street he had known this was the one, and had instructed her to rent it for him. Eugène Carrière was his favourite artist.

The apartment had been his base for the weeks leading up to the opening night, weeks he had spent in quiet contemplation and physical and dietary preparation. He had spent as much time as he could walking the streets, reacquainting himself with the city upon which he had turned his back. Apart from a single case containing clothes, all he had brought to the apartment was a set of dumb-bells and a print of Carrière's painting *Enfant avec casserole*. He had had it enlarged to fifty times the size of the small original, and the huge canvas leaned against the bedroom wall. The first thing he had done on arrival was to go through the apartment and take down all the pictures that had been hanging there: the Eiffel Tower, the Sacré Coeur, Béatrice Dalle, and other such famous sights that the holidaymakers who usually rented the place would have been delighted to see on the wall. Now this huge baby, sitting in the shadows as he scooped the scrapings from an overturned pot, was the only adornment in an otherwise spartan bedroom.

It had been the work of Eugène Carrière that had made him want to pick up a paintbrush, and his earliest efforts had been attempts to emulate Carrière's style, particularly his use of colour, which many described as monochromatic, but not Le Machine – he saw whole worlds within the browns and greys. After years of trying, he had given up. One day he had made a split-second decision and left Carrière alone in his twilit world. He knew he had to find his own way, which he had done, and this was how he had come to be lying naked on a mat on the floor while a woman he had met just twenty minutes earlier waxed every hair from his body.

The first time he had presented *Life* he had shaved off his body hair beforehand, but he now preferred waxing. It took longer for the hairs to grow back, and when they did they were less abrasive than stubble. For the course of the show he would begin to shave every third day once the hair had reached an appropriate length, using an electric razor that collected the bristles, which would then be transferred into a jar. The woman worked on in silence, smearing on the wax and ripping it off. It was not an enjoyable experience but it would soon be over, and he had become used to it.

The last time he had been waxed like this had been around nine months earlier, shortly after he had returned to London from his last show, which had been in São Paolo. That had been when his current batch of promotional photographs had been taken, after which he had allowed his hair to grow back. The city was full of the chosen picture from that shoot, in the Métro and on bus shelters. He had been walking past himself several times a day.

He wasn't sure how he felt about getting ready to present *Life* once again. He loved what he had created, and was in no doubt about its power to move the people who came to see it, but he had begun to find keeping the secret behind it to be an unbearable burden. It took more and more strength to stop himself from blurting it out in interviews, or even from the stage, telling the world what it was all about. There was also the problem that there was no longer anything new about it. The first time he had done it, it had been like taking a voyage upriver into an unknown land, but now there were no surprises, and there was a very real danger that the show would become stale, for him and for the people who came to see it.

He felt it was unrealistic of people to expect an artist to remain at the top of their game year after year, decade after decade. People repeat themselves, retreating into the comfort of familiar patterns, or they simply lose their grip on whatever it was that had once made their work great, and he didn't see why he would be any different. He only hoped he would have the self-awareness to realise when that was happening to him, or better still to withdraw before the rot even began to set in. He was determined not to outstay his welcome, to kill off *Life* before it lost its power.

Every time, *Life* had unfolded in the same way, and so far Paris had not deviated from the template. He avoided reading about himself in newspapers, but his manager had yawned as she told him that, as with everywhere else, campaigners for public decency had been trying to force the mayor to close them down before they had even opened, but even so it had been allowed to go ahead. These campaigners always generated incredible amounts of free publicity and strong advance bookings, and his manager always worried that there *wouldn't* be an outcry from their host city's upstanding citizens.

It had helped their cause that they had been able to draw the city authorities' attention to their having arranged for *Life* to take place in an area that was known for its risqué goings-on. Nobody could reasonably claim to have been enjoying a wholesome stroll with their family when they happened to pop into an innocent-looking art exhibition at Le Charmant Cinéma Érotique only to be confronted with a naked man squatting over glassware.

While not quite daring to call for a ban, conservative newspapers were already running articles critical of the nature of the exhibition, most of it synthesised outrage written by people whose stock-in-trade was synthesised outrage, none of whom had been to see any of Le Machine's previous exhibitions. A lukewarm debate, based on absolute misunderstandings of the piece, had been running in their letters pages about what does or doesn't (even should or shouldn't) count as art. As ever, nobody in any corner of the press had come out firmly in favour of *Life*: the closest the event had to support were a few articles adopting a let's-wait-and-see stance.

In every other city, when the show had finally opened

people had always come in large numbers, art-minded curiosity seekers on the whole, which was fine with him, and the overwhelming majority of them seemed to end up appreciating what he was doing, just as he had hoped they would. They would often return, bringing their friends, art-minded or otherwise, and over the course of a run he would attract a diverse audience. With a few predictable exceptions the press would surprise itself by responding with warmth, guaranteeing further ticket sales. Then the hubbub would die down, and the run would continue in relative peace right up until the end, when the media tuned back in, becoming fascinated by how full all the phials had become, and potential visitors realised that there would be no extension and clamoured for the remaining tickets.

So far, there was nothing to indicate that this run would pan out any differently from the others. He supposed his twelve weeks on stage would pass as they always did.

Somehow, though it had never been his intention, *Life* had become a money-spinner, a small industry. When this had begun to happen, he had let it go to his head; for a while he had lost his equilibrium, and his reason for doing what he was doing had slipped out of focus. In those days he had given interviews in which he had appeared arrogant, and said things he ought not to have said. He was ashamed to think of it now, but he had even begun to feel that the money and press that his work was attracting was in some way a validation of its artistic worth.

Since regaining his perspective, which had happened during a particularly relentless bout of diarrhoea two weeks into the San Francisco staging, his interviews had been more measured, and *Life* continued to have a very positive, even ecstatic, reception. It had come to be regarded as one of the great recent phenomena of the art world. Perhaps Paris would be the place where this all changed. Maybe his home city would reject him, just as he had rejected it. He was ready for this, and he was also ready for this run to be his final presentation of the work. In some ways he hoped it would be. He was starting to feel he had done enough: to pull down the curtain and move on with his life would be a relief.

Only when it was all over, when the finished exhibits from the final staging had been shipped off to whichever collector had bought them, and when his body hair had begun to grow back, never to be waxed again, would he be able to talk openly and honestly about *Life*. If the people who came were to find out why he was doing what he was doing they would bring so many preconceptions that it would come between them and the work. They wouldn't have the opportunity to read the piece in their own way; they would instead see something else, their minds clouded with words, and he felt strongly that words were the enemy of art.

If the critics were ever to find out why he did what he did, they would do everything they could to tear him down. He knew exactly what they would say, too: they would say it was *sentimental schlock*, and they would be half right. It wasn't schlock, he was sure of that, but it *was* sentimental. Only he knew this though, and he was well aware that if the truth ever got out it would all be over, because there is nothing that angers the custodians of the art world more than simple feelings expressed in a straightforward manner. And it was simple feelings, expressed in a straightforward manner, that were at the heart of *Life*.

The waxing went on and on. He would leave the hair on his head until the last moment. That way he would be able to move around unrecognised. He still had a lot to do. He had put off too many things until the last minute. In addition to all the organisational issues that needed to be dealt with, there were two people he had to see before it all began. He had already made several discreet visits to one of them since his return to the city, but he still needed to see them one last time. The other was somebody with whom he had unfinished business.

He had been putting off this particular meeting ever since he had arrived back in the city, but he knew he wouldn't be able to relax on stage unless he had had an opportunity to get what he needed to say off his chest. It was something that had been bothering him for years, and which he had been delaying ever since he had returned to the city: he needed to track down a man called Professor Papavoine.

The woman continued ripping off strips. He would wait until two hours before the doors were due to open before having his eyebrows waxed off, along with a final full check for any missed body hairs from this session. Last of all, the hair on his head and face would be shaved to the skin. He wanted to be as smooth as an egg for his public. Only his eyelashes would remain, and even these he would collect and display as they moulted over the course of the twelve weeks.

He thought back to his visit to the venue. It had put his mind at rest. He had been impressed with the space, and was sure he was going to be comfortable there. His last show had been in the round, in a two-thousand seat boxing arena, and he had never quite been able to relax into the surroundings. This production was going to be smaller in terms of capacity, but he and the crew had worked hard to see that it had a good chance of success. His manager had told him that early sales were fairly strong but they still had a long way to go before they would be able to relax. Soon he would be finding out whether or not he had conquered his home city.

Eugène Carrière's enlarged baby looked on as Le Machine presented his scrotum for waxing. This was his least favourite part of the procedure. He closed his eyes, and braced himself.

VIII

It was almost dark by the time Aurélie and Sylvie started walking down the hill. Sylvie was taking a turn at pushing a drowsy Herbert, and having left Lucien and the Akiyamas eating at the restaurant, they could at last talk freely. Each was impatient to find out what the other had been up to since they had last met. Sylvie told Aurélie about the antics of some of her tormented former lovers and, particularly, their mothers. Sylvie had continuing problems with her ex-boyfriends' mothers who, it seemed, were as keen to have her as their daughter-in-law as their sons were to have her as their wife.

In her middle teenage years, when she had dated only troublemakers, this hadn't been a problem. Her older lovers had never introduced her to their families, preferring to keep her in a dark room and tell her to keep her mouth shut and not go anywhere until they came back, which would often be days, sometimes even weeks, later. When she reached her late teens, she had realised once and for all how quickly things became tedious with bad boys, and stopped bothering with them. She experimented with dating boys of around her age who were more or less normal, and it was then that the mothers had started to come into the picture.

Each of this second wave of boyfriends had been keen to show off his incredible new girlfriend to his family, who without exception would be instantly won over by her looks and her sunny disposition, and when they began to learn snippets from her unhappy history, the boys' mothers clung to her. *She'll be looking for a surrogate family*, they said to their husbands. *Orphans are like that.* They were determined to make theirs the surrogate family they were sure she so desperately craved.

The mothers were right, Sylvie did want a husband so badly because she yearned for the stability of family life. The only person she had ever spoken to about this in any depth was Aurélie. 'I'm not stupid,' she had said. 'I know what's going on; it's pretty basic psychology.' But as much as she wanted the husband and children, she knew that family life with the wrong person would be a lot worse than being alone. She only ever accepted dates from boys she could see herself staying with, boys with an awful lot going for them, but every one had revealed himself to be in some way lacking. Usually it would be nothing obvious, she would just be struck by a feeling that something was not quite right, that he was not the one.

'Maybe it's just typical orphan behaviour,' she had told Aurélie. 'It's not as if I set out to break their hearts, I set out hoping that I'll love them.' That was something she had come to learn was a mistake: hope was not enough. She had pursued the possibility of love, rather than waiting for love to find her, and by the time she accepted that it had failed to materialise, as had happened with every one of them so far, the boy would be so deeply in thrall to her that she could only abandon him to his misery. Sometimes the romance would have lasted for months, sometimes only a few days, but in all cases the depth of despair she left behind was the same.

'Sometimes I'll wonder afterwards whether he *had* been the right one, but I was just so frightened that things would be snatched away that I sabotaged the relationship before it had a chance to be taken away from me.' She had laughed at herself as she said this, and Aurélie hadn't known what to say.

These romances always ended the instant she came to the realisation that the boy was not the one she was going to end up with. She felt this was the right thing to do, that stringing him along for a second beyond this moment of revelation would be dishonest and only make things worse for everybody. She would say, simply, *It's over, I'm sorry,* and leave the room. One time the epiphany had struck her halfway through sex, and another time at the Christmas dinner table in front of the boy's entire extended family. Both had wept, one into the pillow, the other onto his roast goose.

On every occasion, the mother found Sylvie's departure difficult to accept. Often they would be the ones who would call her in the middle of the night to tearfully beg her for a reconciliation, and as Sylvie pushed Herbert down rue Ravignan, her impersonation of the latest poor heartbroken woman made Aurélie clutch her sides with guilty laughter: *I hope you never find out how it feels to lose a daughter.*

She told Aurélie she was going to avoid these situations as much as possible from now on, that she was sure she had finally got the hang of identifying inappropriate men before even agreeing to go on a date with them. She hadn't accepted a date for two months, despite having been asked out over fifty times.

When it was Aurélie's turn to provide an update, she told Sylvie how much she hated Sébastien, and provided her with a creditable pastiche of his plans to *subvert the zeitgeist.* Then she told her about the advances of her creepy old professor, and just as she was making a kind of gagging noise to illustrate the extent of her revulsion, something occurred to Sylvie.

'That squelching sound you're making reminds me – I kept meaning to ask earlier, but never quite got round to it: what's going on with the baby?'

'I got him this morning.'

'Whose is he?'

'Mine for now, I suppose.'

'How did the poor thing end up with you?'

'I threw a stone at him by mistake, and as a punishment his mother's making me look after him for a week.'

'I've not heard of that happening before.'

'Me neither. But maybe it happens all the time – it might just be one of those things that people never talk about. Next time you see a baby with a bruise on his face, have a look at whoever's pushing him along and see if you can spot a trace of panic in their eyes. Anyway, I'm just going to have to live with him. It's been a busy day, but I'm getting the hang of it. I managed to work out how to fold that thing,' she tapped the buggy, 'and we came in on the bus. We were a bit early, so we went to a bookshop and I looked to see if they had one called *How to Keep a Baby Alive for a Week*, but they didn't. I found this, though.' She reached into her bag and pulled out a paperback called *Your Baby & You.* 'Hopefully it'll help. Are you any good with children?'

'I'm not sure. I've never really looked after one, but I kept a Tamagotchi going for three years when I was in the children's home, so I reckon I'd manage OK. I'm doing a world-class job of pushing the buggy, anyway.'

'You're a natural. Hey, I've got a great idea – why don't you keep him for the week? I can see you two have a special bond. You've always said you want to have children one day, so it'll be good practice.'

'Thanks, but no.'

Aurélie found herself quite relieved. She had only been joking, but even so as the words came out the thought of relinquishing him had made her shudder. Herbert was her responsibility, and besides she had her project to think of. She had become fond of him, too. It was strange, but she really had. Ever since she had seen that the stone was about to hit him in the face she had wanted only the best for him.

Sylvie carried on. 'I once heard someone giving someone else a piece of advice about babies, and it seemed to make sense. I can't remember what it was, though. I'll let you know if I remember.'

'Thanks. I'll need all the tips I can get my hands on.'

They reached the neon lights of Pigalle. 'Hey, look.' Sylvie pointed at a big banner hanging outside an old porno cinema. 'Le Machine. Are you going to go?'

Aurélie shrugged. 'I wouldn't mind seeing what all the fuss is about.' It had been impossible to escape all the talk about *Life*, and like so many people they were both inclined to go along so they could make up their own minds about it.

They stopped for a while. There was a queue at the box office, and busy-looking people, wearing black fleeces with *Life* written across them in white lettering, were going in and out of the place as they made final preparations for the opening on Friday night, just two days away. Some of them were wearing walkie-talkie headsets. As fond as she had become of Herbert, Aurélie wished she had chosen to do something as simple as shitting in public for her project. It would have saved her a lot of trouble.

'He's got a good body,' she said.

Sylvie nodded. 'I suppose so.' But the only body she was interested in was the one that belonged to Toshiro Akiyama. 'I prefer a man with eyebrows.' Toshiro Akiyama had eyebrows. 'So where to now?'

'The shop.'

'You mean you actually want to go shopping?'

'Kind of.'

'What for?'

'Baby stuff, mainly. We're running out. There's a supermarket around here somewhere. Do they sell baby stuff in supermarkets?'

'I can't say I've ever given it much thought. I suppose they must do. Let's find out.'

The three of them carried on, past the sex shops, the peep shows and the sushi bars.

* * *

Before she had applied to go to art college Aurélie had visited it on an open day, in the hope of finding out what it was all about and seeing whether or not she would be happy there. She had come into the city on her own for the first time, and had been nervously milling around the refreshments table, trying to work out whether to have some bread and cheese or a biscuit. She had even begun to wonder whether she could find it within herself to be so daring as to have some bread and cheese *and* a biscuit, when she had felt a presence by her side. A smiling girl had appeared, and proceeded to stuff her shoulder bag with as much food as she could. Bread, big chunks of cheese and handfuls of biscuits. It all went into a plastic bag within the shoulder bag, as if the girl had planned the heist in advance.

'I'm hungry,' the girl explained. 'Well, I'm not *actually* hungry, but I expect I will be at some point. It's best to stock up while you can.'

Aurélie didn't know what to say. The girl had such an innocent face that it seemed almost surreal to see her doing something so mischievous. The girl zipped her bag shut, and without a word she took Aurélie by the hair. She inspected it, rummaging through it in a way that was so natural that Aurélie didn't feel affronted or alarmed. There was even something reassuring about her touch.

'Are you checking for lice? I think I'm clear.'

'No, I'm just having a look at your roots. I'm thinking about becoming a hairdresser if I don't get in here,' she explained. 'What would you say your natural colour is?'

Aurélie had bleached her hair a few weeks earlier, and it was time for a touch-up. 'Er . . . mousy, I suppose. A kind of nothing colour.'

'No, it's blonde.'

'No, it's mousy.'

'Listen to me – I'm the professional. Well, not exactly, but you know what I mean. It's dark blonde, but still – you're a natural blonde. What could be better than that?'

'To be a natural light blonde?'

The girl thought for a while. 'Yes, I suppose that would be ideal. But still, your hair is a much better colour than you think it is. What's your name?'

'Aurélie. Aurélie Renard.'

'Sylvie. Sylvie Dupont.' She extended her hand. Aurélie offered hers in return, and Sylvie pumped it in a business-like manner. 'Aurélie . . . that means golden, doesn't it?'

'Yes.'

'That's a lucky name for your hair colour. I wouldn't say your hair is actually golden, let's not get carried away, but it's not too far off.'

'Well, that's good to know.' Aurélie meant it, too. She resolved to have a long think about her hair; maybe she would even start liking it for the first time in her life. 'I have a cousin called Blondelle who had the fairest hair when she was born, but by the time she was three it had turned about your colour – really dark brown. Imagine if you were called Blondelle.'

'That would be really funny for everybody else.'

'I know. She never knows what to do with it – I think it's ruined her life.'

Sylvie couldn't help but laugh at this tale of poor Blondelle's misfortune, and she and Aurélie spent the rest of the day together, walking around the college, attending talks and looking at the work of the current students.

After the open day they went to a bar, and then to save money they headed back to the small hotel room that Aurélie's dad had booked for her, where they talked, ate their way through Sylvie's stash of food and drained glasses of cheap red wine.

Those had been Sylvie's serious drinking days, and Aurélie found it hard to keep up. Aurélie had decided that art college was absolutely for her, and Sylvie had decided that it absolutely wasn't for her. Sylvie wasn't surprised by this. She hadn't expected to end up applying, and she explained that she had only really gone along to make her art therapist happy and to get some free food. Besides, you didn't get paid to go to art college, and she needed money to get by. She was having second thoughts about hairdressing too. Its main appeal had been that there would always be hair so there would always be work, but she wasn't sure she quite had the feeling for it. Her personal ambitions were set in stone, but professionally she didn't know what she wanted to do.

As the night went on they had opened up to one another, bonding over all sorts of things. Aurélie told Sylvie about the boyfriend she had in her home town, saying they were going to stay together even though she was moving away.

'Yeah, right,' said Sylvie. 'Like that's going to work.'

'No, we really are staying together. We've discussed it.'

'Well, good luck with that.' She drained her wine, and topped up her glass.

That was the moment when it dawned on Aurélie that she hadn't been honest with herself, or with her boyfriend. Sylvie was right: she really didn't love him enough to keep things going. How could Sylvie have known that? She wondered if she had psychic powers. 'Shit,' she said.

'He's going to be so . . .' She pictured the scene that she now knew had to happen. She was going to tear his world apart. 'Poor Guillaume.'

'He'll survive. They usually do.'

Sylvie decided this wasn't a good time to tell Aurélie about the exes of hers who hadn't quite made it. Twice she had taken a call from a weeping mother. Both boys had perished in what had been officially declared accidents. One had set up a warehouse dehumidifier in his bedroom, apparently in order to keep condensation off the windows while he slept. It had sucked all the moisture from his body, and he was discovered a few days later, a paper-dry corpse. The other appeared to have slipped on a leaf and fallen head first into a barrel of water from which he had been unable to escape.

Both, though, had left detailed recent wills, which suggested that these hadn't been accidents at all. They had both expressed their wish for Sylvie to be at the church, and specified what they wanted her to wear; both times it had been something inappropriate for the situation – too short and too tight, and bright red even though she never wore clothes that were short, tight and bright red.

She didn't see what she could do but accept these invitations and go along with their wishes. They had both requested that she sing as their coffins were lowered into the ground. She had a beautiful voice, which she rarely used, and as she stood by their gravesides, singing like a lark in her slutty clothes, everybody wept.

On both occasions she had been approached by the boy's mother, who very kindly told her that she was not to feel responsible and that she bore her no ill will. She was glad that they had taken the time to do this, but even if they hadn't, her sense of guilt would have been minimal. It was tragic, of course; they had both been nice boys and it was awful that they had died, but her role in it all had merely been realising that she didn't love them after all, and telling them so. She wasn't to know they were going to end up this way, and she didn't think for a moment that she had done the wrong thing, that she should have stayed with them. She never spoke about these feelings to anyone, because she knew they would think her cold. She was just being realistic though, and not burdening herself with a guilt that didn't belong to her.

As the bottles emptied, Sylvie and Aurélie had started to dwell on their difficult backgrounds. Aurélie had drunk a lot more than she usually did, and she became maudlin as she told Sylvie about her mother's illness and her slow, sad death, which had finally come when she had been nine years old, and how from that day her father had raised her and her younger brother alone.

Sylvie came in with a challenge to this: both her parents had died on her eighth birthday, victims of an unexpectedly pure batch of heroin that had hit the streets that summer. They had been good people, she told Aurélie, and talented – her father a jazz drummer and her mother an accomplished stripper. They had loved her from the start, playing her jazz and classical music while she had been in the womb, even though it hadn't been trendy back then. She smiled as if recounting a trip to the seaside as she told Aurélie how she had been the one to find them lying cold in bed, how from that day she had been alone, how her memories of them grew less and less distinct with each passing day, and how she had spent the rest of her childhood being batted around between foster families, feckless distant relatives and children's homes, and how she would often run away, inevitably into a situation that was worse than the one she had just escaped from.

'If your father was to drop dead tomorrow,' she said, 'I would still be more orphan than you'll ever be.'

She made this pronouncement in such a way that Aurélie had to laugh and admit defeat. She had been comprehensively out-orphaned. She wondered how she would have coped if her father hadn't been there to love, support and encourage her, if she didn't have her brother to live for – if, like Sylvie, she had been all alone in the world, without a safety net.

At the end of the night they parted company, but not before exchanging numbers. When Aurélie was alone again her heart filled with pity for the boy from back home, who right now would be sleeping with her picture by his bedside, having gently kissed it goodnight. She cried. *At least*, she thought, *these tears prove I have a heart.* Soon she was reconciled to the inevitable, and fell asleep.

Aurélie had not been able to stop thinking about her day with Sylvie. It helped her to know that she would have a friend when she got to the city, someone who knew her way around. Months later, when she arrived, she called her straight away. 'It's Aurélie,' she said.

'Aurélie? Aurélie who?' Sylvie had encountered a fair number of Aurélies in her life.

Sylvie had spared her very little thought since they had parted company. She met a lot of people, and had no reason to assume that she would ever see the girl again. Very quickly her time had filled up with work and drama, and their day together had been buried under a mound of subsequent experiences. Unlike Aurélie, she had not spent the intervening months longing for a reunion.

'Aurélie Renard.' There was silence at the other end of the line. 'You grabbed my hair.'

'I used to grab everyone's hair.'

Aurélie was crushed. Sylvie Dupont was slipping away from her. She carried on. 'I'm the failed orphan you met at the art college. We drank wine in my hotel room.'

'Oh. Let me think.' A faint recollection had appeared, and begun to grow. 'Yes, I remember. Blondelle's cousin, right?'

'That's it.' Aurélie had never felt so relieved.

'How is Blondelle?'

'She's still pretty pissed off about her name.'

Sylvie laughed. 'And how about you?'

'Well, I'm in Paris now, and I was wondering if you were around at all?'

Sylvie could barely recall a thing about the girl, but she knew she had her filed in her memory alongside people she liked well enough. She didn't want to be mean to her. She would invite her out for coffee and be friendly for thirty minutes and then drop a heavy enough hint for her to leave her alone from then on. She was always happy to meet people, but she was wary about getting close to anyone. She wasn't in the market for making new friends, and she didn't want this girl who was just in from the country to make a nuisance of herself by thinking they were closer than they were. If necessary she would get her off her back by setting her up with an ex. They arranged to meet the following day.

Once she had put down the phone, Sylvie was surprised to find memories of her day with this Aurélie Renard coming back to her, as if they had really been friends, and she even surprised herself by looking forward to seeing her again. She wanted to find out what had become of Guillaume.

Guillaume had met Aurélie at the railway station on her return from Paris, and though she had hoped to wait until they were in a private place before initiating the Big Conversation, she found she couldn't. As they walked through the town on the way back to her house he had kept making references to their future, and how wonderful it was that their love was so strong that they were going to be able to stay together in spite of living hundreds of miles apart.

'Ah, yes,' she had said. 'About that.'

'About what?'

'About our future together . . .'

'What about it?'

'Well, I've been thinking about that.'

'Me too. It's all I ever think about.'

'No,' she said. She stopped walking, and he stopped too, and she looked away and spoke softly. 'I've been thinking about it in a new way.'

In an instant, Guillaume felt everything that was good about his life slip away. A tear ran down his cheek and, choking with emotion, he begged her to reconsider. Passers-by stopped to watch him as he clung to the wreckage of love. He fell to his knees. 'All I ask is that you give me one last chance.'

She hated to see him making such a spectacle of himself. 'Well, OK then,' she said. 'I'll give it some thought, but don't hold out too much hope.'

He stood up, and they walked back to her house in silence. She waited until they were indoors before telling him he had to be brave, and ending things once and for all.

That night Guillaume built a fire on his front lawn, and fed into the flames everything he had that reminded him of her. Love letters, once cherished photographs, clothes she had left behind when she had stayed over, gifts she had given him in happier times. He went back inside, but everything he saw reminded him of her. The pan he had used to make them hot chocolate, the mattress they had lain on as he held her in his arms, and the television on which they had watched their favourite shows. By the end of the evening there was nothing left but the clothes he stood up in, and then he realised she had helped him choose these clothes, she had touched them with her soft, slender and occasionally paint-splattered fingers, and so they came off too and went on to the fire. By this point news had spread, and people had come to watch. They leaned on his fence. Some offered words of encouragement, urging him to think positively and telling him that there were plenty more fish in the sea, while others were unkind, telling him they weren't surprised that she had left, that she was probably going to look for somebody with a bigger penis.

Aurélie had felt awful for poor Guillaume, but it was only when she related the story to Sylvie that she finally allowed herself to see the funny side. Soon the girls were crying with laughter, and the thirty-minute coffee turned into six hours. By the end of it Sylvie had allowed herself to become as enamoured of Aurélie as Aurélie was of her.

Aurélie grew closer to Sylvie than she did with anyone from art college, and this was why she had been the one she had called when she found herself in trouble, and she was the one whose apartment she was in, surrounded by shopping bags as she scooped purée into the mouth of a small boy whom she had, as Sylvie gleefully pointed out, sort of abducted.

Sylvie lent Aurélie her backpack to help her get everything home, and together they filled it with nappies, bottles of special milk and all the other things they had bought for him at the supermarket, mainly duplicates of what had been in the bag. They had needed a spare set of clothes too, but hadn't been in the best of neighbourhoods for that kind of shopping. The rubberwear emporia wouldn't be much use to them, so they had found themselves with little choice but to go to a souvenir shop. They picked out a T-shirt with a picture of the Eiffel Tower on it, and some trousers made from Mona Lisa fabric.

The owner, a gruff and gigantic man with a walrus moustache, came over and asked them what size they were looking for. Aurélie had no idea how to answer.

'What do you mean *what size*?'

'I mean how large or small would you like the clothes to be?'

'Oh. I see.'

After a long silence, the man took the initiative. 'Are they for your baby?' He nodded in Herbert's direction.

'Er . . . yes, he's my baby. And it's all for him. He loves his home city. He's very proud to be a Parisian.'

Herbert confirmed the extent of his civic pride by blowing a raspberry.

'So,' the man continued, 'what size is he?'

'Well,' she pointed at him, 'he's that size.'

'But how old is he?' His face was beginning to betray extreme impatience.

'Oh. That's a good question.' She had no idea. 'Thank you for asking.' She thought back to what Herbert's mother had told her: 'He's . . . er . . . Aquarius.'

The owner raised his hands into the air, and clenched his fists. His face lit up with delight. 'A-ha!' he cried. 'A puzzle! I love puzzles. As my wife always says to me, *If there is one thing you love, Théophile, it's puzzles.* So, Aquarius . . .' He bunched his enormous fists over his eyes. 'He must be about . . .' His fists unfolded to reveal delighted eyes. '. . . nine months old?'

Aurélie supposed he was right. 'Yes, exactly.' She applauded, and jumped on the spot. 'He's exactly about nine months old.' It sounded close enough, and she was glad to know.

'And what's he called?'

'Herbert.'

'*Air-bear?*'

'No – *Herbert.* H-H-H . . .' She pulled the mirror from her bag.

The backpack was crammed with baby stuff. Aurélie couldn't believe how much she had spent. The money she had saved from working over the summer, money she had hoped would last her until at least Christmas was evaporating fast. She wondered how anybody could afford to have one of these things all year round. She had cancelled her regular weekend shifts to give her time to concentrate on her project, so that would mean even less money coming in than usual. She was going to have to ask her boss for any work going once she had given the baby back. She was about to buckle the backpack closed when Sylvie stopped her.

'Wait,' she said. 'One more thing.' She raced into her bedroom, and came back out with something in her hand. 'It's a mean world out there,' she said, 'and you might need this.' Smiling, she held her offering out to Aurélie.

It was a gun.

Aurélie froze. It took a while before she could speak again. 'What's that?'

'Er, it's a gun. I know it's small, but it's still a gun. It works just the same as a big one.'

'But . . . what's it for?'

Sylvie looked at her as if she had just asked her why Spain was so full of Spaniards. 'It's for shooting people.'

Aurélie still didn't reach out for it.

'Well, if you don't want it, that's up to you. If you think you can take care of Herbert all by yourself. It's fully loaded and ready to go.'

Aurélie stared at it. 'Have you ever used it?' She dreaded the answer.

'Yes. I've waved it around a bit. I've not shot anyone with it, though. I've not had to, they generally just run away. It's got me out of quite a few difficult situations. I carry it around quite a lot of the time, just in case, but I can live without it for a few days. And don't look at me like that. If you were on your own in the world you might want a bit of protection too. It's my security blanket.'

Aurélie looked at the gun. She had always had a feeling that there were sides to her friend that she would rather not know about, and she had uncovered one of them right here. She wondered how many times Sylvie had been armed when they had been out and about together. 'Where did you get it?'

'From some guy. He was the protective type. When I told him I was leaving he tied me up for a while, but he was a big softie underneath it all and after a couple of days he let me go. It had finally sunk in that I really wasn't going to stay with him, and he gave it to me then. He said he would feel he was always taking care of me if he knew I had it, that if anyone ever tried anything funny I would be able to pop a cap in their ass. It was quite sweet, really. Apparently it's a *ladies' gun*. That's what he told me, anyway.'

It was small enough to fit in a handbag, and it had a blue finish.

'I don't know . . .' Aurélie could feel herself shaking.

'You don't have to shoot anyone with it. Just point it at them and they'll go away. If anybody bothers Herbert . . .' She released the safety catch, and finished her sentence with a chilling clunk.

Aurélie still didn't look convinced, and Sylvie continued her pitch. 'If you really have to use it, which you won't, just point it in the right direction and – *blam*. Just make sure you only use it on someone who deserves it. You don't even have to kill them if you don't want to. Just hurt them. Go for the knees if you really want them out of action. I've tried it out in the countryside, so I know it works. I shot a few tree stumps.'

Aurélie hated guns. She had never wanted to be around them, let alone carry one. But she thought of how ill equipped she was to protect Herbert from the world at large, and all kinds of improbable but petrifying scenarios flashed through her mind. It struck her that she hadn't been joking about keeping Herbert alive for a week. It really was an urgent responsibility. The following Wednesday she was going to hand him back to his mother in one piece, and she wasn't going to let anybody get in the way of that.

She reached out and took the gun, and the moment she did her apprehension melted away. She felt a surge of power and excitement, and it was not an unpleasant sensation. Nobody was going to come near Herbert now. She put her finger on the trigger, to get a feel for it. The gun fitted her hand perfectly: seven hundred and fifty grammes of cold blue steel.

JEUDI

IX

Nearly twenty years earlier two boys of eight, best friends and next-door neighbours, had been allowed out by their mothers on two conditions: that they stay together at all times, and that they keep out of trouble. They had not hesitated in accepting these terms. Trouble was the last thing on their minds. Being out in the city alone was enough excitement for them, and they set off through the streets to the Canal Saint-Martin to watch the boats go by.

The boys, Dominique Gravoir and Léandre Martin, knew the canal well, having walked there with their families for as long as they could remember. Léandre Martin liked that it shared his name, and he had always thought of it as *his* canal. They threw stones in the water, stood beside locks as barges made their way up and down the waterway, and when the canal disappeared underground they walked through the streets until they got to the point where it re-emerged, at Port de l'Arsenal, where the boats, owned by rich people, were bigger, and were there to be stared at. Dominique Gravoir and Léandre Martin identified the one they liked above all the others, and agreed that one day they would sail a boat just like it along the Seine to Le Havre and out on to the open sea.

From the Port de l'Arsenal, they walked by the river, along the Quai Henri-IV, and watched the big tourist boats go by.

It was Léandre Martin who first saw the cormorant. He watched it dive, then waited for it to come back to the surface. After a while, it reappeared. Léandre Martin said nothing, but he kept his eyes on the bird. It dived again, then, after a long while, rose once more to the surface. It gave him an idea for a game.

Dominique Gravoir liked games. If anything, he liked them a little too much. He was a personable child, but whenever there was a challenge before him he would rise to it with a single-mindedness that was absolute. People had noticed this about him, and had often commented on his *determined streak*. It wasn't the kind of determined streak that would ever result in a display of bad temper, but on the rare occasions when he was not victorious in whichever game he was playing, he would quietly and seriously reflect on his performance, and work out ways to do better the next time. Nobody knew until it was too late quite how deep his determination ran.

When Léandre Martin told him his idea, Dominique Gravoir accepted the challenge straight away. Léandre Martin had thought carefully before mentioning the game, and had only decided to tell his friend because it wouldn't pit them against one another, and their day, which had been such a success so far, would not be blighted by competition. Instead of boy against boy, it would be boys against bird.

The challenge was simple: they would watch the cormorant, and when it went under the water they would each hold their breath until it rose again. The aim was for them to beat the cormorant every time. They would work as a team, and as long as one of them beat the bird, they would both consider themselves victorious.

The cormorant dived, and the boys held their breath.

It was too easy. The dive was short, and disappointing, and they wondered whether it would be much of a game after all. They kept their eye on the bird, hoping for a tougher round, and soon it went down again. This time it was under for longer. Their eyes scanned the water, waiting for it to reappear. It seemed to be staying down forever.

When at last it popped back up, a few metres from where it had gone down, the boys finally breathed again, and were elated at having beaten the cormorant again, this time in a closely fought battle. As they regained their breath they kept their eyes on the bird, waiting for the next round. Before long it went underwater again, and again Dominique Gravoir and Léandre Martin held their breath.

Their eyes scanned the surface of the river as they waited for the bird to reappear. Léandre Martin often thought back to this third round of the game, and when he did it was as if he was still there, standing on the quay with Dominique Gravoir by his side. He felt the pressure building inside him as he willed the bird to return to the surface, and this pressure turning to pain in his lungs, and his head. It felt as if his eyes were about to pop out, and the veins in his temples were ready to burst open. The bird remained resolutely underwater as Léandre Martin fought his instincts. His body was crying out for breath, and he knew that he needed it, but he would not let the bird beat him. He crouched into a foetal position, hoping this would help him, but it was no use. He could stand it no longer. His mouth opened, and air flooded back into his lungs. Dizzy, he stood up, accepting defeat.

He looked over to Dominique Gravoir, and saw that he was standing still, with a familiar look of complete determination on his face that told him that while Léandre Martin may have given up, *he* was not going to let this bird beat them. The boys were as close as brothers, and Léandre Martin knew that his friend would never cheat. There was no way he was secretly breathing through his nose, as other boys might have done. Every day since then, Léandre Martin had wished he had somehow stopped him right then. If only he had playfully bumped him, or tickled him under the arms, or even punched him in the belly. Anything to get him breathing again. It might have put him in a bad mood, but he would have got over it and they would have been friends again by the end of the day.

Dominique Gravoir's skin turned a shade of purple that Léandre Martin had never seen on a face before. His eyes were almost closed, staying open just enough for him to survey the surface of the water. His fingers clenched into fists. Léandre Martin started to worry.

'Well, you've beaten me,' he said. 'You and the cormorant have won.' Dominique Gravoir gave him an angry look, and Léandre Martin understood why. They had gone into this as a team, not in competition with one another. Dominique Gravoir had not beaten his teammate; he was now holding his breath for both of them.

His face betrayed the pain he was experiencing. 'I think you should stop now,' said Léandre Martin.

Dominique Gravoir shook his head.

'I expect the bird's surfaced downriver.'

Again Dominique Gravoir shook his head.

Léandre Martin knew that the bird hadn't surfaced. There was an expanse of water before them, and the cormorant was nowhere to be seen. He was worried now. 'Is that it over there?' He pointed. 'I think I can see it.'

Dominique Gravoir was not fooled. There was no cormorant. With a horrifying mixture of determination and panic on his face, he fell to his knees. It was as if he had known what was going to happen.

'Give up,' said Léandre Martin. 'We can't win every time.' By this point he was shouting. He looked up and down the quay but it was quiet. The nearest passers-by were a long way away, and walking in the wrong direction. 'Breathe. Just breathe.' At least he had said this. At least when he looked back on this day he knew he hadn't stood silently by and let it happen. He had done as much as an eight-year-old boy realistically could. He looked helplessly around him, wishing he had never thought of this game.

Dominique Gravoir slumped on to his side, but his eyes stayed open, fixed on the water as he waited for the bird to surface. A man had appeared, walking in their direction along the quay. 'Hey, you,' called Léandre Martin, defying his mother's instruction not to speak to strangers. 'Come here.' The man saw the collapsed child and rushed over. 'Make him breathe,' said Léandre Martin.

The man tried to force a finger into the boy's mouth, but it was clamped shut. Dominique Gravoir shoved the man away, and was still again, looking out at the water. The man assumed he was having some kind of fit, and he called to a woman who had appeared on the deck of a boat that was moored some way along the quay. The woman could see that something was wrong, and she called out to them, saying she would radio for an ambulance.

Dominique Gravoir kept on looking out across the water, his eyes now wide open. And then something happened to them. They were still wide open, but there was a glassiness to them. Léandre Martin could tell that his friend was no longer looking for the cormorant. He was still.

The bird had beaten them.

The man didn't know what to do. He pumped the boy's chest, and tried to breathe into his lungs, but his mouth remained clamped shut. Léandre Martin shouted for his friend to wake up, to start breathing again. He was frantic, and he was crushed by guilt. This had been *his* game, *his* idea, and Dominique Gravoir had been holding his breath for the two of them.

Minutes later the paramedics arrived, and Dominique Gravoir was at last surrounded by people in uniform who knew what they were doing, and who tried their very best for him. Léandre Martin went with them to the hospital in the back of the ambulance.

Later that day, Dominique Gravoir's mother wept as she was told by a doctor that her son had *symptoms consistent with asphyxiation.* At this point they had no idea whether or not he would regain consciousness.

He never would.

Léandre Martin never looked for a friend to replace him.

And he never found out what had become of the bird.

X

At eight thirty in the morning, Aurélie Renard sat on a bench in the garden at the centre of the Place des Vosges. She had not slept well.

It had been almost midnight by the time she and Herbert had got back to her apartment the night before. As they headed home from the bus stop, Aurélie had stopped to buy a kebab. This was something she did every once in a while, and normally she thought nothing of it, but it hadn't seemed quite right having a baby with her as she waited alongside the motley collection of late-night customers for her pitta bread to rise.

When they had at last made it home, it had taken her a long time to get the baby settled. She realised he didn't have pyjamas, so after she had put him in a fresh nappy and brushed his teeth, procedures he yielded to with nonchalance, she dressed him in his new Eiffel Tower top and Mona Lisa trousers. Their fabric was soft, and she hoped he would be comfortable.

He was wide awake, and showed no sign of wanting to go to sleep. She hummed fragments of lullabies to him, she read him passages from inappropriate books, and she cuddled him, but nothing would wind him down. He seemed hell bent on staying up for an all-nighter. She didn't like the idea of him sleeping on the floor, and had decided to have him by her side in bed. Hoping to inspire him to become at least a little bit tired, she turned off the main light, leaving only the kitchen spotlight on, with the door open so she could just about see. She tucked him under the duvet, and he lay there staring at her.

This was the first time they had spent time together without there being some kind of immediate drama about the situation. It was nice, but even so it was time to sleep. It had been an extremely long day. She took a close look at him. The bruise hadn't got any bigger, which was a relief. She closed her eyes, and hoped this would encourage him to start thinking about drifting off. It didn't work. He rolled towards her, and kept patting her face. She took his hands in hers, and not for the first time she marvelled at the difference in size. Then she closed her eyes again, and once again he patted her face until they re-opened. His eyes were open wide in the near darkness, and he looked beautiful.

'You are a handsome boy, Herbert,' she said. She knew it made no sense, but she felt proud of him. He pulled a face and made some noises in return. Some of them almost sounded like words.

She wondered what on earth his mother was doing, handing over her beautiful boy to a complete stranger for a week, no matter how kind that stranger's face. She must have been having a breakdown. She had certainly been acting strangely, her mood shifting every few seconds. If that was the case, Aurélie told herself, then she was doing valuable social work, taking the pressure off a stressed mother, allowing her some breathing space. Maybe the call she had made had been to her therapist, who had told her that handing the baby over to a stranger who had just thrown a stone at his face was a terrific idea, that it would give her just the opportunity she needed to relax. She hoped that when the week was up and the time had come to hand him back, she would find her fully refreshed and ready to take care of her son again.

It was half past one by the time he finally fell asleep, and Aurélie at last began to drift off. She was jolted awake by the sound of her phone's ringtone. She had recently changed it, and realised now that she hadn't made a good choice. It was an ear-shattering sequence of apparently unrelated beeps. As she leaned over the side of the bed and fumbled to find the phone in her bag, she heard a gurgle. Herbert had been woken by the noise, and was rubbing his eyes and looking around in the darkness. Aurélie found the phone, but it had already stopped ringing and had gone to voice mail. She checked it.

It was Sylvie. She had remembered the piece of child-rearing advice she had once heard, and was calling to pass it on: *Sleep whenever the baby sleeps, because when they're awake you won't have a chance.*

'Thanks for that,' croaked Aurélie, into the unlistening phone. 'Goodnight.'

She turned the phone to silent, and looked at the baby.

'Go back to sleep, Herbert,' she said gently. She rubbed his tummy. 'Go back to sleep.'

And that is just what Herbert did, an hour and twenty minutes later.

Aurélie had managed three and a half hours' sleep when she was woken by a tiny hand on her face. It took her a while to realise what was going on, and when the events of the day before replayed in her mind she felt a knot in her stomach. It hadn't even been twenty-four hours. For the first time that day, and it would by no means be the last, she wondered what she had got herself into.

'Hello, Herbert,' she said. 'And how are you this morning?'

He didn't have to answer. She could tell by looking at him that he was very well indeed. There was a big smile across his face, and he was ready for the day. All she had to do was get him through it. She recalled that on the bus home the night before she had written a list of the important things to keep on top of when taking care of an approximately nine-month-old baby. They were:

1. Food
2. Drink
3. Nappy
4. Teeth

She had bought a spare baby bottle at the supermarket and, still coming to, she left Herbert on the bed as she got it ready. She boiled some water in a pan and dropped the bottle in, sterilising it just in case, and she put an egg in beside it for herself. Once the bottle had cooled down a bit she filled it with his special milk. She took it through to him, and he latched on to it quite happily.

While he was getting on with that, she got his breakfast ready: a jar of puréed fruit and rice. She dipped her finger in and tried a bit, to see if it tasted as revolting as it looked. It was a lot nicer than she had anticipated, and she needed to exercise a surprising amount of self-control to keep from taking a big scoop for herself.

She propped Herbert into a sitting position, and fed him. He finished the lot with gusto. Then he took the bottle again, and when he had had enough he dropped it on to the bed. She found his toothbrush, and cleaned his teeth, and then she changed his nappy, which was heavy after his night's sleep.

She had done everything on the list. Looking after a baby was a lot easier than she had ever thought it would be, and she wondered why people made such a fuss about it.

Feeling a little self-conscious with Herbert watching her from the bed, she undressed and attempted the world's fastest shower. She stepped under the water, shampooed her hair, rinsed it, and had begun to rub shower gel over her body when from the bedroom came a loud thump, followed by a horrible, yet familiar, silence.

By the time Aurélie had made it through to the bedroom Herbert was crying his heart out, face down on the floor beside the bed. Frantic, she scooped him up and tried to console him. His makeshift pyjamas got wet as she pressed him to her body. She checked him for signs of bruising. There didn't seem to be any new marks on his head or face, which was a relief. She hoped he hadn't broken any bones. She would have to wait and see. She held him close, and whispered to him, and told him she was sorry, and that it was all her fault.

It took a long while for his wails to turn to sobs, and the sobs to mild grizzling and his mild grizzling to a sullen demeanour. She checked his bones by running her fingers along his arms and legs and pressing on various parts of his body. He seemed OK. She built him a nest of pillows on the bed, hoping it would stop him from rolling off again, then she jumped back into the shower, which had been running all this time, to rinse off the shower gel. She dried herself, and pulled on some clothes. At last, Herbert was smiling again. He was fine. She lay down beside him, and looked at him, and he looked at her.

And then something inevitable happened: there was a knock at the door.

Aurélie had managed to get Herbert upstairs twice and downstairs once without passing anybody. Their isolation from the neighbours had been a small miracle, but now the miracle was over. The knocking continued. 'Open up, I know you're in there.' Aurélie recognised the voice of the woman from across the hall, strident for someone who must have been at least ninety years old. It was Old Widow Peypouquet.

Like everybody else in the building, Aurélie had no idea that Old Widow Peypouquet had never lost a husband. She had never even married, but even so everything about her screamed *widow*. On the day she had moved in, it had not entered the concierge's mind that she could be anything other than a widow. On being asked about the new neighbour by existing tenants, he had casually referred to her as Old Widow Peypouquet, and because of the way she dressed and carried herself, nobody had thought for a moment that this was in any way far-fetched, and so that was what she had been known as ever since. She was unaware that this had been going on for the preceding two decades; as far as she knew, to them she was merely Madame Peypouquet, as this was how they addressed her to her face.

The people who lived there were decent folk by and large, and none of them wanted to intrude on a widow's sorrow. Beyond showing her everyday politeness, they left her alone. *Hello, Madame Peypouquet*, they would respectfully say as they passed her on the stairs. They rarely engaged her in further conversation but she wasn't to know that this was because they had no idea what else they could possibly say to her. All the words they thought of seemed somehow inappropriate for one who was evidently in such deep mourning, and they stopped themselves before they came out. No matter how they phrased their questions in their minds, in essence they were all the same: *Hello, Madame Peypouquet. How are you coping now that your husband is in the ground?* They chose instead to make no enquiries, hoping their smiles and gentle greetings would be enough to provide her with at least a little warmth to help her through her bleak, empty days.

Even the few people who passed through the building who could not be counted as decent folk gave her no trouble. After all, it was never good luck to get on a widow's bad side – nobody wants to be tormented by the protective ghost of a dead husband. And so she had lived there, year in and year out, with nobody really getting to know her.

Aurélie had been the same as everyone else. She had greeted her on the occasions when their paths had crossed, and sometimes they had gone as far as exchanging comments on the weather, but that was all. Aurélie had no idea that Old Widow Peypouquet had taken quite an interest in the girl from the apartment across the landing.

The knocking continued. There was no escape.

'I'm coming, Madame Peypouquet,' she said. 'I'll be with you in a moment.'

She opened the door just a crack. 'Hello, Madame Peypouquet,' she said. 'How are you today?' At once Aurélie regretted the question. Every day must have been a living hell for Old Widow Peypouquet as she lamented the loss of her husband, and to enquire after her wellbeing had been tactless.

'I'm the same as always.'

'Good. I mean . . . at least you're not any worse than usual.'

Old Widow Peypouquet stared at her.

'So how can I help you this morning, Madame Peypouquet?'

'Do you have a baby in there?'

She might have been old, but she wasn't deaf.

'A baby? No. There's no baby here.' She opened the door and swept her arm around, indicating the entire apartment in a single gesture. She had folded the buggy and put it in the shower, and put all the other incriminating evidence on the bed and thrown the duvet over it. There was no sign of a baby.

'Ah. Then the sound must be coming from somewhere else.'

'Yes. Now, you have a good day, Madame Peypouquet. I think it's going to be sunny.'

'Yes. Well, it's got off to a clear start. I'm sorry to have bothered you, Mademoiselle Renard, but I could have sworn I heard a baby's cries coming from your apartment, and I've been wondering what was going on, that's all. You will forgive an old woman's curiosity.'

'Oh, Madame Peypouquet, you're not old.'

Old Widow Peypouquet gave her a look.

'OK, yes, you are quite old.' Aurélie was about to close the door when a gurgle came from the other side of the room. Before she could do anything about it, Old Widow Peypouquet had invited herself in, and was looking around for the source of the noise. She soon found it, lying on a blanket on the floor on the far side of the bed: Herbert.

'What's this, then?' she asked, pointing a bony finger. 'What's this if it's not a baby?'

'Oh, that? It's, well, you know . . .' Her mind raced as she tried to think of a reasonable explanation.

'Yes, I do know. It's a baby.'

'A baby? That thing?' Aurélie faked a laugh. 'No, that's not a baby.'

'Not a baby?'

'No.'

'Then what is it?'

They stood looking down at Herbert, who smiled up at them, and expanded on his previous gurgling. Aurélie was about to panic when the brainwave struck. She was out of trouble. 'It's rubber,' she said.

'Rubber?'

'Yes.'

Old Widow Peypouquet scrutinised Herbert, who was looking up at her with his big blue eyes. 'Are you sure?'

'Yes. I'm sorry, Madame Peypouquet. It's all rather

embarrassing, and I was hoping you wouldn't find out.'

'It looks very realistic to me.'

'I know. It's quite incredible really. It's a wonder of modern science.'

'But why, exactly, do you have a rubber baby?'

Aurélie recalled Sylvie's tales of the years of her childhood when her only friend had been a Tamagotchi, and her thoughts began to fall into place. 'Madame Peypouquet, please sit down. I have something to tell you.' Old Widow Peypouquet lowered herself onto the edge of the bed, and Aurélie continued. 'I'm broody. I really want to have a baby of my own.'

'A baby? But you're not ready. You don't even have a husband. As far as I can see you don't even have a boyfriend. There was that handsome boy, the tall one who came to see you a few months ago, but I've not seen him since.'

Sébastien. So Old Widow Peypouquet really was the observant type.

'No,' said Aurélie. 'No, he didn't. And I'm so glad you understand my problem. I went to the doctor, and told him that even though I don't have a boyfriend I'm desperate to have a child, and he gave me this. It's a computerised baby simulator. It's full of wires and things like that. I have it for a week so I can find out exactly what's involved in looking after a baby, and then I'll be able to make an informed decision about whether or not to have a real one myself. They're hoping it'll put me off the idea, for the time being at least.'

'I hope they're right. So how does it work?'

'With technology, mainly.'

'Technology, you say?'

'Yes. And the technology makes it do lots of babylike

things. All the babylike things, in fact. It cries in the middle of the night, it demands to be fed . . .'

'What do you feed it?' Her eyes were narrow.

'Milk, baby food.' She realised what she was saying, and came to her own rescue. 'It's a sort of electronic computer milk. And computer food. It's all very scientific, and I don't quite understand it. Somewhere inside is a microchip the size of a grain of sugar, and it records everything that happens to it, and at the end of the week I'll take it back and they'll plug it into a computer and it'll give me a mark out of ten for my parenting skills.'

Old Widow Peypouquet was silent for a while. 'May I have a closer look at it?'

'Yes, of course.' Aurélie bent down and scooped him up. 'Here it is.' Herbert was looking around the room. He smiled at Old Widow Peypouquet, who still looked suspicious.

A bony hand reached out and grabbed the baby's leg. 'Hmmm . . . It looks right, but it doesn't feel right. It feels too rubbery. I can't believe some of the things they make these days. I tell you – things were different in my day. I only hope it does its job, Mademoiselle Renard. Your time to have a child will come, though. Why not invite that handsome boy here again? Just be sure and wait until you're married to him before you get one of these though.'

'That's very good advice, Madame Peypouquet. Oh, and please don't tell anyone else about this. I'm a little ashamed about the whole business.' She lowered her eyes. 'And it is rather a delicate medical matter, so confidentiality is paramount.'

'Of course. One last thing, though. What's its name,

this rubber baby?' But before Aurélie could answer, Old
Widow Peypouquet made a disgusted face, and held her
nose. 'Vive la France! The manufacturers have gone too
far – no real child makes smells as awful as that.'

Old Widow Peypouquet shuffled out of the apartment, and
Aurélie shut the door behind her. She gave Herbert a big
cuddle. Already she was quite used to the extraordinary
aromas he was capable of producing. 'That was close,' she
said. She was feeling claustrophobic, and knew then that
they had to stay out of the building as much as possible.

Fifteen minutes later, Herbert was in a clean nappy and
proper clothes, and just as they were about to leave she
glanced around the room and saw, lying as innocently as
anything on her bedside table, Sylvie's gun. Old Widow
Peypouquet couldn't have noticed it, as she had said
nothing. She picked it up. She didn't feel as confident about
it as she had the night before. It seemed a lot heavier,
and more awkward in her hand. She put it in her bag,
but it seemed to weigh her down, as if it was telling her
to leave it at home, that only trouble would come if she
took it out with her. Resolving to stick to only well-lit
public places, she opened a drawer, took the gun out of
her bag and hid it under some clothes.

She and Herbert left the apartment, and soon they
were at the foot of the stairs. Just as she was about to
leave the building, she heard a man's voice. 'Ah, it's the
rubber baby.'

She turned to see Monsieur Simoneaux from the second
floor, standing in his pyjamas and slippers, his grey hair
wild, as if he had only just woken up. Monsieur Simoneaux's grey hair always looked like this, and she had

only ever seen him in his pyjamas and slippers. She had often wondered whether he owned any proper clothes. He must have heard them coming down the stairs, and rushed out to see the phenomenon. News of the delicate medical matter had already reached that far.

'May I see?'

Monsieur Simoneaux approached the buggy, and looked at Herbert. 'Amazing,' he said. He reached out and pinched the baby's cheeks a little bit too hard. Herbert pulled a face. 'Is it a boy or a girl?'

'A boy.'

'He looks very realistic, but Old Widow Peypouquet's right – he doesn't feel like the real thing. He feels too rubbery to be a proper baby. I have an idea – let's find out what happens if you grab him by the ankles and smash him against the wall.' He crouched down and squinted as he searched for the buckle that would release him from his buggy.

Aurélie wrestled him away. 'Er, no, Monsieur Simoneaux. Please don't. I would lose points if you did that.'

'Then maybe we could throw him to one another for a while, like a rugby ball?'

'Best not to. I'm not that good at catching, and it would be picked up on the microchip. I'd lose points.'

'We could go to the top floor and dangle him out the window, like Michael Jackson did that time. I bet that wouldn't be picked up by the computer. And if we drop him, it won't matter too much. He's only rubber, after all.'

'No, Monsieur Simoneaux. I have my score to consider, so no smashing, no throwing and no dangling. Please. And if we break him, I'll be liable for the cost of a replacement.'

Monsieur Simoneaux sighed. 'Fair enough.' He scratched

his head and looked a little rueful. 'To be honest, I was trying to lower your score. Old Widow Peypouquet asked me to see what I could do to help. She'd prefer you to fare badly. She's worried that if you do well you'll get yourself a real baby, and she's convinced you're not ready.'

'It's nice of her to be concerned,' said Aurélie, 'but I think I'll be getting a low enough score without anyone's help.'

'I hate to go back to Old Widow Peypouquet without any kind of result, though. She was almost weeping with concern for you, Mademoiselle Renard. She said she doesn't want to see you make a terrible decision. I promised her I would do whatever I could. Could you not just put him on the floor and let me stamp on his head a couple of times?'

Aurélie shook her head. 'That's a definite *no*, Monsieur Simoneaux.'

'Very well. I have to say though, he's quite a machine.' He smiled and nodded his approval of this technological wonder. 'It's just as well he's only rubber. It's close to zero outside this morning, and he hasn't got a hat on. If he were real he would freeze to death in minutes. And so will I if I don't get back in my apartment. As you can see, I'm only wearing my pyjamas and slippers. I've not put on my proper clothes yet. I do have proper clothes, you know.'

'I'm sure you do, Monsieur Simoneaux.' Aurélie said goodbye, and she and Monsieur Simoneaux hurried away in opposite directions. He had been right about the weather – summer was definitely over. She reflected that if Herbert really had been a rubber trial baby, she would have lost points for taking him outside bare-headed.

Monsieur Simoneaux had missed a trick there – the built-in thermometer would have recorded her mistake.

While she waited for the bus to come she felt her way through the baby's bag in search of his hat, which she put on his head. As she did so, she was haunted by *l'esprit de l'escalier*: she would have saved a lot of bother if she hadn't hidden Herbert from Old Widow Peypouquet, and had just told her that she was looking after the baby for a friend who was out of town for a few days. It would have made a lot more sense. The bus came, and they struggled on.

It was still too early for the shops to be open, but she was going to head for Le Marais anyway. She wanted to get Herbert some slightly more normal outfits than yesterday's effort, and she knew there were some children's boutiques around there. And besides, she hadn't been able to stop thinking about his mother's scarf. She had been spending so much that money had almost become abstract, and she decided she might as well treat herself. She was going to find La Foularderie. She planned to be waiting on their front step when they opened.

It had been miserable walking the streets of Le Marais with all the shops shut. The last time she had been in the area she had been with Sylvie on a typically busy Sunday afternoon, and they had gone from shop to shop looking at clothes, shoes and all kinds of things they couldn't afford. For some reason they had both been fixating on expensive chairs that day. It was only later, over falafels, that she found out that Sylvie had recently worked for one of the shops they had gone into, a high-class stationer. When she had left the job, the owner had refused to give her a day's pay that she was due. She never let anybody get away with ripping her off, so on this trip she had stolen stock worth three times as much as she was owed, to get her own back. She had also, without Aurélie noticing, discreetly taken a bottle of ink and emptied it on to the carpet. 'Nasty bosses deserve to be screwed over,' she said, smiling, and Aurélie had to agree. She showed off her haul – two fancy pens, a novelty pencil sharpener and a silver-plated letter opener. She gave one of the pens to Aurélie, who was delighted to be a part of Sylvie's deft and righteous revenge.

That had been a good day, but it had been no fun seeing all the shops with their lights out. A few key holders had come in early, and were shuffling around as they prepared for the day, but nowhere was open for business. She looked for La Foularderie, but she couldn't find it. She would ask someone later on.

She made her way to the Place des Vosges, lit a cigarette, put the used match back into the box and thought about how her project was going. It wasn't going very well at all, and it was only then that she realised she had come to the wrong place to dwell on that. The square was lined with commercial galleries containing work by artists who had made it, or who at least had made it far enough to have their work on sale in the Place des Vosges. She had walked around these galleries on happier days and seen pieces with big price tags. She had never been interested in the show business side of art, but she was neither wealthy nor stupid, and she realised that if she was going to take her work seriously she would have to make at least some money from it as she went along. She tried to picture her current project fitting into one of these galleries, and it didn't even begin to. It was stupid and misconceived, and so far it had been poorly executed too; she wasn't drawing nearly as well as she knew she could.

She decided not to depress herself by taking Herbert to look in the galleries' windows. In the past she had been very impressed with a lot of the work she had seen there, work that had a point, or beauty, sometimes even both. She could really imagine people wanting some of these pieces in their homes, and the thought made her all the more disappointed in her own efforts. Nobody would want to look at it for a moment, let alone own it. She had given up on the idea of her project ever being a triumph: throwing stones at babies was never going to make for good art. Who in their right mind would ever want to hang a picture of a wounded child on their wall?

She didn't want to be kicked out of college. It would break her dad's heart. She had no choice but to carry on – even if the project was doomed to fail, she wasn't going to give up on it. If she could just make it good enough to get the mark she needed to pass her year she would be OK.

Herbert had fallen asleep, and she stubbed out her cigarette, put the butt in the matchbox and brought out her sketchbook. It would be yet another drawing of a sleeping baby, but it was going to be the best one yet.

When the concept had first struck her, as she had waited for her appointment with Professor Papavoine, she had imagined her stone bouncing gently from the shoulder of someone who would make an ideal subject. Her number one choice would have been a Jesus-type, a tall, handsome man with shaggy hair and a beard, and with eyes that were at once piercing and warm. He would invite her into his hygienically Bohemian life for a week, taking her back to his large apartment where he would recline naked on the parquet reading Balzac and de Beauvoir as she drew pictures and took photographs of him before putting her pencil and camera away, and taking off her own clothes to join him in a union of the artistic and the sexual. And when the week was over he would ask to see her again, and she would think for a while and say, *Maybe*.

Even as she had been imagining this scenario, she had known that it wasn't going to happen. It was just a daydream. The other possible subjects she had hoped for, these ones a touch more realistic, were an incredibly photogenic old person so she could somehow trace their personal history through their day-to-day activities, or someone from a marginalised ethnic minority so she could document their trials and triumphs, or even a worn-down office worker so she could follow a narrative trail through the most humdrum working week imaginable. It wouldn't even have been too bad if her stone had hit The Russian. Then she would at least have found out how he spent the rest of his day. At no point had she imagined that her subject would be a baby, let alone that she would be in sole charge of that baby.

It was falling apart on so many levels. The most obvious difficulty was that a baby's activities are very limited, and she was personally orchestrating his every movement. An adult would have gone here and there under their own steam, around a life that they had carved out for themselves. She could have captured them at home, at work and at play. But not Herbert. Herbert was just a baby, and the project was supposed to be all about exploring other people's choices as they built a world around themselves. He was a cute baby, very cute, but that was all he was: a baby. He had people, in this case her, to make his decisions for him. She couldn't even draw him at play in his own home. It was all wrong.

He was always there, as well. If the stone had hit somebody else, anybody but a baby, she would have been able to maintain at least some distance from them. There would have been opportunities for them to have a break from one another. She would have been able to get some sleep, and it would have been unlikely that she would have had to wipe them down after they'd gone to the toilet.

Her eyes closed, and she put down her pencil. She fell asleep.

Something Aurélie Renard was coming to learn was that there is a certain kind of old woman who has granted herself a licence to take an aggressive interest in babies with whom they have no personal connection. It is as if these old women spend their days doing nothing but walking around public places looking out for them and, uninvited, leaning over their buggies and offering exuberant compliments. Most of them will leave it at this, but there are some who don't know when to stop, who will take too much of an interest in the child, an interest which manifests itself in the offering of unsolicited and long outmoded advice, and the asking of all sorts of personal questions, the answers to which couldn't possibly be considered any of their business.

Aurélie's experience with Old Widow Peypouquet, as well as her encounters with various old women on the street and on buses, had taught her that she was going to have to get used to these assaults, and assess each one as it occurred and deal with it in the best way she could. She had found that the most efficient thing to do was to agree with everything they said, no matter how ridiculous, and wait for them to move away. So far she had assured one old lady that she would wrap Herbert in vinegar-soaked brown paper at the first sign of a runny nose, nodded while another told her to prevent him from becoming homosexual by sending him to boxing lessons the moment he could walk, and bowed her head in insincere admiration as yet another boasted about how all nine of her children had been fully potty-trained by the time they were Herbert's age. She had even disguised her indignation at the implicit swipes at her mothering abilities. It was relentless.

She had no idea how long she had been asleep when a nearby presence roused her. A shadow had fallen over Herbert. She looked up and, sure enough, there was the latest old woman.

She was staring at him, and smiling. She saw that Aurélie had woken up. 'Is it a boy or a girl?' she asked.

Aurélie rubbed her eyes. She was still half asleep, and her question, while simple, seemed so stupid that Aurélie wondered if there was a trick to it. 'Er . . .' She looked at Herbert. He was a boy, wasn't he? She thought back to changing his nappy. Yes, she wasn't in any doubt. 'He's a boy.'

'And isn't he a handsome boy?'

'Er, yes.' She wanted her to go away, but the old woman seemed to think that her presence was somehow welcome.

She addressed Herbert directly now. 'Aren't you a handsome boy?' Seconds earlier she had not even known he *was* a boy. 'Aren't you?'

Aurélie decided she would tell the next old woman who asked after his gender that Herbert was a girl, just to see if they then went into raptures about how pretty he was.

He was still asleep, and the old woman's voice was loud. Aurélie hoped she wouldn't wake him up.

'And how old is he?'

She spoke softly, almost whispering, in the hope that the old woman would follow her lead. 'He's Aquarius.'

'Aquarius?' If anything her voice was now even louder. 'Which makes him . . .?'

Aurélie thought back to the souvenir shop. 'Er . . . about nine months old. Roughly speaking.'

'You've been drawing a picture of him.'

'Yes.' Aurélie looked at what she had done. It had been going well. 'It's only half done.'

The old woman said nothing, but her face registered her disapproval of Aurélie's work. It really was time for her to go away.

She looked intently at the baby, and as she did, something about her changed. She was no longer a random old woman cooing over a baby in a public garden. There was something more threatening about her.

'How did he get that bruise on his face?'

Aurélie started. She should have had an answer ready for this. There was no way she could tell the truth, so she scrambled for an answer. 'He's been fighting.' The old woman stared at her, and she added, 'You know what boys are like.'

The old woman stared at her. Aurélie decided she would use some of her concealer on Herbert, and if anyone noticed it she would tell them it was eczema.

'And is he *your* baby?'

Aurélie was stunned by the question. It went far beyond the usual level of interference. 'Yes, of course he's my baby.' The old woman just stared at her. Aurélie wondered whether she had made herself clear enough, and carried on. 'He came out of here,' she said, pointing at the place from which babies emerge. Then she realised what she was doing, and remembered she was in a public garden. She folded her finger away.

The old woman seemed to accept this. She was quiet for a moment, then she said, 'What's his name?'

'Herbert.' She braced herself for the usual exchange, but this time it didn't happen. The old woman pronounced it correctly first time.

'Herbert? Why Herbert?'

'That's a good question. I'm glad you asked me.' She raced to think of a plausible answer. 'I called him Herbert because I thought it was a nice name.'

'Really?'

'Yes.'

'Well, there really is no accounting for taste. What's his surname?'

Aurélie realised she had no idea. She was beginning to panic under the weight of the old woman's pitiless inter-rogation. She was tired, her defences were low, and she felt she had to say something. She wasn't going to use her own name, so she used the first one that came to mind. 'Cruchaudet-Gingembre,' she said. She had no idea where that had come from. Even as the words were leaving her mouth she knew they sounded ridiculous.

'*Herbert Cruchaudet-Gingembre?* The poor child. What a terrible start in life.'

'Yes,' she nodded, 'it is terrible.' This old lady seemed more relentless than her other attackers. Nodding and agreeing was not enough to satisfy her.

'Yes?' she asked. 'Yes? So you agree? Then why did you give him such a ridiculous name? I understand that you can't choose his surname, but why *Herbert*? Why not Jean-Pierre, or Jean-Luc, or Jean-Louis, or Jean-Paul? Surely even Jean-Marcel would have been better than Herbert?'

For the first time, Aurélie found herself actually agreeing with an interfering old woman, rather than just pretending to agree. Herbert *was* a ridiculous name for a French baby, and she had to somehow formulate a defence of it off the top of her head. She hadn't helped herself by saddling him with such a preposterous surname. 'It just seemed like the right decision at the time.'

'And this was a decision you came to along with his father?'

'No.'

'Where is his father?'

Aurélie was running out of patience. She shrugged. 'I don't know.'

'Who is his father?'

'I don't know.'

The old woman crossed herself. 'How can you not know?'

'Well, it's because . . .' Aurélie had had enough. She wasn't going to put up with this. 'Oh, mind your own business, you nosey old bat. Get lost.'

'Right,' she said. 'That is the final straw. I am declaring you to be an unfit mother. This baby is not in safe hands, and I am taking him straight to the authorities.'

The old woman kicked off the buggy's brake, and at high speed she made off with Herbert across the square.

He saw the baby first from the other side of the square. His eyes were drawn to the child, who was just waking up. There was something about him, about his serious expression and line of his brow that he found mesmerising. He was so absorbed by the sight of the boy that it was a while before he noticed the commotion surrounding him. The first participant he saw was the old woman, determinedly pushing the buggy across the square. And beside her, at first protesting, then trying to wrest control of the buggy, was the girl. *The* girl, the one he had been waiting for all his life. Until this moment he'd had no idea that he had been waiting for anyone all his life, but now he knew he had been, and here she was.

As they drew closer, this was confirmed. She was right before his eyes, arguing over a child with a bad-tempered old woman. His heart should have leapt, but instead it sank. Just moments earlier he had considered himself to be a lifelong loner, someone who would never lose his heart, someone for whom there was no love, just occasional sexual interludes that he regarded as a medical necessity as much as anything else. But now he realised this was not the case at all, that there was a girl out there he could love. His carapace had crumbled, and as it did he was exposed to the weakness it had been hiding. Every love song he had ever heard suddenly made sense, and at last he knew what people were talking about when they spoke of broken hearts: somebody else had found her first.

They drew closer to him, and he could see that this was

no normal domestic argument. The girl was frantic. She looked up and saw him. She appealed to him.

'Please don't let her take my baby.'

She looked at him. He was tall, with shaggy hair and a short, full beard. He had eyes that were at once piercing and warm. There was no getting away from it – there was something Christ-like about him, though this Jesus was wearing jeans, training shoes and a black puffa jacket. Something about him seemed familiar, and comforting; it was as if they were already friends. If anyone was going to help her, it was him. Without a word he held up his hand, signalling them to stop, and they obeyed. He looked at the three of them for a long while.

'Madame,' he said to the old lady, 'it is wrong to take people's babies away.'

'It is for the child's own good. This young lady has no maternal instinct. I've seen evidence of this with my own eyes. First I saw her puffing on a cigarette with the child right beside her, then she fell fast asleep and the baby was sitting there completely unprotected. It's unnatural for a mother to put her child at risk in this way. There are strange people out there, you know – people who are perverts for babies – and what's more she doesn't even know who the father is. And you should hear the name she's given the poor child – *Herbert Cruchaudet-Gingembre*. I mean to say . . .'

Gently he put a finger to his lips, and the old woman stopped talking. He tried to hide his delight at this information about the girl's personal life. If the father was out of the picture, maybe he could step in. 'Go now,' he said to the old woman.

'I . . . well . . .' She didn't know what to do or say.

'That poor child.' She turned to Aurélie, and said, 'Don't go thinking I'm not going to report you anyway.' She looked at the man, and said, 'And look.' She pointed. 'His shoes are on the wrong feet.' With a look of disgust, she went away.

Aurélie looked at Herbert's feet, and realised with shame that the old woman was right. She really had put the shoes on the wrong way round. She crouched, took them off and swapped them over.

'Thank you,' Aurélie said, looking up at the man as she fastened the Velcro straps. With the old woman gone, she felt a rush of guilt. While she still considered her to have been a nosey old bat, she knew she had been right: she *wasn't* fit to be in charge of a baby. She shouldn't have been smoking so close to him, and she shouldn't have fallen asleep while she was supposed to be taking care of him in a public place. There really were people out there who were perverts for babies. Maybe it would have been the best thing for everyone if the old woman had been able to hand the boy over to the authorities.

She looked at the baby, and thought again. No, she wasn't going to let any interfering old bat take Herbert, and for as long as he was in her care she was never again going to leave home without the gun. When she got home she would put it in the big inside pocket of her coat, and there it would stay until Herbert was safely back with his mother. As her anger bubbled away, she told herself that if another old woman came for him she would shoot her kneecaps out sooner than allow her to take him away.

The man could see she was upset. 'You've had a horrible experience,' he said. 'Come and sit down.'

They went over to a bench, and sat side-by-side. Aurélie

looked at him, and he looked at Aurélie, and they both felt the same thing. They felt as if they had known one another all their lives. It was a feeling that was warm and, more than anything, overwhelmingly arousing.

Aurélie thought about the chain of events that had brought them together. If it hadn't been for her project, this wouldn't be happening. She supposed that there was something to be said for throwing stones at babies after all.

He noticed the sketchbook in her hand. 'May I see?'

She showed him her half-finished picture of Herbert. He liked it very much. 'It's really . . .' He didn't finish his sentence.

It was the rarest of things – a kiss with no instigator. He didn't kiss her, and she didn't kiss him. They both just kissed. Aurélie clung on to him, and he held her as though she was a precious object. Which, to him, she was.

Minutes later, when at last their lips parted, they suddenly became keenly aware of the watching eyes of an approximately nine-month-old boy. The man felt it was time to introduce himself to his new acquaintances. 'I'm Léandre,' he said. 'Léandre Martin.'

'Aurélie Renard. And this one here is Herbert.'

'I know. Hello, Herbert,' he said. He too had pronounced his name correctly first time. Aurélie felt that things were getting better in a big way. 'Herbert . . .' He looked sceptical. 'Herbert Cruchaudet-Gingembre?'

'Er . . .' Aurélie thought she had better come clean. 'No. That's not his real surname.'

He laughed. 'I thought not.'

'I was lying to the old woman. I didn't think his name was any of her business, so I made one up.'

'You did a good job.'

'He is called Herbert, though.'

'Herbert Renard.'

'No.' She told him the truth. 'He's not my baby. He's
. . .' She wondered whether her new boyfriend, if that's
what he was, was quite ready to hear the whole truth.
'I'm looking after him for a friend who's out of town for
a few days.'

XI

Jean-Didier Delacroix was a happy man for many reasons, four of which were in the forefront of his mind as he lay in his bathrobe on his large bed in the large bedroom of his large apartment:

1. He was called Jean-Didier Delacroix, and a man can hope for no better name than that. Every day the first thing he said to himself was *Good morning, Jean-Didier Delacroix.* Just the thought of his name was enough to lighten his mood, and when he saw it in print it was enough to make him feel like jumping for joy. It was perfect.

2. He was an arts correspondent for a major newspaper, and nobody can hope for a better job than that. Parents leaning over a newborn's crib will barely even dare to hope that one day their child might become an arts correspondent for a major newspaper. They tell themselves that they only want them to be healthy and happy, *although of course if*

he does become an arts correspondent that would be . . .
They will try to stop this train of thought, knowing that it
would be wrong to burden a child with such expectations,
and true enough the parents of his classmates had found
they had no choice but to content themselves with seeing
their offspring embark on the road to such humdrum careers
as airline pilot, heart surgeon, engineer, lawyer, architect,
tennis star, sometimes even artist, taking any path but the
golden one upon which he had embarked.

His parents, unlike most, had been forthright about their
ambitions for their child. From the crib they had refused to
countenance the possibility of him entering another profession. *How is our little future arts correspondent today?*
they would ask him, when his nanny presented him for
his daily appearance before them. And little Jean-Didier
Delacroix had indeed shed his sailor suit and grown up to
fulfil their dream: they had seen their son become an arts
correspondent for *L'Univers*. He would never forget the
day the editor-in-chief of *L'Univers*, his uncle Jean-Claude
Delacroix, had called him into the office and told him,
very sternly, that he wanted him to know that he was not
being offered the job because of any family connection,
he was being added to the staff for no reason other than
his undeniable brilliance. Jean-Didier Delacroix took in
every word.

Now twenty-four, he had been in his position for two
years, and had already had the title *chief arts correspondent* created for him. He was also already in line to
become *deputy arts editor*, and the editorship itself was
widely regarded as an inevitability once the post had
become vacant – something which was due to occur in
around five years' time.

3. He had a beautiful girlfriend. He had just finished having sex with her, and right at this moment she was undertaking a carefully orchestrated shower in the large en suite bathroom. At six feet and one inch she was almost a head taller than him even before she had stepped into her inevitable heels, a height which had helped to establish her on the catwalks of the world. She was a foul young woman of twenty – arrogant, scowling and stone-cold, and this suited him very well. She was his type.

4. And this was the reason which occupied his mind above all others: he, Jean-Didier Delacroix, was the only person from the entire media to have been granted access to Le Machine in the run-up to the opening of *Life*. This was the biggest event of the year in the art world. Everybody was talking about it, and everybody was going to want to read Jean-Didier Delacroix's take on it. This was his most high-profile assignment to date, and to be trusted with something of this magnitude was a sure indicator to the outside world that he had arrived. His piece was going to be a triumph. He had already had a long conversation with the arts editor about it, and they were in full agreement on their opinions of Le Machine. It was as much as they could do to stop themselves from rubbing their hands together and cackling with glee.

Those were four very solid reasons for happiness, and Jean-Didier Delacroix was content as he leafed through the research materials his assistants had collated for him. He drafted the article in his head, smiling at the occasional *mot juste* that drifted into view. He was going to interview Le Machine shortly before he went on stage, and be there for the first two hours of the performance, turning the copy over in his mind as he watched. Then he would retreat to a private booth in a nearby restaurant and while eating his pre-ordered food he would write, incorporating his review of the event into the body of the piece. He had seen the layout, which was just waiting for his words to be added. He would finish the job with lightning speed. He was known for this: Jean-Didier Delacroix did not waste time.

Once it was ready, he would email the article to the subeditor, who would neither dare nor feel the need to change a single word, and it would be emblazoned across the front page of the arts supplement on Saturday morning.

He yawned and stretched, and imagined the looks on the faces of the rivals he was trouncing with this coup. He was well aware that it wasn't possible to reach the position he had reached without ruffling feathers. He knew that people were jealous of him, and he knew that there were those who accused him of taking advantage of the nepotism that is considered to be endemic across the media. But he also knew that his uncle had been absolutely right to employ him – he *was* brilliant. And now, with this article, more people than ever would become aware of this.

His uncle, Jean-Claude Delacroix, was an honourable man who had agonised over his appointment, spending hours in conference with the arts editor as he tried to avoid hiring his nephew, but the conversation kept coming back to the same point: they would not find anyone better than Jean-Didier Delacroix. His mind was incredible, his knowledge encyclopaedic. He could write extensively, impeccably and at lightning speed on ballet, opera, sculpture, classical music, rock, theatre, circus; anything from the world of the arts that was thrown at him. His mind was as sharp and as deadly as Damascus steel, and he wrote with a lightness of touch that belied the incisiveness and the gravity of his analyses. Even the harshest critics of his life story and his modus operandi found themselves obliged to acknowledge, though only ever through gritted teeth, that Jean-Didier Delacroix had an exceptional talent. His freelance pieces had attracted a lot of attention, and it would only be a matter of time before he was snapped up. If *L'Univers* didn't get him, then a rival would, and then where would they be? There was nothing they could do but offer him a generous contract.

His piece on Le Machine was going to be a simple undertaking. It was already more or less written in his head. Without having seen it, he knew that he hated *Life* more than anything he had written about before. He saw it as vulgar, sensationalist and populist, in the worst possible senses of all three. And what's more, he was convinced that it had not one iota of intellectual foundation. The more he read about Le Machine, the more evasive he found him to be. In the interviews he had given prior to his previous presentations of the piece, he had never provided a satisfactory answer to the simplest of questions: *Why do you do what you do?* and *What is the meaning of* Life?, and if an artist cannot, or will not, answer such basic questions when they are put to them by an arts correspondent, then they are not worthy of the name. Le Machine was no artist. He was nothing more than a charlatan. And now, he smiled as he thought about it, he was a doomed charlatan.

Jean-Didier Delacroix's research had not only been into

the man and his supposed *art*. He had also looked into Le Machine's business dealings, sending the newspaper's keenest financial researchers on his tail, a small battalion of business-minded Lisbeth Salanders, all pierced faces and magical powers.

He knew that *Life*'s Paris run was to be an independent production, that the risk of presenting it outside an established gallery had been taken by Le Machine's management, using the profits that had built up over the course of its previous stagings. It had not been a cheap production, either. To read his rivals' previews of the event, it would seem as if the show consisted of nothing more than a naked man and a few bottles. He knew better, though. The technical side was complex, and required a skilled team led by audio-visual experts whose time and expertise were expensive. Some were employees, and others had been embedded within the production from the start, and had stakes in it.

In addition to the payroll for his team, there was the money needed up front to make the cinema suitable for their needs, not to mention round-the-clock stewarding and security. He learned that they had emptied their account to get it all set up, sure that they would recoup the investment and much, much more through ticket sales and merchandising. They had taken out insurance, of course, to cover themselves in the event of a fire, or the star of the show being taken gravely ill. What they could not insure against though, was the abject failure of *Life*. With nobody coming through the doors, they would be sunk.

Le Machine's organisation had confidently bet everything they had on the success of this run. The public might have fallen for this rubbish in London and Tokyo, but he would personally see that Paris did not follow suit.

The interview itself was almost incidental. Jean-Didier Delacroix needed only a handful of quotes from the man with which to flay him, and it would all be over. He would turn Le Machine into a laughing stock, and his *coup de grâce* would be to present him as such a monumental fraud that all the serious art lovers, the curiosity seekers, the armies of people who had professed their determination to see him so they could make up their own minds, the students, the tourists and even the perverts would steer clear for fear of being seen to fall for such a blatant con.

A few days from now, once the unlucky few who had bought advance tickets had come and gone, Le Machine would be standing naked on a stage in an empty porno cinema, desperate for his contractual obligations, and his pathetic excuse for an art exhibition, to end. With nothing to show for it but a mountain of unsold merchandise, he would find himself with little to think about but what he was going to do now that all his money was gone.

Jean-Didier Delacroix carried on reading the research material. It was thorough. He felt a momentary pang of pity for the seedy little man who had leased them the cinema. He had been offered a fair deal by Le Machine's organisation, but as the bulk of his remuneration came from a cut of the ticket sales, he was dependent on the exhibition being as successful as they had assured him it would be. There was no way his business was going to survive the impending catastrophe, but Jean-Didier Delacroix turned the page and forgot about him. He wasn't going to lose sleep over the fate of a middle-aged pornographer. He would be going down with the rest of them. Call it collateral damage.

The one thing that was missing from his pages of

research was a positive identification: they could not verify the real name of Le Machine. It had been buried by a maze of paperwork, a network of holding companies and trails of deliberately placed red herrings. There had been a rumour that the original Le Machine had quit after Tokyo and been replaced by a doppelgänger, and even one that he was really a pair of identical twins who would work in shifts. Jean-Didier Delacroix's researchers had examined official and clandestine photographs, and had found no truth in these stories.

It was not of crucial importance, anyway; he had chosen not to make any mention of the mystery surrounding his identity. To do so would be to play into his hands. Who cared who he was anyway? All that mattered was taking him down.

Jean-Didier Delacroix had already settled on the headline with his editor, who was right behind him in his efforts to contain and destroy this monstrosity.

The article was to be called *The End of Life.*

Jean-Didier Delacroix's girlfriend walked into the room, a tower of perfect skin. She looked at him as though he were a dead spider in a bowl of soup.

What a woman! he thought. *What a day! What a life!*

XII

Sylvie enjoyed all her jobs, but the day of the week she looked forward to more than any other was Thursday. This was when she helped out with the ponies in the Jardin des Tuileries. Extra hands were needed on Thursdays, because that was when the children with special needs came for a ride. She had just finished helping a group of children with Down's syndrome get down from their ponies and out of their gear. She took so much satisfaction from her Thursdays that she had spoken to one of the visiting teachers about the possibility of enrolling on a course so she could begin to get some qualifications and take on more responsibility. She had even begun to think about leaving her job-flitting days behind, and embarking on a career in the field. The teacher had met Sylvie a few times and said she could see her making a great success of such a move, that she had a very natural and easy manner with the children, and that they responded well to her. She said she would be happy to offer advice and provide a reference for her if she were to decide that it really was what she wanted to do.

Sylvie's primary misgiving was that such a decision would be a terrible blow to her exes, many of whom, as a survival mechanism, told themselves over and over again that she was a bitch. She knew this from the letters they sent and the messages they left on her phone (she maintained a special number for these calls, which she checked every few days), but she also knew that in their hearts they knew that she wasn't, that her only crime was not loving them, but the *that bitch* mantra helped them to get through the day. If news was ever to reach them of her taking such a direction, it could be quite disastrous. The thought of her devoting her professional life to being helpful and compassionate towards those less fortunate than herself might prove too much for them to cope with.

It had been a good day so far, and she was getting ready for the arrival of her final batch of riders when she spotted familiar faces approaching. It was Lucien and the Akiyamas. She had told Lucien where she would be that day, and had known he would take the hint and drop by. She felt herself becoming nervous as Monsieur and Madame Akiyama approached. Just being close to Toshiro's parents had given her romantic butterflies. This was a new sensation, but she felt invigorated by it even as it frightened her. She waved a greeting.

She had been grooming one of the ponies, and she introduced him. 'This is Poirot.'

Madame Akiyama raced up and petted him. 'Bonjour,

Poirot,' she said. Her French was coming along. Then she reverted to Japanese.

Lucien interpreted. Madame Akiyama was wondering whether she could have a quick ride.

There were a few minutes before the next group was due, so Sylvie supposed that it wouldn't be too much of a problem. They were small horses though, and their riders were usually children. 'Ask her how much she weighs,' she said.

Lucien turned white. 'No. I'm not going to ask the mother of my future bride how much she weighs. Just let her get on the horse.'

Sylvie laughed. Madame Akiyama had a slight build – Poirot would be fine. A minute later she was being led by Sylvie around the park. Lucien and Monsieur Akiyama accompanied them. Madame Akiyama said something to Sylvie, and Lucien translated.

'Madame Akiyama says that she thinks you are very pretty and very nice, and that one day you will be a wonderful wife for a lucky husband.'

Sylvie was speechless. She felt like crying. It was such a lovely thing for Madame Akiyama to have said. Madame Akiyama carried on, and again Lucien provided her with a translation. 'She says that Monsieur Akiyama feels the same way.'

Monsieur Akiyama looked as cross as ever, but he gruffly nodded his agreement.

Sylvie could stand it no longer. 'Monsieur Akiyama, Madame Akiyama,' she said, standing still with Poirot's leading rein in her hand, 'please tell me everything about Toshiro.'

So they told her: the good news and the bad.

* * *

Aurélie had arranged to meet Sylvie at the end of her shift, and following their long conversation the night before she wasn't too surprised to find Lucien and the Akiyamas in the outdoor café. Madame Akiyama was happy to see Herbert again, and immediately took him on her knee. Aurélie noticed that she was wearing a particularly nice scarf, and through Lucien, she asked her where she had bought it.

'La Foularderie,' she said. 'It's in Le Marais. It's such a wonderful shop – I bought a scarf there for Akiko too.'

Aurélie smiled. With everything that had been happening, she had forgotten about her quest for La Foularderie. With Madame Akiyama's recommendation, though, coupled with the loveliness of her scarf, its legendary status in her life grew to even greater proportions. She would find it at the next opportunity.

Soon they were joined by Sylvie, who had said goodbye to her final group of children and helped put all the equipment away. Aurélie was shocked when she saw her. Her friend looked sad.

In all the time she had known her, she had never seen Sylvie looking defeated. Even at the most trying moments she smiled, and elevated the mood around her. Lucien asked her permission to explain the situation, and she silently nodded her consent. Earlier it had been up to him to translate the news from Madame Akiyama to a shellshocked Sylvie, and it hadn't been an easy task.

Toshiro, Madame Akiyama had told her from the saddle, was twenty-nine years old, and had established himself as an accomplished musician. Working mainly alone, he recorded his own compositions digitally, providing soundtracks for television shows and video games. At this point Monsieur Akiyama had chipped in with a comment about how this was not a steady occupation, and that his son was leaving it too late to take up a position in a large corporation, but this was brushed aside by Madame Akiyama. She continued. Toshiro's work was in demand, and he was – she gave her husband a look – fending for himself perfectly well. This, of course, was good news for Sylvie. As well as being incredibly handsome, he sounded interesting and independent, and what's more his work was portable. He could move to Paris. They would get an apartment with an extra bedroom, and he could turn it into his studio.

Then the bad news began. It started as a trickle, but soon the dam burst and it became a deluge. First of all, Madame Akiyama explained that he didn't speak a word of French. Sylvie spoke no Japanese. Communication was going to be a problem. Sylvie had already considered this, though, and knew it could be overcome. She had Lucien to teach her the basics, and she would enrol in classes at the earliest opportunity. Likewise, Toshiro could learn French. People learn languages all the time.

Then came the death blow.

As Lucien related Madame Akiyama's next misgiving to Aurélie, Sylvie looked close to tears at having to sit through it a second time, and Madame Akiyama gave her a look of sympathy as she bounced Herbert on her knee. For the last four years, Toshiro had been in a serious relationship with a fashion stylist called Natsuki Kobayashi. They weren't engaged or living together but, Madame Akiyama explained, they might as well have been. They had a very modern arrangement, one of which Monsieur Akiyama did not approve. Each had a key to the other's apartment, and they rarely spent a night apart. Madame Akiyama told Sylvie that she and her husband had spoken to Toshiro about this relationship, and he had reassured them that he loved her, and hoped one day to marry her.

The first time Sylvie heard this unhappy fact, Madame Akiyama had just dismounted from Poirot. She had merely nodded, excused herself and taken the pony to get ready for the arrival of the final group of children.

Her abiding feeling had been one of pity, for herself and for other people. She felt a sudden rush of empathy with everybody she had upset throughout the years. She wanted to track down each and every one of the surviving boys whose hearts she had broken, and say sorry for putting them through such a terrible ordeal. It was only now that she truly understood. She had been wrong to ever have allowed them as close as she had, to have given their dreams a chance to grow wings. She should never have let them love her. She should never even have agreed to go on a date with them. It was only as she joined their ranks that she truly realised the depth of the pain she had caused, and the extent of the destruction she had wrought. But those days were behind her now. The universe was exacting its revenge, and it was no more than she deserved. For her, the possibility of love was over. She would be alone for the rest of her life.

She had put on a smile for the children, a lot of whom recognised her from previous visits and were pleased to see her again. For the duration of their stay she was able to function. This was where her future lay. As the children dismounted she arranged to meet their teacher for a coffee and an informal chat about ways into the profession.

She was looking to a future free of Toshiro Akiyama. A future free of love.

As they sat at the outdoor table, Lucien finished updating Aurélie, who reached over and took Sylvie's hand. They all sat in silence for a while, then Madame Akiyama gave Sylvie a determined look, and launched into a short speech in Japanese. Some of the words sounded familiar to the French speakers, and they were eager to find out what was going on.

Lucien smiled as he told Sylvie what Madame Akiyama had said: *I don't want Toshiro to marry Natsuki Kobayashi. I want him to marry Sylvie Dupont.*

Sylvie allowed a tear to run down her cheek. She didn't know if it was a breach of Japanese etiquette, but she didn't care – she threw herself on Madame Akiyama and hugged her tight. Madame Akiyama still had Herbert on her knee, so this turned into something of a group hug, but it didn't matter. She felt Toshiro's mother's hand on her back, holding her tight, and everything melted away, all her toughness and her self-sufficiency. For that moment she allowed herself to be the little orphan girl. She had been searching so long for a family to call her own, and maybe – maybe – she had found it.

Monsieur Akiyama looked on, slightly baffled, as this girl they had hired to drive them around the day before wept tears of joy on to his wife's shoulder. It had been an unusual trip so far, with people falling in love with photographs and so on, but he didn't see what he could do but allow it all to happen. Over breakfast, his wife had given him a stern talking-to. He had spent many years at the head of the family, she had said, setting rules and making decisions, running it like a small department within a large corporation. Now he was retired, and it was time for him to step back from all that, to relax a little and hand some of those responsibilities to her. It all seemed very curious, but he didn't dare raise an objection.

Thinking about it, he supposed he had never really warmed to Natsuki Kobayashi. There had been something hard about her, maybe even calculating. The last time he had met her had been at her apartment for dinner and her cat, an objectionable creature called Makoto, had clawed through his trousers and scratched his leg, and instead of reprimanding it she had picked it up and given it a kiss, and shown him a photograph of it wearing a knitted Viking's helmet. Monsieur Akiyama had pointed out that he had spent many years at a senior position within a large corporation, and if a subordinate at this corporation had scratched the leg of a superior they would not be rewarded with kisses and cuddles, and the superior who had been scratched would not then have to suffer the further ordeal of having to look at a photograph of the subordinate dressed in a knitted Viking's helmet.

Natsuki Kobayashi had taken this innocent observation to heart, and spoken to him in a rather inappropriate tone, saying that her apartment was not a large corporation, and the cat was an equal, not a subordinate. The rest of the evening had passed under something of a cloud.

It had been an unpleasant experience. He supposed his wife was right: Sylvie Dupont would make a better daughter-in-law. She did seem nicer. Ultimately, though, the decision would lie with Toshiro. He had always seemed to be very fond of Natsuki Kobayashi.

151

As the chaos swirled around him, Monsieur Akiyama surprised himself by coming to the conclusion that, on balance, he was having a nice time in Paris, and that maybe there was something to be said for a little bit of disorder after all.

Love was in the air, and when Sylvie had finally untangled herself from Madame Akiyama and Herbert, Aurélie took the opportunity to announce that she had a brand new boyfriend called Léandre Martin.

'I met him in Le Marais,' she said, 'and he looks a bit like Jesus Christ.'

'Not this again,' said Lucien. 'Do all women fancy Jesus?' He looked to Sylvie to find out her views on the matter.

She nodded. She couldn't deny it. 'Yes, it's true. Jesus is incredibly sexy – like you wouldn't believe – but most men who try to look like him don't get it right. They just look like dirty hippies, or folk music people. It's not often you see a *real* Jesus.'

'I know,' said Aurélie 'and the best thing about it is that I don't think Léandre's even *trying* to look like Jesus, he just *happens* to look like him. It's a coincidence. He's definitely not a dirty hippie, and I'll tell you something else: right from the start, from the moment our eyes met, I felt as if I already knew him. There was something about him that seemed really familiar.'

'Well, obviously,' said Lucien. 'He looks like Jesus. Everybody's seen Jesus before.'

'I suppose so. But there was more to it than that. It was almost magical.'

Sylvie gave her a half smile, trying to indicate that they

needed to have a talk about this later on, just the two of them. 'You've got it bad,' she said.

Aurélie smiled. 'I really have.' She told them all about how she had spent the morning and most of the afternoon with him, how they had walked and talked and made each other laugh, how wonderful he had been with Herbert, and how they had arranged to meet up for lunch the next day.

'Tread at least a little bit carefully,' said Sylvie. She recognised something in Aurélie's instant infatuation that she had seen in so many of her boyfriends. And then she thought of Toshiro Akiyama, and realised she was guilty of exactly the same lack of caution.

'For once there's no need,' said Aurélie. 'Nothing can possibly go wrong.'

Sylvie half-smiled again. They needed to talk about all this when it was just the two of them. Or the three of them, as Herbert was certain to be there.

Caught up on this tide of romance, Lucien asked Madame Akiyama if she had mentioned him to Akiko.

'No,' she said. 'Not yet.'

He nodded sadly. He told her he understood. He wouldn't be asking again, at least not until he saw them off at the airport, when he would hand Madame Akiyama a letter and implore her to pass it on to her daughter. He had already begun to draft it. *My dear Akiko Akiyama*, it began. Beyond that, he wasn't sure what to say. Nothing he tried seemed to sound right.

Madame Akiyama continued. 'But I'm going to send Toshiro this picture right now.' She showed him her phone. On it was a photograph she had taken of Sylvie with Poirot before breaking the news about Natsuki Kobayashi.

Lucien looked at the picture, and it was a while before he could bring himself to hand the phone back.

He watched as Madame Akiyama pasted the photograph into an email. He thought Sylvie looked beautiful. Toshiro Akiyama would have to be insane not to fall in love with her.

Madame Akiyama pressed *send*.

VENDREDI

XIII

The doors had opened at six o'clock, and *Life* was due to begin at seven. There was to be no private viewing, no champagne reception, no room full of specially invited movers and shakers from the art world. Thirty press passes had been given out, but when the reporters arrived at the venue they found they had to queue with everybody else, and once they were in the auditorium there was no special enclosure reserved for them. They had no choice but to stand or sit alongside the people who had been fast enough to buy tickets for the opening night. They all complained about this, of course, and two of them stormed out. Though they had been sent by bitterly rivalrous publications, the pair of them presented a united front as they told Le Machine's press officer that they were not prepared to spend their Friday evening standing next to ordinary people while they watched a man do a shit.

The press officer smiled as they threw their passes to the ground and disappeared into the night. There was always an incident like this. She picked up the passes and handed them to the people at the front of the returns queue, who couldn't believe their luck and raced past security to the back of the auditorium.

By six forty-five everybody was in, and the room was buzzing with anticipation. The stage was set. The glass phials were in place, the largest on each side of the stage – the one for urine was on the right, and on the left was the one for faeces, complete with its gas collection mechanism. Smaller containers for less voluminous secretions were placed on a table to the left-hand side, some of them within a refrigerated glass cabinet. As the event went on, viewers would be able to mill around and approach the exhibits in order to get a really good look at them. A narrow runway bisected the front half of the auditorium, so Le Machine himself could go out and stand among his viewers, and they would have the opportunity to approach and examine him.

Also on stage were a bidet and a shower. Answering some criticism they had faced in Tokyo that a small amount of his bodily excretions would be washed into the sewers, Le Machine had arranged for all the shower and bidet water to be put through a filter, a large version of the kind that is found in a coffee machine, and any skin flakes or stray particles of faeces would be collected and put into their own jar. Right at the front of the stage was a clear glass urinal that drained into a clear glass jug. At the back of the stage were a whiteboard and black pen, a bed, a set of weights, specially made from glass, and a small kitchen consisting of a single gas ring, a few miscellaneous utensils, a sink and a small table, beside it a folding chair. This stage, for the next twelve weeks, was to be one man's home.

The loudspeakers were silent: there were no announcements, and no introductory music played. For what would be the last time in a long while, people in this room were able to hold conversations, and the occasion was such that they were talking only of *Life*.

I hope we'll get to see him do a poo, said one. *It would be great to be able to say we were there when it happened for the first time in Paris.*

Elsewhere, somebody was saying that a friend of theirs had seen Le Machine in San Francisco, and that, *Apparently he can do a poo without any wee coming out. Every time, as well. That's pretty impressive.*

There were a number of languages and accents to be heard, scattered among the chatter of the locals: Korean, American, German . . . Somewhere an Englishman was holding forth to a stranger on the French love of urine. *They're crazy about it*, he was telling them. *In fact it's all they're interested in – they call it* eau d'amour. *That's why I could never have a French girlfriend – I'm just not into water sports. They come on to me all the time*, he lied, *but I turn them down.*

To hear what they were saying, it might be supposed that there was little more to *Life* than going to the toilet.

Monsieur Rousset's daughter, Doctor Élise Rousset, had been appointed Le Machine's chief medical supervisor for the duration of *Life*, and backstage in his small private room, which was little more than a cubicle, she was nearing the end of his full medical. She had the power to stop the whole event if she felt there were any doubts about the state of his health, but she found nothing untoward. Le Machine was a fine physical specimen, and he seemed calm as he readied himself.

Her father had become Le Machine's number one fan, and he had been dropping all sorts of unsubtle hints about what a wonderful son-in-law he would make for some lucky father, and how it was inevitable that he and she would become close over the coming weeks as she gave him his regular on-stage check-ups. She felt a little sorry for her father. He wasn't going to get his wish. She supposed that if she had liked men at all then she might well have had a bit of a crush on this perfectly sculpted body. She could appreciate its beauty, but at the same time she felt no desire to press herself up against it.

She had always told herself that she would only tell her father about her preference for women if she was ever to find herself in a steady long-term relationship, and that moment was fast approaching. Things had been going well with Thao all year, and it had been months since they'd had a long and pleasant conversation about how neither was interested in seeing anybody else. They had reached the point where they had been going online and browsing apartments together, and they had drawn up a shortlist of their favourites, and were starting to arrange to view them.

She had wanted to hold off telling her father for as long as she could, not because she worried about his reaction – she knew he would always love her no matter what – nor because she was in any way insecure about the way she was, but because she knew how much he enjoyed girl on girl porn, and she didn't want to do anything that might risk spoiling it for him. It was a central part of his life, and she worried that the knowledge that his daughter was a lesbian would permanently alter his relationship with it. For him, lesbians weren't really people, they were purely sexual beings that were put on earth to take their clothes off and roll around together in improbable scenarios for the titillation of men. It seemed unfair to the point of cruelty to bring them from the realm of fantasy into his everyday life. He was a good and caring man, and as she pondered the worst-case scenario, it might even be that this knowledge about his daughter would lead to such a psychosexual minefield that he would no longer be able to bring himself to watch his favourite films, and that saddened her. But with Thao on the scene, she knew the moment was approaching when he would have to know.

When she was small she had rummaged through his pile of preview videos, and worked out from his personal star ratings which films he liked the best. It was the covers of these films that told her it was OK for women to be together, that she was not the only person in the world who felt the way she did. It was only later in life that she realised that the scenes she saw on these video cases had very little to do with real life, but even so just knowing that somewhere in the world there were girls who kissed other girls had helped her become comfortable with herself from a very early age. Her mother had always known, and she sympathised with her daughter's reason for keeping her father in the dark. She had met Thao many times though, and had grown fond of her, and had already begun to think of her as part of the family. She knew as well as Élise that the time was coming when he would have to find out.

Le Machine coughed twice, and she relaxed her grip on his silky smooth testicles. Everything was in order. She signed the necessary papers from the insurance company, wished him well and left the room. They had been running late, but had caught up. The show would begin on time. He had requested a few minutes alone.

He paced up and down, and ran his hand across his newly razored head. He had too much to think about, and didn't know where to start. There was Professor Papavoine, there was the strangely furious journalist from *L'Univers,* who had barked all sorts of questions at him, there was . . . there was everything. He had left too much until the last minute, and the time he should have spent in quiet preparation for the weeks ahead had instead been filled with places to go and people to see, and too many difficult conversations. He had even arrived at the venue half an hour late, to find a frantic crew wondering where he had got to.

So much had happened to leave him shaken. He felt he had experienced every possible emotion that day, some of them brand new to him, and they had left him in a state of turmoil. He wondered whether the doctor would have been quite so ready to declare him to be in full health if she had been able to see inside his head. He had done his best to appear calm, but he had never felt this way on an opening night, his mind a maelstrom of conflicting thoughts. He knew he had to hold himself together. The last thing he wanted to do right now was stand naked in a room full of strangers, but too many people were depending on him, and he couldn't back out. He had no choice. He was going to do it. He only hoped he wouldn't need a phial for tears. There were always a couple of spare receptacles to hand, in case of unexpected secretions; in Tokyo he had caught a bug and repeatedly vomited into a glass bucket, but he had never yet needed one for tears.

He picked up his phone, and made a call. It went to voice mail. He left a brief message, and hung up. Then he switched the phone off and put it in his holdall with his clothes, which he locked inside the medical cupboard. He wouldn't be needing any of his stuff for the next twelve weeks.

He closed his eyes, breathed deeply and did what he could to ready himself. He called for his masseur and his sound designer. There were ten minutes to go.

When he was a child, Jean-Didier Delacroix's father had told him over and over again that one of the most valuable weapons in an arts correspondent's armoury was inscrutability. *There is no point in having your opinion written all over your face*, he had told him, and Jean-Didier Delacroix had found this to be among the most valuable of his father's lessons.

His renown had spread, via his appearances in *L'Univers* as well as the photographs of him in the society pages, posing alongside his equally celebrated lover, and recently he had even begun offering highbrow punditry on television shows. His had become a known face at cultural events, and he often caught people stealing glances at him to see if they could somehow read his response to whatever it was he was reviewing. Sometimes they were rivals trying to pre-empt his copy, other times disinterested but mildly curious members of the public, and sometimes even the subjects themselves. Whoever it was, he made absolutely sure they didn't find out. If they wanted to know what Jean-Didier Delacroix thought, they would have to read the newspaper.

His father had tested him throughout his teenage years. Whenever his son was back from boarding school he played him music that he knew he would loathe, and waited to see if so much as a flicker of disgust crossed his face. Likewise, he would sit him in front of a favourite painting and make absolutely sure that his expression betrayed not one iota of approval. His father had introduced a degree of torture into this regime, attaching electrodes to various parts of his son's body and administering shocks as punishments for betraying a critical response through a slight nod, a raised eyebrow or a pursing of the lips. *You call that being inscrutable?* his father would bark, as he pressed the buzzer and sent his son's body into spasm. *How are you ever going to make a success of yourself as an arts correspondent if your review is written across your face for the world to see?*

Sometimes the electric shocks were an exercise in themselves – his father would press the buzzer and see if his son could withstand the charge without his face revealing any pain. Over the course of several years he became able to do this every time, and his father told him that he was now ready for the ultimate test. He chose not to reveal the nature of this test, but late one night he had crept into his son's bedroom, held a razor-sharp knife to his throat and told him he was going to kill him, drag his body to the woods and have repeated oral and anal sex with his butchered corpse.

By this point Jean-Didier Delacroix had been drilled to perfection, and he gave no visible reaction. His father put the knife back into its sheath, and congratulated him. His work was done.

Jean-Didier Delacroix was grateful for these lessons. There can't be many children whose fathers are prepared to give them such an immersive and effective programme of instruction in their future career. As he stood in Le Charmant Cinéma Érotique, one of five hundred and thirty people waiting for Le Machine to appear, he knew that his father's groundwork would be more valuable than ever before. He checked his watch, and what a watch it was. There were two minutes to go. Sure enough, people had recognised him, and were casting glances in his direction.

He gave nothing away.

The audience had no idea how *Life* was going to begin. In all its previous presentations, Le Machine had simply walked on from the wings and stood centre stage, looking out. This time though, he had worked in close collaboration with his lighting and sound designers, and his appearance was going to be much more dramatic.

At six fifty-nine the house lights and the stage lights were shut off, and the room was plunged into total darkness. Silence fell. And then, at exactly seven o'clock, and yet so suddenly that people jumped with shock, *Life* began.

In a single, perfectly timed burst, the stage lights and the speakers came on. The room was filled with the heavily amplified sound of a body at work. And there in the middle of the crowd, at the very end of the runway, stood Le Machine: naked, hairless and still.

*   *   *

165

This was not what they had been expecting. From his name, and the posters they had been seeing around the city for weeks, they had thought they were going to see someone who was as much automaton as human, something like the Silver Surfer. To see Le Machine this close was disorientating. They could see the lines on his fingers, the texture of his skin. But most unexpected of all were his eyes: he looked out at the people surrounding him, not with the eyes of a robot, but with eyes that had real expression to them. Eyes that were seeing them, just as they were seeing him. As he surveyed his new home, these eyes made fleeting contact with those of the people who had come to see him.

At once the audience was struck by the reality of what was going on. Le Machine was a man. As one, they wondered why they had expected anything else. People were not machines. They had paid money and taken time out from their lives to stand in a darkened room and look at another human being.

They were mesmerised.

Their preconceptions already dispatched, they waited to see what would happen next. There was a palpable tension in the air.

A few tiny state-of-the-art flesh-coloured radio microphones of the kind popular in Hollywood and Moscow were attached to various parts of his body. There were also ultra-sensitive microphones dotted around the stage, and the sound designer could switch from one source to the next. He was able to channel different sound sources into different speakers, to divide or blend the noises together in any way he thought sounded right. There would be plenty of scope for improvisation in the coming weeks, but he and Le Machine had decided to begin *Life* with a concentration on individual sounds, the same one coming from each corner of the room. He had begun with the pounding of his heart, and minutes later had faded this into the sound of his breath. Then the sound coming through the speakers changed to the gurgle of his stomach. It let out a long whine. Le Machine had not eaten very much at all that day. Already it was time for some food.

He walked back along the runway to the stage, and over to the whiteboard, where he picked up the marker pen, and wrote:

PIZZA, THIN CRUST, FOUR CHEESE, EXTRA ANCHOVIES & JALAPEÑOS. SPARKLING WATER. THREE LARGE BOTTLES OF ITALIAN LAGER.

There was a runner on the staff ready to fulfil such requests. Le Machine stood on the edge of the stage and looked out at all the faces staring up at him. He rarely drank alcohol during *Life*, but today he felt he needed a beer. Maybe he would order some more bottles later on. It was Friday night, after all.

Very few people in the audience had anticipated this aspect of the exhibition. Again they wondered what they *had* been expecting, and supposed that they had thought he would be fed via a tube, or that he would eat some kind of pill-based astronaut food that would be delivered to him once a day by a robot dog. They wondered why they had thought so little about what it was they had bought tickets for, and why they had come with such basic and misguided expectations. They stood spellbound, waiting to see how this would all unfold.

They were no longer too bothered whether or not they witnessed Le Machine going to the toilet. Of course they still hoped he would, but it didn't matter nearly as much as they had thought; this strange and wonderful display was enough. The sound of his beating heart would have drowned out any attempts at conversation, but it made no difference. Nobody felt like speaking anyway, they were all too busy taking it in. They could feel something incredible was going on, but they weren't quite sure what it was. They didn't worry though; they just let it all happen.

Five hundred and thirty pairs of eyes looked to the stage as a naked man waited for his pizza to arrive.

XIV

With everything that had been going on, Aurélie still hadn't made it to a children's boutique, so Herbert was back in his Mona Lisa and Eiffel Tower pyjamas for the third night in a row. It was eight o'clock, and since getting back home she had managed to get on top of her chores. On opening the door she had been struck by the rancid atmosphere. The smell of the soiled nappies had begun to seep out of the plastic sacks they had been tied into, so she had taken them out with the rest of her rubbish and opened the window until the smell had gone. She handwashed some of Herbert's clothes and hung them up to dry, and the dirty sheets were soaking in a bucket in the shower room. She wiped down the tiny stretch of work surface in her kitchen, and when this was done she saw that Herbert had fallen asleep in his nest of pillows on the bed. He had only had one nap all day, and she wasn't surprised that he had fizzled out.

She looked at him from across the room. He was absolutely motionless, lying on his back with his mouth a little open and his head slumped to one side. She felt a rush of panic. She darted over and lay on the bed beside him. She stared at him. She was under no illusion about what she was doing: she was checking to make sure he was breathing, that he was still alive. He was so still that she couldn't tell. What if she had somehow managed to kill him by mistake? What if he was severely allergic to fast food, or the fumes from her cleaning products? She was about to prod him to see if there was any response, but the rising terror abated when he closed his mouth, licked his lips, opened his mouth again and sighed. He was fine.

She wondered what she would have done if he *hadn't* been fine. Maybe she wouldn't be so lucky next time. There was no getting away from it: she had got herself into a terrible situation, and at any moment it could get even worse. She supposed she ought to give up while he was still alive, and take him to the police, and tell them how she had come to be in charge of him.

I see, they would say. *So why did this stranger give you the baby?*

Because I threw a stone at his face.

Is that how he got the bruise? It was still there. It had started to turn yellow. That morning she had been about to apply some concealer to his face when she had stopped, as if she was being prevented from continuing by an invisible force. She had accepted there and then that the invisible force had a point – it would never be right to put make-up on a baby.

Yes, that's how he got the bruise.

So am I right to conclude from what you have told

me that you are the kind of person who throws stones at babies' faces?

Yes, I suppose I am.

Are you aware that society doesn't look kindly on the likes of you?

And so it would go on. They would take Herbert away from her, slap on the cuffs and bundle her off to a cell. Then they would search her apartment and find the gun, and then they would telephone her father, and he would race to see her.

It was this, above everything else, that was stopping her from confessing. She imagined the look of disappointment on her dad's face as he saw her through prison bars. She knew how much he loved her, and how proud he was that she had gone to art college in Paris, and the thought of him seeing it all come crashing down this way was too much to bear. She had to get through the week.

There wasn't much she could do around the apartment without risking waking Herbert, so she showered, shaved her legs and underarms and, wrapped in a towel, lay beside him. 'Oh Herbert,' she whispered, 'you're the only man I can trust. Well, that's not strictly true. I trust my dad as well. But you two are the only ones I can trust.'

She had bought two bottles of wine on her way home, and she was already near the bottom of the first. She got up from the bed, went over to the kitchen and poured what remained of the bottle into her glass.

Lunch with Léandre Martin had not gone well. She wouldn't be seeing him again.

*   *   *

She felt stupid. She had really thought she had found a boyfriend, but with an efficiency that was almost impressive he had proved her wrong. He wasn't even second date material, let alone boyfriend material.

She had been hoping that their lunch would gracefully segue into an afternoon together, the three of them throwing back their heads in laughter in a series of scenic locations, but before it had even begun she couldn't wait for it to end. She wondered what had become of the man she had met the day before. It was as if he had exhausted his repertoire, using up anything about him that had been interesting, charming, funny or warm on their first meeting, and having nothing at all left over for the second.

He had been agitated and distracted from the outset, and had kept looking at his watch. When Aurélie asked him why, he told her that straight after lunch he had an appointment he couldn't break. He didn't offer any details about this *appointment*, he just looked away as he told her about it, and she hadn't pursued it. It was obvious to her that it was with a woman, that he was already in a relationship, a relationship that he wasn't going to give up for her, and that all he was doing was sounding her out in the hope of coming to some kind of arrangement. She despised men like that – the ones who slithered around behind women's backs. Men like him and Professor Papavoine.

Conversation moved on to the menu, and they spoke blandly of favourite dishes while avoiding eye contact. He asked her how Herbert was doing, and she told him he was fine. She was glad that he was sleeping beside her in his buggy throughout this excruciating ordeal.

As if things weren't already awkward enough, in the

seconds before it turned one o'clock he had told her he was about to hold his breath for two minutes, that it was something he did twice a day, at exactly one o'clock in the afternoon and then again at one o'clock in the morning. He checked the second hand on his watch, took a deep breath and sat stock-still. The first minute passed uneventfully, but as the second minute progressed he began to look uncomfortable, then in some pain. When the time finally ended, he fought to regain his breath.

As this display had gone on, Aurélie had decided once and for all that he was a creepy weirdo, and even though he was an incredibly handsome creepy weirdo, his handsomeness wasn't nearly enough. She resolved to get away from him at the first opportunity. She said nothing.

'Excuse me,' he said, in between gasps, 'but I never miss my one o'clocks. I usually find somewhere private for them. Yesterday I went to the toilet at that café, remember?'

She recalled that he had excused himself at one point. She looked away, uninterested.

'I have a reason for it,' he said, his eyes closed, 'but it's always been something I haven't talked about.'

'Well, aren't you mysterious and fascinating?' she said.

The sarcasm was inescapable. 'I'm sorry,' he said. 'I'm obviously not very good at this kind of thing. I . . . I should tell you all about it, though. I would like to. May I?'

She yawned. 'Don't bother,' she said. 'I really couldn't care less.' She stood up. There was no point in dragging this out any longer. 'Come on, Herbert,' she said. The baby was still asleep, but she spoke to him anyway. 'Let's leave the hairy man to his enigmatic routines and mystery appointments.'

'Aurélie, I'm sorry,' he said. 'Please stay.' He stood up as well. 'I'll tell you absolutely everything. I don't want to hide things from you.'

Aurélie wasn't in the mood to hear him talk about his other lovers or his pathetic hippie rituals. 'No, forget it,' she said. 'Thanks for lunch. It's been fun.' The food had only just arrived, and it sat there barely eaten. 'You can finish mine.'

She started to manoeuvre Herbert's buggy towards the door. Léandre Martin opened his wallet and threw some euros on to the table to settle the bill. She couldn't help noticing that he carried a thick wad of cash. Of course he did. He didn't want to leave a trail of evidence on a credit card statement for his real girlfriend to find and ask questions about. Maybe the poor woman was even his wife. Either way it was unfortunate for her that she had ended up with a man like this. Aurélie could sense him following her out of the restaurant.

'Just go away,' she said.

'Aurélie, I've been an idiot.'

'You don't say?'

'I've become so used to hiding things from people that it's become second nature to me, but I'm not going to hide anything from you . . . I'm going to tell you everything about myself. For a start, my appointment is with an old friend . . .'

'I'm sure it is. And you'll be telling the gendarmerie about your old friend if you don't leave me alone.' She saw two policemen ahead, and started walking in their direction. 'And while you're at it you can tell them why you're harassing a woman and a baby.'

'I'll call you.'

'Well, that's good to know. As my grandmother says, it's always nice to have something to look forward to.'

'Please don't give up on me. Aurélie . . .'

She walked away, but she heard what he said next, and it made her furious.

'I think I'm falling in love with you.'

He was exactly the kind of vermin who would say that to a girl and not mean it. She didn't look back until she was next to the policemen, to check that he wasn't following. He was standing where she had left him, looking at her.

'Go away,' she shouted.

He seemed to get the message. He had such a pained looked on his face that she almost felt sorry for him, but she knew he was only sad because his attempt to add her to his list of lovers had come to nothing. He turned and walked back the way he had come. He must have been embarrassed at having his man-of-depth-and-mystery routine fall so comprehensively flat. She was glad she hadn't fallen for it, and that she had seen right through his attempt to turn things around by professing love; it was nothing more than a desperate attempt at emotional manipulation. And anyway, what difference did it make even if he did love her? She didn't love him, so that was the end of it. Until an hour ago she had been falling for him in a big way, she had been a bag of nerves all morning, but she knew now that she'd had a lucky escape.

One of the policemen spoke to her. 'Is that man bothering you, Madame?'

'Not any more.'

She remembered she had a loaded gun in her coat pocket, and decided she had better not spend too much time hanging around with the gendarmerie. She walked on, and now she had left Léandre Martin behind she realised how naïve she had been to surrender so quickly and so completely to such a cretin. It wasn't as if it was the first time.

She banged a fist against her forehead, furious with herself for having failed to learn her lesson. She could feel she was about to cry, so she went into a fast food restaurant, found the toilet, locked herself and Herbert into a cubicle and let it all out. After a few minutes he woke up, and looked at her, quizzically, as he came to. The sight of his big blue eyes, blinking in the harsh light, made her realise she had to pull herself together, for his sake. She blew her nose, went back out and ordered some food.

She and Herbert ate fries together. He seemed to like them.

Léandre Martin punched himself on the forehead too. He had been such an idiot, and Aurélie had been absolutely right to react the way she did. He had deserved every barbed comment and every withering look. He should have told her everything, but instead he hadn't told her anything, and of course this had made her angry. Why wouldn't it? Who would want to spend time with someone as distracted, evasive and inarticulate as him?

He relived every uncomfortable silence, and replayed his mumbled dialogue, and he could only respect her all the more for walking away from someone who was such a waste of time. Whenever he had spoken it was only to say something that made him sound like a dullard, or a ball of slime. He had become used to closing off chunks of his life, but he really had planned to tell her everything. He had been waiting for the right moment, but it had all loomed too large, and shyness had taken hold of him and he hadn't realised until it was too late that he should have taken her in his arms the moment she arrived at the restaurant, kissed her, and said, *Aurélie, there's something I have to tell you.*

He should have told her where he was going, and why he was going there, and all about everything else that had grown out of such a terrible situation. That way she would have been able to come to a decision about him that was based on who he really was, not one based on him being a nervous, shifty mess.

He should even have invited her and Herbert to come along with him. But instead of doing this he had first avoided the subject altogether, then tiptoed around the edge of it. He wasn't at all accustomed to talking about it, particularly not to people he had only recently met, but that was no excuse. This was Aurélie. He wanted her to know, she *had* to know, and he had gone absolutely the wrong way about telling her.

His regrets began to pile up on one another. For her, he should even have postponed his one o'clock breath-holding session, or at the very least he should have told her exactly what it was all about beforehand. It could have been a way into his story. But instead he had just mumbled something about how it was time to hold his breath, and got on with it. He would never forget her face as he had been timing himself. She had looked at him as if he was an attention-seeking bore, then looked away. He supposed she was right, too. That was all he was – an attention-seeking bore.

With a jolt he realised that she must have thought he was involved in something preposterous – drug dealing, perhaps.

He had been so secretive about his movements, why would she not have thought that? Or maybe she thought he was part of a breath-holding sex cult, and was trying to recruit her and Herbert. Whichever way he looked at it, he knew that she had been right to give him the cold shoulder. Her immediate refusal to take any shit from a man only elevated her in his esteem. If only he hadn't been that man.

He hoped she would give him another chance, but it wasn't looking good. He tried to find a way forward. Maybe a break of a few weeks would work for them. He supposed she would need at least that long to stop being so angry with him. This train of thought juddered to a halt. He was fooling himself. In a few weeks' time he would be nothing more to her than a faint and unpleasant memory, surviving in her life only as the subject of an anecdote that she would tell her friends when they were exchanging stories about disastrous dates.

He walked on to the appointment he had been so nervous about explaining to her. He was going to the home of the only person he had ever really talked to about what happened in his life, the only one who knew everything there was to know about him. And today he would be talking about a girl called Aurélie Renard, and how right she was for him, and imploring them to ignore everything he had ever said before about how he would never fall in love. And then he would go on at some length about what a mess he had made, and how angry he was with himself.

He picked up the path alongside the Canal Saint Martin, *his* canal. He was tempted to throw himself in, to swim down to the bottom and burrow into the silt, never to surface again. But he didn't. Instead he walked on, every step taking him closer to the bedside of his best friend. To the bedside of Dominique Gravoir.

Aurélie looked at a sleeping Herbert, and drank her wine. She knew she ought to be sleeping too, but she couldn't. Her mind was too busy. She was having trouble reconciling the Léandre Martin of yesterday with the Léandre Martin of today. Yesterday they had seemed to belong together, but today he had been so different. Yesterday they had gazed into each other's eyes, and kissed on bridges, but today he seemed only to look at his fingernails, or into the middle distance. Yesterday conversation and laughter had flowed so naturally between them as they talked about everything and nothing, as if they had been old friends picking up after a long break and feeling as if no time had passed at all. Today though, their conversation had fizzled out before it had even begun; on the rare occasions when he had spoken it had been in code, and she hadn't been able to muster the enthusiasm to try to decipher it. She tried to tell herself it was just a bad second date like any other, but it was worse than that. Her hopes had been so high, and she felt so defeated, and alone. She blamed herself for having been so stupid as to let herself be carried away by romantic notions.

Longing for company, she reached for her phone. She had switched it off before she had met Léandre Martin, not wanting their afternoon to be disturbed, and she hadn't switched it back on since. There were two messages: one voice mail and one text. She listened to the voice mail first. It was from him. *Aurélie, I'm so sorry about earlier*, he said. *I handled things so badly . . .* She wasn't going to listen to his insincere grovelling. She deleted him. He was right though, he *had* handled things badly. He had been with a girl who was all packed up and ready to fall in love with him, and he had let her slip through his fingers. At least, she thought to herself, she had found him out early on. It would have been terrible to have discovered his scheming ways too late.

She scrolled through a few menus until she found out how to block his number. That was it. Done. She wouldn't be hearing from him again.

The text, though, was unexpected. It was from Sébastien. He wanted to see her: *I've been thinking about you.*

So he'd had her number all this time.

She thought back to the night they had spent together on this bed, and how wonderful she had felt as she had lain in his arms. Maybe something could be salvaged from the day. She took another swig of wine, and thought for a while. Then she texted back: *Come right away.*

XV

Le Machine's pizza arrived, but before he ate it he picked up a small capsule from the table. It had been there all along, but nobody had paid it any attention until now. He tapped it, and the sound boomed around the room. It was a microphone. Whenever *Life* was staged, he and his team made sure they added a few new elements, and this was going to be the first time he had used the microphone outside a trial situation. He unscrewed the bottle of sparkling water, and took a swig. He held it in his cheeks, then put the microphone into his mouth and let it sit there. The crackle of the bubbles as they fizzed in his mouth swept through Screen One of Le Charmant Cinéma Érotique in full surround sound, and the audience was rapt. He swallowed, and the microphone was inside him. Its journey had only just begun.

Le Machine sat at the table and readied his utensils, all

181

of which were made of glass. He always wanted as much of the equipment on stage as possible to be made from glass, and wherever he went he made sure to have the pieces made by manufacturers from the host nation, and after a lot of research, he and his team had found the people they believed to be the finest bespoke glassmakers in France. In Tokyo he had felt the glass was too thin and delicate, that it might not be up to the task. He had been particularly worried that either the faeces bottle or the urine bottle would crack. If it had done, the mess would have been so great that the exhibition would have had to be abandoned. He had always been on edge about this, but his worry had been misplaced; the glass had been perfectly engineered, and fit for its purpose. He had no misgivings about the quality of the craftsmanship now though – all the glassware was visibly sturdy, and though it lacked the delicacy of the Japanese pieces, it had been beautifully designed. Pieces by the same glassmaker were on sale in the gift shop: cutlery, crockery, replica specimen jars and various unique pieces for collectors. Piles of extra stock were stored in a warehouse, and their factory was on standby to fulfil further orders. One of the utensils was a bottle-opener. He used it to snap the cap off a bottle of lager. He took a long drink, the sound thundering around the room.

Before long, he had finished the first bottle of beer, and the large pizza was half eaten. Le Machine stood up, and walked to the end of the runway. He looked around at the people who had come to see him, and for the first time that day he felt comfortable with what he was doing. His worries that the show would seem stale were unfounded. Here were over five hundred people, and most of them would have been experiencing *Life* for the first time. For them it was fresh and new, and he knew that every one of them was coming to their own conclusions about what it was all about. It meant something different to everybody. He knew he had been right not to give the journalist from *L'Univers* what he had been looking for. He had been looking for a single answer to the question: *What is the meaning of* Life? He had told him only that there were as many answers as there were people who came through the door, and for him to tell people how they were supposed to feel would be to insult them, to blinker them and strip them of the joy of the experience. Looking out, he was glad that he had held his ground.

The reporter had not been delighted by his subject's reluctance to cooperate, but when had saying the right thing to reporters come to be considered a part of the artistic process, anyway? It was all nonsense.

Le Machine wasn't going to worry about him now. How much harm could one person do?

The audience watched Le Machine as he walked back along the runway to the main body of the stage. With all the water and beer inside him, it was at last time for the exhibition to live up to its reputation. He walked over to the glass urinal, and held his penis in his left hand.

The audience watched in wonder as it came out, a pale yellow that was highly visible in the stage lights. His bladder had been full, and as the stream went on and on the visitors began to cheer, so loud that it could be heard above the sound coming out of the speakers. Then they began to chant his name: *Le Ma-chine! Le Ma-chine! Le Ma-chine! Le Ma-chine!*

* * *

When he had shaken the final drops away, Le Machine bent down and picked up the jug into which it had all drained. He held it up. He knew everybody would be keen to see how much had come out. He walked over to one of the large glass vats, then he stood on a stool, took off a stopper and poured in the contents of the jug. He waited until every drop was in, then he replaced the stopper. *Life* had really begun now, and things seemed to be going well. For the first time in a long while he had a good feeling: he was doing something worthwhile.

Somewhere towards the back of the room there was a flicker of movement. It caught Le Machine's eye, and he watched the reporter from *L'Univers* push his way past the other onlookers and leave the auditorium. He tried to work out from the look on his face what he had thought of the little he had seen of *Life*. He couldn't. He was unreadable. Still, there was nothing he could do about him now.

He swept the reporter from his mind, and looked out at the hundreds of people who had come to see him. For a moment he allowed himself to feel imperial. *Paris belongs to me*, he thought to himself. But this moment passed. There was a piece of Paris, the most important piece of all, that would never belong to him. He was going to have to spend the coming twelve weeks trying his best not to think about it.

The cheering died down, and Le Machine returned to his pizza. He cracked open a second bottle of lager, and tried to make himself comfortable.

XVI

Aurélie worked fast. She fashioned a makeshift crib for Herbert out of folded blankets, and placed it in the same place where she had hidden him from Old Widow Peypouquet, on the floor behind the bed. He stayed fast asleep as she lowered him down and tucked him in. She thought back to what she had been wearing on the night she had finally managed to get Sébastien into her bed. It had been a party night, and she had dressed accordingly, in a short skirt and high-heeled boots. She looked through her drawers for a similar outfit. She didn't want to disappoint him.

She chose a tight black minidress, and slipped into it. Then she put on a bit of lip gloss and checked herself in the full-length mirror. She knew she looked good. Just the way he liked her. She kept her feet bare. She remembered that once she had got him home and stepped out of her boots he had spent quite a lot of time on her feet. That seemed to be one of his things.

She checked herself from a number of angles. Before meeting Sylvie she would never have had the confidence to dress this way. Sylvie had told her time and again how good she looked. *I don't have a lesbian bone in my body*, she had said one time, when appraising her outfit for a night out, *but if I did, even if it was one of those really small bones you get in your ear, I would be all over you right now*. She had told her that there must have been something wrong with Sébastien for not wanting her. When Aurélie had bemoaned her uneven teeth, Sylvie had explained at extreme length why, on balance, they were a good thing, and that they only enhanced her looks. She knew that Sylvie had not been sparing her feelings; she was never a great one for sparing feelings, and had been absolutely sincere. Since that day, Aurélie had never felt self-conscious when she smiled, and she no longer regretted refusing the offer of braces when she was thirteen. She had no idea how her self-image would have fared if it hadn't been for Sylvie. Maybe she would have ended up such a wretched mess of insecurities that she would even have yielded to the advances of her nine-hundred-year-old professor. She felt nauseous at the thought.

And it turned out that Sébastien did want her. He wanted her badly, and as she looked in the mirror she could see why. She felt a pang of sadness when she thought of the Léandre Martin of yesterday. She had caught glimpses of the two of them reflected in shop windows, and even though he was so much taller than she was, she had thought they fitted together well. She wondered whether they would have spent the night together if it hadn't been for Herbert. She would have been ready to. She'd had a lucky escape.

She pushed these thoughts away. Sébastien was on his way over, and very soon she would be exacting her revenge on Léandre Martin.

Aurélie and Sébastien exchanged a few more messages, and she told him to come up quietly, not to ring the bell or knock on the door. She didn't tell him why it was so important to be quiet. Soon he texted her to say he was outside on the street, and she buzzed him in. Her heart raced as she opened her door to him.

And there he was, back again, all cheekbones and height, and expensive clothes. He smelled good, too.

Aurélie motioned for him to whisper, mouthing that the walls between the apartments were thin. She directed him to the kitchen, where she shut the door behind them and perched on the worktop, crossing her legs. The room was so small that she and Sébastien had no choice but to be close together, almost touching.

'You look good,' he said.

She acknowledged this with a smile. 'To what do I owe the pleasure?' she asked.

'I think you know.'

'Oh, do I?'

'I want you, Aurélie.'

'You've got a funny way of showing it,' she said. She knew he would be expecting a demand for an explanation, and she didn't want him to think she was being a pushover. 'You've been ignoring me ever since you were last here.'

'Things have been complicated.'

'And now they're not complicated any more?' She smiled. 'So you're getting rid of Sculpture Girl?'

He looked her in the eye. At least he had the decency to do this. 'No,' he said.

Aurélie was unsurprised by this revelation, and she was glad. It was going to make things so much easier, and more fun.

'She and I are going places,' he said. 'We make a good partnership – we're both artists on the rise, we're both highly cerebral people.'

'And me?'

'Well, you know . . . I wouldn't say we were compatible artistically, or cerebrally. I mean, your drawings are nice, I suppose, but they're not really . . . out there, like our work. They're charming, in their own way, but it's obvious that you lack our ambition, our fire. And that's fine; we can't expect everybody to be working at our level. There's only room for so many people at the forefront of contemporary art – it's basic mathematics.'

She looked at him and smiled. *Typical Sébastien*, she thought.

'Hey, what's this?' he asked.

She realised that the list of Sébastien's qualities that she had written on the back of an envelope was still stuck to the fridge door by a magnet. She hadn't made much of an effort with it, and had forgotten all about it very shortly after writing it. She really should have taken it down before he got here, and she tried to work out a plausible explanation.

He took it off the fridge and looked at it. She read it too, to remind herself of what she had written:

Positives: Good-looking.
Negatives: Bad at art, nobody likes work, stupid,
horrible, only ever talks shit, embarrassment to self,
no real friends, will amount to nothing.

'Hey,' he said, 'you shouldn't be so hard on yourself. I mean, you got the first one right, and that's the main thing for a girl, isn't it?'

She smiled. 'You're such a charmer.'

'You know what I want, Aurélie.'

'I think I do. You want to stay with Sculpture Girl, but you also want a bit of blonde in your life.'

'I'm so glad you understand me. And you know it's got to be secret. Nobody must know. Especially not her.'

'So let's strike a deal,' she said, fixing his gaze. 'Whatever happens in this apartment stays in this apartment. OK?'

'That sounds fine by me.' It sounded more than fine. It was exactly what he had wanted.

She surprised him by holding out a hand, to shake on the agreement. This was getting better and better. He took it. It was soft, and smooth, and he was pleased to think about where her fingers would soon be.

He moved towards her, and took her in his arms. She could feel that he was ready to go. 'I'm so glad we've been able to come to an understanding,' he said.

'Oh, we've come to an understanding,' she said.

He felt a blunt jab in his side. He looked down, and straight away his burgeoning excitement shrivelled to nothing. The barrel of a gun was pressed against his ribs.

* * *

'Don't make a sound, Sébastien. As I said, these walls are paper thin and we wouldn't want your squealing to disturb the neighbours.'

He trembled, and nodded. She lifted the gun, pointing it at his head, and he took a step back. That was as far as he could go – he was pressed up against the kitchen door.

'Give me one reason why I shouldn't blow your brains out, you sleazy piece of shit,' she whispered.

'Because . . . because . . .' His mind was blank. 'Aurélie, put the gun down, please. Let's just . . . talk.'

This was great. The wine had really kicked in, she was feeling sexy in her dress, and Sébastien was getting the fright he deserved. He would think twice about sneaking around behind girls' backs from now on.

'This is what happens when you don't call for months, and then come crawling round for sex, Sébastien.' She took a step towards him. All the anger she felt for him, for Léandre Martin and for Professor Papavoine merged into one delicious chunk of revenge.

He took a step back, turned the door handle and darted into the main room. Aurélie followed him. In his haste to get away he had taken a wrong turning and fallen on to the bed. She pointed the gun at him and, for dramatic effect, she released the safety catch. The clunk sounded beautiful.

He looked up at her, pale as a ghost. There were tears running down his face. 'Don't,' he said. 'Please.'

'Shhh . . .' she said, putting her left forefinger to her glossy lips. And with her right hand she pointed the gun at his head.

'Oh God,' he whispered. 'No.'

*　*　*

She was surprised by just how little pressure had been needed to fire the gun. Whenever she thought back to this moment, she knew that she really hadn't meant it to go off. She only had her finger on the trigger for the sake of appearances, but after what had seemed like the slightest of squeezes the bullet had come out.

She remembered being very calm as it had blasted from the barrel. She felt the kick, and the report rang in her ears, and then there was a silence so total it was eerie. Sébastien was slumped on the bed, his face pressed into the duvet.

Slowly he opened his eyes, and looked up at her. She had missed. She could see he was unhurt, and she stood there smiling her sweetest smile. He was petrified. The silence continued, and now there was something familiar about it. It seemed strange that an absence of noise could have a particular quality, and then she realised what it was. It was the same as the silence that had followed the times when Herbert had been hurt, those awful quiet moments before he cried. But this time no cry had come.

Frantic, she scrambled past a whimpering Sébastien and looked on the floor on the other side of the bed.

She saw what she had done.

She had shot Herbert.

XVII

In a restaurant three streets away from Le Charmant Cinéma Érotique, Jean-Didier Delacroix sat in the private booth that his assistant had reserved for him. He had a talent for typing with one hand and eating incredibly expensive food, paid for by *L'Univers*, with the other, and he had been doing this ever since getting to his table over an hour before. He checked the clock on his computer screen, but unsatisfied with the quality of time it offered, he looked at his recently acquired 1974 Blancpain watch instead. That, he thought, was much better. Both told him the same thing: he had three minutes until the deadline. Back at the office the sub-editor would be nervously staring at her inbox, wondering if she would have to run the back-up article after all. This would be a disaster: Jean-Didier Delacroix's piece on Le Machine had been heavily flagged all week, and to fail to run it would irritate their readers and embarrass the paper in front of its competitors.

He had expected to have had it finished by this time, to have put the piece to bed at least fifteen minutes ahead of time. He should have been in a taxi by now, on his way back to his apartment to have vigorous sex with his horrible girlfriend, but here he was, still wrestling with the copy. A white-gloved waiter refilled Jean-Didier Delacroix's glass with wine from the very top of the list as he read through the article, making adjustments here and there. Still acutely aware that he was in public and could be observed, his face betrayed nothing.

One minute to go. The sub-editor would be frantic by now. Thirty seconds. He opened a blank email, and attached the file. Twenty seconds. He wrote a brief covering note. *Add question mark to title. It now reads: The End of Life?*

Five, four, three, two, one . . . He pressed *send*. Jean-Didier Delacroix had never filed copy late. His reputation, for punctuality if nothing else, was intact.

He closed his computer, finished what remained of his food, and drank his wine. Normally he would have simply gathered his things and left, but he felt too exhausted to stand. Never before had a job left him so drained. Very soon his wine glass was empty again.

He called for a brandy.

XVIII

After turning in for her customary early night, Old Widow Peypouquet had woken at the sound of a loud bang. Not one to be woken by a loud bang and then just roll over and go back to sleep, she listened for further sounds. None came. She wondered for a moment whether it had been a car backfiring, or a frying pan falling in a neighbour's kitchen, but she dismissed these possibilities. She was accustomed to those sounds, and while she would sometimes be woken by them, it was never with quite such a jolt. There was something unusual going on. In a flash she recalled her visit to the girl across the corridor, and she jumped out of bed and into her slippers.

She pulled on her robe, went out into the hall and pressed her ear to her neighbour's door. She heard voices. Mademoiselle Renard had a man in there, and they were whispering. She couldn't work out what they were saying, but it didn't feel as if she was eavesdropping on a romantic scene.

Herbert's eyes were open, but they seemed not to be registering anything. He was completely still, and the tears that had followed his previous traumas had not come. There was blood on his blanket, and a panicked Aurélie lifted it up to find out what had happened. The shoulder of his Eiffel Tower top was red, and she pulled it back to reveal the wound.

Sébastien leant over to see what she was looking at, then leapt back at the sight of the wounded baby, as if thrown by an explosion. 'I'm getting out of here,' he said. 'You're fucking mental.'

'You're going nowhere,' snapped Aurélie. In a flash her rising panic had evaporated. She was beyond that now. The effects of the wine had vanished, and her head was absolutely clear. She had an urgent task in front of her, and there was no time for hysterics. She looked at where the bullet had hit. It had grazed his shoulder, close to where it met his neck. 'Get his bag from the back of his buggy. It's in the shower. Empty it on to the bed and find the first aid box.'

She reached down and scooped Herbert up, and held him tight. She was relieved to see his eyes start to look around the room. He was alive. Then he looked at her. His eyes seemed to be saying, *Why, auntie Aurélie, why? Why did you shoot me?*

'I'm so sorry, Herbert,' she said. 'And don't you worry, the nasty man's going to get you some antiseptic and we'll have you cleaned up in no time.'

'I'm the nasty one, am I?' snapped Sébastien as he

carried out his orders. He found the first aid box and opened it. Aurélie reached in and took out an antiseptic wipe. 'You're the one who shoots babies, and *I'm* the nasty one?'

Aurélie found herself obliged to concede that he had a point. Maybe they were both as nasty as each other.

'What did you say his name was?'

'Herbert.'

'*Air-bear?*'

'Yes.' She wasn't going to bother teaching his name to Sébastien. It wasn't as if the two of them would be hanging out together a great deal after today.

'How old . . .?' Sébastien turned a shade whiter still as he tried to work out whether or not he was the father of the child. In his dazed state it took him a while to compute the numbers and work out that there was no way they could be related.

She took off Herbert's top, and prepared to wipe the wound. That was the moment Old Widow Peypouquet chose to make her presence known. They both jumped as she banged on the door.

'Open up,' she said. 'Open up – I know you're in there.'

Aurélie wiped Herbert's shoulder, and this jolted him from what must have been a state of shock. His mouth opened wide, and out came the most primal howl she had heard from him yet. She had never been so relieved to hear the sound of a child in pain. She cleaned his shoulder, took out a cotton wool ball, dipped it in antiseptic and dabbed the wound. Herbert wriggled to get away. As the blood cleared she told herself that the wound wasn't as bad as it could have been; that it would scab up nicely, and probably scar, but he was going to be OK.

Old Widow Peypouquet knocked again. 'What are you doing in there?' she shouted through the woodwork.

'I'm coming, Madame Peypouquet,' she said. 'Just a moment.'

The old woman banged on the door again.

Aurélie threw the bloodied clothes behind the bed, and turned to Sébastien. 'Get a towel.' He went through to the shower room, took the towel from the back of the door and threw it to her. She wrapped it around Herbert, taking care to hide the wound from view. His crying was subsiding now. She hoped that after the initial sting the antiseptic was having some kind of soothing effect. She looked at Sébastien. He was still white, and trembling.

'Right,' she said. 'Follow my lead, and don't give anything away.'

Carrying a bundled-up Herbert, she hid the gun under a pillow, scrambled over the bed and opened the door. 'Hello, Madame Peypouquet,' she said. 'What can we do for you?'

She looked around, taking in the situation. It was the boy she had seen before, but he seemed a little paler this time. Still, it had been summer back then. He was still very handsome, though. 'What was that bang?' she asked.

'Yes, I'm sorry about that,' said Aurélie. She had become accustomed to thinking on her feet. 'It was Sébastien. He thought it would amuse the baby if he set off a firecracker. He's not very good with children.'

Old Widow Peypouquet turned to Sébastien. 'So you thought it would be a wonderful idea to set off a fire-cracker?'

He nodded.

'Indoors?'

He nodded again.

'While old people are trying to sleep?'

He nodded.

'In front of a baby as well?'

Old Widow Peypouquet stared at him, and he knew he had to say something. He did as he was told, and followed Aurélie's lead. 'I thought babies liked that kind of thing,' he said.

'No, you didn't. I can see right through you. You were teasing it. You thought that just because the baby's made of rubber it wouldn't mind being given the fright of its life – that's it, isn't it?'

He looked at Aurélie, who, out of Old Widow Peypouquet's line of vision, tapped her head, indicating that the old lady was prone to flights of fancy. She didn't want Sébastien to complicate everything by letting it slip that Herbert was real.

'Yes, you're right.'

'But it's cleverer than that. Look at it – it's upset. It'll all be recorded on the microchip, you know. It's only the size of a grain of sugar, but nothing gets past it. It'll all be in there.'

'Yes. I suppose it will.' Sébastien looked at the floor as he accepted his telling off, and tried to make sense of what she was saying.

She carried on. 'You're quite right to look ashamed, making a row like that, waking up old people and upsetting a rubber baby.'

'What's going on?' Monsieur Simoneaux had heard the disturbance and come up to investigate in his pyjamas and slippers. His head appeared around the door, his grey hair wild, as if he had only just woken up.

'Don't worry, Monsieur Simoneaux,' said Old Widow Peypouquet. 'It's just the boyfriend of the girl with the rubber baby setting off a firecracker. I've given him a stern talking to. He won't be doing it again in a hurry, I can tell you.'

Monsieur Simoneaux called down the hall, to the neighbours who had congregated. 'Panic over, ladies and gentlemen. It was just a firecracker, a student prank that's upset this rubber baby you've all been hearing so much about. Old Widow Peypouquet has dealt with it, so we can all return to our homes.'

There was a choral intake of breath from the onlookers, and Monsieur Simoneaux realised at once what he had said. It was his turn to lose all the colour from his face.

Old Widow Peypouquet gave him a look that could shatter a diamond, and he felt his knees weaken.

'*Old Widow Peypouquet?*' she rasped. '*Old Widow?* Who are you calling an *old widow?*'

'I'm sorry,' he said. 'You're not old.'

She gave him a look. 'Of course I'm old. I'm ninety-four if I'm a day. But for your information, not that it's anybody's business but my own, I'm not a widow. I never married. But,' she waved a long, bony finger at them all, 'that doesn't mean that I never had a boyfriend. Oh no. Don't you go thinking *Old Widow Peypouquet* never had any fun in her day. Far from it, as a matter of fact. I was quite the girl about town. I got around – if anything I had something of a reputation. There was no stopping me. I even caught VD a couple of times.'

The assembled neighbours looked at her, ashamed. Each one of them knew they were guilty of the same crime, and they felt a mixture of pity for Monsieur Simoneaux and gratitude that it had been he and not they who had made the slip.

Aurélie was relieved, because it took the focus away from her. Now this would no longer be the night her boyfriend had startled a rubber baby with a firecracker, but the night Monsieur Simoneaux had called Madame Peypouquet an old widow. She now had just a supporting role, like all the others.

'Be off with you,' she said, and they all scuttled away.

Madame Peypouquet, as she would now be known by all her neighbours, looked at the young people. 'Honestly,' she said. '*Old Widow Peypouquet.*' She saw the funny side, and started to laugh. 'If I'm in mourning for anyone, it's for the girl I once was. I was quite something back then. You might not think so to look at me now, but I'd have given even you a run for your money, Mademoiselle Renard.' Once again, she lifted a bony finger and pointed. 'And even though this ear sticks out a bit more than the other one, and your teeth aren't exactly straight, I still count you as a very pretty girl.'

Aurélie smiled as she accepted the compliment.

'I consider myself to be quite the judge of the female form,' continued Madame Peypouquet, 'and I never knew you had quite such a good body – you should wear slutty clothes like that more often.'

Despite the strangeness of the situation, Aurélie found herself buoyed by Madame Peypouquet's compliments.

'Well, I'll be going,' said the old woman. She poked Sébastien's chest. 'And no more firecrackers, young man.' She turned back to Aurélie. 'For a moment there I thought you'd been firing that gun of yours.'

Aurélie froze. So she *had* seen the gun on her last visit.

'Mine's so old I can't find anyone who sells the bullets any more. I've been thinking about asking if I could borrow yours so I could shoot the pigeon that sits on my windowsill and wakes me up every morning. That would teach it a lesson. I don't suppose I should, though. I bet they don't even let people shoot pigeons any more, now they've brought in the Common Market. Anyway, I'm glad you've taken my advice and invited the young man around again. Just don't let him get you pregnant.' She poked Sébastien's chest again. 'Don't get her pregnant. Even if the computer says *she's* ready for a baby, you're not. I'll leave you two lovebirds alone now.'

And with that, she went away.

Sébastien sat on the bed and breathed a sigh of relief. He was pretty sure he had managed to sort out fact from fiction. 'Damn, you're cruel,' he said. 'You almost had me believing that was a real gun, and a real baby.' He looked at Herbert, who was lying on the bed with his eyes half open. 'He's quite realistic from some angles. Latex, right?'

She nodded as she refilled the baby's bag with all the things that Sébastien had poured all over the bed.

'I've heard about these. I might use one for an art project. I could take him around and take photos of him as if he was a real baby. I could really push the envelope. I could attach a magnet to his back, and stick him to the side of the Eiffel Tower. It could be like robotics meets a barbed comment on the quasi-sexual fetishisation of the child in contemporary society.'

'And what makes you think you'd be the first person to do that?'

'Shit. So that's why you've got him?'

'No, you know me – I just hang around with animatronic rubber children for fun.'

Sébastien allowed himself to be impressed. 'Maybe you're not as hopelessly unadventurous an artist as I thought you were. I had the impression that you were hidebound by convention, but it looks as if you're challenging some boundaries here.'

'I'm really honoured that you would think that.'

Sébastien had no idea that she wasn't being a hundred per cent sincere. 'You deserve the praise,' he said. 'I've got to admit you've not done too bad a job. The blood and everything . . . it's almost realistic.'

'It was easy,' she said, 'I prepared the blood before you arrived. It's actually a tomato sauce from my cousin's farm.' She began to wonder why she was lying to him, and why her lie was so elaborate. She didn't have a cousin with a tomato farm. There would be very little point to all her efforts if at the end of it he went away thinking it had all been a big hoax. She owed it to Herbert's shoulder to make sure Sébastien was scarred for life too.

He moved towards her, in a movement that she recognised as *sidling*. 'I was just playing along,' he said. 'Of course I knew it wasn't a real baby or a real gun.'

Something caught the corner of her eye. 'Oh really? Not a real gun? Then what do you call this?' She pointed to a hole in the sheet, then pulled it back to reveal a hole in the mattress. It must have gone right through before hitting Herbert. She followed the angle of its trajectory, and there in the rug, just where Herbert had been lying, the blunt end of the bullet was visible. She reached down to get it. It was wedged into a floorboard, and she had to use some effort to remove it.

She held it up in front of his face. It was streaked with blood. 'So this isn't real?'

He was mesmerised by the bullet. 'You are a crazy, crazy bitch. I had no idea.' He took her hand, the one holding it. 'And I have never wanted you more than I do right now.' He leaned in for a kiss, but before his lips reached hers he felt a now familiar sensation in his side.

She sighed. 'Haven't you learned anything?'

He got up, and she kept the gun trained on his head as he backed his way over to the door.

'And you're not that great with materials, are you? It's not only the gun that's real. The baby's not rubber – he's real too. And the blood wasn't sauce, that was real blood from a real baby, and he was bleeding because I shot him.'

Just when it seemed Sébastien couldn't get any paler, he managed it.

'You remember our agreement, Sébastien?'

'Yes.'

'Remind me, what was it?'

'What happens in this apartment stays in this apartment.'

'And we shook on that, right?'

He nodded.

'If a single word – *a single word* – about any of this gets out you're going to find yourself with a lot of explaining to do to Sculpture Girl, and that'll just be the start of it.'

'As if I'd tell anyone about what just happened. Aurélie, you are a fucking psycho.'

'Thank you,' she said. She made sure she was beautifully arranged across the bed. 'One last thing, Sébastien,' she purred.

'What is it?'

'Can you draw hands?'

He shook his head.

'I can draw hands.'

Normally this would have been a cue for Sébastien to launch into an extended monologue about how the old ways are redundant, that to expect an artist to be able to draw hands was the same as expecting a designer of synthesisers to be able to whittle panpipes, that times had moved on. But today, mainly because a madwoman was pointing a gun at his head, he just stood there, not knowing what to say.

Aurélie gave an ostentatious yawn. 'Now go, Sébastien.'

'Yes.'

And he was gone.

Aurélie stroked Herbert's tummy. He was sleepy, exhausted by all the action of the day. She unwrapped him from his towel and checked his wound. It was no longer bleeding, but it was ugly: shiny and open, and about two centimetres long and half a centimetre wide. She opened his first aid box and started to dress it. He wasn't happy about that, and a brief and noisy wrestling match ensued. Aurélie was victorious, and got the dressing on.

She put him in the only one of his T-shirts that wasn't hanging up to dry, then decided he had earned some food. She opened a jar of pasta and vegetable puree, which was followed by an apple and peach puree. Then she filled his bottle, and he had a long drink of milk. She took off his clothes and nappy and washed him with a warm damp flannel before dressing him again in hopelessly inadequate nightclothes, then she brushed his teeth and tucked him into bed.

She stroked his hair, and sang him the only song she knew all the way through – Charles Aznavour's 'Hier Encore'. He seemed to enjoy it, so she sang it again. She wasn't such a bad substitute mother after all.

She watched him drift off to sleep, and when he was finally under she felt very much alone again. She knew this was her cue to break down, for the realisation of what had happened to hit her, and for a landslide of guilt and shame to crush her. It didn't happen. She had shot a baby, very nearly in the throat, she accepted that. It had been a mistake, but she had learned from it. She had hurt Herbert though, and while she felt awful about it, she also knew she couldn't turn back the clock, and there was nothing to be gained from beating herself up about it. It had been stupid of her, but he was going to recover and she was going to make double sure she never shot a baby again. He would have a scar there, probably for the rest of his life, just where his shoulder meets his neck, but women like men with scars so, if anything, she had probably done him a favour in the long run.

She had proved quite decisively that she couldn't be trusted with firearms, and she was going to give Sylvie her gun back. The lessons had been learned, and everyone was going to be OK. And besides, she had given Sébastien the fright of his life. He had been well and truly revenged.

She stood up, poured another glass of wine and looked at herself in the full-length mirror. She was pleased with what she saw: a gun-toting femme fatale. Madame Peypouquet was right – she did have a good body. Léandre Martin and Sébastien had really blown it. She walked right up to the mirror, and stood eye-to-eye with her reflection.

That was when the landslide happened. It all came crashing down.

She had shot Herbert.

Sébastien was right: she was a fucking psycho.

She spent the night curled up on the bed in her short, tight black dress, a sobbing mess of guilt and shame.

SAMEDI

XIX

In July, Natsuki Kobayashi had bought a cat. He was not a pleasant cat. He had mean, narrow eyes and a sour, arrogant nature, and she had named him Makoto.

Toshiro Akiyama had not found out about Makoto Kobayashi until he had gone to visit Natsuki's apartment and been hissed at the moment he walked in. It was a hiss both aggressive and disdainful.

'He's just getting used to you,' Natsuki had said, but this hissing had continued all evening, and started up again the moment he stepped out of her bedroom the next morning, and it had not abated since. Natsuki seemed to love Makoto though, and the cat tolerated her in return. She spent a lot of time tickling his belly, and making him small hats, helmets and headdresses, and posting photographs of him wearing them on the Internet. In each of these photographs Makoto had an unpleasant look in his eye, and even the people of the Internet, so many of whom love nothing more than commenting favourably on photographs of hat-wearing cats from around the world, were reticent in their praise. Each picture received only two or three hundred responses, and though they were always positive they seemed only ever to come from people who had specifically set out to find pictures of sinister-looking felines in unorthodox handcrafted headgear. The rest of the Internet maintained a diplomatic silence on the subject of Makoto Kobayashi.

One evening, after weeks of this, Toshiro was at Natsuki's place and the cat had scratched him through his trousers, drawing blood yet again. Finally, he asked the question he had been holding in for such a long time. 'Natsuki,' he said, at last, 'why didn't you tell me you were going to get a cat?'

She shrugged. 'I don't have to tell you everything.'

'No, of course you don't, but things are pretty serious between us, and it's a big deal.'

'Since when was getting a cat a big deal? It's just normal. And anyway, it doesn't matter how serious we are, I don't need to ask your permission if I want a pet.'

'But we've already agreed that at some point we'll be living together. What happens to the cat then?'

'He'll live with us. Anyway, we're not even engaged. I'm still an independent woman and I can do what I want. And if you love me you'll love my cat.'

'I'm never sharing a home with that thing. He's mean. This is something we should have talked through together. He could live for another twenty years.'

'I hope he does.'

'But I don't want to spend the next twenty years of my

life being hissed at by a furry ball of negativity. I work from home, so when you're out all day I'll be stuck in the apartment with him. And I've noticed that since you got him you don't come to mine so much because you don't want to leave him alone, and to be honest I haven't looked forward to coming round here as much as I used to.'

'Well, that's your problem.'

'It's not just *my* problem.'

The bickering continued throughout the evening.

A few more weeks went by without the subject being raised again, but it was always there, looming over them. Toshiro thought about it a lot, turning the dilemma over in his mind. He didn't want to stifle his girlfriend's independence, but the more he dissected the situation the surer he became that she really should have spoken to him before making a decision that was going to affect them both in the long term. Even if the cat had turned out to be a tolerable creature, a conversation should have taken place. The whole episode had revealed a side to her that he supposed he had been in denial about. She was selfish, and perhaps even sly, and no matter how much she tried to make him look petty for complaining, this *was* a big deal. And what if they were to have a baby? He wouldn't want this hissing cat anywhere near it. And if they couldn't even agree about looking after a cat, then how could they ever agree about raising a child?

Makoto had been a test of some sort, he was sure of it, part of a mind game. He had found himself looking forward to times when he wouldn't be seeing his girlfriend, because seeing her meant being hissed at, and he knew that wasn't how things were supposed to be. Even

211

when they went out it would be as if the cat was there with them, a ghostly presence snaking around his mistress's ankles and readying himself to scratch his legs. There was a constant tension.

He had even begun to find Natsuki Kobayashi less attractive. He had always found her so beautiful, but now there were times when he didn't want to look at her. Until Makoto's sudden arrival she had never shown any signs of being a cat person, but her conversation had become almost exclusively about this unpleasant creature, be it worming tablets, flea collars or her plans for fashioning novelty headgear: her latest project was an English policeman's helmet sewn out of felt, and she had told him about this plan as if he would have wanted to hear about it. She had even had some photographs of the cat printed onto fabric, which she then made into clothes. It was as if she and the cat were merging into a single intolerable entity. He had started to wonder quite seriously whether he could bring himself to be with her any longer.

And then it hit him: she was deliberately driving him away. Whether she knew it or not, she was sabotaging their relationship. On some level, conscious or unconscious, she was putting up a force field around herself. Suddenly everything seemed clear. It was over. He felt sad about that, but his sadness was for the passing of what had once been, and it was outweighed by a sense of relief that the stand-off was over. He was glad to put an end to the tension of the last few months. He was also relieved to know that deep down or otherwise, this was what she really wanted. No hearts were going to break. If anything, it was going to be a happy occasion.

He decided right away that he was going to be single for the foreseeable future.

He opened his laptop for the first time in a while, and checked his mail. His agent had been in touch to tell him that a television quiz show for which he had written the theme music had been given a second run, and he would be paid accordingly. That was very good news. He tried to remember the last time he had met his agent. It had been at least a year ago. All his business was done online now. He checked the next message. He had lost an auction for a 1983 Korg drum machine, and was annoyed about that. He had never quite got along with his 1984 Korg drum machine and had been hoping the 1983 model would be an improvement. It didn't escape his notice that he felt more upset at having lost an auction for a drum machine than he had at having lost his girlfriend. Finally he opened a mail from his mother, headed *News from Paris*. He had never been to the city, and had been wondering how they were doing.

The message was short, sent from her phone. It just said: *Your father and I are having a good time. We have made a new friend: Sylvie Dupont. She is very nice. I hope you and she will meet one day.* Below the text was a photograph. It was sideways, because his mother always seemed to manage to send her photographs sideways, but even before he had spun it around his heart sped up. When he had aligned the photograph, it was even more incredible than he had thought. There she was, Sylvie Dupont, the prettiest and happiest girl he had ever seen, her arm around a small horse.

His plan to remain single for the foreseeable future had been forgotten.

*   *   *

213

Toshiro Akiyama picked up his phone and dialled Natsuki Kobayashi. He arranged for them to meet at her place. There are some things, cat scratching his leg or no cat scratching his leg, that need to be done face-to-face. He was elated. His soon-to-be-ex girlfriend had won. Her game had worked, and she had forced him into a position where he had no choice but to break up with her. It was going to be a good day for both of them.

The appointment made, he called his travel agent. While he was on hold he printed out the photograph of the girl and the horse, pinned it to his notice board and got back to work. There was no point in wasting time. A piece he had been working on for a month, and had been close to abandoning, was finished within an hour. He sent it off to his agent, who emailed straight back to tell him how perfect it was. The client was going to love it.

There were three hours left before he had to be at Natsuki Kobayashi's apartment, and his plane wasn't taking off until the morning. He downloaded a *Teach Yourself French* audio book, and started learning straight away.

'Bonjour,' he said, looking at the photograph as he packed his suitcase. 'Bonjour, Sylvie Dupont.'

XX

At ten twenty in the morning, Professor Papavoine's wife picked up the phone.

'Hello?'

—*Ah. Yes. Hello. Please could I speak to Professor Papavoine?*

'I'm afraid he's not available at the moment. May I take a message?'

—*How unavailable is he? Is he in the house?*

'He's in the shower, if you have to know.'

—*Tell him not to leave.*

'Not to leave the shower?'

—*No, not to leave the house. Tell him I'll be arriving in about twenty minutes.*

'Oh really?'

—*Yes. And I'll be bringing a baby. The professor knows about me, but he doesn't know about the baby.*

'Does he not?'

—*Tell him he'll be watching the baby for a few hours while I catch up on sleep. I've not slept all night. Are you his wife?*

'Yes.'

—*Then maybe you can help with the baby too.*

'Just out of interest, not that it's any of my business or anything, but who are you?'

—*I'm one of his students.*

'You're not this Aurélie Renard, are you?'

—*Er . . . yes?*

'Interesting. He told me he'd given you our number. I didn't think you would call, and neither did he. But he's told me everything about you.'

—*Everything?*

'Well, everything he knows. Which isn't much. Mainly what you look like, I'm afraid – how your blue eyes sparkle, how your smile lights up the room and so on. I can't wait to meet you, to see if it's all true.'

Aurélie put the phone down. *Shit*, she thought. As if it wasn't bad enough that his wife had answered the phone, it turned out that she was just as bad as he was. They were both sex maniacs, hell bent on having a threesome with her. Why did everything have to be about kinky sex? Still, she thought, if his wife was his accomplice then at least she wouldn't have to invent stories to spare her feelings.

Her bag was packed, she and Herbert were both dressed and ready, and the baby seemed to be looking forward to the adventure. Aurélie weighed up her options. She hadn't slept at all, and the combination of exhaustion, mortification and hangover was too much for her to deal with. Unlike Herbert, who was more energetic than she had ever seen him, she could barely keep her eyes open.

It was Saturday, so Sylvie would be working on a floating restaurant on the Seine and wouldn't be able to take care of the baby. There were a few vague friends from college she could call, but she didn't really feel close enough to any of them to ask such a favour. They would all be busy anyway, the rich ones having fun and the normal ones working their weekend jobs, and even if any of them weren't busy, she was fairly confident that they wouldn't be impatient to take sole charge of a nine-month-old boy at a moment's notice. And there was still the complication that she wanted as few people as possible to know what was going on. She wasn't overwhelmed by the variety of options available to her.

Sometimes when Sylvie needed a favour, she would call on an ex who was still in love with her. She would explain from the start that she wasn't going to get back with him, that she was only calling to ask him to help her out, but because he would be so desperate to see her he would be powerless to refuse. This was mainly how she managed to move heavy objects around; the last time she used this tactic had been to get a wardrobe up four flights of stairs.

Aurélie didn't have such resources available to her, though. The day after he had burned all his belongings, Guillaume had borrowed his uncle's boiler suit and left for a town a long way away, somewhere he wouldn't know anybody. News had reached her that he had married the first woman he met when he got there, a frantic divorcee with four children, who had a tendency to hang around the railway station waiting for new arrivals in the hope that she would find one who would be prepared to take them all on. She had heard through the grapevine that it had worked out well for them, that he had won a medal for being his adopted prefecture's most devoted stepfather, and that he had even added a child of his own to the mêlée. She wasn't about to go barging back into his life and demanding that on top of his existing responsibilities he also take care of Herbert. And even if she had felt inclined to utilise him, it wouldn't have helped that his new home was over four hundred kilometres away.

Guillaume was the only boyfriend of any significance she had ever had, certainly the only one whose heart she had broken, and by all accounts he had moved on. He wasn't like Sylvie's exes, going from day to day doing nothing but longing for a reconciliation. She would have to make do with what she had available: an elderly academic who had sweaty palms over her. And so she had called Professor Papavoine.

He was already involved, whether he knew it or not, and he owed her. With a bit of squinting, it was even possible to look at the situation from an angle where it seemed as though it were his fault: he was supposed to have been the responsible adult, and he should have prevented her, a mere child of twenty-one, from throwing the stone. He was creepy and he was sleazy, and she had felt her flesh crawl as she dug out his card and dialled his number, but she didn't see what else she could do. There was no way she could take care of Herbert in her condition. He was her only option, and she didn't have any choice but to make him useful.

'OK, Herbert,' she said. 'Here's the plan. We'll get to Papavoine's, I'll break the news straight away that he and his wife aren't going to be doing anything funny with me, then I'll hand you over to them . . .' She stopped. She wondered whether it was right to leave Herbert in the care of a pair of swingers. She quickly decided that it wasn't a problem. They were clearly into young women, not babies. 'And as soon as you're with them, I'll find a quiet corner and fall asleep.'

She struggled down the stairs. Two neighbours whom she knew by sight but not name passed her, offered greetings and looked intently at the baby. *Incredible*, said one. *Not that realistic*, said the other. *It's got a kind of waxy look about it.*

Aurélie and Herbert stood on the corner of a busy street, where there were always taxis going by. Now though, for the first time ever, there were no taxis going by. As she waited and waited, the world around her started to lose focus. She wondered whether it was possible to fall asleep while standing up, and received her answer when she fell asleep while standing up. The loss of balance woke her, and when she opened her eyes it was to see an empty cab going by, just too late to hail.

Minutes later another one came along at last, and she wrestled Herbert's buggy into the boot and got into the back seat, clutching the baby close and hoping the driver was a safe one. She gave him the address, and the next thing she knew they were in an unfamiliar but pleasant street, and the taxi driver was laughing at her. She sensed that her mouth had been hanging open, and she had probably been snoring. At least she had instinctively kept a tight grip on Herbert.

She paid, retrieved the buggy and found the door. She

stopped for a while. She thought of her dad, who would never have dreamed of cheating on his wife, and had never found anyone to replace her. He lived his life alone, while these Sébastiens and Léandre Martins and Professor Papavoines oozed around, getting it wherever they could. It was sickening. At least Professor Papavoine's wife knew what was going on, and even seemed to be an enthusiastic supporter of his behaviour. That was a small consolation. But even so, it was wrong of him to turn sleazy on his students, and she was going to feel no guilt at all about turning up on his doorstep and using him as a babysitter, and his home as a crash pad.

She pressed the bell, and the man himself answered. 'Hello?'

'It's Aurélie Renard,' she said.

'Mademoiselle Renard!' He sounded delighted to hear from her. Of course he did. He thought she had been driven out of her mind with desire for him, and was desperate to take off her clothes and rub herself against him, and maybe even his wife at the same time. She wondered how their conversation had gone, and whether his wife had mentioned that she would be bringing a baby with her, and what they were going to do about that, logistically. Maybe they were prepared to wait for the child to fall asleep before stripping her and licking her up and down, or perhaps they had agreed to take turns with her, rather than both going for it at the same time. She didn't really know how things like that worked, but whatever they had in mind, they were out of luck. 'I'll be right down,' he said.

He buzzed her into the building. The lobby was a lot more spacious than the one in her building, and it was better kept. She didn't have long to inspect her surroundings though, as Professor Papavoine was running down the steps two at a time.

'Hello, Mademoiselle Renard,' he said. 'What a pleasant surprise. And you've brought a friend. Let me help you. We'll be here all day if we wait for the lift.' He took Aurélie's bag and the buggy, and together they went up the single flight to the Papavoine home.

Aurélie looked around. Their hall alone was bigger than her entire apartment. The parquet shone, and instinctively she took off her shoes. It was that kind of place. Dotted around were beautiful artworks.

He saw her looking at them. 'All by students of mine,' he said. 'We buy them discreetly. I don't want to fuel any resentment or rivalries. You know what artists can be like.'

Aurélie smiled. She knew. She tried to imagine her work alongside these highly accomplished pieces: a video projection of a stone hitting a baby's face. It didn't really fit.

'Come in,' said Professor Papavoine. He ushered her through to the lounge, another large room with yet more art on the walls and an enormous sofa. She sat down, and lay Herbert beside her. He started happily rolling up and down. He had been doing that a lot more today than he had on previous days. It seemed to be his latest hobby. He was going to need a lot of watching to make sure he didn't do another of his plummeting tricks.

'So,' said Professor Papavoine, 'can I get you anything? Coffee?'

Aurélie shook her head. 'Where can I go for a cigarette?'

'You don't have to go anywhere. I'll bring you an ashtray.'

He took one from a sideboard and put it on the coffee

table in front of her. He also produced a lighter. It seemed very civilised to be smoking indoors, and in such surroundings. It felt like lighting up in a museum. She blew the smoke away from Herbert.

'I can't have you smoking alone,' said Professor Papavoine. He lit a pipe. Aurélie loved the smell of pipe tobacco. It reminded her of her grandfather.

It was a very comfortable sofa, and as she smoked on she felt her eyes going again. She wondered where his wife was. Changing into her sex gear perhaps, or quietly fuming somewhere. She could well have been bluffing about how pleased she would be to meet her. Aurélie thought back to their conversation; there was every possibility that her voice had been dripping with sarcasm. Maybe she was sharpening an axe, ready to behead the girl she was sure was trying to steal her husband. Then she appeared, all smiles and warm greetings. Automatically, Aurélie put her cigarette in the ashtray and stood to greet her.

Professor Papavoine's wife kissed her, but Aurélie felt no sexual charge. It seemed she was just being friendly, and putting her at her ease. She was all *It's so nice to meet you*, and *Please call me Liliane*, and *I hope I didn't sound brusque on the phone, but I'm always a little perturbed when I don't know who I'm talking to* and *Can I get you anything?* She was youthful for her age, slim, ash blonde and very well dressed. Aurélie felt crumpled and red-eyed in comparison.

With both Papavoines there, she said what she knew she had to say. 'I'm sorry to disappoint you, but I don't want to have sex with you. No threesome, OK?' She looked at Professor Papavoine. 'Not even a twosome. It's nothing personal; it's just not my thing. All I want to do is sleep. And that's not *sleep*. I mean *actual* sleep. Oh, and just so you know,' she addressed Professor Papavoine's wife, 'there's nothing going on here.' She pointed at the professor.

Professor Papavoine and his wife looked at one another, then burst into laughter. 'You were right,' said Professor Papavoine's wife. 'She *did* think that.'

Professor Papavoine looked embarrassed, but amused at the same time. 'I'm very sorry, Mademoiselle Renard,' he said. 'You'll have to forgive my total incompetence when it comes to life in general. There's no need to worry – we're not trying to have sex with you.'

'Why not? What's wrong with me?' They laughed, and Aurélie was surprised at having been able to joke while only partially conscious. The release of tension from the atmosphere was palpable. 'But seriously, that's a relief. So do you hand out cards to all your students?'

'Er, no. Please let me explain.' The professor's embarrassed look returned.

'You can tell me later. I'll sleep first, and give you a few more hours to work on your innocent explanation.' She remembered the conversation she had been rehearsing as she had lain awake all night, and returned to her script. 'And because it's all your fault,' she said to him, 'you'll be taking the baby until I wake up.'

'It's all my fault, is it?'

'Yes.'

'What is?'

'Everything. Him, for a start.' She pointed at the baby. 'He's not mine, by the way. I'll explain when I'm awake. But maybe you'll be able to work it out for yourself.'

'OK, I'll get thinking.'

'He's so cute,' said Madame Papavoine, picking him up and bouncing him.

Aurélie agreed. She tried to imagine how her week would have gone if Herbert had been a plain baby, or lacking in personality. She wondered whether she would have cared about him less. She hoped not, but she suspected she probably would have. She would never know.

'What's he called?' asked Madame Papavoine.

'Herbert.'

'*Air-bear?*'

'No. *Herbert.*'

'Is he English?'

'Does he look English to you?' Aurélie was on autopilot.

Madame Papavoine examined the baby, then shrugged. 'Maybe a little, around the chin.'

'But never mind that now,' said Aurélie. 'I'll tell you everything when I wake up.' She ran through the other points she had intended to raise with them. 'Oh yes,' she said. 'Before I forget, one more question – you're not child molesters, are you?' She had decided that they didn't look or act like child molesters, but she felt she had better ask anyway.

'No,' said Madame Papavoine, 'we're not interested in anything of that nature. We'll take great care of *Air-bear* . . . *Hair-bear* . . .'

'*Herbert.*'

'We'll take great care of . . .' She closed her eyes in concentration. '. . . Herbert. Now you come with me, I'll pop you into bed, and you can tell us all about it when you wake up. Don't you worry about your . . .' She gave the baby a squeeze. '. . . incredibly cute little boy.'

'Well, as I said, he's not *my* little boy. I'm . . .' On

reflection, she didn't want them to do too much speculating about his provenance and get suspicious and call the police, so she used what was becoming her signature line. '. . . I'm looking after him for a friend.'

'Whoever's he is, we're going to have great fun together.'

Madame Papavoine led Aurélie through corridors into a small but immaculate guest bedroom at the back of the apartment. She told her to hang on for a minute, then came back with a large glass of water, which she placed on the bedside table. There was an en suite shower room. 'Towels here,' she pointed, and Aurélie could tell from looking at them that they were so much softer and fluffier than the laundry-hardened ones she had at home. 'There's a robe on the back of the door. You sleep as long as you like, and don't you worry about Herbert. Is there anything else I can get you?'

Aurélie shook her head. 'Thank you,' she said. 'We'll go as soon as I wake up. I just need to get some sleep.'

'I understand.'

Madame Papavoine left the room, and for the first time in days Aurélie was alone. She closed the curtains. They were thick, and the room was now almost pitch dark. Madame Papavoine seemed so nice. Her blue eyes sparkled, and her smile lit up the room. Even Professor Papavoine seemed OK. He was a lot less sleazy than he had become in her mind. She was ready to believe that he hadn't been trying to seduce her, that it had all been a big misunderstanding. She would unravel everything when she was able to think straight again.

She supposed she ought to have a shower, but first she would try the bed for comfort. She lay down. It was just right. She fell asleep.

* * *

225

In the living room, Professor and Madame Papavoine looked at the boy as he lay on their sofa. He was grinning up at them. For a long while, neither of them spoke.

Professor Papavoine broke the silence. He turned to his wife, his face drained of expression, and his voice little more than a whisper. 'Though I am ashamed of it now,' he said, 'I had begun to lose faith. I had been starting to wonder whether this day would ever come.' He returned his gaze to the baby as he continued to address his wife. 'We must not waste time. I shall prepare the altar, you fetch the knife and ready my robes.' He looked upwards, to the ceiling and beyond, and closed his eyes. He raised his hands high. 'Thank you, oh great one,' he said, addressing an unseen higher power. 'Thank you for bringing us the boy child.' He fell to one knee, his arms still raised but his eyes closed and his head bowed. 'We shall do as we have been bidden.'

He was knocked out of this apparent state of religious ecstasy by his wife, who jabbed him sharply in the ribs with her knuckles. She couldn't stop herself from laughing, though. 'Enough of that, Papavoine,' she said. 'Sometimes I think it's just as well we never had one of our own. You'd have scarred the poor thing for life with your *jokes*. I'm still not quite sure how you've managed to land us with a baby for the day, but this is a big responsibility. Now, let's get the toys out.'

She pulled out the hamper containing the things that they kept for visits from their grandnieces and grand-nephews, and started to sift through it. She found a plastic battery-powered tortoise, which, when pressed, played ear-splitting electronic renditions of nursery rhymes. Herbert loved it.

Professor Papavoine looked on. 'So what do you think of our Mademoiselle Renard?' he asked his wife.

'She seems very nice, if a little unhinged. Let's hope it's just the sleep deprivation. I wonder if we'll ever find out what her visit is all about.'

'We'll have to cancel lunch with the Thibodeaus,' he sighed.

'What a shame.' She hid her relief. She couldn't stand the Thibodeaus, and had been dreading this lunch ever since it had been arranged, just as she had dreaded every appointment they had ever made with the Thibodeaus. She looked at Herbert. He was much better company than they would ever be, and her relief grew into elation. She was so happy at getting her day back that she could no longer contain herself. 'Tell you what, let's not reschedule.'

'But they're your friends.'

'No, they're not, they're *your* friends.'

'I thought it was *you* who liked them. I can't stand them.'

'Neither can I!'

'Why have you never said anything?'

'Why have *you* never said anything?'

They fell about laughing at the realisation that for over thirty years each had been stoically enduring these people for the other's sake. Once they had even gone on holiday with them, spending an entire week on a failed hiking trip, sheltering from the rain inside a Bavarian log cabin, each Papavoine believing themselves to be the personification of self-sacrifice as they tolerated the other's interminable, humourless friends. They were both drunk on the relief they felt at the thought that they would never have to see them again.

Madame Papavoine had an idea. 'Instead of meeting them four or five times a year, let's have four or five Thibodeau days – days when we do something we wouldn't otherwise have done. Something that would be more interesting than spending time with them.'

'Eating my own kneecaps would be preferable to spending time with the Thibodeaus.'

Her plan began to take shape. 'For our first Thibodeau day, let's go to Euro Disney.'

'Yes!' cried Professor Papavoine. 'You're a genius, Liliane! I knew I married you for a reason. I've always wanted to go to Euro Disney – I'm going to have my picture taken with Goofy. Fuck the Thibodeaus!'

'Language.'

'Oh. Yes. Sorry, Herbert, I was getting carried away.'

The baby looked up at them, gleefully clutching his excruciating tortoise.

'You are a highly valued visitor,' continued the Professor. 'If it hadn't been for you, we might have been stuck with those boring bastards for the rest of our lives.'

'Papavoine! Watch your tongue.'

'Oh. Yes. Sorry again, Herbert.'

Herbert acknowledged this apology by pulling a face. Then there was a squelch, and a smell.

'Your turn,' said Madame Papavoine.

Professor Papavoine emptied Herbert's bag on to the floor, and picked out everything he would need to change a nappy. As he got ready to wipe the child's bottom, he found himself recalling his unexpected meeting with Le Machine. It all seemed quite serendipitous.

XXI

The arts editor of *L'Univers* always rose late on a Saturday. His butler was under strict instruction to leave him in peace until precisely noon, at which point he was to bring him his silver breakfast salver and, beside it, an ironed copy of the paper.

When the butler had made his delivery to the four-poster bed, accepted his customary scolding and left the oak-panelled room, the arts editor of *L'Univers* chewed on a chunk of croissant, and picked out his supplement. He could see at once that something was not quite right. But what was it? He moved the paper around, looking at it from a number of angles, and at last he found the offending detail. It was the headline. For some reason it now read: *The End of Life?* Where had the question mark come from? First thing on Monday morning he would track that sub-editor down and have their guts for garters.

He was eager to find out how Jean-Didier Delacroix had skewered his subject. He knew he could trust him to have done it with a delicious deftness, and no little humour. That was why he had chosen him for this assignment.

He began to read. *Pure Jean-Didier Delacroix*, he thought. *This is why we pay you so much, you little scamp*. But as he neared the end and realised what his chief arts correspondent had done, he inhaled a chunk of croissant in shock, and began to choke. Turning purple, he reached out and rang his golden bell, and moments later his butler glided in, and after a few hard but futile white-gloved pats on his back, followed by a far more fruitful Heimlich manoeuvre, the errant bolus was dislodged.

'Save me faster next time, you ghastly little man,' wheezed the arts editor of *L'Univers*. 'Now get me my telephone.'

The butler left the room, and returned moments later, wheeling a gigantic and ancient telephone on a silver trolley. He plugged it into the wall, and went away.

Jean-Didier Delacroix was also in bed, and like his superior he was reading the arts supplement of *L'Univers*. His was a little crumpled. He had always felt sure that one day *he* would be the arts editor, and he would have a butler to iron it for him, but now, for the first time in his life, he wondered whether that would happen. Everything seemed upside down.

He had woken in a panic, sure that he had made the biggest mistake of his career. As he thought back to the evening before, he felt he must have been having some kind of breakdown. Was there any way he could really have written what he had?

He stared at the paper, and began his fourth read-through of the morning. It was pure Jean-Didier Delacroix: perceptive, passionate, wise and grammatically beyond reproach, and it was all suffused with his trademark wit. And yet it seemed to go against everything he had ever believed in; he felt as if he had entered a new world, a world in which the old certainties had been swept away.

His bedside telephone rang. He knew who it would be. His girlfriend was lying beside him, naked but for the slices of cucumber on her eyes, and she tutted loudly at the disturbance. He held the receiver to his ear. It was a deafening voice.

'*De-la-crrrrrrooooooooiiiiiixxxxxx . . .*'

'Good morning,' he said, swallowing nervously. 'So you've read my piece?'

Jean-Didier Delacroix had never had the intention of stitching up Le Machine. He had not planned to go in and use the time-honoured journalistic tactic of making friendly conversation and engaging him in lively banter, all the while feeding him just enough rope to hang himself. No, he was going to go straight on the offensive, putting him on the back foot from the start.

He had been ushered into a small room backstage in the seedy little cinema, and come face-to-face with the man. He was wearing a white towelling robe and a distracted expression. There were angry red marks where until minutes earlier his eyebrows had been, and his head and face were barbershop smooth.

Jean-Didier Delacroix looked him in the eye, switched on his Dictaphone and, without so much as introducing himself, began the interview: 'So,' he said, fixing

Le Machine with an ice-cold glare, 'how does it feel to be a living joke?'

When it was over, Le Machine felt he had not fared particularly well in the interview, but that he had not disgraced himself either. This first question had taken him by surprise, but he had not considered it unfair. He had thought for a moment before giving an answer about how it was understandable that most people would see him that way, bearing in mind the way his work was presented in the media. 'If all I did was take my clothes off and go to the toilet in a bottle, then it would be right for people to regard me as a joke. But anyone who comes to *Life* will find that there is so much more to it than that.'

'For example?'

Le Machine went into a spiel about the technical side of *Life*: praising the work of his sound designer, whom he saw as an equal collaborator, and the importance of the lighting and the craftsmanship involved in the glassware.

Jean-Didier Delacroix yawned, and did not ask to be pardoned. 'Loudspeakers, light bulbs and novelty glassware,' he said. 'Fascinating.'

Other questions followed. Most of them Le Machine had anticipated, though he had expected them to have been posed in a less combative manner.

You have said that you feel you were rejected by Paris, so what makes you think that Paris is going to want you now?

Apart from the inevitable perverts, what sort of audience are you expecting?

Do you honestly believe that what you do deserves so

much attention when compared to work of a less sensa-
tionalist and scatological nature?

And so it went on, for around twenty minutes. He had
pat replies for most of the questions, all of them civil
but bland, and was soon tired of the sound of his own
voice. Jean-Didier Delacroix showed no sign of interest
in anything Le Machine said, and Le Machine could tell
this, but he stayed calm and answered the questions as
efficiently as he was able, though never to his interrogator's satisfaction. To him it was just another interview,
and all interviews were ordeals of one kind or another.
This time they had sent an attack dog, but that was OK.
It wasn't the first time. He even had some admiration for
the man; at least there was no bullshit about him.

Jean-Didier Delacroix kept going, waiting for Le
Machine to slip up, to give the line that he could quote,
the one that would reveal him as a fool. So far he had
only been a bore.

Time was running out, and Jean-Didier Delacroix knew
he had to start wrapping things up. Out came the big
question, disguised as a sardonic throwaway line: *So*, he
yawned, *what is the meaning of* Life?

Le Machine knew that this was where, if he wasn't
careful, he could let himself down. He was just about
satisfied with the answer he gave, but his interrogator
was clearly not.

Jean-Didier Delacroix was all for egalitarianism, just so
long as he didn't have to be involved, but Le Machine had
taken things too far with his suggestion that everyone who
came into the room was welcome to interpret the piece
in their own way, and that he didn't want his words to
influence them, to cloud their minds. Jean-Didier Delacroix

knew for sure that the general public – road sweepers, Métro drivers, schoolteachers, office workers – could not be trusted to draw intelligent conclusions about a piece of art by themselves, and for the artist to refuse to offer them direction was a dereliction of duty. But then again, this wasn't art, and if people were stupid enough to spend money coming to this show, then they deserved to be left floundering as they tried to come up with their own interpretations.

Why are you so reluctant to talk about the theory behind your performance?

For the first time in an interview Le Machine acknowledged that he was being evasive, that there was a theory, and even a story, behind it. He didn't want to explain his work, he re-emphasised, because to do so would be to strip away any magic it might have. If an artist needs to explain their work, he said, then they have failed, and if they choose to explain it then they choose to spoil it for people, denying them the possibility of connecting with the piece in their own way. He had started to feel like a dog chasing its tail. 'It comes back to that word again,' he said. '*Magic*. If you are an artist then you must believe you have it, otherwise why would you bother? And if you have it why would you want to snuff it out by picking it to pieces?'

'And you believe that you are an artist?'

'Yes.'

'And you truly believe that your work has . . .' he spat the word, '*magic?*'

'Yes, I do. But you are welcome to disagree, Monsieur Delacroix.'

'As if I need your blessing to disagree with you.' Jean-

Didier Delacroix smiled for the first time. It was not a pleasant sight.

Le Machine was starting to disagree with himself. The words had been coming out as they always had, but he wasn't sure he believed them any more, and he had given so many similar answers in so many interviews that they sounded to him like platitudes. The encounter had descended to the verge of quarrelling, but there was every possibility that the reporter was right. Maybe there would be no magic. Maybe there never had been, and Paris would be the place where he would find out that there really was no more to *Life* than a naked man shitting on stage.

'So what are you going to give me, then? This is your only interview, and I've got nothing – just a load of drivel about microphones and thermostats and some repetitive whining about how terrible it is to have to answer questions in interviews.' Jean-Didier Delacroix folded his arms and waited.

'OK.' Le Machine thought. A part of him wanted to tell this strange and furious man what it was all about, to reveal the true reason why he did what he did. After all, he had already told one person that day, and it had felt good to unburden himself. That had been in confidence though, and he knew he mustn't tell the same story to a journalist. And even if he was to, they only had a minute of interview time left. It had taken him a long time to tell the story to Professor Papavoine, and that had been the reason for his late arrival at the venue. It certainly wasn't something that could be dispatched in a sound bite. He stopped wavering, stuck by his principles and kept the story to himself.

He always liked to make sure he gave reporters something, though, even the ones he didn't care for; it would be bad manners to send them away with nothing to work with. In his younger days he would give them a rant about his rejection of Paris, or how he had embraced his position as an outcast from the art establishment. Those days were gone, though. Today the angle he gave the reporter was straightforward: 'After this run, I have no intention of presenting *Life* again.'

'So this is the end?'

'Yes, I believe it will be.'

He expected the reporter to ask him what his plans were. But he didn't. Instead he switched off his Dictaphone.

The two men stood facing one another.

'I am afraid I am unable to wish you well for your show,' said Jean-Didier Delacroix. 'I had thought you were a con artist, an old-fashioned grifter, but now I know you're not. It's a shame really, because I would have had some respect for you if you were simply a scam merchant. There is an art to that sort of behaviour, after all. You have a real sincerity about you though, don't you? I think you truly believe that what you are doing has great artistic worth. You're deluding yourself, of course.'

Le Machine looked him in the eye. 'Thank you for your time,' he said. 'I hope you have enough material for your article.'

The moment Jean-Didier Delacroix had left, there was a knock at the door. His manager introduced Le Machine to Doctor Élise Rousset, and left them alone. He did as he was asked, and took off his robe. Once again he found himself naked in front of a woman he had only just met.

XXII

Lucien sat with the Akiyamas as they finished their lunch in an old-style bistro. Already that day they had been to the Catacombs, and now they were looking for a way to fill the afternoon. Lucien had bought a copy of *L'Univers*, and he pulled out the arts supplement, to find out what was going on around the city.

On the front cover was a photograph of Le Machine. He didn't think he would be recommending his show to the Akiyamas. He had seen the posters and heard a lot of chatter about the man, and like a lot of people he had already come to the conclusion that he was a pretentious attention-seeker who thought that just because he called what he did *art* that it suddenly made him an artist. And what made it worse was that he was exactly the kind of pretentious attention-seeker that girls are suckers for, all moody expressions and meticulously tended musculature.

He smiled when he saw that the profile was by Jean-Didier Delacroix. Lucien enjoyed reading his work; for all his pomposity, he did have a brilliant mind, and he was always entertaining. He was going to rip Le Machine to shreds.

As usual, the piece was as much about Jean-Didier Delacroix as it was about his subject: it started with a description of what he had eaten for lunch, then moved on to a detailed report on the length and texture of his girlfriend's legs, which he followed with an account of an altercation he had had with a valet at a top hotel. He had, of course, cut the valet down to size. It wasn't until the sixth paragraph that he even mentioned Le Machine: *The man who has famously, and in the name of 'art', gone to the toilet on stages around the world.*

Then he spent two paragraphs ruminating about a forthcoming trip to Vienna, before embarking on a short and savagely comical passage about his backstage meeting with Le Machine, during which his subject had given very little away, presumably because there was very little to talk about. It had seemed to Jean-Didier Delacroix that he had attempted to create a reticent, enigmatic persona in order to deflect attention away from the simple fact that he had nothing much to say. Lucien laughed at that; in his days of dating non-Japanese women he had lost plenty of girlfriends to people like Le Machine – empty vessels hiding behind a facade of artistic mystery. And then, Jean-Didier Delacroix reported, the star of the show had announced that this was likely to be his final presentation of *Life*: *He looked at me intently, evidently expecting me to ask what he planned to do next. I simply did not care. It took all my self-control not to laugh in his face and wish him good riddance.*

Lucien was loving this. Le Machine would be reviewed all over the place, but it was Jean-Didier Delacroix that everybody would be looking to. Piece by piece, he was tearing *Life* down. Muscle-boy would be a failure in Paris, and girls the world over would stop fancying men like him, and start taking an interest in slightly gawky interpreters instead.

The article moved on to a vivid, riotous and wildly snobbish account of Jean-Didier Delacroix's experience of standing in the auditorium amid the kind of people whose idea of a great way to spend a Friday night was to pay money to stare at a naked man while hoping they'll get to see him go to the toilet. And then the lights went down.

Jean-Didier Delacroix confined his praise to the final paragraph. When the stage lights had come on, and the sound of a human body pulsed through the room, he had been stunned to find himself profoundly moved. In a moment, he had understood why Le Machine had been so reluctant to talk about his work, for to try to explain *Life* would be to try to explain life. It was all there, in front of him, and it was within him too, and he felt a oneness with the people around him, and that was something that had never happened to him before; he had never made a secret of his feelings of almost superhuman superiority to people who happened to be around him, but now there he was, feeling a oneness with a group of strangers about whom only moments before he had been sculpting a series of derisory *bons mots*. He had never been quite so aware of himself as a human being, and this was a feeling both incredible and unsettling. *The religious will point to* Life *as being sure proof of God's presence in all of us; the atheists will point to it as an illustration of the human body as an amazing bag of chemicals. But don't listen to them*, he wrote. *Don't listen to anybody, not even me, except as I implore you to go. And let us all hope that* Le Machine *does not mean what he says, that this is not the end of* Life.

Well, thought Lucien, *that was unexpected.* Jean-Didier Delacroix had made him want to buy a ticket. He still wasn't going to recommend *Life* to the Akiyamas though.

'Ah,' said Madame Akiyama, noticing the photograph on the newspaper. 'It's that man. He came to Tokyo. Akiko went to see him, and said he was very good. Lucien, could you book us tickets for today?'

'Are you sure? Do you know what he does?'

'Yes, he takes all his clothes off and does his business into a bottle.'

'Well, if that's what you really want to see . . .'

'Oh yes,' she said. 'It'll be fun.'

Monsieur Akiyama shook his head, resigned to his fate. He had lost control of his life, but he wasn't going to let it get him down.

There was a science to selling tickets for *Life*. Each one came with an allocated time slot for admission, but once inside, the ticket holder could stay as long as they wanted. As no food or drink was allowed in the auditorium, the organisers banked on people getting hungry and thirsty, then drifting away. In the previous stagings, the average length of stay had been between one hour and forty-three minutes (London) and two hours and four minutes (Tokyo), though some people stayed for much longer, even sneaking off to the toilets to eat discreetly hidden snacks. One boy in São Paolo had stayed for four days. He hadn't been quite as furtive as he had thought, and had become something of a celebrity among the crew; when he finally left they surprised him with a free pass so he could come and go as he wished for the remainder of the run.

Following fairly predictable patterns, they were able to sell several thousand tickets a day. For the Paris run they were aiming to sell a total of two hundred thousand, at between ten and fifteen euros a time. They saw no sense in anticipating a sell-out. Historically there had been most demand on weekends and in the evenings, and at off-peak times it was usually possible to simply walk up and pay on the door. In the early hours of the morning the room would often be quite empty, but there would always be at least a few people there, watching the naked man as he slept, and listening to him as he breathed, as his heart beat and his stomach gurgled.

Lucien tried calling the ticket hotline, but he couldn't get through. Following the piece in *L'Univers*, their lines had jammed. He borrowed Madame Akiyama's smartphone and checked their website, but there was no availability until eight o'clock on the Tuesday morning, and they would be on their way to the airport by then. People were so impatient to find out what it was all about that even the graveyard slots were full for the coming couple of days.

'I'm so disappointed,' she said. 'Maybe, Lucien, you would be so kind as to make things better by taking your clothes off right now, standing on the table and . . .' She picked up their empty water bottle and held it out to him.

Lucien laughed, and Monsieur Akiyama looked startled. He was beginning to wonder who it was he had married all

241

those years ago. And then he smiled, because he couldn't help but be amused by her bawdy humour.

'We could send a photo to Akiko,' she teased.

Lucien no longer felt like crying at the mention of Akiko's name. He was even starting to wonder whether his love for her had run its course.

Madame Akiyama wasn't going to let the lack of tickets for *Life* ruin her day. They settled on a trip up the Eiffel Tower instead. It had to be done. 'And after that, where should we eat our dinner?'

'I know a good floating restaurant,' answered Lucien.

XXIII

Aurélie was woken by the smell of cooking. She had a long shower, using the very nice soap and shampoo that the Papavoines left for their guests, then she dried herself on a towel that was just as soft as it looked. She put on the white bathrobe. There were white slippers for her too. She felt cleaner and dryer than she ever did after showering in her own home. She looked at herself in the mirror. She was human again, and she felt an urgent need to see Herbert, to make sure he was OK. She opened the door, and stepped into the corridor.

She followed the sound of laughter to the master bedroom, where she found him lying on the bed being amused by Madame Papavoine, who was repeatedly covering her head with a pillow case before whipping it off to reveal a different funny face each time. She noticed Aurélie, and was all *How did you sleep?* and *Was the bed comfortable?* and *Are you sure you're ready to get up, because I can take Herbert for longer if you'd like?* and *Please, you really must call me Liliane,* and *You must stay for dinner – we've set a place for you.*

Professor Papavoine was a good cook, and Aurélie, still in her robe, started on her soup, pleased to be eating a proper meal after days of grazing on whatever was close at hand. Herbert sat in his high chair, eating peas with his fingers, banging his spoon against the tray and squawking. Newly bathed, he was doing a good job of making himself sticky again. Then his eyes crossed, and he put down his spoon and started looking very serious. Madame Papavoine picked him up and whisked him away, and a minute later she walked back in, reporting that he was taking a nap.

'I've been meaning to ask,' she said, 'how did he get that nasty scab he has just here?' She ran her finger along the point where her shoulder met her neck. There was no trace of accusation in her voice, nothing to suggest that she wasn't just making general conversation.

Aurélie didn't want to hide anything from the Papavoines; they had been so good to her, and to Herbert.

'I shot him,' she said.

Professor and Madame Papavoine froze, Madame Papavoine with her finger still pointing at her shoulder, and Professor Papavoine with his soup spoon halfway to his mouth.

'But he's going to be OK,' Aurélie reassured them.

They stared at her.

'Everything's gone a little bit out of control,' she said, and once again it all caught up with her, and she buried her face in her hands.

Madame Papavoine unfroze. She walked up to Aurélie and put her arm around her shoulder. 'What's going on, Aurélie?' she asked.

Aurélie pulled herself together and told them the bare bones of the story, from throwing the stone in the square to being given the baby, and then being given a gun by a well-meaning friend, to Herbert being snatched away from her by the old lady in the Place des Vosges, to the rescue by a mystery man, to the visit from an unnamed ex, to the gun going off in her hand, to the sleepless night.

'And that's why I came to you. I had nowhere else to turn.'

'Even though I'm a sex pest, desperate to get my hands on young flesh.'

'Exactly.' The mood had lightened as Aurélie's story went on, and they were joking again. 'And since you're already involved, I thought I might as well foist myself on you.'

'Ah yes, I've been meaning to ask – so why *is* this all my fault?'

'Well, maybe it's not *all* your fault. The shooting Herbert part I managed completely by myself. But how I got Herbert in the first place . . .'

'Go on.'

'Well, do you remember our tutorial?'

Professor Papavoine nodded. He remembered aspects of it very well, particularly the extraordinary feeling he had experienced when she had walked into the room, and the way he had almost been blinded by her smile.

'So you remember my proposal?'

'Er . . . no. That part, I'm afraid I don't. Not really.'

'You don't?'

'Well, maybe some dribs and drabs . . . something about archery? Or darts?' He ran his fingers across his stubble. 'I have a confession to make, Mademoiselle Renard: I never pay a great deal of attention to my students' proposals.'

'What? Why not?'

'Because they're irrelevant. A piece can have the highest concept known to man, but still be total rubbish. Or an artist can have an idea that they can't even articulate, but which turns out to be a work of beauty. It's all hot air: all that matters is whether or not the work they produce is any good.'

'So when someone sits in your office and tells you they're going to throw a stone into a crowd to find a random subject for their project, you just wave it through as if it's a perfectly reasonable idea?'

'Ah, that was why you were throwing the stone?' He shrugged. 'It's not history's most sensible idea, is it? But if you say I approved it, then I must have done.'

'I remember exactly what you said. You said, *That sounds fine.* You told me, in your capacity as professor, that throwing a stone into a crowd in the name of art would be *fine.*'

'That's what I say to everybody. *Fine*, I say. Everything is *fine*. But I see your point.' He puffed his cheeks out, then made a kind of clicking sound with his tongue. 'I did give you *carte blanche* to hurl a projectile at a baby, didn't I?' He sighed. 'All this has happened under the watchful eye of the department. I shall probably lose my career over this, Mademoiselle Renard, but that's no more than I deserve. I should have done my job. I should have listened more closely.'

'No, you won't lose your career. I'm not going to tell on you, and as long as I get Herbert back to his mother safe and sound at nine twenty-two on Wednesday morning, which I will, everything's going to be OK. Who's going to know?'

They sat in contemplation for a while. So,' said Aurélie, 'come assessment time I could have presented you with any work at all and you would never have known whether or not it had anything to do with my proposal?'

'Yes.'

'OK then, I'm going to change my project.'

'That doesn't sound like a bad idea.'

'Would it be OK for me to scrub the mixed-media aspect of it?'

'Please, for God's sake, get rid of it.'

'My heart was never really in it, to be honest. All I really wanted to do was draw pictures. I only came in with a big concept because I heard the other students outside your office, and they had all these fancy ideas, and I thought you would laugh at me or kick me out of college if I just said I was going to draw some things that took my fancy, even though I wanted to draw them really well. And that's when I came up with the stone idea, right at the last minute.'

Professor Papavoine laughed. That was the second time in as many days that he had heard something very like this. 'That is all I ever want to hear from my students,' he said, 'that they want to do something really well. I hear such nonsense sometimes that it makes me despair.'

'Then despair no more. I now know what I really want to do. I'm going to do an enormous drawing of Herbert. A really huge one, on a really big piece of paper, three metres square. And if anyone ever asks me what it's all about, I'll look at them as if they're stupid and tell them it's just a giant drawing of a baby.'

'Excellent news. That sounds fine. I mean it *actually* sounds fine this time. Just one thing . . .'

'What's that?'

'This picture . . .' He looked at her intently. 'Don't just do this drawing really well. I want you to do it really, really, really well. I want you to make it brilliant – the best thing you have ever done.'

'It's a deal.'

'Oh, and one more thing.'

'Yes?'

'You and Herbert are staying with us until Wednesday.'

'That's so nice of you. But I didn't bring any spare clothes. My bag was full of Herbert's stuff.' She had been staggered by just how filthy clothes can get when there's a baby around. 'I've got to go back to my place to do laundry and that kind of thing.'

Madame Papavoine came to the rescue. 'We'll wash the clothes you came in, and I've got plenty that will fit you. And while you were sleeping I went out and got a couple of outfits for Herbert.'

Aurélie felt like crying. They were so nice.

After dinner, Liliane told Aurélie that if she called her Madame Papavoine one more time she would shoot her in the neck, then she took her to her enormous walk-in closet, and together they picked out some outfits for her stay. Liliane was determined that Aurélie would not look older than her years, and between them they picked out a pile of clothes that suited her.

*   *   *

Meanwhile, at Euro Disney, the Thibodeaus had finished their second ride on *Indiana Jones et le Temple du Péril*.

'That was most exhilarating,' said an unsmiling Monsieur Thibodeau. 'Your friends cancelling on us at the last minute turned out for the best. We would never have come here otherwise.'

'*My* friends? They're *your* friends.'

'*My* friends? I find them quite exhausting company, with all their joking, and their talk about cultural matters. To be honest with you, I've only ever put up with them for your sake.'

'But I've only ever put up with them for *your* sake.'

'Well, there you are.'

They both gazed into the middle distance for a while as they contemplated their situation.

'Do you remember Bavaria?' asked Monsieur Thibodeau.

Madame Thibodeau shuddered at the recollection of their week in a cabin with the Papavoines. Their continual attempts at lifting the atmosphere with conversation and games had tested both the Thibodeaus' patience to the limit, but neither had said a word at the time, each not wanting the other to think they were intolerant of their friends.

'Oh well,' said her husband, 'it's over now. We'll never call them again, and if they call us we'll just tell them we're too busy to meet up. Would you like one more go on *Indiana Jones et le Temple du Péril*?'

'No,' she said. 'Let's move on. I want to dance with Mickey Mouse.'

Aurélie emerged from Madame Papavoine's large closet in a grey knee-length dress. She felt as if she was about to go to a fancy restaurant, rather than spend an evening sitting around indoors, but she didn't mind. Apart from her little black number the night before, which didn't really count, she hadn't worn a dress for ages. It fitted her perfectly, and she felt as if it had transferred some of Madame Papavoine's elegance to her. It was a good feeling. She decided to wear dresses more often, like Sylvie.

Herbert was stirring from his nap. Aurélie picked him up, and they all went through to the living room, where Professor Papavoine was watching the final item on the news. It was the art show that everybody was talking about.

Television cameras were not allowed inside *Life*, so for visuals they had to make do with footage of the queues at the venue's box office and a montage of promotional photographs of Le Machine. The newsreader reported that the night before, Le Machine had ordered wine after he had finished his beer, and that after a six-hour sleep he had woken with what appeared to be a hangover. Then he had lifted some glass weights, and used a special cloth to collect his sweat, which he then dripped into a bottle. He had a breakfast of cereal and milk, walked up and down a lot with a thoughtful expression, and had a salad for lunch. The very latest reports suggested that he had ordered a medium-sized portion of spaghetti Bolognese for his evening meal, but no alcohol to go with it. The consensus of opinion seemed to be that he was on a health kick following his binge of the night before.

The report kept the big news, what everybody really wanted to know, until last: Le Machine had now done nine wees, but had yet to do a poo. The newsreader delivered this last fact in a critical manner, as if Le Machine had assured everyone who had bought a ticket that they would get to see him evacuate his bowels, and that he had reneged on this deal. He was using the tone of voice he normally reserved for surrounded gunmen who had agreed to give up their weapon, but had so far failed to do so.

Professor Papavoine found this all very amusing. He looked away from the television, and saw his wife and Aurélie standing together, with a very lively Herbert in Aurélie's arms. They could have been three generations of the same family.

His eyes seemed to mist up. 'Excuse me,' he said, quietly, and he left the room.

Aurélie watched the concluding summary of the headlines. She had been in a bubble for days, and it was disorientating to be reminded that there was a world out there, and everything was going on just as it always did, as if she had never thrown a stone at a baby. Furious farmers were blocking roads with their tractors, the police were searching for a killer, and President Bruni-Sarkozy had felt the need to call yet another press conference to deny that he was planning a full-scale invasion of Spain. *As much as I would love to invade Spain*, he was saying, *I have had a long conversation with my Finance Minister, with whom, incidentally, I am not having an affair, and she has told me that with the current economic climate and the doubt hanging over the future of the euro, it is not a viable option for France at the present time.* The assembled reporters groaned with disappointment, and he gave his trademark *What can I do?* shrug. His wife was by his side, wearing a perfect dress as she smouldered into the cameras.

A few moments later Professor Papavoine was back,

just as upbeat as he had been before, and clutching a Monopoly box.

'Right,' he said, 'as soon as the boy's down for the night we're playing this. So who can remember the rules? I know I can't.'

XXIV

The boat had moored after its trip up and down the river, and the diners were disembarking. Sylvie's final table was clear, and her double shift was over at last. As always on a Saturday, she had made a small fortune in tips, and she had decided that this would be one of the jobs she kept on as she took her certificates in child care. She was hoping to hang on to her apartment, and in a good week this day alone would cover most of her rent. With all her tables clear, she joined the Akiyamas and Lucien. She fervently embraced Madame Akiyama, and then Monsieur Akiyama, who didn't know quite how to respond. Then she kissed Lucien and, at their invitation, sat down with them.

Toshiro's parents had been served by one of her colleagues, and as she had watched them from across the room she had decided that they needed to know every-

thing about her. She didn't want them to be shocked by
finding out her history at a later date. She was going to
give them a crash course in Sylvie Dupont, the good and
the bad, and then she would see if they still wanted her
to marry their son.

An hour later they were still there, the last diners left on
the boat, as the cleaners were starting to put chairs on
tables. Madame Akiyama was weeping into her napkin.
She had heard about Sylvie's parents, about her stealing
and her drinking, and about her army of unhappy exes,
and how hard she had worked to overcome her difficulties. Sylvie had finished with the tale of the two young
men who had died. If they wanted to keep Toshiro away
from her, she told them, she would be heartbroken but
she would understand.

At Madame Akiyama's request, she sang the song she
had sung at the unfortunate boys' gravesides. It was a
simple tune that was believed to date from the fifteenth
century. As she sang, Lucien did not translate the words,
which were about a bird that had hurt its wing, fallen
from the flock and perished slowly on the ground, but
the Akiyamas were touched to their cores by the purity of
Sylvie's voice and the melancholy beauty of the melody.
Even Monsieur Akiyama looked close to tears.

She hoped with all her heart that her potted autobiog-
raphy hadn't put them off her. Then she realised something, and felt ashamed. She had been so wrapped up in her
own love story that she hadn't been doing nearly enough
to help Lucien's cause. She steered the conversation away
from herself, and asked the Akiyamas what they had been
doing that day. She made sure every comment she made

reflected well on their interpreter, so they might see him as a potential match for the lovely Akiko. She had grown very fond of Lucien, and was really hoping that he would one day be her brother-in-law.

But Lucien had as good as forgotten about Akiko Akiyama. With every tale of heartache and triumph from Sylvie's life, the girl from Funabashi had drifted further and further from his heart. He knew he was staring into the abyss, but he couldn't find the strength to look away. Nobody who was watching him as he interpreted the conversation would have thought that anything was amiss, but in the back of his mind a song was going round and round: a song about a bird that had hurt its wing, fallen from the flock and perished slowly on the ground.

DIMANCHE

XXV

A urélie had no idea what the time was. She had gone to bed shortly after storming to victory at Monopoly at around midnight. The baby had been tucked up in a travel cot behind a screen in the corner of the Papavoines' bedroom, and Liliane had told Aurélie she could sleep as long as she needed to, that they would take care of Herbert until she rose. She found her phone, and saw that it was half past eleven. Until Herbert had come into her life she hadn't realised it was possible to be so tired.

She dressed in another of Liliane's immaculately tailored outfits, and left her room. Professor Papavoine was in the living room, surrounded by newspaper supplements, and Herbert was rolling up and down on the floor. He seemed to be very excited at having so much space. Aurélie wondered how big his home was, and she was reminded of just how little she knew about him. She didn't even know if he had a father in his life. Maybe somewhere a man was pacing up and down, out of his mind with worry about the whereabouts of his son. He could be in a police station right now, reporting him missing as he wondered why the child's lunatic mother wasn't answering his calls, and failing to stop himself from picturing her tying the baby in chains, bundling him into a bag and dropping him from a bridge.

'There you are,' said Professor Papavoine. 'I was starting to wonder if we would see you at all today.'

It still felt strange that she was at her professor's house, and that her status had been raised from intruder to guest. 'I slept really well. Thank you so much for looking after Herbert.'

He dismissed this with a gesture. 'He was no trouble. He slept until half past eight, and he only woke twice in the night. I think that's a record for someone his age, and we've been having a great time ever since. We've been out together to get the paper, haven't we?'

Herbert carried on rolling.

'And you look ready for an outing yourself. Get some breakfast inside you, and we'll all go for a walk.'

Aurélie and Professor Papavoine stood in the Musée d'Orsay, in front of Eugène Carrière's painting *L'Enfant malade*, in which a mother tenderly cradles her sick child.

'Wow,' said Aurélie. She had been all over the Musée d'Orsay several times and must have seen the painting before, but this was the first time it had stopped her in her tracks. As well as being arrestingly beautiful, it demonstrated that there really was an audience for pictures of unhappy children. She recalled having seen a similarly themed Picasso at some point, and she thought also of Gustav Vigeland's sculpture of the screaming baby. There must have been plenty of others. Until she'd had a child in her life such works had not resonated with her a great deal, but now she wanted to track them all down. Their existence intimidated her, and invigorated her at the same time. She was determined to capture Herbert, bruise and all.

She moved on to the next picture. Another Eugène Carrière, another painting of a melancholy baby. He was brilliant, and she decided he was her new favourite artist. The next one, *Enfant avec casserole*, was more upbeat. This one's subject, a cheeky child scooping leftovers from an upturned pot, reminded her of Herbert; there was something about the contours of his brow, and the determined expression. The sight of all these children on the wall induced occasional bursts of worry, and from time to time she found herself looking around to see where Herbert had got to, and she had to remind herself that he was busy having fun in the café with Liliane.

Professor Papavoine had not given Carrière much thought for some years, but ever since his conversation with Le Machine, he had been itching to get back here. The museum had a substantial collection of his works, and he was pleased to become reacquainted with them. He smiled as he thought of the story Le Machine had told him, of how for his second-year project he had planned to paint a picture of a friend of his that would be, in part, a homage to Carrière, but while sitting outside his office he had overheard the other students talking about their own projects and had become intimidated by the verbose way in which they articulated their ideas. He had abandoned his plan, which he had managed to convince himself would be dismissed as derivative and unambitious. He had thought up a new idea on the spot, an idea that came at the same subject matter from a very different angle. This was the idea that had made Professor Papavoine pull a face, and which was currently the talk of Paris.

The Professor had followed *Life*'s progress, and had hoped for an opportunity to see how far it had come since it had been proposed to him. Now he had a pass that would get him and a guest in on a day of his choosing, and he thought that the coming evening would be as good a time as any. He was almost giddy with excitement. Liliane had been glad to stand aside and let the guest slot go to Aurélie. *That will be a nice surprise for her*, he thought.

He looked over to her, as she stood absorbed in Carrière's *Jeune femme nourrissant son enfant*. Her profile was perfect. Making sure she didn't hear him, he sighed.

They returned to *L'Enfant malade,* and stood together before it.

'Professor Papavoine,' said Aurélie, quietly, 'you were going to tell me why you gave me your card and told me I could call you day or night.' He hadn't returned to the subject, and she felt she ought to know.

Professor Papavoine looked at her, and Aurélie looked up at him. She tried to read his expression. He wasn't embarrassed, he wasn't laughing the question off, and he wasn't full of pent-up lust that was about to boil over in a hideous confession. 'You deserve an explanation,' he said. 'But first, may I . . .?'

He took her in his arms.

Aurélie found herself returning his embrace. She rested

her head against his shoulder, and they stood there for what must have been a minute before they parted.

She tried to work out what had just happened. This was not a romantic pass. If it had been she would have fought him off, she wouldn't have yielded and felt comforted by it. It was the hug she had been needing ever since her disastrous date with Léandre Martin.

She looked up at him.

'I had to get that out of my system,' he said. 'I'm an old man; you'll forgive me my sentimentality.'

She didn't know what to say.

'Liliane and I never had children,' he said. 'This wasn't out of choice. She was pregnant once, but after five months . . .'

Aurélie reached out to him, and stroked his arm.

'She was a girl. We would have had a daughter, and she would have been around your age by now. Aurélie was even on our list of names, but we called her Simone in the end, after Liliane's mother. We tried for another . . .' He felt no need to go on, and paused for a while as he collected himself. 'And then, when you walked into my office, I felt something I had never felt before. You reminded me so much of Liliane when she was younger, and, well, as I said, I'm getting old and sentimental. I'm so sorry I didn't make myself clear to you. You must have thought I was just another lecherous old goat, like . . .' He almost said *like Professor Boucher*, but stopped himself. He didn't want to incriminate his colleague. '. . . like a stereotypical academic going through a belated midlife crisis.'

'Well, yes. That's exactly what I thought.'

'Why wouldn't you? But I suppose I just wanted to spend time with you as a father might spend time with his grown daughter. I wanted to take you out to lunch, to hear your news, to laugh with you, to be exasperated by you, to implore you to stop smoking, to disapprove of the men in your life . . .'

Aurélie laughed. 'You're very welcome to do that!'

'It all seems quite idiotic, doesn't it?'

'Not at all.'

'I told Liliane about you when I got home, and the first thing she said was that you probably thought I was trying to lure you into an inappropriate romance.' Now he looked embarrassed. 'And, as always, she was right.'

Aurélie smiled. 'There are pictures in your apartment of Liliane when she was younger. I can see similarities. And you know what? She gives me hope for the future. If I age half as well as she has I'll be very happy. She's so beautiful.'

Professor Papavoine nodded. 'She is. I'm sorry to have bothered you with all that, Mademoiselle Renard,' he said, 'but I thought I owed you a full explanation.'

'Thank you,' she said. 'Oh, and please call me Aurélie.'

'And you can call me, er, you can call me . . .'

'I think I'd like to call you Professor Papavoine. It has a ring to it.' He was still her professor after all, and when all this had blown over and she was back at college it wouldn't be right for her to go around calling him by his first name.

He appreciated her tact. 'Thank you.'

They embraced once again, and Professor Papavoine closed his eyes. When he opened them, he realised that one of the worst things imaginable had come to pass. Over Aurélie's shoulder he saw, looking at them through the glass door to the preceding room, Professor Boucher.

*   *   *

Professor Boucher came through to their room pulling faces, bugging his eyes out and winking, and Professor Papavoine could tell that somewhere under that unruly beard a grey tongue was running up and down his lips.

'Excuse me,' he said to Aurélie, bringing their touching moment to an abrupt end. 'I have to see a man about a . . . misunderstanding.'

Aurélie turned around and saw Professor Boucher. She watched, amused, as Professor Papavoine darted across the floor and manhandled him into the next room. She liked Professor Boucher. She had been to several of his lectures, and he had always made her laugh.

'Papavoine,' said Professor Boucher, giving his colleague a playful punch on the shoulder, 'I like your style! Leaving the old lady in the café while you come up here for a fumble with your compact blonde. And very nice she is too, very . . .' He went into an array of faces, and made a number of unusual growling noises to illustrate his approval of Professor Papavoine's supposed choice of conquest. 'I must say, I've had my eye on that one myself. If you hadn't got in there, I would have made a play for her, but she's all yours now, you filthy, filthy dog. Speaking of which, my girl's going to be wondering where I've got to. Isn't this the perfect place to bring them? I'm here most week-ends, playing the worldly professor with one little minx or another; if anybody sees us together we tell them we met by coincidence and happened to fall into a conversation about art. What could be more innocent? And then it's off to a nice little hotel I know just around the corner. Very reasonable hourly rates, Papavoine, if you know the right man to talk to. I could put in a word for you . . .'

Before Professor Papavoine could explain just how different his reason had been for coming here, Professor Boucher had imprisoned him in a fraternal headlock. 'I didn't think you had it in you, Papavoine,' he said, rubbing his knuckles against Professor Papavoine's head. 'You dirty, dirty ram! You sex fiend!'

When at last he released him, Professor Boucher pinched Professor Papavoine's cheeks, wobbled them, and said, 'Welcome to Wonderland, Papavoine. And ten out of ten for the blonde. What a girl. I love the way one of her ears sticks out a bit more than the other. It really makes you want to . . .' He made a protracted trilling noise, and for a full minute he went into what looked a bit like a Maori tribal dance. 'Eh, Papavoine?' he said, when the dance finally came to an end. 'Eh?' And after a quick run through his repertoire of faces and sounds, another fraternal headlock and a brief reprise of the dance, he darted back the way he had come, in search of his latest conquest.

Professor Papavoine watched him go. Professor Boucher had a beautiful wife at home too, though she was every bit as amorous as he was, and was probably entertaining one of her silent young companions right now. When, still rubbing his head, he got back to Aurélie, Professor Papavoine didn't know whether to be dismayed or relieved that she seemed to be finding the situation with Professor Boucher hilarious.

'Promise me you will never go near that man,' he said. 'Let's go back to Liliane and Herbert before I get us into any more trouble.'

They walked back the way they had come, and as they

did they ran into Professor Boucher and his date, a start-lingly pretty and fashionably dressed platinum blonde from the year below Aurélie's. They recognised one another from the canteen. The platinum blonde gave Aurélie a conspiratorial smile, which she returned. She didn't want the girl to think she was snooty. And besides, she *was* up to no good with one of the professors, only in a very different way.

XXVI

After her lucrative Saturdays, Sylvie was ready to undertake a less financially rewarding day's work, and Sundays saw her helping out her upstairs neighbour at les bouquinistes, the book stalls that line the Seine. The day would usually begin with her hauling a box of stock from her neighbour's home to the stall, and she would sit there for the rest of the day with her flask of coffee, vending an entirely haphazard range of books at various stages of disintegration.

Her neighbour was getting old, and she was glad to have Sylvie take over as she spent a day indoors. After closing the stall, Sylvie would report back to her apartment and show her the ledger, running through the list of what had been sold, and handing over the takings. There was no way of predicting how much stock would go; sometimes the stall would be as good as stripped by the end of the day, and other times it would be untouched. Sylvie's neighbour would hand her a handful of coins, the weight of which would depend on the general state of the business. It never amounted to a great deal, but Sylvie had grown fond of her neighbour, and had been touched by her readiness to trust her with her livelihood.

Alongside the battered old books, the stall also sold prints of famous artworks, reproductions of antique maps and vintage dirty postcards. It was these sidelines that really kept the business going, and one of Sylvie's favourite things was to sell a postcard of her mother.

In the early eighties, before Sylvie had been born, her mother had posed for a number of photographers. In the picture that had ended up on the postcard she was completely naked apart from a pair of lime green leg warmers, and was holding a baguette at such an angle that it just covered her lower modesty. It was these touches that had helped it find its way on to the tourist stands; it had now attained a kind of retro charm, and it sat quite comfortably alongside the sepia goings-on from the very olden days. She had been amazed to see them among the stock on her first day on the stall, and whenever anyone bought a picture of her mother, she would proudly tell them who she was, and hold it up beside her face so they could see the likeness. Her mother's hair was big, and she had a lot of make-up on – green eyeshadow and purple lips – but there was no denying where Sylvie's looks had come from.

Quite often Aurélie would join her for a few hours on the Sunday, keeping her company and even minding the stall while she took breaks, but today she had texted to say she wasn't going to make it.

—*How's that baby you kidnapped?* Sylvie had texted back.

—*He's fine. Am staying with creepy Prof. Long story, but nothing funny going on. Not creepy any more. On way to see* Le Machine. *Will track you down soon. Much to report.*

It was another cold day, and she sat on her folding chair in her duffel coat and hat as she waited for customers to drift by. So far she had been asked out twice, and each time she had given a firm *no*. One of the boys had been a hopeless case, wide-eyed and trembling as he asked her if he could treat her to a coffee when she had finished work. When she had declined he had thanked her, apologised and run away. The other one, though, had been something else. He looked like a male model, the kind who would pose in corduroy with a Golden Retriever. He was tall and healthy-looking, with a thick head of hair, and he was wearing really great clothes. He had even chosen to buy a battered copy of her favourite book of all time, *Timoléon, chien fidèle.*

'I love the ending,' she had said, as she handed him his change. 'It's not easy to read, but it says something that needs to be said. I don't think I could ever really be friends with anyone who didn't get this book.'

'I've lost count of how many times I've read it,' he said, his smile revealing great teeth and dimples. 'I love the ending too. I'm buying it to depress a friend of mine who's been a bit too happy lately.'

Sylvie laughed, and they fell into a conversation about

the brilliance of the author, and how underappreciated he was, and she told him she had heard a rumour that the last time he had been translated into French his publisher, Editions Stock, hadn't even bothered to send him a copy.

'It's a scandal if it's true,' said the handsome man. Sensing his opportunity, he had asked her if she was going to be free at all that week, and she had told him, very firmly, that she wouldn't be, and that she already had a boyfriend.

He took this graciously, told her it had been nice to meet her, and went on his way. It was only as she watched him go that she realised she hadn't been entirely truthful when it had come to her romantic status. She really had felt as if she already had a boyfriend, though. She realised how ridiculous this was, and hoped she wasn't setting herself up for a broken heart. She replayed their conversation, and she knew that that was all it was – a conversation. She had liked him, he had a pleasant manner and exemplary taste in books, and it was plain to see that he was almost supernaturally handsome, but she hadn't been attracted to him at all, and she hadn't been flirting with him. Not once had her devotion to Toshiro wavered. Nobody could compare to Toshiro.

She sat on her folding chair, and tried to fight the thought that she was being stupid, that it was unlikely that she would ever even meet this man she had fallen for in such a frightening way.

There was something inevitable about the appearance of Lucien and the Akiyamas, and Sylvie threw herself at them. Monsieur Akiyama seemed at last to be getting used to this, and rather than standing like a baffled statue as Sylvie hugged him, he even smiled a little bit, and tentatively returned her embrace.

'Look at you,' said Madame Akiyama. 'A few days in Paris and you've become European.'

Monsieur and Madame Akiyama announced that they were going over the bridge to Notre Dame cathedral, and that they wouldn't be needing Lucien for a while. He pulled up a folding chair beside Sylvie, and tried to work out what to say to her. She had never known him to be so quiet; normally the banter had flowed between them so naturally. To get conversation going, she found the postcard of her mother. She handed one to him.

'What do you think of her, then?' she said.

Lucien looked at the postcard, then looked at Sylvie. Back and forth several times. 'Your mother?' At dinner the night before, Sylvie had mentioned her mother's tendency to take her clothes off.

Sylvie nodded.

Lucien looked at the photograph. The hair, make-up, leg warmers and baguette were distracting, but her face was as pretty as Sylvie's, and her body was timeless. 'She's beautiful,' he said.

Sylvie smiled. 'I'm so proud of her. Sometimes I really miss her,' she said. 'It's funny to think that she was younger than I am now when these were taken. I always seem to sell at least one every week. I'm so glad she lives on in these postcards.'

'She lives on in you as well.'

This was no place to get emotional, so she changed the subject. 'Right – some Japanese, please.'

After learning a few pleasantries, Sylvie called a halt to the lesson. 'So have you made any progress with the lovely Akiko?'

Lucien looked at the pavement. 'No,' he said.

'OK,' said Sylvie. 'We need a strategy.'

Lucien shook his head. 'We don't, Sylvie. We don't need a strategy.' And he gave her the look she knew so well; the look that told her everything.

Sylvie felt like crying on his behalf. 'Lucien, no,' she said. 'You mustn't. What about your Japanese girls? Never mind Akiko. Forget her – go to Japan and find another one. Anyone but me, Lucien, for God's sake. Haven't you listened to a word I've said?'

A customer approached the stall, and picked out a print of an antique map of the city and the postcard of Sylvie's mother. She was in such a hurry to get back to Lucien that she sold them without mentioning the family connection.

'It turns out the girl for me wasn't Japanese after all.'

'Lucien,' she said, 'you're being stupid. I'm not the girl for you. I don't love you, and I never will. Not in that way, anyway.'

'I'm sorry, Sylvie,' he said. 'I'd better get back to the Akiyamas.' He stood to leave, and Sylvie stood beside him. She was so fond of him, and he looked so forlorn. She put her arms around him and held him close.

'Lucien,' she said, 'soon you'll realise that we weren't meant to be together. You're just having an episode. It's all going to be OK.'

'All I want is to marry you on a mutual friend's llama farm in Avignon. Is that really too much to ask?'

'Yes, it is, and you know it is.'

As Lucien held her he closed his eyes. He could smell her hair, and feel the shape of her back beneath her duffel coat. He knew her body would be as incredible as her mother's, and he couldn't help imagining her in a short, tight red dress, the kind a prostitute might wear. She would look unbelievable.

He opened his eyes, and it was his turn to feel that one of the worst things imaginable had come to pass. Standing just an arm's length away as this tender scene unfolded was Toshiro Akiyama.

Sylvie felt Lucien's body stiffen, as if he had suddenly gone into a state of rigor mortis. She hoped he hadn't died in her arms of a broken heart.

'Er, Sylvie,' he said, as she felt his arms slowly let go of her body and return to his side. 'There's someone here to see you.'

He took her by the shoulders, and turned her around. And there he was, Toshiro Akiyama, even more handsome in real life than he had been in the photographs. It all took a moment to sink in. When it did, Sylvie opened her mouth and let out a scream of unbridled horror.

As the scream was going on, a crowd of passers-by gathered, wondering what to make of it. When at last it was over, Toshiro Akiyama said something in Japanese, and he and Sylvie Dupont stood there just looking at one another.

'What did he say, Lucien?'

Lucien said nothing.

'Tell me, Lucien. What did he say?'

Lucien, his eyes glazed, told her. 'He said, *I am sorry. I seem to have misunderstood the situation.*'

'Tell him he *has* misunderstood the situation, but not in the way he thinks.'

Lucien turned over a sentence in his mind: *Yes, you have misunderstood the situation. The lady and I are very much in love, and your presence is not welcome, so please return to Japan on the next available flight.*

But he didn't use it. Instead he marshalled all his inner strength and goodness, and in faultless Japanese he explained the situation to Toshiro, 'Sylvie was consoling me because I am in love with her but she doesn't love me in return.'

'What did you say?' asked Sylvie.

He told her, and the onlookers let out a sympathetic *Aaaahhhh*.

Lucien's statement made sense to Toshiro. He couldn't imagine anybody *not* being in love with Sylvie Dupont. It didn't quite fit the story, though. He had surprised his parents outside the cathedral, tracking them down via a text message exchange in which he neglected to mention that he was in Paris too. Once he had endured his father's lecture, which he had predicted word for word, about how there had never been room for spontaneous behaviour within the large corporation in which he had spent his working life, and once his mother's shock had subsided, his parents had delivered a short presentation, illustrated by photos on his mother's phone. As part of this they had told him that Lucien, the nice but slightly gawky interpreter, was in love with Akiko.

Toshiro had felt sorry for him, because Akiko had told him, though not yet her parents, that she was going strong with a boy she had met at work. When the slideshow was over, his parents had directed him to Sylvie's stall, and

when he got there he found his sympathy for this interpreter had waned quite considerably as he found out just
how fickle he could be.

He supposed he would find out later what was going on
with him, but for now it was low priority. He had flown
halfway around the world with a clear mission in mind,
and the moment had come. Sylvie Dupont was right in
front of him, in a duffel coat and hat, and looking even
more perfect than she had in the photograph. He spoke,
this time in French.

'Hello, Sylvie Dupont.'

'Hello, Toshiro Akiyama.'

'How are you?'

'I am very well, thank you. How are you?'

'I am very well too.'

The language changed to Japanese.

'Hello, Toshiro Akiyama,' said Sylvie.

'Hello, Sylvie Dupont.'

'How are you?'

'I am very well, thank you. How are you?'

'I am very well too.'

And there it is, their first conversation. In years to come
they will re-enact this meeting for their children's amusement. There will be the surprise, and the scream, but they
will always omit one detail: the presence of the heartbroken interpreter looking on.

Sylvie will always wish that things had ended differently for him, that her two boys and her girl might have
known him as *uncle Lucien*, that they would have played
with his own half-Japanese children. They wouldn't have
been Akiko's, because she will have ended up marrying

her new boyfriend, but that wouldn't have mattered. He should have found *somebody*. Her thoughts will often turn to poor Lucien. She had only known him for a short while, but she had liked him very much. She had even loved him, in a funny sort of way.

XXVII

Le Charmant Cinéma Érotique had been more or less consistently full since *Life* had opened its doors, and late on the Sunday afternoon four hundred and seventy-one people were in the auditorium, every one of them looking intently at the bald man's body and listening to the thunderous sounds that were coming from inside him.

Then, at last, it happened.

He picked up a glass tray and placed it in the centre of the stage. Until that moment the few people who had noticed this tray had assumed it was an oven dish. Most of them had not given it another thought, but some had idly wondered why he had an oven dish but no oven. Now, though, it became clear that it was not there for culinary purposes.

Spotting the cue, the sound designer brought the volume right down. The only microphone he kept in the mix was the one Le Machine had swallowed on the Friday night. These moments were to be the only ones in the whole of *Life* where the background gurgling and thumping of a body at work were brought down, allowing the possibility of moments of near silence. Because this microphone was a new addition to the show, the crew were on tenterhooks, hoping it would all work out. They had been wondering whether the audience would get excited and start to cheer or shout things out, but everybody watched in rapt silence as Le Machine crouched over the glass tray.

Aurélie Renard stood in the middle of the crowd. She hadn't known what she would think about *Life*; she thought it could well turn out to be a load of pointless, pretentious rubbish, but it wasn't. To see and hear a body at work, presented in this way, had been really moving. She thought of her mother, and Herbert, and herself. She looked at Professor Papavoine, and he seemed to be close to tears as he watched Le Machine squat down, getting ready for the big moment.

For Le Machine, this part of *Life* had become routine, so much so that he wondered why people went on about it so much. Everybody did it, so what was the big deal? Normally he went once a day, and he had expected to have done it by this point, but for some reason he had been a bit blocked up. As he crouched, it became clear that this was not going to be an easy one. He started to strain. The microphone picked up a small squelch of movement, and the audience gasped in anticipation, but it seemed to be a false alarm. There was still some way to go. There was a loud pop as some gas forced its way out, and a while later there was another squelch as his faeces crept towards the exit. He could really feel it coming now. All he needed was a big strain, and it would be out. He readied himself, and went for it.

Like everybody else, Aurélie was watching him intently, and willing him on. Le Machine had won her over, not only with the nature of his show, but also with his perfectly sculpted body. *Come on*, she was thinking. *You can do it . . .*

Le Machine strained harder and harder, and as he did so the sight of him suddenly made her feel uneasy. But even so she couldn't look away. His pained expression seemed familiar, but she couldn't recall where she had seen it before. And then it struck her. She had seen it two days ago, as she had stood beside a pair of policemen and shouted at him to go away. She pictured Le Machine with clothes on, and eyebrows, and hair on his head, and before she had a chance to stop herself, she started to call out to him: '*Léan—!*' As she heard her own voice reverberating around the room, she put her hand over her mouth.

Le Machine looked up, to see where the sound had come from.

Murmurs began to spread through the crowd: *Who was that putting him off?* and *Some people have no respect for art*, and *Oh no, he's sucking it back in.*

Le Machine stood up. His sound designer wasn't sure what to do as he watched him pace to the edge of the stage and scan the faces in the audience. And then Le Machine did something he had never done before – he put his hands over his genitals, hiding them from view as though he were suddenly ashamed to be naked. He took a step back, a look of horror on his face.

He stood there, covering himself up, his eyes following Aurélie as she made her way out of the auditorium, pushing through the crowd. And somebody was there in her wake, accompanying her through the mêlée with a hand on her shoulder. It was Papavoine . . . He tried to work out what was going on.

He felt an urgent biological need to return to his glass tray and crouch back down. Le Machine strained and strained. The audience cheered, and began a slow but supportive hand clap, and finally out came a small brown pellet, about the size of a kidney bean. It had happened. The room erupted, and the interruption was forgotten. Another pellet dropped into the tray, this one the size of a broad bean, and the chanting began: *Le Ma-chine! Le Ma-chine! Le Ma-chine! Le Ma-chine!* And when these dry lumps and others had finally passed, they were followed by a softer, more substantial stool. The audience was ecstatic. Not only had they been there for his first poo of the run, but the rumours were true – not one drop of wee had come out at the same time.

When he had finished he went over to the bidet and cleaned up, then with a pair of tweezers he picked out the tiny microphone, which had done its job very well. He would swallow another one the next time he drank water. Using his special spatula, he transferred all the waste from the glass tray into the big bottle.

And there it sat, for all to see.

XXVIII

Monsieur Eric Rousset was sitting at the dinner table with his wife, his daughter and his daughter's friend Thao, whom he had met in passing a few times before and had always found to be very pleasant.

'I didn't quite catch that,' he said to Élise, his eyes glassy.

'I think you did. But just in case you really didn't, I'll say it again: Thao and I are moving in together. We've found a place, and we're getting the keys next week. It's a one-bedroom apartment. With one bed in it. A big bed. It has to be a big bed because it'll be for both of us.'

'You mean . . . you and she . . .?' He made what looked like peace signs with two fingers from each hand, then bumped them together like duelling scissors.

Élise nodded.

'I had no idea. Nice place, is it?'

'It's wonderful,' said Thao. 'It's exactly the kind of apartment we've been looking for.'

'So you'll be needing some help with the move. I'll get some cardboard boxes from the cinema. They're taking deliveries of new stock for the shop every day, so they have plenty going spare. And I can drive you around, and help you up the stairs, and all that kind of thing, don't worry about that.'

'Thank you,' said Thao. 'That'll be very helpful. My dad's offered too, so Élise and I won't have to do anything much. We'll just mix some cocktails, sit back and let you two get on with it.'

He laughed, and looked from his daughter to Thao, and back again. 'Well, I never . . .'

'Dad, I'm sorry.'

'You shouldn't be sorry. What's there to be sorry about? I'm very open-minded. I've always said there should be a lot more girls like you two in the world. But above all, I'm glad to see you happy.' He pointed at Thao. 'She's nice.'

'I'm sorry I didn't tell you a long time ago. It's just . . .'

'Just what? You thought it would break your old dad's heart?'

'No . . .' She knew she had to tell him the truth. 'Well, yes, in a way. I didn't want to ruin your love of lesbian porn, that's all. I know how much it means to you, and I thought that if I told you about myself it might make things too real for you and stop you from enjoying the fantasy.'

'I do love my lesbian porn.' He stared into space and smiled for a moment, before snapping out of it. 'You know your old dad too well. But why would it ruin it for me? I know it doesn't have much to do with reality. Unless you two are in any of the films, now that would be a bit much. Have you ever . . .?' he asked Thao.

'Been in a porn film? No.'

'Good. Then everything's going to be fine. You can be too protective, you know.'

Madame Rousset and Élise exchanged relieved glances. He was right; they had been overprotective of him.

Élise smiled, and squeezed her father's hand. Then her pager beeped, and she apologised and checked it. 'I've been called to the cinema. Le Machine has asked to see me.' She kissed Thao and her parents goodbye, hurried out of the apartment and off to work.

Monsieur Rousset hoped Le Machine's ailment wasn't anything serious. Even though he had very suddenly had to abandon his dream of having him as a son-in-law, he was still very fond of him, and wished him only well. So now it was just the three of them: Monsieur Rousset, Madame Rousset and Thao.

'So,' said Monsieur Rousset to Thao, 'you and Élise . . . How long have you been . . .?' Not knowing quite what to say, he made the scissoring gesture again.

'About nine months now, Monsieur Rousset.'

'Nine months, eh? Nine months. Well, fancy that. Oh, and you must call me Eric. Or Papa. Whichever you prefer.'

'Thank you,' said Thao. 'Thank you . . . Eric, I think.'

'Then Eric it is.'

Anybody watching disc 16 of the DVD box set of *Life: Paris* will see Le Machine's Doctor, Élise Rousset, emerge from the wings, and a short consultation take place. In the editing suite they will make sure that none of the words that were spoken make their way on to the soundtrack, and that the angles chosen do not give away any of this confidential encounter to lip readers. One of the strictures of *Life* was that Le Machine was not allowed to make any private communications. Anything he did or said had to be shared with everyone in the auditorium, hence the presence of the whiteboard, and the only exception for this was for his visits from the doctor. The sound designer bumped up Le Machine's heartbeat in the body of the auditorium to almost deafening levels, but because of the positioning of the speakers it was still possible for them to hold a conversation on stage.

After a short talk to Le Machine, the doctor walked over to the large faeces bottle, and had a good close look at what had come out. She returned to her patient, and passed a comment on the condition of his stools. Then he pointed to his knee, and said something to her, and she prodded it, and massaged it, and asked some questions, and he answered them. Three minutes after arriving on stage, she went away.

She didn't go straight back to her parents' place, though. First she went to Le Machine's dressing room, which doubled as the official sick bay, so her presence there would not have been regarded as suspicious. There was nothing irregular about her unlocking the medical cupboard and looking inside. What might have arrested the attention of an onlooker, though, was the sight of her opening the bag that contained the few personal belongings that Le Machine had brought with him to the venue, then picking out his wallet and going through it. Apart from a thick wad of euros, it didn't contain much, and she soon found the card he had told her about, and slipped it into her pocket and zipped the bag shut. Only when this was done did she enter the details of her visit in the official medical log.

As she left the backstage area she ran into his manager, and reassured her that he was fine, that while the first stool had been a little hard it was nothing out of the ordinary, and that he had just sprained his knee a little on his debut crouch.

'There's nothing to worry about,' she said, and she headed back into the night. She turned her task over and over in her mind. She was going some way beyond the boundaries of her duty, but what the hell?

She dropped into a bar that she went to from time to time, ordered a beer and took the card from her pocket.

XXIX

Professor Papavoine hailed a taxi, and he and Aurélie got in. 'So,' he said, 'you know Léandre too?'

'Too?'

He nodded.

'We've met. And it turns out there's plenty I *don't* know about him. He never told me he was Le Machine, for a start. So he's your best friend, is he?'

'He was a student of mine a few years ago. One day I made the mistake of betraying a lack of enthusiasm for an idea of his, and he stormed out of the room and out of college. I hadn't seen him since, not until he surprised me with a visit on Friday, on his way to the venue. That's how we got the tickets. So what did you think of his work?'

Aurélie had reached her verdict before realising she had fallen out with the star of the show, and she had to admit that she thought it was wonderful. 'I loved it. But once I knew who it was up there I had to get out in a hurry. Sorry about that.'

'That's OK. I agree though, I think it's incredible what he's doing.'

'You seemed quite choked up.'

He nodded. 'Léandre came to me to apologise for having been such a hothead when he was younger, as if that was something he needed to apologise for. I can never understand people who *aren't* hotheads when they're young. Then I apologised for not having seen the potential of his proposal, which, incidentally, was for what we just saw, and he apologised for pitching it so crudely. Apparently his original plan was to paint a picture inspired by his hero, who happens to be Eugène Carrière, but in the moments before he came to see me about this, he heard some other students talking a load of pretentious crap outside my office and felt intimidated by it. He thought I would throw him out of college for being unambitious, for just wanting to paint a picture. He thought he needed a grand concept, so he came up with a new idea on the spot. Does that sound at all familiar?'

'I don't know what you're talking about.'

'He went straight to the bodily secretions aspect, and when he started talking about earwax I went like this . . .' He pulled a face. '. . . and said I wasn't sure about the idea. And off he went, and I hadn't seen him since. Anyway, after a while we stopped apologising to one another, and he told me all about *Life*. He spoke about it properly this time. He told me why he does what he does. It was almost as if he was in confession. He said he was glad of the opportunity to talk to me about it after our disastrous previous meeting. It was the first time he'd spoken about it in such detail to anyone except . . .' He stopped himself.

Except his main girlfriend, thought Aurélie.

'As you know I'm old and sentimental, and after what he told me, *Life* really tugged at my heartstrings.'

'So what's it all about then?'

'I'm afraid I can't tell you. He swore me to secrecy.'

'You can tell me. I can keep a secret.'

Professor Papavoine shook his head. 'I promised. I think he's doing the right thing keeping his motivations under wraps. There are far too many words in the art world, anyway; all they do is create an unnecessary fog.'

'So you think people shouldn't talk about art?'

'No, if people stop talking about it we'll be in big trouble. We need to keep critics in business for a start. What if they all lost their jobs and had to work elsewhere? It would be chaos. Would you feel safe travelling in a train driven by a redundant arts correspondent?'

Aurélie laughed. Professor Papavoine had a knack for snapping her out of a bad mood.

'It's the artists themselves who need to learn to keep their mouths shut and leave all the chatter to everyone else. Léandre and I are in total agreement about that. From now on Professor Boucher and I are going to give a big talk to every new intake: we shall make it clear from day one that while we appreciate a modest degree of intelligent discourse, we have a low tolerance threshold for what Boucher so charmingly calls *wank talk*. It's such a shame that we've allowed things to get to the point where the students think that we want them, or even expect them, to use this kind of language. Artists need to stop using words. They shouldn't explain why they do what they do, and they definitely shouldn't use them as part of their work. Even giving something a title is pushing it. If we carry on going down this route we'll end up as bad as the British. I was in Scotland for an exhibition a couple of years ago, and the artist hadn't even bothered making anything, he'd just stencilled a load of wank talk all over the walls. In English, of course, just to make sure I was as alienated as I could possibly be. And as we went in we were all handed a sheet of paper explaining why he'd written all the wank talk all over the walls. It was the worst thing I've ever seen, and I've seen a lot of crap in my lifetime. If it hadn't been in such a nice building I'd have been tempted to burn the place down. Now *that* would have been art.'

'It sounds horrendous,' said Aurélie. 'All things like that do is give ammunition to the kind of people who dismiss all contemporary art. Anyone trying anything different or new is always bracketed alongside pointless shit like that. It's a load of bollocks,' she said. 'We've been swearing a lot, haven't we?'

'Yes, we had better stop that now.'

They sat in silence, and Aurélie reflected upon how she shouldn't become too indignant, because in the scheme of things it was probably better for artists to talk shit than to throw stones at babies.

The taxi reached the Papavoines' street, and as the professor and Aurélie got out they were so deep in conversation that they failed to notice the small black motorcycle that had pulled up fifty metres behind them. The rider was dressed from head to toe in black leather. Their visor was down, so it wasn't possible to tell whether their eyes were following them as they opened the door and walked inside.

* * *

Aurélie and Professor Papavoine were greeted by a delirious Liliane.

'Quick,' she said. 'Come and look.' She ushered them through to the living room, and there on the floor, on his belly, was Herbert. He looked up at them and grinned, his brilliant white teeth shining. 'OK, Herbert,' she said, 'away you go.'

As if obeying the instruction, Herbert stopped smiling, and very seriously began a commando crawl across the parquet. He went about two metres before stopping to examine a piece of fluff he had found.

Aurélie felt so proud she could weep. And then it all came bubbling up. A tear ran down her face, and she wiped it away. She crouched beside Herbert, and gave his back a rub. 'Well done, Herbert,' she said.

'Open a bottle, Papavoine,' said Liliane, joining Aurélie and putting an arm around her. Professor Papavoine did as he was told, and while he was out of the room, Aurélie and Liliane sat side-by-side, watching in wonder as the baby put down the piece of fluff and resumed his journey across the floor.

When Herbert was in bed, the Papavoines and Aurélie sat drinking wine. Liliane left the room for a while, and when she came back she was wielding a bleeping mobile phone. 'Papavoine,' she said, 'shut this thing up.' She threw it to him. 'What was it doing behind the microwave, anyway?'

'Ah,' he said, 'I was wondering where this had got to. Well, in fact I wasn't wondering at all, but now I know I should have been. So, what's going on?' He squinted at the small screen. 'A message. How unusual! And it's from

291

. . . hmmm . . .' He read it, then looked up at Aurélie. 'Our friend Le Machine has got in touch.'

'What? How?'

'Listen to this.' He read the message. '*Le Machine's doctor here. Top secret message from him to Prof Pap. Le M says hello to you and Aur. Prof Pap please tell everything to Aur. Hope she will understand, and remember Thursday and forget Friday and wait for me.*'

'So,' Aurélie smiled, 'I'm being let in on the big secret.'

'It seems you are. And what's all this about Thursday and Friday? Is there something we should know about?'

'We met on Thursday. He was the one who rescued Herbert from the old woman. It was the best day of my life, and on Friday we had our second date and it was a disaster.'

'Lunch, right?'

'Er . . . yes.'

'And you ran off and hid behind a policeman.'

'Were you following us?'

'He told me all about it. He likes you, you know. He *really* likes you. He was feeling terrible about how he'd scared you off. He was kicking himself for being so nervous. I think he was having difficulty finding a way to tell you what he was about to do without you running for the hills. In his defence, it is a pretty unusual situation. I think that's partly why he got so confessional; he was telling me everything he wished he had told you.'

'And now I finally get to hear it.'

'Welcome to the inner sanctum. Now, make yourself comfortable and let *Prof Pap* refill your glass . . .'

Aurélie always called her dad on a Sunday night, and she wasn't going to let Le Machine, Herbert or anyone else stop her. It was later than usual when she got around to it, but she knew he would still be up, and he was as glad as ever to hear from her. She asked after her brother, and about what they had been up to, and when he asked her how she was doing she told him that she was busy with her project. She didn't burden him with too many details, particularly not about how she had commandeered a stranger's baby. Then she told him she thought she might have a new boyfriend.

'Will I approve of him?'

'I think you will.' She decided that this was not the time to tell her father that her new boyfriend's job involved him taking his clothes off and going to the toilet in front of strangers who had paid to watch. And she didn't tell him that this was an artistic tribute to his friend, Dominique Gravoir, who had been in a coma since the age of eight, when the boys had failed to beat a cormorant in a breath-holding contest. One day she would, though, and she would tell him about the hours her new boyfriend had spent by his friend's bedside, helping his mother to take care of him: feeding him, shaving him and cleaning up after him, and becoming fascinated by the sights and sounds, even the smells, of his body as it worked on in spite of his apparent absence. From an early age Léandre Martin had had a heightened awareness of the cells he carried with him everywhere he went, and the chemical and mechanical processes that were happening inside him every moment of every day, and he had always wanted to convey his sense of wonder at this to other people. Neither did she tell her father that his friend's mother was becoming increasingly frail, and that in a frank conversation with her he had pledged to take over his care, should her son outlive her, or if she got to the point where she could no longer cope. He had told her that her son would always be welcome to live with him, and he was going to put most of the money he made from his show into a fund that would ensure he would always be well looked after, no matter what. And when the show was over, he was finally going to paint him, as he had meant to all those years ago, with wasted limbs, and his eyes open and unseeing in the half-light.

'So when will I get to meet this boyfriend character?'

'Let's wait and see if it works out. If we're still together in three months I'll bring him home.'

After her phone call she went back to the living room, where the Papavoines were watching the late news summary. President Bruni-Sarkozy was being interviewed about his chances of remaining in power. *Of course people will vote for me*, he laughed, pointing a thumb at himself. *I'm the one who kicked out all the gypsies.* His wife was by his side, perfectly angled for the cameras. They were indoors, but her hair was fluttering in a breeze, almost as if a wind machine had been placed there for just that purpose.

Once again, the final item was devoted to Le Machine. They told their viewers that his long-awaited bowel movement had finally happened, and went into some detail about the difficulty he had had in passing the stool, and how he appeared to be momentarily interrupted by a member of the audience shouting something out. But, they reassured the viewers, it had all been fine in the end, and after a few early expulsions that appeared to resemble owl pellets, he had laid a conventional-looking cable. They were also able to confirm that no wee had come out at the same time. Following a visit from his doctor, which had seemed to reassure Le Machine that everything was functioning as it should have been, *Life* had returned to its expected pattern. He had ordered sushi and a half-bottle of whisky. The newsreader wrapped up his report in the tone of voice he usually reserved for updates on serial snipers who had been terrorising communities and were expected to strike again at any moment. *So,* he said, *Le Machine has done numbers one and two. How much longer will we have to wait before he does number three?*

Aurélie turned to Professor Papavoine. 'Did he . . . talk to you about that?'

'Apparently up until now it's all been rather agricultural. He's used some kind of apparatus adapted from the equipment they use on rams when they're artificially inseminating sheep. It was all done very quickly and clinically, and it left the audience quite disappointed. He's had a bit of criticism about it not being quite true to the spirit of the show, though, and he's accepted that. So, for this run, he tells me, it's all going to be a little more traditional.'

'Oh . . .' she said, '. . . good?' She wasn't quite sure what to think. She didn't really have a reference point for it; even Sylvie would never have had a boyfriend who got up to things like that.

LUNDI

XXX

The Papavoines had to go back to work. Herbert was sleeping in his folding cot at the end of Aurélie's bed, and by the time he woke her with a protracted gurgle, they had already left. She knew that once she and Herbert had some breakfast inside them the time would have come for her to make some solid progress on her project. They were going to stay out of trouble for an entire day.

The morning passed productively. As the baby crawled around and made his way through the hamper of toys, she made a series of sketches of him, and took a few photographs for reference later on. His bruise was still there, but it had become so faint that it had almost faded into insignificance. The main project would continue long after she had handed him back to his mother, and she didn't yet know if he would be available for future sittings. She really hoped he would be; she had grown so fond of him, and she tried not to think about how likely it was that after Wednesday morning she would never see him again.

After lunch she started to worry that he might be feeling cooped up indoors, and it was a sunny day so she took him out for some fresh air to the park a few streets away from the Papavoines' apartment. She wrapped him up, and off they went.

As she sat on a bench, with Herbert facing her in his buggy, she felt a presence by her side. She didn't even have to look to know that it was an old woman, and that she had come to talk about the baby. As much as she would miss Herbert, she would not miss this.

'What a handsome boy,' said the old woman.

'Yes, he is.' At least the old woman was able to work out his gender.

'I hope you don't mind me saying,' she said, 'but his shoes are on the wrong feet.'

Aurélie winced to find that she had done it again. But this time she wasn't going to let the old woman win. 'He's pigeon-toed,' she lied. 'The doctor says it'll help his condition if he wears his shoes the wrong way round.'

'I see. I'm sorry. I was interfering, wasn't I?'

'Yes, a little bit.' Aurélie looked at the old woman. She was different from the usual ones. She was younger for a start, maybe only in her early sixties, but, when it came down to it she was the same as all the rest, a nosey old woman bugging her about Herbert.

'He reminds me so much of my grandson,' she said.

Aurélie had heard this several times. Sometimes the old woman would proceed to pull out a photograph and expect her to be dazzled by the similarity between Herbert and a baby who looked absolutely nothing like him. They would both have heads, and arms, and all that sort of thing, but apart from that they might as well have been from different species. And because the children in the photographs were never as cute as Herbert, she always felt insulted by the suggestion that he was in any way comparable to an inferior child.

'I saw him from across the park, and couldn't resist coming over for a closer look. I'll show you a picture of my grandson.'

Great, thought Aurélie, *I can't wait.*

The old woman pulled out her purse, and tucked among her shopping receipts was a photograph. 'He's called Olivier.'

Aurélie wondered why Herbert couldn't have been called Olivier. It would have saved her a lot of trouble. The old woman handed her the picture, and she was surprised to find herself agreeing; the baby did look quite a lot like Herbert, only not quite as cute or intelligent-looking. He was sitting on the knee of a woman in a green velvet jacket, with long blonde hair tied back in a ponytail.

'There he is,' said the old woman. 'And that's my daughter Aimée.'

Aimée's hair was so blonde that it made Aurélie feel mousy again.

The old woman held the photograph beside Herbert's face. 'If it wasn't for your little one's pigeon toes it would be hard to tell them apart.'

Aurélie smiled politely, but with a lack of enthusiasm. 'I don't really see it,' she said. 'It's my mother's eye. No other baby looks quite like my own, and this one's definitely mine. I remember the day he was born – he came out of . . .' She stopped herself before she started

301

pointing at inappropriate places again. She was ready to accept that the child in the photograph was better than most, but he still wasn't in Herbert's league; he lacked his *je ne sais quoi*.

'Oh no,' said the old woman, with a look of horror. She slipped the picture back into her bag, and put her hand to her mouth.

'What is it?' Aurélie hoped she wasn't having a seizure. She had too much going on in her life to have to deal with convulsing strangers.

'I've just realised something. I've realised what I've become – I'm an old woman who hangs around in parks harassing young mothers who are only looking for a moment's peace.'

'Well,' said Aurélie, 'at least you realise it. That's the first step; maybe you'll be able to nip this affliction in the bud. I'm sure you'll be able to get help – there are probably support groups, and if you can't find any then you should start one yourself.' Aurélie suddenly saw herself as a catalyst for social change; not for nothing would she have spent a week with a baby she had never met before. 'It has to stop. Mothers of young babies must be able to go to the park and travel on public transport in peace. Go now and start that group, and may it be the first of many the world over.'

The old woman zipped up her bag and stood up. 'I shall. I'm so sorry,' she said. She really did seem to be embarrassed. 'I can only pray that it will never happen again.'

'I wish you every success,' said Aurélie. 'And say hi to Olivier from us. He really is cute, you don't have to worry about that. Some of the photos I've been shown . . .' She pulled a face.

302

The old woman walked away. 'Maybe there is hope for humanity after all,' said Aurélie to Herbert. There was peace at last, and she lit a cigarette. After a few more minutes on the bench, when she was sure the old woman was gone, she put his shoes on the right feet. Then she got up and pushed the buggy around the park.

She didn't notice that someone was lurking in the bushes, dressed only in black leather. And nor did she hear the *click click click* of a camera's shutter.

Aurélie worked through the afternoon, and when Professor Papavoine came home he asked to see what she had done. She was nervous about showing him, but he insisted, and he looked at her sketches intently. He asked her questions about them, and she was relieved to find she was able to give him coherent answers about her intentions and her technique. He was particularly interested in how she was going to approach her final, enormous, piece, and he offered some very useful advice. When he had finished looking through her sketches, he handed them back to her and said, 'Very good. Keep it up.'

She could tell he meant it too, and she was pleased. She was starting to feel confident that she was going to produce something decent from this fiasco after all.

'Professor Papavoine,' she said, 'I hope you don't mind me asking, but I've been wondering – what do you actually do? I mean, what does a professor do, apart from give very occasional lectures? I see Professor Boucher making his rounds of the studios a lot, but I think that's mainly to pick up girls. You seem to stay in your office a lot more.'

'Oh, I keep busy,' he said. 'There's a lot of admin to be dealt with – departmental matters, that kind of thing

– but I do emerge from my cave every once in a while. You'll see me around a bit more the further you go in your course. I'm afraid you'll have to endure a series of lectures from me next year. A bit of art history, and a couple on my pet topic: miniatures and miniaturists. So that's something to look forward to.'

'Well, I am looking forward to it.'

'Do I detect an uncontrollable enthusiasm for miniatures and miniaturists?'

'You certainly do.'

'Then come with me.'

Professor Papavoine had turned a bedroom into his studio. He worked at a table over which hung a bright light.

'Believe it or not,' he said, 'I do a bit of painting on the side. This is what I've been working on for the past few months. I'm almost finished.'

Aurélie had to get close to see it properly. It was a painting of a school of fish on a small copper plate, about twenty centimetres by fifteen. There must have been hundreds of fish, each one painted in what appeared to be microscopic detail.

Aurélie couldn't believe what she was seeing. It was incredible. 'Fucking hell, Papavoine, this is awesome.' She stopped. She realised what she had just said, and turned red. 'Er . . . sorry. What I meant to say was, *Gosh, Professor, what a super picture. You must have a terribly steady hand.* But really, it's incredible. I had no idea . . .'

'Why would you? I'm glad you like it. This kind of work isn't exactly fashionable right now; in fact it hasn't really been in vogue for a few centuries, and maybe it wasn't even all that popular back then, but I'm a long way past caring about that. I've been working in miniature for forty years now. It's just what I do.'

Aurélie felt ashamed at having supposed that all Professor Papavoine did was sit in his office and stare into space. She really admired him as an artist now. She decided there and then that once she was done with her huge drawing of Herbert she was going to have a go at working in miniature herself.

'And how about Professor Boucher, does he paint, or anything like that?'

'He sculpts. Nudes, mainly.'

Liliane had returned from work, and tracked them down to the studio. 'Good, isn't he?' she said, looking proudly at her husband, and reaching up to ruffle his hair.

'Unbelievable,' said Aurélie, still finding it hard to equate the amiable and often baffled academic she had come to know with the creator of this work of intricate beauty.

'Now, before I forget, something landed on my desk today.' He patted his pockets one by one until he found the right one. He pulled out an envelope. 'It's addressed to you.'

Aurélie opened it. It was a pair of passes to *Life*, and a handwritten note: *Courtesy of Le M. Unlimited access. Come and go as you please. Bring your friends.*

He had been talking to his doctor again.

XXXI

A few phone calls and Métro rides later, Aurélie and Sylvie stood outside Le Charmant Cinéma Érotique with passes in their hands. Art exhibitions tended not to open on Mondays, but *Life* was buzzing with activity.

'OK,' said Sylvie, 'let's go in.'

Aurélie had turned white. She didn't move.

'Take a few deep breaths,' said Sylvie. 'I don't know how much it'll help, but that's what people on television say at times like this, so there must be something in it.'

'But what if I see him and decide I don't want to be with him after all?'

Sylvie shrugged. 'If you don't, you don't. That's just hard luck for him. But wouldn't you at least want to give it a try? Remember all that stuff you were saying about how he seemed so familiar, as if you had known him for years?'

'Yes, I do, and now I know why. First there was the Jesus angle – Lucien made a good point about that – but what I didn't know was that I'd been seeing pictures of him all over the city for weeks. I can't help wondering if I've been cheated. Of course there was going to be something familiar about him. It doesn't seem quite so magical when you think about it that way.'

'But what about all the other stuff, about conversation flowing so naturally, and how you made each other laugh, and how good he was with Herbert?'

'Well, yes, that side of things was fantastic.'

'How are things going with Herbert?'

'Pretty well – I haven't shot him once since Friday.' She had told Sylvie all about the Sébastien incident.

'That's good. You're getting the hang of it.'

They looked together at the big banner of Le Machine.

'He's got quite a body,' said Aurélie.

'And that doesn't hurt.'

'I wonder why he felt he had to be so secretive with me. That's a bad sign, isn't it?'

'Usually. But he does seem pretty mortified now. And let's not forget that he wasn't the only one who was holding back tiny nuggets of information. It's not as if you quite got around to telling him how you came to be hanging around with Herbert, is it?'

'I suppose not. But what if he sees me and doesn't like me any more? Every girl in town's going to be after him now he's a hit, and I bet loads of them will be better-looking than me.'

'If a naked man sends you secret texts via his doctor, it's a pretty good sign that he likes you. And look at yourself, for God's sake. You're magnificent. You're going to be every bit as good-looking as any of his wannabe groupies, and he's going to know that you liked him before you even knew he was Le Machine, and that counts for a lot.'

'But what if he notices that my ears aren't quite symmetrical?'

'He'll already have noticed.'

'Is it that obvious?'

'Yes, but as I've explained to you a thousand times before, men like that kind of thing. They find minor imperfections endearing, even sexy.'

'I hope that's true.' Even so, she decided she would try to angle her head in such a way that wouldn't draw attention to them. 'But what am I going to say to him?'

'You're not going to say anything, are you? You won't be able to, for a start. Stick to the plan. Remember the plan?'

Aurélie nodded.

'What is it?'

'I'm just going to go in, and watch him stand around naked for a bit with all the other people. If I'm lucky I'll get to see him go to the toilet, or blow his nose into a test tube. And as soon as he looks in my direction I'll give him a nice smile to let him know I've forgiven him for having had a bad day.'

'Precisely. And then you're going to come with me and meet my new boyfriend – Toshiro Akiyama.'

'So that's something else we have in common – boyfriends we barely know, and who we can't have private conversations with.'

'I know!' Sylvie said this as though it were a wonderful thing, and Aurélie found herself inclined to agree. There was something undeniably romantic about both their situations. Once again, Sylvie's turbo-charged positivity had saved the day.

Léandre Martin, Le Machine, was standing at the end of the runway, and the sound of his breathing thundered through the room. Aurélie froze again, overwhelmed with shyness. Sylvie took her hand, and together they snaked their way through the crowd. Soon she was just feet away from him. He didn't see her. He walked back along the runway to the stage. She watched him, and she also watched the other people who were there. She could tell by their faces that they were being transported by the experience, and she felt so proud of Léandre for doing what he was doing, and pleased with herself for having a brilliant boyfriend with such a great body. They stood there for a few minutes, but he didn't seem to be at all inclined to look in their direction. She wondered how she could let him know she was there.

Sylvie solved the problem for her. As he stood on the edge of the stage and surveyed his audience, she jumped up and down, waving her arms. People standing around them gave her pitying looks, but as soon as Le Machine had noticed the movement she started pointing at Aurélie, and he knew exactly what was going on. He walked back up the runway and stopped as close as he could get to them. Aurélie smiled at him, and at once he knew everything was going to be OK, that she had forgiven him for his pitiful performance at lunch, and was ready to give him another chance. He smiled too, and did something he wasn't supposed to do, that was contrary to the rule he had set himself for *Life* that stated *no physical contact with members of the audience*, but just this one time he would break it. He reached out, over people's heads, and she reached out to him and, just for a moment, they resembled the ceiling of the Sistine Chapel.

Léandre Martin touched the tips of Aurélie Renard's fingers, and Aurélie Renard touched the tips of Léandre Martin's fingers, and they understood one another perfectly. And as they touched, something happened to him, something to do with blood rushing to a particular destination in his body, filling certain sponge-like tissues. But he felt no shame. It was natural and normal, and if he hadn't allowed it to happen from time to time it would have diluted *Life* into pointlessness. Their fingers parted company, and he stood on the runway, looking at Aurélie Renard, and she looked at him and she wished with every cell in her body that it was three months from now. She had a lot to look forward to.

She knew she had to stick to her plan. She had seen him, and let him know, and now it was time to leave. And that was what she did.

Aurélie and Sylvie made their way back through the crowd to the exit, and Le Machine, standing proud, smiled as he watched them go. He walked back along the runway. The feeling hadn't gone away. Soon it would be time for number three.

'Wow,' said Sylvie, as they stood on the front step of the cinema. 'That was quite something. You don't have to worry – he definitely likes you.'

Aurélie couldn't stop smiling at the thought of what she had just seen.

'So,' said Sylvie, 'are you going to come back every day?'

'No, I don't think so. It would seem a bit like spying on him while he's at work. I'm just going to keep busy

310

until it's all over. I may not even go back at all. I'll get in touch with his doctor from time to time though, to let him know I'm thinking of him.' She lit a cigarette.

'Good idea. You don't want to seem needy, or like you've got nothing else to do. Now, let's go and find the Akiyamas and hand over the passes. Madame Akiyama's desperate to see your boyfriend without his clothes on.'

'And I'll get to meet Toshiro at last.'

They walked on to where the others were waiting, so happy with the turns their lives had taken, and so deep in conversation that neither noticed the black-clad figure walking along a few paces behind them, speeding up when they sped up, and slowing down when they slowed down.

Toshiro Akiyama had chosen their base camp for the evening, Café des Deux Moulins on rue Lepic. He knew it was touristy, and he was a little bit ashamed to mention it in front of people who lived in the city, but it was his first time in Paris, and when he read in the guide book that the café actually existed, he had become determined to go there at the earliest opportunity. With Le Charmant Cinéma Érotique just a short walk away, its time had come. He sat at a table with his mother and father and Lucien, and the moment he saw Sylvie he stood up and braced himself. He knew what was coming next. The prettiest, happiest girl he had ever seen was going to fly into his arms and pepper him with kisses. He was enjoying Paris.

Lucien had insisted on interpreting Sylvie and Toshiro's conversations. Both of them had told him that they didn't expect him to put himself through such an ordeal, but he assured them that it fell within the remit of his professional

311

engagement, and that even if it hadn't he would have done it anyway, as a friend, and that they were to look at it as if they were doing him a favour. He explained that being with the love of his life as she excitedly discussed her future with another man would be such an excruciating tribulation that it would help him in the long term – he would gain strength from the torment, and as he was sure it would be the absolute low point of his existence, he would try to find comfort in the thought that things could only get better for him from then on. And, he told them, he had accepted that he could never make Sylvie happy by loving her, but he was comforted by the thought that he could make her happy in other ways, and he would start by helping her to cement her romance with the man of her dreams.

Neither Toshiro nor Sylvie were convinced by his assurances, but he was adamant, and they couldn't see what they could do but allow it to happen. At least this way they were able to hold conversations, and they were sure that Lucien was so sincere that he would never misinterpret anything. They were right to put their trust in him. He never abused his power by putting inappropriate words in their mouths; all he did was translate their conversation as literally as he could, down to the finest nuances.

Sylvie, he said, as the pain tore through his flesh and bones, *I didn't know what love was until I found you*, and *Toshiro, you are the most handsome man I've ever seen*.

Whenever Sylvie or Toshiro used lines like these they would realise halfway through what they were saying, and add the brief addendum: *I'm sorry, Lucien*. He would translate these postscripts as he translated everything else. He saw no reason why he should spare himself.

This was Lucien's last night in the employment of the Akiyamas. The next morning they would be heading back to Japan, and he had another party of visiting tourists arriving straight away. He was going to be accompanying them on a trip around the countryside on a coach, and he was looking forward to getting out of the city.

Without Lucien there, communication between the new couple was going to become a lot harder. They had already planned for this, though. Once they had seen Monsieur and Madame Akiyama on to the plane, Toshiro would move his bags to Sylvie's apartment and while she was at work he would keep on top of his music, and explore the city, and when she wasn't at work they would take their clothes off and lie down together. For Lucien's sake they hadn't gone into further details about what they planned to do once they had taken their clothes off and lain down, but they had agreed on this broad outline. Each wanted to be sure that the other was ready to take that step. So far they had only kissed, but they could tell from this that they were absolutely compatible, that their bodies would fuse into a thing of extreme beauty. And when they weren't lying down together they would play backgammon, and cook for each other, and learn odds and ends of vocabulary, and be happy just being close.

While Monsieur and Madame Akiyama were away watching Le Machine, Aurélie got to know Toshiro. She even asked him the question that Sylvie hadn't dared to ask: *How did Natsuki take the news that you were flying to France to be with somebody else?*

Toshiro didn't take this question lightly. It hadn't been quite as slick a break-up as he had hoped it would be. It turned out that Natsuki had loved him deeply after

313

all, and as he told her he was leaving she had caved in straight away and finally admitted to herself that the cat had been a mistake, that she had bought him in a moment of weakness to keep her company on the long nights when Toshiro was so absorbed in his work that he was barely there. She sobbed as she told him that he was right, that they should have discussed Makoto before she got him. She told him she didn't even like the cat, that she had accepted that he looked mean and had a matching personality, and she had even grown tired of crafting hats for him. He wasn't the kind of cat that looked cute in novelty headgear anyway. She would try to find another home for him, and if nobody was prepared to take in such a nasty creature she would drive him to another city and abandon him, so things could go back to the way they had been before.

'Just don't leave me, Toshiro,' she had said, and he had seen the love and the fear in her eyes.

But he had left her, a sobbing wreck with a cat she didn't like, and he had taken the plane to Paris to meet a girl he had seen in a photograph and who, according to his mother, was very nice.

Via Lucien, he told them he felt sorry for his ex-girlfriend, but he knew he had done the right thing. He had come to realise that he had never loved her the way he loved Sylvie, and that the relationship had to end. If he were to stay, it would only be out of pity for her, as well as being a terrible act of self-sabotage. Lucien's own love for Sylvie was confirmed when he felt no urge at all to fly to Japan with the Akiyamas, and find Natsuki Kobayashi and comfort her. He had seen a photograph of her, and until days ago he would have considered her to be his type, on a par even with Akiko. He would have been ready to dry her tears and help her rebuild her life. He would even have helped her to rehome the cat, if she had asked. But, no, there really was only one girl for him, and there she was, right by his side as he helped her to plan the practical details of her forthcoming life with another man, her face aglow as he confirmed that this other man's previous relationship was definitely over.

At least, he thought, he had lost to a man who was amiable, and talented, and good-looking, and had a decent sense of humour. There was some consolation to be found in the knowledge that Sylvie was right to have chosen him: Toshiro Akiyama was a better man than he would ever be. It would have been harder still to watch her go off into the sunset with a man who was unpleasant, or dull, or who had a moustache, or who didn't love her as she deserved to be loved. Even in defeat he could at least see that there was some sense to the world.

Toshiro was telling her how easily he could move his job to Paris, how most of the people he worked with wouldn't even realise he had gone. She was saying that they could start out using her apartment, but that they would need to look for a bigger place if they were to have a room for them and a studio for him. 'And when the baby comes,' said Lucien, interpreting Toshiro, 'I can rent a studio space elsewhere.'

Sylvie looked at Toshiro, and he looked surprised, as if only just realising how much he had revealed. 'Baby?' she asked. 'What baby?'

Toshiro's surprise turned to a smile. He seemed not to regret his revelation. 'Our baby,' he said, and Lucien interpreted. 'We'll be having a baby one day, right?'

Time was short, and Sylvie and Toshiro hadn't bothered pretending that things were anything other than major between them. They had already spoken about her inevitable visit to Japan to meet Akiko and his grandparents, and to see where he had grown up. Neither had mentioned marriage yet, but Lucien knew Toshiro was only waiting for the right moment to ask her if she would be his wife, and it was clear that Sylvie had already decided upon her response. Toshiro had leapfrogged that particular conversation and moved straight on to babies.

Sylvie said nothing. She was speechless with happiness. She leaned across the table, and kissed Toshiro.

For Lucien, this was even worse than overseeing a marriage proposal. Just when he thought his life had reached its absolute nadir he was proved wrong, and things got worse. At last, it had all become too much for him.

Once their kiss had finally come to an end, he addressed Toshiro. 'Please tell your mother and father that it has been a pleasure working for them. I'm sorry that I'm not going to be finishing my agreed time with them, but I'm sure that under the circumstances they will understand. Please wish them a pleasant journey home.'

And then he spoke to Sylvie. 'I'm sorry,' he said. 'When we met I truly had no idea this would happen. I've really let you down.'

She shook her head. 'No, you haven't. You just need to . . .' She didn't know what he needed, and neither did he.

He carried on. 'You're going to have a great life with Toshiro. He's a good man. I don't know what I was thinking, falling in love with you.' He then translated this exchange, word for word, to Toshiro, just to let him know what had been said.

316

None of them knew what they could do but give him a look of sympathy. He stood, put on his coat and slung his bag over his shoulder. Aurélie, Sylvie and Toshiro said nothing as they watched him go, hunched over in defeat. Of the three of them, only Toshiro Akiyama would ever set eyes on Lucien again.

Monsieur and Madame Akiyama had returned from *Life*. They had been there for an hour, and Madame Akiyama was bursting with excitement. 'I feel like a girl again,' she said, showing them the souvenirs she had bought, mainly official *Life* cutlery for friends and neighbours. Akiko was to get a miniature version of his huge urine bottle to use as a vase. She turned to Aurélie. 'And he's really your boyfriend?' She had heard the story.

Aurélie hadn't understood a thing, and without Lucien there, there was no hope of them being able to hold anything like a viable conversation.

Madame Akiyama was so full of her experience that she carried on anyway. 'Lucky you,' she said. It wasn't until she realised that Aurélie wasn't going to respond that she looked around for her interpreter. 'So where's Lucien?'

Toshiro explained what had happened. Madame Akiyama understood. 'Poor boy,' she said. 'First Akiko and now Sylvie. He doesn't have much luck, does he? But he falls in love fast; I'm sure he'll have moved on to the next girl in a day or two.'

But somehow all of them, even Aurélie and Sylvie, who hadn't understood a word she had said apart from the names, had a feeling that there would never be a next girl, not after Sylvie.

They sat in silence, every one of them overwhelmed with

sorrow for him, and when Aurélie stood up to leave she felt as if she was interrupting a funeral service. She said goodbye to them all. She wished the Akiyamas a good flight. They couldn't understand what she was saying, and just smiled at her. She was determined to bridge the linguistic divide, so she stuck her arms out in imitation of an aeroplane, pointed at them and gave two thumbs up.

It worked. 'Thank you,' they both said, in their finest French.

Resisting the temptation to go back into *Life* for a sneaky look at her boyfriend, Aurélie made her way to the Métro and back to the Papavoines' place. She hoped Herbert would still be awake when she got there. She was missing him, and they only had one full day left together. She knew it would be a good one. She only wanted to keep him well, to have fun with him and to return him to his mother at nine twenty-two on Wednesday morning with a minimum of fuss.

As the Métro rolled on, there was no reason why it would have occurred to her for a moment that Sylvie would call her in the morning and, when she didn't get an answer, leave a message on her phone asking her whether she had seen the papers that day, and that if she hadn't, she might like to head down to a news-stand.

But whatever you do, Sylvie will say, *don't wear that coat you've been wearing, the professor's wife's one. And if there's any hair dye in the house, give yourself a dose. Oh, and do you have a balaclava for Herbert?*

XXXII

O n the pavement outside Le Charmant Cinéma Érotique, the arts editor of *L'Univers* stared at his chief arts correspondent as he waited for his car to arrive. The chief arts correspondent of *L'Univers* could not bring himself to return the stare, and as he looked away he wore an expression that appeared to passers-by, many of whom recognised him, to be one of steely resolve. They weren't to know that for the last two days Jean-Didier Delacroix had found himself suffering from momentary lapses of self-confidence, an experience so new to him that he had been knocked off balance, and neither the steeliness nor the resolve were quite what they appeared to be.

It was such an unusual situation for him to find himself in that it had even begun to affect his home life. That afternoon he had made love to his girlfriend, and she had tutted and yawned as he pounded away at her. There was nothing unusual about that, but for a moment he was sure he could sense a whole new layer of dissatisfaction over and above the default settings from which she had never deviated. He tried to tell himself that this couldn't possibly be, but even so the experience had made him anxious to the point where he had felt himself begin to lose his prowess, and she had very nearly ended up really having something to be disappointed about for the first time in her life. It had been a close shave, but he had pulled himself back from the brink and finished the job with his customary aplomb. Even so, he couldn't shake the feeling that she suspected that something was not quite right with his life, and he knew he would be rejected at the first sign of weakness. To lose her would be an incredible blow; it would be hard, even for Jean-Didier Delacroix, to find another girl as right for him as she was.

Standing with his boss as they waited for the car, he was more nervous than he had ever been, and it took every bit of strength he had to keep his lips in a steadfast line and his chin set at a defiant angle. He was determined for his inability to return his superior's gaze to seem like a refusal rather than a failure. Just as had been the case with his girlfriend, he knew that no matter what was going on in his mind he must at least appear to be strong.

They had spent ninety minutes in the auditorium, and Jean-Didier Delacroix knew that this time had been pivotal to his future. His editor had been so incensed with him for reneging on their agreed assault upon Le Machine that in that first, furious phone call he had fired him. As soon as he had slammed the phone down, he had called the newspaper's head of dismissals and had Jean-Didier Delacroix's termination papers drawn up and faxed to his apartment.

Jean-Didier Delacroix had waited a while before getting back in touch with his superior and, taking pains to make sure that at no point did it appear as if he was begging, he asked for a final chance to remain in his post. He had told him that he would accept the terms on offer without fuss, on one condition – that they go together to *Life*. If, after an hour and a half in the room with Le Machine, his editor still thought the man deserved to be destroyed, then he would go quietly. The arts editor knew that news of a scuffle over Jean-Didier Delacroix's departure from the paper would get around the business within seconds, and be the source of a feeding frenzy for their rivals. He had no option but to accept this challenge.

The chauffer-driven limousine pulled up, and in silence the men got in. They were taken directly to the arts editor's private club; a club so exclusive that even Jean-Didier Delacroix would not be considered for membership. He had only been there a handful of times, and until he was established as, for example, the arts editor of a major newspaper, he would have to suffer the indignity of being signed in as a guest. That day seemed farther away than ever as he made his way past marble busts to a private dining room.

They sat across the table from one another. A waiter entered, and poured them each a glass of wine. The arts editor of *L'Univers* found fault with the way he had done this, and with an explicit threat to the man's body and livelihood he had efficiently put him in his place. The waiter apologised, as if for his very existence, and left the men alone.

'So, Delacroix,' he began, 'I gave you the biggest break of your career when I took you on. And I took a great personal risk; I would even go so far as to say that I put my reputation on the line, and you of all people know how highly I value my reputation. I knew that if it was to backfire, if your work was to be anything short of exemplary, your uncle Jean-Claude and I would be accused of engaging in the most brazen nepotistic practices. You were always well aware of this. I put my trust in you, Delacroix. And how do you repay me? Let me tell you: by going behind my back and praising an *art show* which we had explicitly agreed had nothing to do with art, and which needed to be destroyed. By putting a love letter to a naked man who shits into bottles on the front page of *my* supplement. By undermining me, Delacroix.'

Jean-Didier Delacroix knew that the time had come for his veneer of defiance to be succeeded by a more appropriate expression: one of humility. He had to look as if he knew his place, and he tried to draw inspiration from the waiter's expression. Humility didn't sit well with Jean-Didier Delacroix – it required facial muscles that had never been exercised before, and as these muscles struggled to settle into place the arts editor almost spat his champagne out in mirthless laughter at the sight. Jean-Didier Delacroix said nothing, allowing his superior to compose himself and continue.

'And you forced me to go along to a seedy pornographic cinema, and stand – yes, stand – alongside some rather questionable . . .' He pulled a face and spat the words, '*members of the public* to watch this naked man do . . . do what, Delacroix? Tell me what we saw.'

This wasn't looking good. Jean-Didier Delacroix decided not to go into his feelings about Le Machine, feelings which even days after his first encounter with him were still taking shape, and to go instead for a literal recounting of events. He cleared his throat. 'He stood there naked for while, in a state of some considerable arousal, then he took out a test tube, and closed his eyes, and had a brief affair with himself. And when he had finished he put the results on display for all to see.'

'And that was just the start of it. What else did he do while we were there, Delacroix?' The arts editor of *L'Univers* thumped the table. 'What else?'

'He had a shower, then he made and ate a terrible sandwich. And he drank some water and a glass of white wine.'

'And then?'

Jean-Didier Delacroix knew what he meant. 'And then he urinated, and poured it into a big bottle, where it merged with several litres of urine he had already poured in. After which, he crouched down and . . .'

The arts editor of *L'Univers* held up a hand to stop him. 'And you still stand by your recommendation of this . . . *artwork*?'

Jean-Didier Delacroix had been just as impressed by *Life* on this second visit as he had been on his first, but he knew his neck was in the guillotine. The time had come for him to stand by his beliefs, for integrity to reign. Either that or the time had come to do what he could to save his career.

He looked his editor in the eye, and said, 'Yes, I stand by what I wrote.'

The arts editor of *L'Univers* leaned back in his chair, fixed Jean-Didier Delacroix with an icy gaze, and very, very slowly raised an eyebrow. Then he spoke. 'It *is* very good, isn't it? I'm rather glad we didn't close it down. Somehow they've pulled it off. I can't quite put my finger on why it works, but it does. What's that Goethe quote? The one about art and life?'

This reminded Jean-Didier Delacroix of the interrogations he had received as a child, and he felt invigorated by it. He knew the answer, of course: 'Art and life are different; that is why one is called art and one is called life.'

'Why didn't you use that in your review?'

'Because it's far too obvious, and I knew everybody else would.' He had read his principal rivals' take on *Life*. Several of them had used this line, and gone on for a number of pointless paragraphs about how Le Machine blurred these boundaries.

'Correct.'

'And besides, it's hardly Goethe's finest hour; I don't suppose he ever found himself top of his Venn diagram class.'

The arts editor of *L'Univers* put a hand into his jacket pocket, and pulled out a cheque. 'I brought this with me, in settlement of your dismissal terms. I was in no doubt that this conversation we are having now would have been about severance, and severance alone, but from the moment I walked in, it was clear that what I was seeing was art of the highest order. God knows why, though. Thinking back to your piece, I can tell you don't either. But something is going on there. Never ever quote me on this, Delacroix, not to anybody, but I even found myself asking some fundamental questions about my own life while I was in there. And I came to a decision.'

Knowing he had been vindicated, Jean-Didier Delacroix's humility had already evaporated, and his self-assurance was back, stronger than ever. It was as if his flirtation with insecurity had never happened. 'Do tell.'

'I can't say my decision was entirely inspired by Le Machine; in truth I've been weighing up my options for some months now. But around the time he was eating that sandwich, and my God it was a terrible sandwich, everything seemed to crystallise. It made me acutely aware of how little idea I have of how many days I have left. I am becoming old and emotional, Delacroix, so it is time for me to leave the stage. I have taken my career as far as it can go, and I am going to retire earlier than I had planned. I shall be stepping down in a year's time, and that's going to leave something of a vacuum. I don't see why we should go through the charade of making you deputy arts editor; I can't think of a single reason why you shouldn't go straight to the top. Of course I shall have to clear it with your uncle Jean-Claude, but I don't see him raising too many objections. You have the ability, you have the profile, et cetera, et cetera, and thus far you have yet to put a foot wrong. How do you feel about becoming the nation's youngest ever arts editor of a major newspaper?'

Jean-Didier Delacroix allowed himself a smile. Just minutes ago he had felt as if he was leaping from the top of a tall building, but now his birthright was more secure than ever. 'That is welcome news,' he said. 'And I have you to thank. I've had the finest grounding imaginable in my career, and in many ways you shall be carrying on. As my mentor, my successes are your successes.' He raised his glass. 'Father, I wish you a long and happy retirement.'

'I'm sure you do, Delacroix,' he said. 'I'm sure you do. But don't go thinking I'm going to be spending my days on the croquet lawn. Oh no, I'm going to be sitting on every committee you can think of. I'll be advising the government, and taking up every foreign exchange junket I can worm my way on to. I'm going to be a menace, Delacroix.' He raised his glass in return. 'To the future.'

They drank.

'So, Delacroix,' said Jean-Didier Delacroix's father, 'enough shop talk. I see you're still with that young lady.'

'I am.' She had accompanied him to a weekend get-together at the family's ancestral château a few weeks earlier, during which she had only smiled once, and that had been when she had made one of the servants cry.

'You do know, don't you, that she is absolutely vile?'

There was something admiring in his father's tone, and Jean-Didier Delacroix smiled. 'Oh, yes. Very much so.'

'You ought to think about sticking with that one, Delacroix. She's my kind of girl.'

Jean-Didier Delacroix smiled. 'So tell me, how is Mother?'

He looked triumphantly to the ceiling. 'Just as appalling as ever,' he said.

They raised their glasses, and drank to their women, and to their wonderful lives.

MARDI

XXXIII

L e Machine had not been quite as absent from Paris as his reputation suggested. Often over the past few years, Léandre Martin had left his home in London and taken a train beneath the Channel to Gare du Nord, where he would go down to the Métro and straight to his old neighbourhood.

Telling no one of his presence but those closest to him, he would stay at his parents' apartment for a few days at a time, sleeping in his childhood bedroom. He never ventured into the city, but every morning he crossed the landing to spend the day by Dominique Gravoir's bedside. He talked to him, read to him and took care of him, feeding him and cleaning up after him. He was glad of the opportunity to give his mother a break from her responsibilities. Every time he saw her, she seemed older, and more worn down.

When *Life* had started to go into profit, he had bought his friend a new bed, a new mattress, cotton jersey sheets and flannel pyjamas, and he had paid for a carer to come in twice a week. As his success had grown, he was able to provide even more for him; now the carers came every evening and stayed all night, keeping watch over him while his mother had a chance to sleep uninterrupted, and his mattress, bedclothes and pyjamas were renewed a little more often than they needed to be.

On his visits he always brought piles of CDs, and loaded his friend's MP3 player with audio books. He had no idea how his tastes would have developed, so he tried to provide him with as wide a range as possible, from classical poetry to spy thrillers, and the latest pop music to avant-garde orchestral pieces. He road-tested everything for quality before introducing it to him, so they were all personal recommendations. It helped that his own tastes were broad; he was always looking for the best of everything. In between visits he would send him packages containing bits and pieces that he thought he might appreciate, and prior to each staging of *Life*, when he wouldn't be in touch with him for months on end, he had made sure he had a good supply of books and music.

Every once in a while, Dominique Gravoir's condition would be reassessed. The doctor would always say that there was no hope of a recovery, that it was surprising he had lived as long as he had, and that it was very unlikely that he would be able to comprehend a word that was spoken to him. Léandre Martin and Dominique Gravoir's mother had no cause to disbelieve the doctors, and neither was waiting for a miracle. They knew he wouldn't be coming back, but at the same time they felt that even if the words they spoke to him were never heard, they were not wasted, because every one of them was spoken with love.

As *Life* had taken off, and he had stood naked on stage in front of decent-sized and apparently appreciative crowds in London, Léandre Martin had a good feeling that his primary motivation had not been misplaced, that Dominique Gravoir was not living in vain. If it hadn't been for him, the exhibition would never have taken place: his friend was as much a part of it as he was, and when he heard stories about how people had responded to the work, he felt gratified on his behalf as well as his own.

Ever since the battle with the cormorant, Léandre Martin had felt that he was living for both of them, and during the bleaker moments of *Life,* when loneliness took hold, he often had a feeling that Dominique Gravoir was helping him to get through it. He had little patience for tales of the supernatural, but he had a sense that his friend's condition had become such a huge part of his own life that it was ingrained within him, and somehow he was able to draw inspiration from whatever strength it was that had been keeping him alive for all these years.

At the end of each run, Le Machine would be handed a large box of mail, with translations attached if necessary. It was always a mixture of demented scrawlings, sexual propositions from women (some of which he would accept, on the understanding that there was to be no chance of a relationship), sexual propositions from men (who were out of luck), and tales of how *Life* had improved the days of so many people who had been to see it.

These tales touched him to his core. He would read letters from people who had become more aware of their bodies than they had ever been. Some would tell him that they had started fitness regimes; others had found themselves eating healthier food than ever before. Other responses were more oblique, from people who, while watching him, had found themselves thinking deeply about their own lives, and had made big decisions of one kind or another: some had extricated themselves from bad relationships, others had decided to move house, some had abandoned their jobs and applied for nursing degrees. Dozens had pledged to get companions for their pet goldfish. Many people had said that while they had been watching him they had realised how simple life can be, and how cluttered their own life was, and that they had decided to pare back their belongings and lower their material ambitions.

None of these outcomes had been specific intentions of his. All he had wanted to do was display the human body at work, in all its familiarity and wonder, and let the audience think whatever they wanted to think. But still, he was glad to hear these stories. There had even been people who had written to tell him that they had decided against suicide after watching *Life*, realising that the body was too incredible a machine to destroy. And every time, without fail, he would receive a handful of letters from people who told him that *Life* had knocked them out of a state of denial about a medical issue, that they had finally gone to see a doctor about something that had been worrying them, and learned about an underlying condition that would only have worsened if they had left it any longer. *It could be that you helped save my life*, they wrote.

Léandre Martin weeded out the sexual propositions and the demented scrawlings, and read these letters to

Dominique Gravoir before handing them to his mother to keep. She looked at her son with pride as she made her way through them. In ways that they could never have foreseen, *Life* had been a triumph.

To his mother, and to Léandre Martin, and to a lot of people who would never even know, Dominique Gravoir was a superhero.

Dominique Gravoir did not look like a superhero. His limbs were wasted sticks, his face lacked definition and expression, his eyes saw nothing, and his torso was little more than a bony row of ribs. Every doctor who had ever seen him told his mother that one day he would catch an infection and his body would be too weak to fight it. But for now, something inside was keeping him alive.

His mother sat beside him, as she had done every day for almost twenty years. She held his hand as she read the paragraph from the newspaper about Le Machine's latest activities. She and Léandre Martin had never spoken about his reason for creating *Life*, but they didn't need to. She knew exactly why he did what he did.

'It seems to be quite an eventful run this time,' she said. 'He's even selling out the early morning slots. And there's been some gossip that he's found himself a girl. Apparently a blonde with a baby has been seen hanging around the show. Do you know anything about this?'

Léandre Martin had told Dominique Gravoir all about how he had found somebody, that she had been blonde and as pretty as it was possible to be, that he loved the way her teeth were slightly wonky and one of her ears stuck out a bit more than the other, and that she had been looking after a friend's baby. He told him he had noticed the baby first, and the child had reminded him so much of the one from his enormous print of Eugène Carrière's *Enfant avec casserole* that he had become quite mesmerised by him, and when he finally looked up and saw the girl, he had immediately been ready to be with her, to share his life with somebody at last.

I thought of you, Dominique, he had said, *and I know it sounds stupid, but I felt as if you were there with me, giving us your blessing. It all happened so suddenly, and it was as if you were right beside me, telling me that she was the one, that it was time for me to let somebody in. I know that kind of stuff isn't real, but I really do think you would have wanted us to be together.*

He had told him about what a wonderful day they had had, how she had made him laugh, and how he had even made *her* laugh, and for the first time since he was eight years old he felt he had a playmate, someone with whom he could be himself. And then he had ruined everything. He told his friend how awful he felt for messing things up. He told him how hopeless the situation was, and that he was sure he would never see her again.

'There's a picture here of her standing outside the venue,' said Dominique Gravoir's mother. 'She's very pretty. She looks nice, too. I always hoped Léandre would find somebody nice one day. He deserves it.' She often found herself worrying about him, concerned that he spent too much time feeling bad about Dominique, and not enough time living his own life. He had been such a happy boy until that day, but ever since he had been so serious. She hadn't blamed him for a moment, and she just wanted to see him smile again, to see him enjoying life as he had all those years ago.

'Let's hope she can bring him out of himself a little. But who knows? It could just be a load of rubbish made up to sell papers. Maybe they've never even met.' She looked at her son. Something about him had changed. 'Are you OK, Dominique?'

It seemed to her that at that moment he looked more comfortable and content than usual. She thought she could see a light in his eyes. She checked herself. He looked just the same as he always did. She had only ever wanted to deal with the situation as it was, and she often warned herself against getting carried away by silly notions. She was still his mother, though, and she still allowed herself moments of sentimentality. Even though he was a grown man, there were times when she looked at him and all she could see was her little baby boy.

She kissed his forehead, and left the room to make a mug of coffee. She kept the bedroom door open for him. He had always liked the smell of coffee.

XXXIV

When Aurélie switched on her phone and picked up Sylvie's message, she abandoned her plan to spend another quiet morning sketching Herbert, and hurriedly got ready to go down to the news-stand to find out what was going on. She knew there wasn't going to be any hair dye in the house, so instead she borrowed one of Liliane's hats and pulled it low over her eyes, and in the absence of a balaclava she arranged Herbert's hood around his face so that only his eyes and nose were showing. As cute as he was, he really could have been almost any pink baby.

Just as they were about to leave, she spotted a pair of enormous sunglasses, and put them on, and hanging on a hook by the door was a magnificent scarf of Liliane's. She wrapped it around her face until it was almost completely covered. It wasn't the usual way she would wear a scarf, but she wouldn't worry about that now. She liked the pattern, and the material felt really good. She found the label: it said, of course, La Foularderie. She told herself that as soon as all this was over she would go there. She looked at herself and Herbert in the hall mirror. There was no way anybody was going to recognise them.

They got to the news-stand without any drama. She looked around to find out what Sylvie had been going on about, and there she was, on the front page of *L'Étoile*, smiling as she pushed Herbert through the park. Underneath were the words:

EXCLUSIVE! Has this mystery blonde captured the heart of Le Machine? This pretty single mum has been seen hanging around *Life*, flirting with the naked artist. Read the full story on page 5.

Aurélie took the paper to the counter, and the woman picked it up, looked at her, looked at Herbert, and looked back at the paper. Then she did it again. And again. 'It's you?'

Aurélie shook her head.

'Yes it is. It's you.'

Aurélie didn't have the energy to make a second denial. She nodded.

The newsagent put her hand to her heart, and trembled. 'In thirty-six years I have never had a celebrity come to my news-stand. My husband is always complaining. *Henriette*, he says, *why do celebrities never come to your news-stand?* But now those days are gone. This is a new beginning. Please, please, would you sign a copy of the paper for him? Right now he's suffering from an appalling bout of haemorrhoids; if you were to see his anus, even from a distance, you would weep with pity for the man, and I just know that a kind word from you would do more to relieve the pain than any medicine. I can see him now, bouncing up and down with delight on his special cushion.'

The woman handed her another copy of the paper and a pen, but her hands were shaking so much that Aurélie had trouble taking hold of them. When, at last, she had both the newspaper and the pen in her hand, she couldn't think of a word to write. She stared out at nowhere from behind her enormous sunglasses.

'Hurry,' said the newsagent, 'before you have a chance to change your mind. His name is Alphonse.'

Aurélie found a blank spot near the photograph, and wrote: *Dear Alphonse, I hope your unfortunate condition improves in the near future. Best wishes from Le Machine's mystery blonde.*

The newsagent saw what she had written, and was speechless with emotion. Aurélie handed her the money for her copy of *L'Étoile,* and with a gesture she refused to take it. Mumbling through her scarf, Aurélie thanked her, and she pushed Herbert back the way they had come, wondering all the way how many other people had seen through their disguises.

Back at the Papavoines' apartment, she spread the newspaper on the dining table and had a proper look at it. It could have been worse. She could have been described as a *mousy-haired mystery girl.* And while *pretty single mum* wasn't particularly accurate, at least they had said she was pretty, and they seemed to have no idea that Herbert's presence in her life was in any way questionable.

The story inside didn't add much to the front-page caption; it was just a bit of lightweight filler. All they had to say was that their embedded reporters had seen her twice, once apparently calling out to him, and another time *sharing a fleeting romantic moment*. They had clearly sent a photographer on her tail too, but they chose not to go into details about that. They said that *sources close to the controversial artist* had reported that he was smitten with her.

She knew well enough that newspapers are inclined to invent such sources to suit their needs, but after everything she had heard from Professor Papavoine she was sure they had got this right. Léandre really did seem to be smitten with her, and she had even seen some very solid evidence to back this up.

She read on. They used the rest of the piece to give their daily update of what he had been up to, mainly cataloguing what had gone in and what had come out. They finished with an interesting observation: they had been the first ones to report that he seemed to be holding his breath twice a day, at one o'clock in the morning, just before going to sleep, and again at one o'clock in the afternoon. *He lies down*, they noted, *and seems to turn purple for a while*.

The main article was accompanied by another photograph, of Aurélie standing on the front step of the cinema, *confiding in a close friend*. Sylvie looked aglow with love for Toshiro. She wondered whether the photographer was still following her. If they were, she would have to shake them off before handing Herbert back. The last thing she needed was someone lurking in the shadows and capturing the mother and child reunion on film.

She still hadn't got around to changing her horrendous

ringtone, and when it went off she almost jumped out of her skin. She jumped again when she saw who was calling. It was her dad. She had a feeling she was in trouble, and for a moment she thought about not answering, but she couldn't do it. She couldn't bring herself to send her own father to voice mail.

'Hello, Dad.'

—*Hello, Aurélie.*

'How are you?'

—*I'm fine. How are you?*

'Fine. How are you?'

—*I'm still fine. Nothing much has changed in the last two seconds.*

'That's good.'

He got straight to the point.

—*So are things still going well with your new boyfriend?*

'Yes, they're going very well, thanks.'

—*So tell me all about him. What does he do for a living?*

'Oh, you know. A bit of this, a bit of that.'

—*And while he's doing a bit of this and a bit of that, does he wear any clothes?*

So he had seen the newspaper. 'As a matter of fact, no. No, he tends not to during working hours.'

—*And if he needs to, say, go to the toilet, does he discreetly withdraw to a private place, or . . .?*

'No, Dad. He just does it in front of everybody. I know it doesn't sound very good on paper, but there's so much more to it than just taking his clothes off and doing a poo. He's doing something beautiful.'

—*If you say so. It all sounds a bit unusual to me, but I only have myself to blame. I guess this is what happens*

*when you encourage your daughter to go to Paris to be
an artist. She starts hanging around with people who . . .
well, who do things like that.*

'He's nice, Dad. You'll like him.'

—*Are you absolutely sure he's not just a pretentious
idiot?*

'I'm sure.' It was good of him to ask. If he had posed
the same question about Sébastien he would have been
on to something.

—*Well, if you say so. Just make sure he treats you well.
You know what famous people can be like.*

Herbert, who had been slithering up and down, chose
this moment to make some quacking sounds.

—*Oh yes, that's next on my list. What's going on with
this baby? Since when were you a 'pretty single mum'?*

Aurélie braced herself. She was going to tell her dad a
big fat lie. He seemed to be taking things in his stride so
far, but she knew he would be on the next train to Paris
if he found out about the stone, and if he ever found out
about the gun it would break his heart. 'I've been looking
after him for a friend.'

—*How's that going? I have to say you look like a
natural. At least you put his shoes on the right feet – I
never quite got the hang of that with you two.*

She silently thanked the nosey old woman for her interference. 'It's going fine. She's back in town tomorrow, so
I'll be back to full strength with my project.'

—*It sounds like you're busy. I'll call again in a few
days to see how you're getting on. For now I'll trust your
judgment over the naked man. Say hi to him from me.*

'I will, when I get a chance. He's quite busy with work
at the moment.'

—Oh, and there's one last thing on my list: what's that in your hand in the second photo?

It was a cigarette. The last time she had seen him she had assured him that she was going to give up. It was only now she had Herbert that she realised how awful it must be for a parent to see their child do something that had a good chance of making them very ill. Her father had watched his wife's slow decline, and he had told her that he was kept awake at nights with worry at the thought of his daughter volunteering to go down the same route. She had felt a bit guilty when she heard this, but it was only now that she could begin to comprehend the depth of his concern. She felt awful.

'I'm sorry,' she said. 'I will give up. I promise.' She had said that before, and had thought she had meant it, but for the first time she knew she *really* meant it, that she wasn't just fooling herself.

—And are you littering?

'No!' When she was fifteen her dad had found out she was smoking, and she had told him, with all the petulance she had inside her, that she wasn't going to stop. He had made her promise, though, that she wouldn't ever throw litter on the ground. He told her that littering was the scummiest thing about smokers. What they did to their health was up to them, but he hated the mess they made. Since that day, Aurélie hadn't dropped a single match or cigarette butt on the ground. She still let her ash fall, though. She didn't count that as littering, and told herself it was good for plants.

She felt good to be able to tell him the truth about this. It was something he felt so strongly about that she would sooner tell him that she had been shooting babies than dropping her cigarette butts on to the pavement.

They said goodbye, and Aurélie picked up her sketchpad. She was going to be a good girl for the rest of the day. A model daughter. A minute later she put her sketchpad down, and reached for a cigarette. She lit it. Then, remembering her dad's words, she stubbed it out in the ashtray, vowing never to smoke again. Then she picked it out of the ashtray, and lit it again. Today was not the day.

XXXV

Sylvie Dupont drove back into the city, with Toshiro Akiyama by her side. Neither of them spoke, but neither felt the need to speak. She had managed to convince her Wednesday boss that it would be a great idea for him to lend her a 2CV for the morning, so she could take Monsieur and Madame Akiyama to the airport. It had done a good job; it had started at the first try, there weren't too many ominous rattles, and they had made it to their destination with time to spare before the flight. The only problem had been the lack of luggage space, which meant that her passengers had been buried under piles of bags. None of them seemed to mind, though. Even Monsieur Akiyama had been sanguine about the situation. Lucien had taught Sylvie the Japanese for *senior position* and *large corporation*, and he hadn't used the words once. Instead he had just sat there quite serenely, a heavy case squashing him into the back seat.

Without its passengers and their baggage it looked as though the car was going to get the two of them back to the city without any drama, too. At red lights she and Toshiro looked at one another, and held hands, relying on the honking horns of other drivers to let them know when it was time for them to move on.

That morning, Madame Akiyama had been impatient to get back to Funabashi and tell Akiko all about Toshiro's new romance, and she had used the journey and check-in queue as an opportunity to take as many photos of the couple as she could, for inclusion in her forthcoming illustrated lecture on the subject. She was determined to make the most of what little remained of her time in France, and she used all the phrases she had learned over the preceding week, no matter how irrelevant they were to the situation. *Two tickets, please*, she said to nobody in particular, or *Please excuse my husband, he speaks no French*. She planned to become fluent as quickly as possible, and she was going to start taking lessons as soon as they got back. Through Lucien, she had already explained that she and her husband planned to be regular visitors to the city, now that Toshiro was going to be settling there.

It was Madame Akiyama who had spotted the picture of Aurélie and Herbert on the front page of the newspaper. She had been so excited that she had bought a copy straight away, and when she opened it and saw the picture of Aurélie and Sylvie on the steps of *Life*, she was so ecstatic that she bought five more copies to distribute among friends and family. While Madame Akiyama was queuing, Sylvie had called Aurélie and left a message to let her know she had suddenly become a media star. And while she had her phone in her hand, she had sent a quick text to Lucien, saying hello and asking how he was doing.

She would never receive a reply.

When the time had come to say goodbye, she had embraced Monsieur and Madame Akiyama with all her strength, and she had vainly fought tears as she watched them vanish behind the security doors. She was really going to miss them, but she consoled herself with the thought that they would be meeting again before too long. In a couple of days she would be ringing around all her bosses, arranging time off for her visit to Japan. She already knew which bosses would be OK about it, and which would cause trouble, but the difficult ones could get stuffed. She would just leave. She wasn't going to let anyone come between her and her trip to Toshiro's homeland.

They drove up the steep and narrow west end of rue Norvins, and this time the clutch held out. She dropped the car off with her boss, and took Toshiro's arm as they walked down the hill and through the streets to her apartment. He always glided quite naturally to the kerb side of the pavement, and she appreciated that. Quite a few of her suitors had been dropped after taking a lackadaisical approach to positioning as they walked along the street. One of the last things her mother had said to her was: *Sylvie, never give yourself to a man who walks on the inside of the pavement. It's a signifier: if he won't even offer you this small act of consideration, how will he treat you in other aspects of your life?* She hadn't really known what she was talking about at the time, but she had remembered these words and come to regard this as

346

important advice; she always looked with pity at women whose men wouldn't follow this simple code. She didn't feel a sense of relief with Toshiro, though; she had known from the moment she had seen his photograph that he was the kind of man who would walk on the outside.

On Tuesdays she normally worked a late shift on the door of a drag cabaret show, but she had arranged for one of her colleagues to take her place. This was to be her first full day off in months, and she was going to spend it in the best way imaginable.

Toshiro had not been to her apartment before, but she chose to leave the full guided tour of its three tiny rooms until later. When the door closed behind them, they stood and looked at one another. They were alone together for the first time. She unbuttoned his shirt, and he pulled the poppers on her dress, and everything was as wonderful as they had known it would be.

XXXVI

Aurélie spent a quiet evening in with the Papavoines. They took turns amusing Herbert, all of them trying hard not to think about how they would be saying goodbye to him forever the next day.

While Liliane was in the shower and Professor Papavoine was busy sending the baby crawling after a ball with a bell in it that had been a favourite toy of a long-deceased cat of theirs, Aurélie sent a message to her boyfriend, via his doctor, in which she told him that she wouldn't be going back to the venue until the very end of the run, and that she wasn't going to be sending him regular texts or expecting messages from him. She told him she was going to be busy for the coming weeks, that she had a major project to absorb her. He, of all people, would understand this.

She didn't want him to worry that she wouldn't be there

for him at the end, and she would be in touch from time to time, just to let him know she was thinking of him. She didn't want to bother his doctor too much, either. She was sure she had better things to do with her time than secretly pass on romantic notes while pretending to attend to a very slightly sprained knee.

She insisted on making mashed potato for dinner, and was pleased with the rapturous reception it received. Even Herbert shovelled his down quite joyfully and banged his spoon for seconds. After dinner, as Herbert began to flag, so did she. She decided on an early night. She had to be up first thing in the morning, to go back to her apartment to collect some of Herbert's clothes that she had left hanging up to dry, before returning to the scene of the crime. As long as she was in the square by nine twenty-two, everything would be fine.

She had already set her alarm for six. The Papavoines offered to get up with her and make her breakfast, but she insisted they had done enough and should stay in bed. She knew her way around the kitchen well enough. It was time to say goodbye.

She told them she didn't know how to thank them, and the four of them came together in a group hug. Apart from Herbert, who blew a long, clear raspberry, nobody quite knew what to say.

As soon as Herbert was in his freshly laundered Eiffel Tower and Mona Lisa pyjamas (the blood had washed out, but she hadn't patched the bullet hole in the shoulder) his eyes, which had been barely open, pinged wide awake. He gave Aurélie a big smile. He was ready for fun.

Aurélie read to him from the pile of picture books that

Liliane had put by her bedside, and sang 'Hier Encore' a few times, and cuddled him and tried her best to soothe him. Whenever his eyes seemed to glaze over, she tried putting him to bed, but he thrashed and wailed and would not put up with it. It was past midnight by the time he finally flaked out. Aurélie gently picked him up and lowered him into his cot. The instant he touched the mattress he woke up, and was immediately furious.

She calmed him down by showing him his photograph on the front page of the newspaper. He was mesmerised. When his attention began to wander, she found the horoscopes. 'This is how we'll find out what you've done today, Herbert,' she said. She read his out to him. '*Aquarius*: Money has been on your mind a lot lately. A big decision will soon be made, and you will feel a great sense of relief. A stranger in yellow brings good luck.' Aurélie thought back through the day. She was fairly sure there had been no stranger in yellow. It was a shame. They could both have done with some good luck.

An hour later Herbert fell asleep on the bed again, and this time she left him there, and lay beside him. Her mind was busy turning over everything that had been going on, and for all her exhaustion it would not switch off. When it finally did, her sleep was fitful, and punctuated by unpleasant dreams. At one point she woke to feel her heart racing, and she was gripped with a fear that Herbert was no longer there. It was a while before her eyes adjusted to the dark and she could see him by her side, sleeping peacefully. The adrenaline kept her awake for a long time afterwards.

The next time she woke up she checked the clock on her phone. Her alarm was going to be going off in twenty minutes, and then she was going to have to go halfway across the city to give Herbert back.

She didn't want to give him back.

She watched him in the dark, this beautiful, strange and innocent creature she had grown to love. She thought of his mother, who hadn't even kissed him goodbye. What kind of life would he have with her?

MERCREDI

XXXVII

Aurélie Renard checked the time. She had got there twenty minutes early. She sat on the bench adjacent to The Russian's. He was playing his Russian instrument in his usual spot, and the music they were making together was so melancholy that it cut right through her. It was the perfect soundtrack for her state of mind. Herbert had fallen asleep in his buggy, so she wasn't even able to bond with him in these last precious moments they had together. All she could do was look at him as the music crashed over her. It was heartbreaking.

She was dreading the arrival of his mother. She hoped she would have calmed down over the preceding week, and would be pleased to see her son safe and well, and would scoop him up and kiss him and cuddle him. She needed to be reassured that she wasn't handing him over to a horrible person, that he would be growing up with someone who would give him all the love he deserved.

She and Herbert had taken the Métro from the Papavoines' to her apartment. The place was just as she had left it, only colder and with a bit of a musty smell. She found everything of his that she had left behind, and stuffed it all in his bag. Sitting on the bedside table was the copy of *Your Baby & You*. She hadn't even opened it. She would read it when she got back, to find out what she should have been doing all this time.

She was about to leave when she thought of something. The gun was still in a drawer, hiding under some clothes. She found it, and held it. It felt so much heavier than before, as if weighed down by its unhappy history. She found a tea towel and rubbed it, wiping off her fingerprints, as she had seen criminals do in films. Then she wrapped it up and put it in her bag. She would track Sylvie down later on and hand it back with thanks, and tell her she never wanted to see it again.

As she left her apartment, she came face-to-face with Madame Peypouquet.

'Hello, Madame Peypouquet,' she said.

She looked at Herbert. 'That thing's been quiet these last few days,' she said.

'I found a volume switch,' said Aurélie. 'I think I'll lose points for turning it down, but it doesn't matter. I know I'm not ready for a real one. Not yet, anyway. As a matter of fact I can't stop because I'm off right now to get him plugged into the computer. They'll take all the information from the microchip and give me a mark out of ten for my mothering skills.'

'Let me know what you score. I'm not going to wish you luck, because you know my thoughts on the matter. Oh, and by the way, did you see yourself in the newspaper yesterday? Monsieur Simoneaux came up here in his pyjamas and slippers to show me. They thought the baby was real!' Madame Peypouquet smiled, revealing more gums than teeth, and the few teeth there were stuck out at extraordinary angles, like abandoned gravestones. 'If only they knew!'

Aurélie returned her smile, and backed away. 'I must be going, Madame Peypouquet,' she said.

'And you're doing it with that naked man behind the handsome boy's back? Or is it the other way round? Either way, I like your style,' she said. 'I always thought you were too prim for your own good, but you've proved me wrong. And good for you – if you can't have fun while you're young, when can you?'

Still gliding backwards, Aurélie nodded. She would explain the situation, or at least some of the situation, to Madame Peypouquet when she had more time.

As she made her way downstairs, Madame Peypouquet's voice reverberated around the building. 'I can't say I blame you – he's got a good body. You know, you remind me of me when I was your age. I was just like you – there was no stopping me. I went with anyone I could get my hands on. When you get back I want you to tell me every detail – and I mean *every* detail.'

It was nine fifteen. The Russian at last steered his haunting melody to a heart-rending finale, and without the rattle and drone the square seemed almost silent. He didn't start another tune; instead he gently packed his instrument back into its battered case, and clicked it shut. He stood up.

'Well done,' he said.

Aurélie looked up at him. 'Pardon?' she said.

'Well done. You kept him alive.'

So he had witnessed the incident the week before. 'Only just,' she said.

'I knew he would be OK,' he said. 'I could tell you weren't the kind of person to mistreat a baby. Anyone could see you hadn't meant to hit him with the stone. It was an incredibly stupid thing to do, but I've always had a very low tolerance for people who don't do incredibly stupid things from time to time. She's right, you know – you do have a kind face. She's insane, but she was right about that.'

'Thank you,' she said. 'He and I had a good time together.' She decided not to go into the darker details of Herbert's time in her care. She changed the subject. 'What's your instrument called?'

He patted its case. 'It's a hurdy-gurdy,' he said.

'Is it . . . Russian?' She'd noticed that The Russian didn't sound particularly Russian.

'Maybe a little bit. Nobody's quite sure where it's from; it seemed to evolve from all over the place. Maybe bits of it came from there . . .' He realised why she had asked. 'Ah, I see. No, I'm not Russian, but my hat is. I was once working on a boat that docked in Vladivostok, and I got it there. I've worn it ever since. I feel naked without it. As for the hurdy-gurdy, I won it in a dice game one night in Saint-Chartier three years ago. I'd never played a note of music on any instrument at that point in my life, but I thought I'd give it a go, and I haven't stopped since. Apparently it's even older than I am, if you can imagine that.'

'Are you busking?'

He shook his head. 'I have a landlady whose nerves can't stand the noise, so I come here every morning to play it. It's as good a place as any.'

'I really like the music.'

'Thank you.' He seemed genuinely gratified by the compliment. 'Now I'd better get off to work.'

A part of her wanted to ask him where he worked, what he did when he wasn't playing his hurdy-gurdy. But she stopped herself. She didn't want to be like an old woman in a park, asking unwelcome personal questions. She would have found out all about him if the stone had hit him instead of Herbert. He would barely have felt it land, too; it would have just bounced softly off his Russian hat. He seemed friendly, and she was sure he would have let her follow him around.

She was glad it hadn't hit him, though. There had been one or two bumps in the road, but the more she thought about it, the more confident she became that it had been a good week, that on balance she had done the right thing in taking Herbert, rather than just running away from the situation. She had spent time with an incredible baby, she had managed to get herself a boyfriend, she had got to know the Papavoines, and even though she wasn't going to be doing the project she had set out to do, she had a good feeling that her new plan was going to go well. If the stone had hit The Russian, or anyone else, she would have ended up producing an unfocused mixed-media mishmash. Now, though, her week was coming to an end, and her life was going to return to something resembling normal.

'Good luck with everything,' he said.

'Thanks. You too.' She wanted him to stay for a few minutes, to wait with her until Herbert's mother arrived, but she said nothing, and with a touch of his forelock, he left. The rush had died down, and she was alone.

It was nine twenty-one. With one minute to go, there was no sign of Herbert's mother.

Nine twenty-two came and went, and there was still no sign of her. Herbert slept on, and Aurélie started to wonder what to do.

XXXVIII

L e Machine could tell that *Life* was going very well. In
all his previous presentations of the piece, the room
had started to empty in the early hours of the morning,
and would only start filling up again around midday. In
Paris, though, it had been full all the time. He had even
found this a little disconcerting. Every night he fell asleep
to the thunderous sound of his heartbeat, or the gurgling
that was picked up by the microphone deep inside his belly,
and as he did he felt a thousand eyes upon him, and
when he awoke he felt a thousand eyes upon him, and if
he ever got up for a glass of water he would look with
bleary eyes at a room packed full of people watching him
stumble from the bed to the sink and back again.

In the mornings it always took a few moments for him
to adjust to the new day, as he sat on the side of the bed,
stretching and looking at his surroundings. When he was

ready he would pick out any sleep that had built up in his eyes, and sprinkle it from his fingertips into a jar. Then he would wash his face, brush his teeth and walk over to the urinal. His morning ritual had become known as a highlight, and anybody who was there for it felt they had spent their time and money wisely.

Today he had slept late. It was almost half past nine by the time he woke. He went through his usual routine, which culminated in an extremely long wee. As it went on and on, the early morning crowd began the chant that had become traditional at this point in the day, the combined volume of their voices just about beating the sound coming from the speakers: *Le Ma-chine! Le Ma-chine! Le Ma-chine! Le Ma-chine!*

It was a good feeling. The run was going to be a success, and when it was over his girl would be waiting for him. This warm feeling was interrupted by a shudder of doubt. What if she wasn't there as she had said she would be? What if she had second thoughts about being with him? What if she met somebody else? What if she fell ill? What if she was arrested, found guilty of a serious crime and sent to jail for several years?

This last thought snapped him out of this state of mind. He was just worrying for the sake of it. Aurélie wasn't going to be arrested, and he felt stupid for thinking such a thing. As he shook off the final drops, and bathed in the cheer of the crowd, he smiled at his propensity to dwell on such far-fetched scenarios. He picked up the jug and poured its contents into the big urine bottle, which was filling up very nicely.

He wasn't going to worry any more. She would be there.

*   *   *

Backstage, Le Machine's manager was experiencing a tangle of emotions. *Life* was going exceptionally well. Most of the reviews were in, and with very few exceptions the critics were agreed that it was something worth seeing. Among the naysayers, *Today's Technology Now* magazine had declared that Le Machine's reluctance to engage with social media had fatally undermined *Life*'s status as art, and *Urban Puritan* had warned its readers that while the piece was not without its merits, the sight of a gentleman in all his glory might be a bit much for their delicate sensibilities. On the whole, though, the reviewers, many of them waiting for Jean-Didier Delacroix's verdict before following his lead, had been very positive, and attendance had been exceptional.

They were only a few days into the run, but with the advance bookings and strong sales of merchandise they were already well on the way to breaking even. If they could just maintain this momentum they would be making a lot more money than they had anticipated. That was all good, of course, but her worry was that after this it would all be over, and to drop a production that had so much potential remaining went against her every instinct.

Le Machine had told his manager plenty of times that he was planning on quitting, that he couldn't face another run, but his interview with *L'Univers* was the first time he had expressed this in public. For years she had worked with musicians, and she knew that the dramatic retirement announcement was standard practice in show business, and that going back on that same retirement announcement was as normal as having a cup of coffee. She hoped he would be the same, that his decision wasn't final.

The trouble she had found since starting to work with

artists, or people who regarded themselves as artists, was that they had a propensity to delude themselves, to think that what they did lay beyond the boundaries of show business. Whenever she had found herself with such a client she had let them carry on thinking this, while handling their business affairs in exactly the same way she would have done if she had been looking after a rock band, a conjurer or a gardening star. As with any branch of show business, the art world had its own context, and some of the details would be unique to it, but the fundamentals of the business remained the same: her client did whatever it was they did, and it was her job to ensure that people paid them to do it. She hoped his decision was a reversible one, that he wouldn't feel he had some kind of high artistic obligation to stick to his declaration.

Paris had proved that there was still a large and appreciative audience for *Life*. Yesterday Sweden had called, offering an enormous amount of public money for him to appear on a plinth on the concourse of Stockholm Central Station the coming year. She had wondered aloud whether it would be considered suitable for a naked man to be getting up to all sorts while children and old people walked past on their way to catch trains, and she had been reassured that it wouldn't be a problem at all, that nobody in the country had ever been shocked by anything. There was already an offer on the table for him to present *Life* at Sydney Opera House the year after that, and a few weeks earlier she had received an invitation from somewhere called Aberystwyth, where the manager of their camera obscura had written to her, saying that *Life* would be an ideal show to put on there in the winter months, when they were normally closed. *We have a capacity of forty*, he had written, *though sadly the fire inspector will only allow twenty-six in at any one time, which I suspect is because my wife once ran over his foot. She didn't mean to do it, but try telling him that. As for facilities, we have a toilet (one cubicle – mixed ladies, gentlemen and disabled), and though our café will be closed for refurbishment, there will be a machine. We also have a funicular railway to bring visitors to our cliff-top location; it offers stunning views of the bay, though sadly it doesn't run during the winter months and people would have to take the steps, or come up the back way along the road, though it's only fair to point out that this is widely regarded as cheating. We would of course have to get permission from the mayor, but she would have a cheek to give us too much trouble about the nudity aspect as she used to be an actress – you might have seen her in* The Life of Brian, *where she takes all her clothes off, right down to her biffer.*

Le Machine's manager had gently turned this offer down.

Aberystwyth aside, there was a lot of money still to be made, but she would make no mention of that when she was persuading Le Machine to carry on. He liked to keep conversations about finances to a minimum. Instead she would tell him how he had moved so many people, and had enriched so many lives. What everybody in show business really wants to hear is that they are making the world a better place, to be reassured that they are so much more than a desperate, cash-hungry show-off. She would tell him how sad it would be for people in the future not to have their lives enriched by his work, and then she would look at him with puppy-dog eyes, and sigh as she wondered out loud what would happen to his loyal crew.

She knew well enough, though, that his crew would all understand, and respect his decision. His lighting designer filled the time between exhibitions by touring the arenas of the world with various acts, and he would have no trouble keeping himself busy. Prior to this run of *Life*, he had spent nine months on the road as a technician for Lady Gaga, during which time over three million people had seen his work, and he had undergone sex with the star of the show four times – in her dressing room, on a plane, in a cupboard full of fire extinguishers and, best of all, as part of a threesome under the bleachers at the Quicken Loans Arena in Cleveland, Ohio, while an impatient audience stamped their feet, and chanted her name. Le Machine's principal creative collaborator, his sound designer, would be quite content to go back to his day-to-day life, playing his gigantic saxophone as part of a quartet in half-empty bars while living off the royalties that still came in from some soft rock radio hits he had co-written back in the nineties. His manager knew she was the one who would miss *Life* the most, and it wouldn't only be the business side of things that she would be sad to see come to an end.

She had been with him from the beginning. Although he had been actively seeking representation, he had exhibited the artist's customary wariness of people from the business side. She had seen potential in what he planned to do, and gradually she had convinced him that they could work together. She didn't really understand what *Life* was all about, and she had never felt the need to know, but from the start she'd had a feeling that people would want to see it. She had never asked him about his motivations, and he had never volunteered to talk about them. Her role was to see that the production ran smoothly, and to maximise the money it made. She had been able to convince him that her desire to turn a substantial profit was in no way in conflict with his ambitions for the piece. There was no doubt that they were looking in the same direction: their conversations were often about how they both wanted it to reach as many people as possible.

Léandre Martin saw just as well as she did that the art world, just like any other tentacle of show business, was a playground for the wild and the weak; a gruesome tableau of grifters and chancers and rich folk at play; a grim pit of desperation, vanity and despair, where nothing was thought of trampling on the lives of those who couldn't keep up. If it hadn't been for people like his manager, if it had been run solely by artists and born-wealthy dilettantes, the art world would never have been anything more than a hotbed of intrigue, failing livers, lost fortunes, unfulfilled potentials and herpes.

The intrigue never abated, livers continued to fail, fortunes were lost all the time, potentials continued to go unfulfilled and herpes remained a constant menace, but she was able to bring order to his working life, to shield him from the chaos. She had convinced him that the last thing an artist needs is a manager who believes that self-expression is an end in itself. She had steered him on a course that kept him productive, and his profile high, and which, particularly now this run was set for success, had made him a good living.

He was happy with her, and something he had thanked her for many times was her ability to cover up his true identity. He didn't like the idea of people snooping around his private life. She supposed that like a lot of artists he was under the impression that he had a big secret. She had never asked about it, but unless he had killed somebody it probably wasn't as big a deal as he thought it was, and even if he had killed somebody, she doubted it would have made that much difference.

And then there was the girl. He hadn't told her about the girl. Maybe she was behind it all. What if she was the clingy type, and had persuaded him to give it all up so they could spend more time together? It could be that she didn't want to share him; she wouldn't be the first girl who didn't like the idea of other women seeing her man without his clothes on. Le Machine's manager had not been there when she had made her appearances in the auditorium, and she knew nothing more about her than what she had read in the newspaper, but she didn't like the idea of her one bit.

After every showing of *Life* so far, Le Machine and his manager had withdrawn to a luxury hotel suite for three days as he adjusted back to normal life. They had an understanding that any sex that took place between them, and there was always a lot of it, was mechanical, that there was no emotional aspect to it at all, and that outside these days they would never mention it, or let it become an issue in their working relationship. But that didn't mean that it wasn't incredible, and that she wouldn't miss it if it stopped happening.

Once his reacclimatisation was over, she would go through his fan mail with him and help him pick out the best of his offers from other women. Together they chose the ones who looked beautiful and hygienic, and she would call and arrange for them to meet him. She felt no jealousy towards them; she just accepted the situation. After all, they meant nothing to him. It wasn't as if he loved them.

But if the girl was there when he came off stage, things would be different and that would be a great pity. She hoped she wouldn't be around, that something would happen to come between them. She wanted to be the one Le Machine turned to when he walked off the stage.

For now, though, the production was going very well. She checked the box office statistics. They had sold almost two thousand tickets overnight.

XXXIX

Everybody involved in *Life* knew that it wasn't possible to please everyone who came through their doors. Some people arrived with what they had thought was an unassailable cynicism, only to find that by the time they had left they were steadfast admirers of the work, but others would not be swayed, and would leave the venue spitting fire.

Le Machine's fiercest critic so far sat in a café round the corner from the exhibition, drinking the most obscure coffee on the menu. Most people would not have dared to order it, believing its name to be unpronounceable, but he had pronounced it not only correctly, but also with extreme nonchalance. His girlfriend had ordered a cappuccino.

Before he had crossed the threshold of Le Charmant Cinéma Érotique, Sébastien had already made his mind up about *Life*, and had been furious when his girlfriend had told him she had bought them tickets. He had only gone along in order to prove himself right.

'That was pathetic,' he said. 'I'm streets ahead of that clown. If he can shift that many tickets, I'll have no problem when the time comes. My work's in a league of its own.'

Sébastien's girlfriend said nothing. She sat there looking at her spoon, turning it over and over in her fingers. She thought of her boyfriend's latest piece. He had drawn three circles in black felt-tip pen on a sheet of A3 paper, then he had coloured them in, also with felt-tip pen: one red, one blue and one green. At some points he had gone over the edges. That was all he was going to submit for his project.

His fellow students were going to spend the coming weeks absorbed in their work, trying their best to produce something exceptional, but he was confident that he had already left them standing. She agreed that his circles were in a league of their own; it just wasn't the league that he thought it was. This work, he had told her, undermined every preconception that people had about art. *To call it revolutionary would be an understatement*, he had said. *It obliterates everything that's come before it*. He had gone on at great length about his thinking behind it. He was very, very pleased with it, and with himself.

'Anybody who doesn't get what I do is an idiot,' he said, 'and who wants to make art for idiots?' He almost laughed as he thought of an answer to his own rhetorical question: 'Le Machine, that's who.'

He sipped his coffee. 'God, that's good,' he said. He

looked at his girlfriend's humble cappuccino. 'I don't know how you can drink that stuff. It's so obvious.'

She carried on turning her spoon over, and weaving it through her fingers.

He continued. 'I guarantee that in a couple of years' time I'll be getting crowds twice that size to see my work. You won't be anywhere near as high-profile as me so don't go expecting queues round the block, but you'll still do well. Your sculpture has a rare quality to it – that small piece you're working on right now, the one that looks a bit like a whelk, has more to it than twelve weeks of *Life*. And as for my work . . .'

Sébastien had told her many times that although she was an accomplished sculptor she would never quite catch up with him intellectually or artistically, but he had always followed this with a reassurance that she wasn't to feel bad about it because his was the great mind of his genera-tion. Whenever he spoke to her about her work, he went to extraordinary lengths to tell her exactly what she was doing, and why she was doing it. She could never make any sense of what he said; it never tallied with what she was really doing, or why, but he was so good-looking that she had let him carry on. He would sometimes break off from a monologue to tell her that he hoped she was taking it all in: *It's so important for you to be able to talk intelligently about your work.*

Sébastien was widely acknowledged as the best-looking boy in college, and he was her first proper boyfriend, and she had been so proud that he had chosen to be with her over all the other girls, but the power of his looks had begun to wane, and she had grown exhausted by him. As he sat in the café and went on and on, the last molecules of her admiration for him evaporated. She had given him the benefit of the doubt over so much, but for a while a hairline crack had been appearing, and now the dam had burst: he was bad at art; nobody liked his work; he was stupid; he was horrible; he only ever talked shit; he was an embarrassment to himself; he had no real friends; and no matter what he thought, he was going to amount to nothing. All these failings eclipsed his looks to the point where they had just stopped working. When he had unveiled his latest piece, she had been horrified by how pathetic it was. No amount of intellectualising or posturing could disguise its complete lack of redeeming qualities. That he thought it had any kind of power or worth had made her squirm on his behalf.

As he lectured her about her own work, he never failed to remind her that she was a quarter Cambodian, and to tell her that this somehow connected her to a mythical past which fed into her work. She was fed up with this. She had told herself that she would leave him the next time he used the phrase *Khmer energy*. It didn't mean anything, it was just nonsense. She knew she wouldn't have long to wait.

He sipped his unpronounceable coffee, and carried on. 'Our work sits well together. Yours has this rare and tremendous Khmer energy that links it to the past,' he said, 'and as for mine, well, I work in a realm so far beyond the imagination that it can only be the future. It's as if together we complete a circle.' He thought for a while, then corrected himself. 'Well, it's not so much that we complete a circle, it's more that we coexist amid the same parallax. So anyway, what did *you* think of that Machine idiot?'

She put down the spoon, and brushed her long, black hair away from her face, tucking it behind her ears. 'Well, for a start, I wouldn't say he's an idiot. I wasn't sure about him before we went; there was a good chance it could have been a load of pointless rubbish, but I don't think what he does can ever really make sense until you experience it. I thought the sonic aspect in particular was incredible; his sound designer is a genius, there's no question of that. It all comes together so perfectly. It's the kind of piece that can't be captured in words, and that's partly what makes it so great. It just *is*. If you believe the press you would think it's just some guy shitting on stage, but there's so much more to it than that. It really moved me. It made me think about my own life, about my body, and I found myself asking, and answering, some pretty serious questions. I thought it was excellent.'

Sébastien was incredulous. 'Didn't you listen to a word I said?'

She nodded. 'I did. I listened very closely.'

'Then what are you talking about?'

She continued as if he hadn't spoken. 'Did you see the papers yesterday? It looks as though he's dating a girl from our course. She's called Aurélie something-or-other. You'd recognise her. She's blonde. I've never spoken to her, but I really like her work. Do you know her?'

Sébastien turned white, and started to tremble. He tried to cover this up by shaking a salt cellar, as if separating clumps.

His girlfriend thought of the questions she had asked herself in *Life*, and the conclusions she had come to. And she thought about her body, and how she had decided that she was going to keep it to herself for a long time to come. 'Le Machine is a better artist than you'll ever be,' she said. 'And if anyone's an idiot around here, Sébastien, it's you. You are a jealous, talentless, boring idiot.' It felt so good to say it.

His eyes were as wide as they could be. 'You don't mean that.'

'Yes, I do. Why do you think we coexist amid the same parallax, anyway? What does that even mean? You talk such shit, and I'm fed up with you.'

He stared at her, unable to speak.

'Sébastien,' said his girlfriend, 'I think it's time we had a long conversation.'

For the first time in a long while, she smiled. She couldn't help it. She was so happy at the thought that she wouldn't have to put up with him any more. They wouldn't need to have the long conversation. He had got the message. She reached into her bag to get her wallet out, so she could settle the bill and leave.

As her hand began to withdraw from the bag, he held up his arms in surrender. 'Don't shoot,' he said. 'Please. Don't shoot.'

She took out her wallet, and when he saw it he lowered his hands.

'I was only joking,' he said.

'But you've always told me that you never joke, that joking was incompatible with the gravity of your intellect.'

'I was just trying to lighten the mood,' he said.

She knew he was lying. Sébastien had never tried to lighten a mood in his life.

'I think you must be unwell,' he said. 'Get some rest, and we'll talk again later.'

She left enough money to cover the bill, then stood up and checked her watch. It was ten past ten, time to go to the sculpture room at college and get back to her project. And this time it would just be her and her work, with no interruptions, no pointless buzzing in her ear. She was so glad to think that even when she had been crazy about him, even when she had thought he was talking sense when he had told her that she must never smile because to do so would be to devalue her art, she had never let him influence her work. In the days when she had thought there was a grand intelligence behind his soliloquies she had let his words wash over her, and gone in her own direction.

'You'll be nothing without me,' he said, as she walked away. 'I gave you all your best ideas. I created you.'

She stepped out into the day. It was cold, but it felt like springtime.

XXXX

It was eighteen minutes past ten, and in four minutes' time Herbert's mother would be an hour late. The baby was still asleep after his busy night, and Aurélie had a sickening feeling in her gut. She wanted to cry.

She felt like a child who needed a grown-up to tell her what to do, and she had decided that she was going to wait until Professor Papavoine and Liliane had finished work, and she would wait for them on their front step, and when they got in they would take her upstairs and sit her on their sofa and help her make the decision. She already knew what they were going to say. They would tell her that the only thing she could do now, for Herbert's sake, was go to the police and show them the baby, and tell them that they had to find his family. She already knew that was the sensible and the right thing to do, even the only thing, but she needed to hear it from somebody else

377

first, because walking into a police station would bring her whole life crashing down, and she didn't feel strong enough to take that step alone.

The Papavoines were so nice that she knew they would go with her, and see that she was OK. The police would ask her all sorts of questions, and once the doctors had sent back the results of their examination of the boy they would ask her how he had come to have a wound on his shoulder. Whether she told the truth, or shrugged and said she didn't know, she wouldn't be seeing him again. They would search her apartment, which would be understandable since at that point they would be suspecting her of having snatched a baby, and they would find bullet holes, and tiny spots of Herbert's blood. What chance would she have then of ever seeing him again, or of keeping her new boyfriend, or of not being kicked out of college, or of ever making her dad proud?

She knew so little of Herbert's life. Maybe he had been reported missing straight away, and a police search had been going on all this time. She knew the police didn't always immediately publicise such cases for tactical reasons, or out of sensitivity, particularly when broken families or people with mental difficulties were involved. And if Herbert didn't have a father in his life, if they couldn't find someone who could be relied upon to take care of him, he would be sent to a children's home. If she had just controlled herself, if she hadn't started playing with guns, then maybe they would have let her keep him. She wanted to keep him. She was ready. She didn't want him to be raised by anybody who didn't love him with all their heart.

She wished The Russian had stayed. He seemed like the

kind of worldly character who would have been able to dispense wise and practical advice. Maybe he had once been left holding a baby on his travels. *Ah, it reminds me of my experience in San Salvador in 1982*, he would have said, before telling her exactly what she ought to do. But even he would have told her to take him to the police, to tell them everything that had happened.

She followed the clock on her phone. The minutes seemed to last forever, and none of them brought Herbert's mother. It turned ten twenty-two, and she knew the time had come for her to give up. She was going to spend the day walking around with the baby, filling time until the Papavoines were due home.

'Let's go,' she said to the sleeping child. She would start by heading up to Montmartre, to see if she could talk Sylvie's boss into allowing her a coffee break. She had all day, so she decided to walk there. She lit a cigarette, stood up and kicked the buggy's brake off.

She got halfway along the side of the square when, from the corner of her eye, she saw a madwoman zigzagging around, and making a kind of whimpering noise. She felt sorry for her, but now was not the time for her to be actively compassionate towards the mentally ill, and she quickened her step, but as she did so the madwoman stopped zigzagging and started racing towards them. Aurélie sped up, but the woman was faster, and fell to her knees in front of the buggy, staring at Herbert with wild eyes through a tangle of long brown hair. Aurélie turned the buggy around, and started back the way she had come, but the madwoman scrambled to her feet, raced around and threw herself to her knees in front of them again. Again Aurélie manoeuvred the buggy away, and again she found her path blocked. Now she didn't need a grown-up to tell her what to do. She had to get rid of her as quickly as possible.

She felt for the gun. She hadn't sorted her bag out for a long time, and it had fallen to the bottom and was lost among days of accumulated rubble. 'Wait,' she said to the madwoman. 'It's definitely in here somewhere.' She found it. It was still in its tea towel, and feeling a strange sense of calm, she unwrapped it and pointed it at the woman, who froze. A moment later Aurélie covered it with the tea towel again, so it wouldn't attract the attention of passers-by, and held it close to her body. 'Get away from us,' she said quietly. She knew that she could never shoot such an unfortunate character, but if it came to it she would fire the gun, to scare her away. 'Just go. Nobody needs to get hurt.'

The madwoman looked at the covered gun, and shook her head.

'Get away from the baby,' barked Aurélie. 'Don't touch him.' She didn't move.

Aurélie decided that she might be able to shoot her after all. She wouldn't kill her, but as a last resort she would take her legs out. She wouldn't care if it got her into trouble; there was no way she was going to let her get her hands on Herbert.

The madwoman returned her gaze to the sleeping baby. Even though a gun was pointed at her, she seemed relieved and happy. And she didn't seem to be quite so insane any more. She brushed her hair away from her face.

'Oh, Olivier,' she whispered. 'It is you. Olivier, you're OK.' A tear fell from her eye, and ran down her cheek. 'I've missed you so much.'

'What? Who's OK?' The woman didn't answer, but Aurélie didn't need her to. She had heard perfectly well. Aurélie looked closely at the woman. She looked familiar. 'Did you used to have blonde hair?' she asked.

The woman nodded.

'And do you ever wear a green jacket?'

The woman looked at her, quizzically and still apparently unafraid of the gun. 'Sometimes.'

'A velvet one?'

'Well, it's not actually velvet but I suppose it could look a bit velvety from a distance. I'm not sure I like it very much.'

Aurélie looked hard at her again. It all made sense to her now. 'Aimée?'

The woman nodded, and went back to gazing at the baby.

'I've seen a photo of you,' she said. She put the gun back in her bag, and showed the woman her empty hands. There was no need for it any more. She crouched beside her. 'I thought the jacket looked good on you. You've dyed your hair. I didn't recognise you at first. It looks nice. The blonde was natural though, wasn't it?'

She nodded. 'I fancied a change. I've been blonde all my life.'

'Most women would kill for your hair colour. I would, for a start. It's so fair. Look at mine – it's mousy.' She waited for Aimée to reassure her that her hair wasn't mousy, that it was dirty blonde, but she said nothing. Aurélie supposed she had other things on her mind. Either that or her hair really was mousy and she had been kidding herself these last couple of years.

'Oh, Olivier,' said Aimée, reaching out to touch the sleeping child.

'Ah, yes,' said Aurélie. 'About that. There's been a misunderstanding: I'm afraid he's not Olivier, he just looks a bit like him. He's called Herbert.'

'*Air-bear?*'

'No, Herbert. *Herbert.*'

Aimée shook her head. She was very calm. 'He's Olivier. I would know my baby anywhere.'

Aurélie didn't know what more she could say to convince poor Aimée that she was mistaken. She really didn't want to have to get the gun out again. Maybe she could get her to call her mother, who could come and meet them and confirm that Herbert was indeed the baby she had seen in the park. She pictured the three of them laughing at the misunderstanding. 'Shall we . . . go for coffee?'

Aimée looked at her, and nodded. 'Maybe we should.'

Herbert chose that moment to wake up. His eyes were bleary, and he blinked a few times as the world came into focus. The women watched him. He looked up at Aurélie and smiled. Then he looked at Aimée, and Aurélie saw a look on his face that she hadn't seen before. He had an upbeat disposition, but she had never known him to be quite so overflowing with happiness. It was an incredible sight.

'My baby,' said Aimée. She unclipped him from his buggy, and scooped him up and held him close, and he held on to her tighter than he had ever held on to Aurélie. They slotted together so naturally, and he was so delighted to see her that Aurélie felt no compulsion to wrestle him away from the woman. She knew she was no expert, but this looked to her like an authentic reunion between a mother and a child. She couldn't imagine the woman she had been waiting for ever holding him this way, or Herbert looking so pleased to see her. She would have just grabbed the buggy, checked he was there, maybe said, *Hello, Herbert*, and walked away. She began to accept that Herbert might not be Herbert after all.

'I've missed you so much,' said Aimée, her voice breaking with emotion. The baby continued to hold Aimée tight, as if he loved her more than anybody else in the world.

Aimée cuddled the baby close, and rocked him, and when she held him in front of her so she could get a good look at him, he pressed his fingers into her face, and she said, 'I'll never leave you with that horrible woman ever again.'

'Hey,' said Aurélie, 'I'm not that bad.'

Aimée smiled. 'It's OK, I wasn't talking about you. You don't seem too unpleasant when you're not waving guns around.'

With the mention of guns, Aurélie relived the shooting incident. She felt ashamed that she had bothered to defend herself. She *was* that bad. She watched Herbert hugging this woman, and carried on trying to unravel everything that had happened.

'I wasn't expecting you,' she said.

'Then who were you expecting?'

'Someone else. She was a bit shorter than you, and she was wearing this really nice turquoise scarf.'

'So that's where my scarf went. Typical! I'd only just bought it, too – from La Foularderie, as well. And you don't even know her name?'

'I didn't really have time to get to know her. She just told me I had a kind face, then she handed me the baby, told me to come back here today, and went away.'

'And when was that?'

'A week ago.'

Aimée shook her head. 'Unbelievable.'

'So . . . she wasn't Herbert's mother?'

'There's no such baby as *Air-bear*.'

'*Herb*—' She stopped herself. She had given the last of her pronunciation tutorials. It really was looking as though he was Olivier after all. 'It's all a bit of a mess, isn't it?'

Aimée nodded. 'At least I can see how far you were prepared to go to protect Olivier from lunatic child-snatchers. You weren't to know I was his real mother.' She smiled. 'I suppose that on balance you did a good job by pointing a gun at my head. So . . . thanks?' She stopped smiling. 'I shall throttle her when I catch up with her.'

They stood in silence, and Aurélie felt she should say something. 'Just so you know, I wasn't going to kill you – I was just going to fire a warning shot. At worst I'd have taken your legs out.'

'Oh. Right.'

Aimée continued to hug Olivier, and Aurélie didn't know quite where to put herself.

'So,' said Aimée, 'we've got a lot to talk about. Will you tell me what he's been up to for the past week?'

Aurélie nodded.

'We only live a few minutes away. Will you come back for coffee?'

'OK.'

With Olivier loaded back into his buggy, they left the square.

'Did you know he can crawl?' asked Aurélie.

'What?! He crawled?!' She leaned over and looked down at him. 'You crawled?'

Herbert was modest, and declined to confirm the report. Aurélie answered on his behalf. 'Yes, he's pretty good at it. I expect he'll show you when we get to yours.'

'And you were the first person to see him?'

'Well, no. I'd left him with . . .' She didn't want to name the Papavoines, just in case things weren't ending as smoothly as they seemed to be. '. . . with some people.'

'What people? Your family? Old friends?' She looked genuinely worried, as if she had just started to ask herself why Aurélie had been carrying a gun in the first place, and where she had got it from. 'Drug dealers?'

'No, they're not drug dealers. I didn't know them very well, but they turned out to be really nice people.' She laughed. 'It's a funny story, but at first I thought they were sex maniacs.'

'Jesus!' Olivier's mother looked horrified.

'Oh no, don't worry. They're not. They were fine. They were really good with him.'

They walked on. Aimée didn't seem entirely reassured. Then she noticed something, and stopped. She turned to Aurélie. 'Why are his shoes on the wrong feet?'

Aimée's apartment was full of pictures of Olivier. In one of them he was being held by the woman she had seen a week ago, the one she had thought was his mother, and in another he was with the old woman she had met in the park. There was no question that the baby in the photographs was Herbert, and that Herbert was really Olivier. Now she knew who he was, she could see that the baby in the photos had *je ne sais quoi* after all. And his grandmother hadn't been quite the interfering old woman she thought; all she had done was recognise her own grandson.

385

They drank their coffee as Olivier showed off his new crawling skills to his delighted mother, and as she watched him in wonder, Aimée told Aurélie all about her younger sister, how she had insisted on taking him for the week while she was away being the maid of honour at a friend's wedding in America, a wedding that had been booked before the baby had even been conceived, and from which children were banned. Her friend had turned out to be the worst kind of Wedding Nazi imaginable, and Aimée, her savings drained, hoped never to see the joyless harridan or her dismal, cowed husband ever again.

In the run-up to the trip, Aimée's sister had become indignant when it had been suggested that their mother would be the obvious choice of sitter. 'She's never been the most responsible person, but she assured me that everything would be fine, that I needed to trust her. Look . . .' She reached for her phone. 'She kept sending me these texts.' She read them out:

—*Olivier is very happy – we've been doing potato prints.*

—*Olivier has a little bit of a cold today, but don't worry – I'm giving him lots of cuddles.*

—*Olivier and I did baby Reiki today, and he responded to it very well.*

—*Olivier seemed to say 'I love my mummy.'*

Aimée put her phone down. 'All made up. God knows where she sent them from. And today, this.' She scrolled through her messages.

—*Oops, I can't make it round to yours as planned. Hopefully Olivier will be with a girl – mousy hair, kind face, one ear sticks out a bit more than the other – in that square by the Métro about now. Go and get him, quickly. Hope you're not too late.*

Aurélie had never liked that woman, and now she liked her even less.

Aimée continued. 'She'd told me she would be here at nine with Olivier, that was always the agreement, and I was tearing my hair out when she didn't show up. I must have called her twenty times. She didn't even send that message until it was gone ten o'clock, and it drove me out of my mind with worry. I've never run so fast in my life.'

Aurélie was relieved to think that she looked good in comparison to Aimée's sister.

'The sad thing is, I can guess what she's done. She'll have run off on tour with a drummer. It's always a drummer. Maybe I wouldn't mind so much if she had gone off with a proper musician for once in her life, but a drummer . . .'

'That's really sad – she must have very low self-esteem. But maybe she's moved up in the world. Maybe it'll be a guitarist this time.'

'I doubt it. At best it'll be a bass player. Let's see.' She switched on speakerphone, and dialled.

—*Hi, Aimée,* came a perky voice.

'Hi, Justine.'

—*So you got Olivier back?*

'Yes, he's here now.'

—*Sorry I couldn't be there. I'd run out of something and had to go to the shop at the last minute, so my friend stepped in.*

'What did you run out of?'

—*Er . . . cheese.*

'Well, that explains it. I can see how important it must have been for you to get some cheese. It's terrible running out, isn't it?'

—*It is, yes.*

'But thank God your friend was there to help you out. She's very nice, isn't she? What's her name, again?'

—*Her name? You don't need me to tell you that.*

'Don't I? Why not?'

—*Well, this is typical, isn't it? I've known her all my life – she's my best friend. She was always there when we were growing up, but you never even noticed her. You and Mother were too busy coddling the baby to ever pay attention to anything that happened to me.*

'So the middle child syndrome's still raging?'

—*I don't have a syndrome, I just see the facts as they are.*

'But never mind all that now. Her name has completely slipped my mind. You must remind me.'

—*It's . . . er . . .*

'You can't remember it either, can you?'

—*Well, it's just . . . we always used to call her by her nickname.*

'Which was what?'

—*Dumbo.*

'Dumbo?'

—*Well, Semi-Dumbo.*

'Semi-Dumbo?'

—*Yes, Semi-Dumbo – it's because of her . . .*

'I know why you would call her that, but I find it hard to believe that you've forgotten your best friend's real name because you only ever think of her as Semi-Dumbo.'

—*Well, I do remember her name, as a matter of fact. She's . . . er . . . Véronique. Yes, that's right – Véronique. She's definitely quite Véroniquey. Some people just suit their names, don't they?*

'Are you sure she's called Véronique? I thought she

said it was something else. It's just I was so pleased to see Olivier again that I lost concentration.'

—Ah, no, it's coming back to me now. It's . . . wait . . . she's . . . er . . . Aurélie, that's it. I always get those names mixed up.

'If you say so. Anyway, how's the drummer?'

—He's fine . . . Hang on, no, I mean, what drummer?

'What's his group called?'

—I don't know what you're . . . She knew the game was up. She sighed. *Herbert,* she said. *They're called Herbert.*

'Air-bear?'

—No, Herbert. Pronounced the English way. They've never made it as a French band, so their manager has made them reinvent themselves as an English band, and they've given themselves the most English name they can think of. They sing in English, and pretend they're from The Deepings, apparently that's a place in England, and they tell people they're called things like Desmond and Roy. My one pretends he's called Rodney. And it's worked, too. They made up all these fake press cuttings about how everyone in England thinks they're the new Beatles, or the new Smiths, and they're getting the bookings.

'And where are you now?'

—Somewhere between, er . . . Toulouse and Toulon, I think.

'How's the tour going?'

—Pretty well. They had sixty people in last night, which is a record. I work the stall, and I even sold a T-shirt – their first one. We were all pretty excited about that. And nobody's realised they're French yet. If they ever think someone's starting to suspect, they just start acting as English as they can by bumping into things and saying

'crikey', or drinking too much and being sick all over the place.

'I'm delighted for them. I'm sure they'll become really, really famous. But never mind all that. Guess what I've found out: I know for a fact that you'd never met Aurélie before you gave her Olivier. She could have been anyone. You do know, don't you, that I'm never going to trust you with him again?'

—*What? Why? You can't stop me from seeing him. I'm his aunt – I have legal rights, and anyway he's OK, isn't he? I don't know why you're being so uptight. That girl looked after him, didn't she? I knew she would. She has a kind face.*

'She has an exhausted face right now. She's done a good job under the circumstances. And what about all those texts you sent, telling me what you and Olivier had been up to?'

—*Well, pardon me for putting your mind at rest. Hey, did that girl tell you about how she threw the stone? That was so funny. How could that ever be a good idea for an art project? What an idiot!*

Now she was telling tales, in the hope that she would begin to look better in comparison with Aurélie. Fortunately, Aurélie had already confessed to the stone throwing. Aimée hadn't been delighted by the story, she had even cried a little bit, but Aurélie had been so mortified that Aimée couldn't help but forgive her.

'She told me everything.'

Aurélie looked at her shoes. She hadn't told Aimée everything. The sisters' conversation carried on, but she stopped listening and started worrying.

*　　*　　*

Aimée put the phone down. 'Well, that's answered the big question. Who is to blame for this mess? It's me! I'm the one who entrusted Olivier to a pathological liar with terminal middle child syndrome. That's the problem with the government's big scheme to get people breeding. It's all very well giving people tax breaks to have a third child, but they haven't thought of future generations. How is the country ever going to function with an underclass of middle children with chips on their shoulders, creating dramas to draw attention to themselves, living in fantasy worlds and lacking direction in their lives? For one thing there won't be enough drummers to go round. Whatever was I thinking, giving my eight-month-old baby to my messed-up sister?'

'Isn't he a nine-month-old baby?'

'He's a eight-month-old baby. He won't be nine months old until next week.'

'OK, let's work this out. If he's Aquarius, then . . .'

'Aquarius? Who said he was Aquarius?'

Aurélie didn't have to answer. Aimée sent a text to her sister: *What is new boyfriend's star sign?*

Seconds later, the answer came back: *Aquarius. Perfect for me, I know!*

At least this cleared up the mysterious non-appearance of the stranger in yellow.

As Aimée and Aurélie talked, Aimée went through her suitcase. She had bought some clothes for Olivier while she had been in America. Picking them out for him had been the only aspect of her stay that she had enjoyed, and she was impatient to see him wearing them. She pulled out a red-and-black striped sweater.

'Let's put this on you,' she said.

Aurélie turned cold with fear. 'I should go now,' she said, and stood up.

'No, you sit down. You have to see Olivier in his new sweater.'

'No, I've taken up enough of your time.'

'Nonsense. Sit down.'

Aurélie didn't see any alternative but to do as she was told.

She popped Olivier on her knee, and took off the top he was wearing. He sat there in his vest, and she put the sweater on her hands, ready to put it on him. Then she noticed something.

'My God,' she said. 'Olivier . . . how . . .?'

She pulled back the strap of the vest, and stared at the wound. It was worse than Aurélie had ever seen it. It was healing, but the scabbing looked awful, almost black, and there was a yellowness and a tightness to the skin surrounding it.

'Aurélie,' said Aimée, 'what happened to him?'

Aurélie looked at her shoes. 'He fell.'

Aimée looked at the wound, then back at Aurélie.

Aurélie could see from Aimée's face that her explanation hadn't been adequate, that she needed to know more. And she knew Olivier's mother needed to know everything, *really* everything this time. But to tell her everything would be the end of her. She tried to find the courage. 'He fell . . . on to . . . a bullet.' Aurélie realised how stupid this sounded. She had to stop slithering around, and start telling the truth. 'I shot him.'

Aimée held her baby tight. 'Olivier,' she said, 'what have I done?'

Aurélie carried on looking at her shoes. 'I'm so sorry,' she said.

She could feel Aimée looking at her, and she looked back.

'Aurélie,' said Aimée, 'this is too fucked up. I can't deal with it any more.' She took Aurélie's bag, with the gun in it, and put it between her feet. 'I'm going to call the police.' She picked up the phone.

Aurélie felt no urge to wrestle her gun from her bag and point it at Aimée's head to get her to put the phone down. She never wanted to touch the thing again. She felt awful. She was beyond feeling sorry for herself; now she just felt sorry for her dad. He was going to find out what she had done. She loved him so much, and he didn't deserve to have such a ridiculous and horrible daughter.

'I was drunk,' she said. 'It was a big drunken mistake. Maybe you've never made a big drunken mistake. If you haven't, you're lucky.'

Aimée put the phone down, and went back to getting Olivier into his new sweater. It suited him very well. She lowered him on to the floor, and watched him dart away. She clamped a palm to her forehead and slumped back in her chair. 'So tell me what happened,' she said.

Aurélie told her everything. Aimée listened in silence, and when she had finished, Aurélie said, 'Are you going to call the police now?'

'I ought to. People who shoot babies should go to prison.'

'I know.'

'But when you asked me if I had ever made a drunken

mistake, well, guess what – I have made a few in my time. Most of them were pretty trivial in the scheme of things. But sometimes . . .' She picked up Olivier, and held him close. '. . . good things come from drunken mistakes. Wonderful things, even.'

Aurélie wondered what she meant.

Aimée continued. 'A couple of years ago my work transferred me to England, and I made the basic error of embracing the local culture. You've probably heard what it's like over there.'

Aurélie nodded. She had never been, but she had heard plenty of stories; life across the Channel seemed to be one big drunken mistake.

'One night I drank much too much, much too fast, and nine months later this little character came along. I never even knew his father's name. I can barely even remember what he looked like. All I remember is that he was English.'

'So Olivier is half English?'

'Yes. You can see it from some angles – particularly around the chin. But he's still my baby, and I love him no matter what. Anyway, when I found out I was pregnant it felt as if it was going to be the end of the world, and it's not been easy, but I can't imagine life without my little boy.' She looked long and hard at Aurélie. 'Maybe something good will come from all this too. What do you think?'

Aurélie nodded. She was going to make sure of it.

XXXXI

While Sylvie Dupont was working, Toshiro Akiyama had gone to spend a few hours at the House of Soundwaves, a permanent exhibition of sonic marvels that had been established by a group of enthusiasts, including Le Machine's sound designer. He had sent her a text message, in comprehensible French: *Museum very good.*

She was missing him like mad, and couldn't wait for her shift to end. She came to the end of a trip around the neighbourhood, and pulled up at the top of Montmartre. She waved off her passengers, and the moment they were out of the car, her friend Aurélie Renard got in, diving on to the back seat.

'Just drive around the block,' she said, 'and pretend you don't know me.'

Sylvie drove off.

'I've got your gun,' said Aurélie. 'Thanks for lending it

to me. You can have it back now.' She took it out of her bag and dropped it on to the passenger seat, still wrapped in its tea towel.

Sylvie drove on, thinking hard. Then she pulled over to the side of the road. She picked up the parcel, and put it in a paper bag that was full of wrappers from her lunch. Three soldiers were walking by, on one of their regular patrols that were designed to reassure tourists that the streets were safe. Two held rifles, the other carried a pistol. She got out of the car, went over to a litter bin, and right in front of them she dropped the bag in. She smiled at them, and they smiled back. She got back in the car.

'I don't need it any more,' she said. 'I have Toshiro now.'

They drove on.

Aurélie looked at her friend. She knew she wouldn't be seeing much of her for a while, as she and Toshiro spent time getting to know each other. But that was OK. She was so happy for her to have found him.

'Sylvie,' she said, 'don't worry. I'm not going funny on you or anything, but there's something I want you to know.'

'What is it?'

'Actually, no, I'm not going to say. You'll just laugh at me.'

'Well, you have to tell me now.'

'Promise you won't laugh.'

'I promise. So what is it?'

'I love you.'

Sylvie laughed. 'Have you been drinking?'

'No. I just wanted you to know, in case you were wondering.'

'Well, you're in luck, because, if you must know, it

just so happens that I love you too, you baby-shooting nutcase. Now get out of my car, I've got a living to make.'

They were back where they had started. Aurélie opened the door, and found a middle-aged German couple waiting to take her place. They had a happy black Labrador with them, and Aurélie gave him a quick cuddle as they passed. She was used to having someone to put her arms around, and she was going to miss it. She let the dog go, and it jumped on to the back seat, and sat between his owners. She watched them pull away. When they had vanished over the brow of the hill, she began her long walk home.

THE LAST DAY OF LIFE

XXXXII

Aurélie walked around the same hall where she had first met Sylvie at the college open day. Today it was filled with the second-year students' finished projects, and they were all there to see what everyone else had produced. She had been really impressed with everything she had seen: people had been working hard and coming up with decent work. She stood in front of her favourite so far – one of the girls had painted what looked from across the room to be a quartet of giant penises, but on closer inspection they turned out to be detailed physical maps of places that just happened to be penis-shaped: Manhattan Island, Sweden, the Republic of Benin and the Kintyre peninsula. They made her smile, and reminded her, as if she needed reminding, that Léandre Martin would be bringing the curtain down on *Life* at seven o'clock that evening.

She had mixed feelings about that. It was going to be so

strange seeing him again, and she had butterflies whenever she thought about it, which was most of the time. She didn't know if they would ever be able to recapture the magic of their first meeting; she mainly hoped it wouldn't be too awkward.

She moved on from the maps. Another student was holding a free raffle every few minutes. Whoever held the winning ticket got to load up a small cannon with the fist-sized paint pellet of their choice, and fire it at a giant canvas that was leaning against the wall. Aurélie won the round she entered, and she chose bottle green. She aimed and fired, and while she was relieved that it had hit the canvas, it had splattered a long way from where she had been aiming. She decided there and then that her days of marksmanship were definitely over. She was given a round of applause, and was pleased to see that her splatter looked pretty good among all the others. She wasn't sure what he was going to do with the canvas once it was covered, but she told herself that one day when she had a bigger place she would get him in to help decorate. She hadn't expected there to be quite so much fun going on.

She walked on, past her own exhibit. She had been working on it almost non-stop since she had given the baby back, and she was relieved to feel she had done something that held its own alongside her fellow students' work. There was Olivier, crying his heart out, his enormous bruised face in charcoal on a sheet of incredibly expensive white paper, three metres square. She had captured him. She thought back to her original idea, to simply draw some pictures of things she saw and felt like drawing, and was glad that she had changed it. It had been unpretentious, but she could see now that it had also been unambitious, even timid, and she was glad she had pushed herself to do something different. The Russian was right, and so was Justine, and everybody else who had found out about it: the stone idea had been really stupid. But if it hadn't been for that she would never have made this work that she could be really proud of, and there were an awful lot of good things in her life that wouldn't have happened had it not been for her hopeless plan. She even felt a flash of gratitude to Sébastien for having daunted her with his lofty intention to *subvert the zeitgeist*. She still didn't know what that meant, but she hadn't spent a great deal of time trying to work it out.

She had drawn several versions of the piece, starting small and getting bigger and bigger before attempting the really big one. The last time she had gone round to babysit Olivier, she had presented Aimée with the final trial version, one metre square, the one when she had known she had finally captured him. She saw them every couple of weeks, usually when Aimée was out with her new boyfriend, trying her best to have something resembling a conventional date, free of nappy changes and screaming fits. She still caught herself calling the boy *Herbert* from time to time. The two of them were getting along very well. He recognised her, and gave her a big smile whenever he saw her. He was walking now, and his wound had healed, leaving a narrow scar that looked as though it would be there forever.

She didn't want to spend too much time hanging around her own piece, so she moved on. Someone had drawn three circles in felt-tip pen, and coloured them in quite badly. It seemed so sloppy alongside everyone else's work. She couldn't see any point to it, and tried to work out what was going on, to see if she could detect a redeeming quality in there somewhere. She couldn't find one. She rubbed the bump on her head; maybe she had concussion, and wasn't seeing it properly.

Justine had returned the stone to her, and that morning she had punished herself by taking it to the park, throwing it as high as she could and letting it land on her head. It had hurt, she had seen stars, and now she had a bump, but she was glad to have done it. Concussed or not, she still couldn't find any worth to the circles, then she looked at the name of the student, and it all made sense. Someone came and stood by her side.

'It's terrible, isn't it?'

Aurélie turned to see who she was talking to, and it took a while before she recognised her. It was Sculpture Girl. She had never seen her smiling before.

'I wouldn't say that.'

'Wouldn't you?'

'Well, actually I would. I was just being polite because he's your boyfriend.'

'Not any more!' Even though weeks had passed since she had left him, she was still elated.

'Well, in that case I don't mind telling you I think it's boring, lazy shit.'

Sculpture Girl laughed.

'I don't think I've seen him today,' said Aurélie.

'No, you wouldn't have. He's dropped out.'

'Really? Why?'

'He was called in by the assessment panel yesterday, and they told him he was going to have to repeat the year. They said the work he had submitted didn't display any evidence of technical ability, thought or effort.'

'I can see where they're coming from.'

'I had him blubbing to me on the phone. Of course he's convinced that they just can't see his genius. He says his concepts are so far beyond their understanding that he feels pity for them. He refused to repeat the year, so he's out of here. He says he's going to go to London, where he tells me they understand the value of artistic genius. I think by that he means that there are a load of millionaires there who'll buy any old shit. I think his work's too pathetic even for London millionaires, though.'

'You could be right. It's fucking dreadful, isn't it?'

Nobody had been given their marks yet, but those who hadn't been called in could be confident that they had passed. Aurélie wasn't worried. That morning, as she had wandered through the corridors, she had met Professor Papavoine for the first time in a long while, and he had whispered to her that he had been very impressed with her piece, but he had thought it judicious to keep a low profile during the assessment, and to go along with the consensus. He couldn't resist telling her, in strict confidence, that his fellow assessors had been very positive, and that she had nothing to worry about. He had asked after Herbert, and she told him that he was now called Olivier, and that she and he were great friends and she would be babysitting him on the coming Sunday. He had invited the two of them round to their place for lunch. 'Liliane's been begging to see you again. Oh, and bring Léandre too, if he's around. He's off duty from tonight, isn't he?' It had been impossible to escape the news. With *Life* winding up, the media had gone into overdrive, with news programmes offering representations of the contents of the bottles in colour-coded computer graphics.

405

Aurélie had accepted the invitation, and told him she was looking forward to it, and he had scuttled away.

The members of the assessment panel weren't the only ones to appreciate her work. 'I love your giant crying baby,' said Sculpture Girl. 'I've always liked what you do, but this is the best I've seen yet. You've really nailed it.'

'Thanks. I've not got to yours yet, but . . . I'm sure I'll like it too.'

She was relieved to find she did. She thought it was beautiful.

Everyone started drifting away, and Aurélie and Sculpture Girl, who she had discovered had a real name, Sandrine Gall, found themselves drifting away together, to share a bottle of wine in a bar. Music was playing and a television flickered silently in the corner. Apparently President Bruni-Sarkozy was about to hold yet another press conference.

They ignored it, and carried on talking, about college, and Le Machine, and anything else that came along. A song came on.

'Hey, I love this,' said Sandrine. 'It's this new English band called *Air-bear*.'

'I like it too,' said Aurélie. The song was called 'Such Ghastly Weather', and she had first heard it at Aimée's. Justine had sent it to her, along with a note telling her that she had left the drummer, Rodney, and moved on to the bass player, Jean-Pascal, aka Clifford. Aimée considered this a promotion of sorts, and hoped it was a sign that her sister was finally getting her act together. Aurélie had been hearing the song being played all over the place. It was a hit. Apparently nobody had yet discovered that they weren't quite as English as they appeared.

'It's funny – for such an unsophisticated nation, the English produce some pretty good music.'

Aurélie wasn't going to be the one to blow their cover. They carried on talking. Aurélie liked Sandrine Gall. She was nice, and funny. She could tell they were going to be friends.

The television flickered away behind them, and neither paid it the slightest attention.

XXXXIII

The President's media secretary hushed the assembled members of the world's press. 'Gentlemen, gentlemen,' he said, 'pipe down.' At this all the women started to make a racket in protest. He shook his head in dismay. 'Ladies too.' When at last he had quiet, he began. 'You all know the routine. In a moment's time President Bruni-Sarkozy himself will emerge from the wings. He will sit in this very chair, whence he shall deliver a short statement, and then you will have the chance to ask one or two relevant – that's *relevant* – questions.' There was a groan. 'The President has asked me to forewarn you that he will not – I repeat *not* – be announcing that he is going to invade Spain, and he will not be drawn on the subject.'

There was an even bigger groan, and everybody looked at Julio Gonzales from *El Pais*. 'We'll get you one day, Gonzales,' hissed the economics editor of *Le Monde*.

The media secretary gave a signal, and the lights went down. A laser shone on to a mirrorball, and the room filled with swirling light. They all wondered what the President would use as his walk-on music. At his last press conference, when he had been announcing a series of drastic fiscal measures, he had chosen the twelve-inch remix of 'Buffalo Stance' by Neneh Cherry. Everybody agreed that it was a great song, though given the circumstances it was somewhat overlong and inappropriate in tone: for seven minutes he had stalked the edge of the stage, waving at the press, pulling shapes and high-fiving and fist-bumping the competition winners and specially invited fans in the front row. Most of all they just hoped it wasn't going to be Tina Turner singing 'Simply The Best'; he had played that one to death, and they were all sick of it. Today, though, he had chosen a classical theme, and as the opening bars of Wagner's 'The Ride of the Valkyries' drifted through the room, the assembled reporters turned to one another and nodded their approval. The President walked on stage, waving and punching the air, and after little more than a minute of shape-pulling, high-fiving and fist-bumping, he took his place at the table and the music faded out. It appeared someone had had a word with him.

The President began. 'Ladies and gentlemen of the press,' he said, 'thank you all for coming. I am going to start with a very special announcement – today I shall be joined on the podium by my third wife.' The women sat stony-faced at this news, but the men fidgeted in anticipation. 'Will you please welcome to the stage, the model turned actress Carla Bruni-Sarkozy!'

The mirrorball came on again, and her walk-on music

started. They had chosen Serge Gainsbourg's 'Je t'aime
. . . moi non plus'. They faded it in halfway through
the song, just as Jane Birkin's gasps were really getting
going. Madame Bruni-Sarkozy emerged from the wings,
resplendent in a really tight red dress with a slit up the
side that gave a superb view of a magnificent leg. The
women sat stock still, and the men rocked back and forth
in their seats. The First Lady walked over to her husband
and whispered something in his ear. The music faded out.

'I do apologise,' said President Bruni-Sarkozy. 'I have
a correction for you – my third wife is of course a model
turned *singer*. I always get that wrong. Although you are
going to be in that Woody Allen film, my petal. Do you
remember? I thought you were rather good.'

She dismissed this compliment with a coquettish bat
of her hand.

'To business, gentlemen.' At this, the women raised a
hubbub. 'And, of course, ladies. Now, I have not brought
you here today without reason. No, I am here to tell you
that yesterday Madame Bruni-Sarkozy dressed up as a
man.'

There was a gasp from the assembled members of the
press.

'You would do well to gasp. And I ought to point out
that I have never . . .' He furiously banged the table with
his fist. '. . . NEVER . . . felt a homosexual urge in my
life, but I have to say that she looked rather fetching in
her three-piece suit and false moustache. I wore a Breton
fisherman's outfit – you should have seen me in my beard
and cap – and together we stood unrecognised and un-
molested among the audience at *Life*, this art show you
will all have heard so much about.'

There was a murmur through the room.

'You would do well to murmur,' he said. 'We were made aware of this show through the wonderful review by a certain Jean-Didier Delacroix. And I have to say that it quite opened my eyes. You see, ladies and gentlemen, while we were there we witnessed the star of the show, Le Machine, make a sausage.'

The room erupted in laughter, and he banged a fist hard on the table, to remind everybody who was President. Immediately there was quiet. His eyes were blazing with fury. 'Not that kind of sausage!' he barked. He took a moment to compose himself before carrying on. 'We witnessed him frying an actual sausage, and here is the amazing part: he cooked it using gas that had been collected from his own faeces.'

There was another gasp from the members of press.

'You would do well to gasp. Do you see what this means? Instead of letting the methane from our faeces drift into the air, we, the Republic of France, are going to capture it and harness the power of human waste. The Russians think they've got everybody's backs to the wall with their gas pipelines and so on, but they're in for a big surprise. I have had a long meeting with my Energy Minister, with whom, incidentally, I am *not* having an affair, and she tells me that there are a number of ways in which this can be achieved. Pilot schemes begin tomorrow. Soon we shall be a totally self-sufficient excreta-powered nation, world leaders in the field, and we'll be able to tell the Russians to get lost.'

There was a big cheer throughout the room, and cries of *Vive la France!*

Everybody looked at Yevgeni Romanov from *Izvestia,*

411

who stared straight ahead, his face frozen. 'What do you make of that then, Romanov?' hissed the economics editor of *Le Monde*. 'Not so smug about your pipelines now, eh, Romanov? Eh?'

The President waited for the hubbub to die down before continuing. 'We'll even be able to export our gas to more prudish nations, such as Switzerland. Did you know that the Swiss are so modest they don't even have a word for faeces? They have a hundred and seventy three words for urine, but not one for the brown stuff. We'll make millions of euros, or whatever currency we happen to be using in the future – probably not the euro, let's face it. And for once the farmers will have something to be happy about. When we've taken off all the gas we'll be using the leftovers for fertiliser. There will be so much, they'll be more or less able to help themselves, and they'll be growing runner beans the size of hockey sticks. It's what they did in the olden days, and according to some parchments I've been looking over, it worked perfectly well. So there will be no need whatsoever for them to block the roads with their tractors.'

The president sat back, and his media secretary returned to the spotlight. 'Any questions for the President?' Plenty of hands went up, and the media secretary pointed at the most eager-looking journalist.

—*This is exciting news, Monsieur le Président. Whatever next? Piss-powered combine harvesters?*

'I shall consult my scientists about the viability of such a scheme.'

—*So this was all inspired by your trip to* Life? *Can we expect somebody to be receiving high recognition?*

'Well, I can't give too much away, but I expect a certain

someone will soon be made a Chevalier of the Legion of Honour.'

—But where will he pin the medal? He doesn't wear any clothes.

'No, not him,' snapped the President. 'I am talking, of course, about Jean-Didier Delacroix. His writing is really first-rate – without him we would never have gone along, would we, my butterfly?'

Madame Bruni-Sarkozy smouldered her agreement.

The President's media secretary raised his hands, palms forward. 'That is all we have time for today, unless, Monsieur le Président, you have any more announcements?'

The President looked into the air for a moment. 'Ah, yes, there was one more thing. We've merged our army with Britain's.'

A roar erupted through the room.

'It's just a small detail, and nothing to worry about. Any questions on the subject can be addressed to my Minister of Defence, with whom et cetera, et cetera . . . Now, I have to be going. If you will excuse me, I have a country to run and an Englishman to sue. I shall leave you in the capable hands of my stunning third wife, to whom I shall make love, and probably impregnate, later on.'

He stood, and with a wave and a bow he was gone. His media secretary took over. 'She is President Bruni-Sarkozy's third wife, but she is our beautiful First Lady. You are welcome to ask her anything you like, but please keep it decent for once. No questions about Eric Clapton's private parts this time.' Again, there was a collective groan. 'Now, who will start us off?' The women crept out of the room to file their stories about the President's methane plan and demand a press conference from the

Minister of Defence, while the men bobbed up and down in anticipation, their hands raised. The media secretary pointed to the lucky winner.

—*Madame Bruni-Sarkozy, please tell us – are you French or Italian?*

'I'm afraid I am unable to answer that question at the present moment. However, I can tell you that my new album, *Burning Desire*, will be out in two to three weeks, and will be available from Fnac, Amazon, iTunes and all other music retailers.'

—*Would you be so kind as to give us a preview, Madame Bruni-Sarkozy?*

She blushed. 'I wish I could, but sadly I didn't bring my guitar with me.'

The media secretary stepped in. 'By extraordinary co-incidence I happen to have brought my guitar with me – I was bashing out some Rod Stewart numbers backstage. You would be very welcome to borrow it, Madame Bruni-Sarkozy.'

'I couldn't possibly.' She looked surprised and bashful, but encouraged by whoops from the audience, she acceded. 'Very well.' She took the guitar, and perched on the edge of the table as demurely as she was able with so much leg showing. 'This is a song about somebody who means so very much to me, and I hope it will finally put an end to the rumours of my infidelity. It's called "Mon petit Président".'

The cameras rolled, and the gentlemen of the press settled back and let the lilting folk-tinged ballad wash over them. Though they would deny it if confronted, some were seen to wipe tears from their eyes.

XXXXIV

Monsieur Eric Rousset and Doctor Élise Rousset stood in the wings of Le Charmant Cinéma Érotique, peering out at *Life*. It had been a good run for both of them, and they were going to miss it.

The doctor's duties had been light. Le Machine had been in good health throughout, his only difficulty being a mild but persistent cold over Christmas. His imaginary knee trouble had given her more to do than anything. He hadn't wanted to inconvenience her, and after the first times, he had always waited for her to be on a routine visit to the venue rather than ask to see her. She always went away with a message for his new girlfriend, and Élise usually had a message to deliver to him. She had thought this was very romantic, and she hoped it worked out for them. She thought his girl was playing things very well, staying in the background and not bugging him, while letting him know just often enough that she was thinking of him, and would be there when it was all over.

Her only uncomfortable task had been to relay the news to his manager that after the show he would be met by his new girlfriend.

Le Machine's manager had taken the news coldly, and Élise had read between the lines. The doctor had become a familiar face among the crew, and was kept up-to-date with the backstage intrigue; she had just found out that the sound designer was going to be taking Le Machine's place in the luxury hotel suite, and that both he and the manager were surprised by how much they were looking forward to it. They had even practised a couple of times behind his mixing desk.

Élise was looking forward to giving Le Machine his final medical. They would at last be able to talk freely. She felt as if they had become close over the course of the run, and she was interested in finding out whether or not they really had done. Maybe once they were able to talk they would find they had nothing to say. However things turned out, it had been a great twelve weeks for her. She felt proud to have played a part in such an incredible event.

Monsieur Eric Rousset could not have been happier. The venue had been packed for the entire run; people had even gone there on Christmas Day, and a full house had seen in the New Year with Le Machine, who on the stroke of midnight had fired a champagne cork into the crowd. All the old cinema seats and spare memorabilia had been sold, and he now had more than enough money to make his refurbishment something quite spectacular. His cut of the box office proceeds had been paid out as they had gone along, and he had spent the preceding weeks booking in the works, and falling in love with the Internet as he built a website with an online box office.

The programme was filling up, as he got ready for the big relaunch in the summer. He was going to turn one of the small screens into a bar, papered with salvaged vintage posters, and fill the main screen with a smaller number of incredibly comfortable chairs. People would be invited to take their drinks through. He wanted his old customers to return, but he also wanted to attract a younger clientele. The art crowd had been a good place to start, and by leafleting *Life* he had already built up a mailing list of thirty thousand. Tickets were already selling for his re-opening season, which was going to feature the French debut of the 1960s Welsh language classic, *Girls Doing Each Other's Hair*. The director, Aneurin Lewis, was now ninety-nine years old, but he had agreed to leave his nursing home in Llandeilo and mark his one-hundredth birthday with an appearance at a Q&A session after a screening. Nearly all the tickets for that were already gone.

He peered out at the man he had to thank. He couldn't wait to shake his hand, look him in the eye and thank him from the bottom of his heart. He was going to present him with a free lifetime pass so he could come to any film he wanted, whenever he wanted. He hoped they would always be in touch. He had been dropping hints to Élise and Thao, telling them what a fine specimen he was, and how his sperm would be ideal for baby-making purposes. *It's good stuff*, he had told them over dinner the night before. *You can tell just by looking at it.*

From his vantage point, Monsieur Rousset could see

417

some of the audience. The place was packed. He could hardly believe that very soon it would all be over, and he made the most of these last few minutes.

Aurélie Renard and Sylvie Akiyama had found seats in the balcony. They watched Léandre Martin as he paced up and down, and Aurélie's butterflies were now constant. It was so strange to think that very soon she and he would be alone together. He had requested her presence backstage, asking her to visit him after his medical, when he had put his clothes back on. She had accepted.

For days she had been agonising over what to wear, and on Sylvie's advice she had decided on the exact clothes she had been wearing the first time they met. Added to this was a scarf that she had bought at La Foularderie. The shop had been exactly the wonderland she had been led to believe it would be, and it had taken her over two hours to make her final choice; not a minute of that time had been wasted, because she had narrowed their entire stock down to exactly the right scarf for her. Whenever she had worn it, which had been every day since, she had felt her spirits lift. It wasn't just cosmetic either; there was snow on the ground, and it was doing a good job of stopping her from freezing.

She wondered what she and Léandre were going to say to each other. She wished there was a way of telling whether things were going to work out between them, but whatever the future held, she was looking forward to giving it a try. She just hoped he would grow his hair back straight away. He looked a lot better with eyebrows.

With minutes left to go, Le Machine walked over to the urinal, and out came a light yellow stream, to the familiar

accompaniment of cheers and chants. Even Sylvie and
Aurélie found themselves joining in. *Le Ma-chine!* they
chanted, *Le Ma-chine! Le Ma-chine!* Everybody knew it
would be the final one.

Something about this sight made Sylvie remember something. She dug into the pocket of her duffel coat, and
pulled out a parsnip. She handed it to Aurélie, who took
it, and smiled her thanks. She quite liked parsnips whenever she found herself eating one, but she rarely thought
to buy them.

It was too loud in there for Sylvie to tell her the story
behind the vegetable; she would have to do that another
time.

The day after saying goodbye to Sylvie, Lucien had joined
a coachload of Japanese tourists as they started a week-
long trip through the French countryside. He held himself
together as best he could, telling them all about the places
they were going to see, and answering their questions,
but sometimes he couldn't help but let slip a sigh, and
every once in a while a tear glided down his cheek. Soon
the holiday makers had found out everything that had
happened. They all felt very sorry for him.

Two days into the trip they had arrived at a monastery
in the Loire Valley, and the tourists had disembarked
to spend some time looking around the grounds before
heading to the shop to buy the monks' famous honey.
When it was time to go, they all got back on board, and
just as they were about to leave they realised that Lucien
was not with them. *Wait*, they shouted to the driver,
wait for Lucien, but the driver seemed not to understand
them. Just as the coach pulled away, Lucien appeared at

the monastery gate, dressed in a habit, and with a perfect circle shaved into his hair. He raised his hand in goodbye.

They all hoped he would find the contentment he sought. They waved until the coach rounded a bend and he was lost from view. They all agreed that he seemed to have a new serenity about him. They would have to make do without an interpreter for the rest of the trip, but everybody understood, and nobody complained.

Lucien settled into monastic life very quickly, and after a few weeks he found it in his heart to write to Toshiro, to ask him to visit and tell him how things were going with him and Sylvie. Toshiro made the journey, and stayed at the monastery for the night. He spent several hours walking around the grounds with Lucien. Neither of them said very much, but Lucien was grateful to Toshiro for travelling all that way. Toshiro told him about Sylvie starting her course, and their move into a new apartment. He waited for a good moment to tell him about the wedding, but it never seemed to arrive. He was relieved when Lucien beat him to it. He had noticed Toshiro's ring, and asked him about it.

Lucien offered his congratulations, and asked to see some photos.

Toshiro took out his phone, and scrolled through a few pictures from the day. The wedding had taken place on Sylvie's trip to meet his family, and she had worn a traditional Japanese dress. She looked so beautiful, and she and Toshiro looked overjoyed to be with one another. It was good to see Monsieur and Madame Akiyama again, too. Even Monsieur Akiyama was smiling broadly. Akiko was in some of the photos, and she looked beautiful too, but it was Sylvie who really shone.

420

'Thank you, Toshiro,' said Lucien, handing the phone back to him.

As a parting gift he had offered Toshiro some vegetables. He explained that he spent most of his day tending the crops, and he was looking forward to the spring and summer, when he would be kept very busy. He told him he still wasn't entirely convinced by the religious aspect of monastic life, but the winter vegetables had been a great comfort to him.

Toshiro accepted his gift of eight parsnips and a swede, and assured Lucien that he would be back in the summer with more news from their lives. Lucien told him that the harvest would be a little more enticing at that time of year, that he would be able to send him home with plums, courgettes and runner beans.

Toshiro told him he was looking forward to them. He said goodbye, and began the long journey back to his wife.

Le Machine emptied the jug into the big urine bottle, which he sealed for the last time. There was an incredible amount of liquid in there. Likewise, there was a deep brown slurry in the faeces bottle. The other containers were less spectacular, but interesting nonetheless. He had scooped out no more than a raisin-size globule of earwax, his fortnightly toenail and fingernail clippings amounted to very little, and his cold had resulted in a fairly substantial green slime in a jar. There were body hairs and skin flakes, and there was semen and sweat.

He walked up and down, looking at it all. This was what he had left behind these last twelve weeks. He could see that people were astonished and disconcerted by the thought that they too would have left a comparable trail over the same period of time. They had been working, and sleeping, and making love, or not making love, and doing whatever else they had done, and without giving it any particular thought they had left so much behind. Above all, though, they were amazed – by their own bodies, and by the strangeness of life.

Léandre Martin had no idea what was going to happen to him. It was too early to say whether he would ever be ready to present *Life* again, and he had butterflies whenever he thought of Aurélie, which was all the time. He had no idea whether or not they were going to end up together, but he couldn't wait to find out. Most of all, he just wanted to see her again, to put his arms around her and find out what the future had in store.

He checked the time on the clock in the wings. There was one minute to go. He walked to the end of the runway. He looked around, trying to pick out Aurélie's face from the five hundred and thirty that were staring at him. He couldn't see her, but just the thought that she was out there was enough for him to end his exhibition on a high. He smiled as he listened to the sound of his body, and just as suddenly as it had started, the lights went down and the sound shut off.

Before anybody's eyes had a chance to adjust to the darkness, Léandre Martin walked back along the runway, across the stage and into the wings. Applause thundered through the building.

And that was the end of *Life*.

XXXXV

A few kilometres away from Le Charmant Cinéma Érotique, another light went out.

Dominique Gravoir had not been well for weeks. He had caught a winter cold, which was nothing unusual, but this time it was as if he had invited it to stay. His mother held his hand. He was thinner than he had ever been, and his breathing was so shallow it was barely perceptible. She let go of his hand, and placed her fingers on his forehead, gently rubbing it, and as she whispered words of love, she felt the room turn cold.

She carried on rubbing his forehead, and whispering words of love. She hoped he had known how much of a difference he had made to so many lives.

'Goodbye,' she said. 'Goodbye, my baby boy.'